SERVANT
OF THE
CROWN

SERVANT
OF THE
CROWN

DUNCAN M. HAMILTON

TOR

A TOM DOHERTY ASSOCIATES BOOK

NEW YORK

SERVANT OF THE CROWN

Copyright © 2020 by Duncan M. Hamilton

A Tor Book
Published by Tom Doherty Associates
120 Broadway
New York, NY 10271

www.tor-forge.com

Tor® is a registered trademark of Macmillan Publishing Group, LLC.

Library of Congress Cataloging-in-Publication Data

Names: Hamilton, Duncan M., author.
Title: Servant of the crown / Duncan M. Hamilton.
Description: First edition. | New York : Tor, 2020. | Series: The dragonslayer; 3 |
"A Tom Doherty Associates book." |
Identifiers: LCCN 2019052038 | ISBN 9781250306852 (trade paperback) |
ISBN 9781250306845 (hardback) | ISBN 9781250306838 (ebook)
Subjects: GSAFD: Fantasy fiction.
Classification: LCC PR6108.A5234 S47 2020 | DDC 823/.92—dc23
LC record available at https://lccn.loc.gov/2019052038

Our books may be purchased in bulk for promotional, educational, or business use.
Please contact your local bookseller or the Macmillan Corporate and Premium
Sales Department at 1-800-221-7945, extension 5442, or by email at
MacmillanSpecialMarkets@macmillan.com.

First Edition: March 2020

Printed in the United States of America

0 9 8 7 6 5 4 3 2 1

SERVANT
OF THE
CROWN

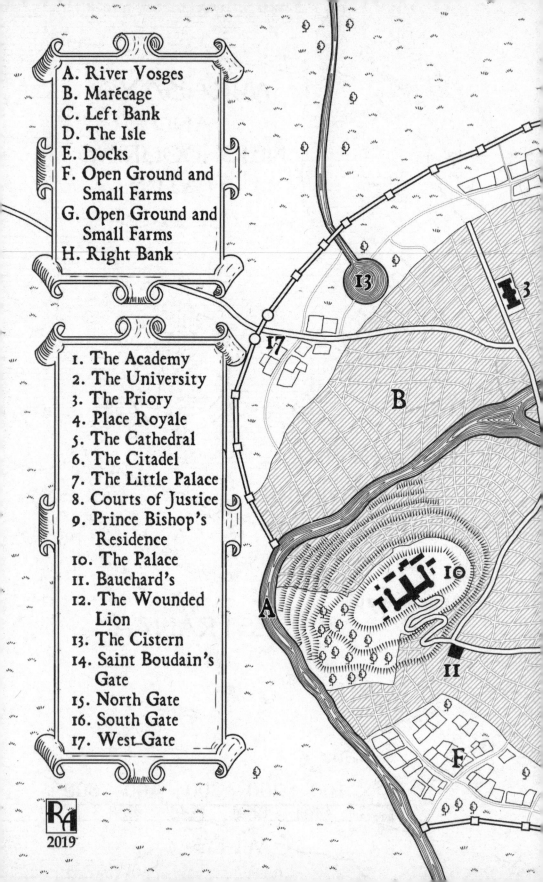

A. River Vosges
B. Marécage
C. Left Bank
D. The Isle
E. Docks
F. Open Ground and
   Small Farms
G. Open Ground and
   Small Farms
H. Right Bank

1. The Academy
2. The University
3. The Priory
4. Place Royale
5. The Cathedral
6. The Citadel
7. The Little Palace
8. Courts of Justice
9. Prince Bishop's
   Residence
10. The Palace
11. Bauchard's
12. The Wounded
    Lion
13. The Cistern
14. Saint Boudain's
    Gate
15. North Gate
16. South Gate
17. West Gate

RA
2019

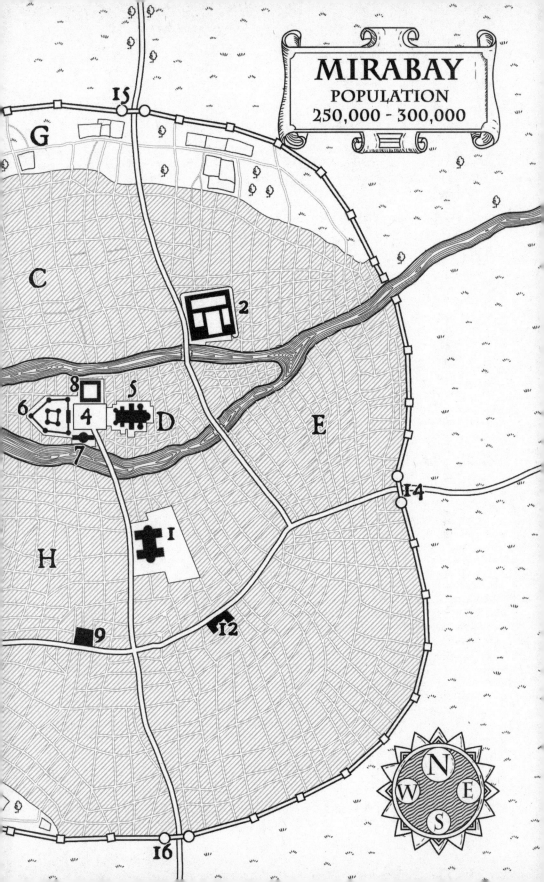

PART ONE

CHAPTER
1

Val had always dreamed of the city of Mirabay, the glittering capital of their country. Home to the king, his lords, ladies, knights, and dames. He wasn't naive enough to think of it as a place of wonderment, where streets were paved with gold, where dreams became reality. He reckoned it would be little different from Trelain—good bits and bad bits—albeit on a far larger scale.

He stopped his horse when the city first came into view, the king's palace sitting majestically on the hill overlooking Mirabay. Even from that distance, Val could see the twin campaniles of the cathedral, as well as some of the turrets of the old castle on the Isle. He had never been here, but felt as though he knew the city well. Almost every story of Chevaliers and heroes he had ever been told had started within the walls of the city before him. To finally visit was at once exhilarating and terrifying. He felt some pride, too. He was going to take his place at the Academy and seize the future he had always desired, but thought would be forever beyond his grasp.

As he urged his horse forward and continued toward the city's gates, he thought over the last few days. They had been a true taste of the life that lay ahead of him. Val wondered which of the three bannerets he had recently kept company with he would come to most resemble: the bragging Beausoleil, who showed his true worth at a critical moment and shamed everyone for not having thought highly enough of him; Cabham, who had seemed competent, but proved to be nothing more than a fame-hungry coward; Gill? Val had spent more time with Guillot than with either of the other two, but still didn't know what to make of the man.

On the one hand, Gill seemed like a man who had given up on life, or one whom *life* had given up on. Either way, he was as unlikely a candidate to ride off to save a village from marauding dragons as Val could imagine. He certainly didn't fit the image of the old Chevaliers of the Silver Circle, who were, according to legend, handsome, decked out in shining armour, and armed with courage that never wavered. Yet Gill had all the substance that was needed.

In the old stories, the Chevaliers never got knocked down. Gill did. Often. But he got up every single time and tried again. He had kept getting up and trying until he'd won. Val wondered how Guillot had fared against the last dragon. That matter would have been long decided by now. Val felt rotten having left him to face it alone—it didn't seem like something an aspiring banneret should do. He understood why Gill had sent him away, though. Ostensibly it was to deliver a message, but he knew what Gill's intention was, something that was confirmed when Val noticed that the letters Gill had given him were addressed to the master of the Academy. Gill had lost people, and didn't want to lose any more. He had sent Val away to keep him safe. More than that, he was a man who did his best to make good on his promises, and knowing he faced death, he was keeping the one he'd made to Val: sponsorship to the Academy.

After that odd little cup, the one used in the Silver Circle ritual, was stolen, something in Gill had changed. Val had been so caught up in the idea of finally realising his own dream that he hadn't noticed at first, but he'd worked it out eventually. Resignation was something Val had seen often in Trelain—people doing the same thing, day in, day out. They accepted it because they knew there was nothing else for them. Resignation might have made the drudgery easier to bear, but it killed something inside. The thought made him feel nauseous. He should have stayed. Should have helped, but he hadn't. Gill had known exactly how to tempt him away, and he'd gone. Regret wasn't much use now.

Val knew he'd likely be dead now, if he'd ridden out after that last dragon with Gill. No one had ever done a selfless thing for him before. That was why Gill was a hero, more so than any of the old Chevaliers with their glittering breastplates and magical swords. He put others before his best interests, and Val knew it had probably cost him his life. He loved Gill for that.

He stopped his horse again, and turned south, looking back at the mountains he had come from. There, he knew, Gill had fought the last dragon, near a village no one had ever heard of. But Val knew. He knew the village was called Venne, and he would be sure to tell anyone who would listen what had happened there. Where the last of the Chevaliers of the Silver Circle had faced the last of the dragons.

Val chuckled to himself. He knew he gave far too much weight to the old stories. Now he was getting carried away by having been a bit player in a new one. Even he, a lad of sixteen summers—perhaps seventeen, he couldn't be sure—was too pragmatic to take all that romantic nonsense at face value. He'd need to empty his head of such thoughts before he entered the Academy, or the other students would think him a country fool.

Giving the mountains one final look, Val prayed to all the gods that Gill still lived, that the dragon was slain, and that there might be some hope of the man finding whatever it was his life was missing.

▲▲▲▲▲▲

Val was determined not to look like a wide-eyed country bumpkin as he rode into Mirabay. He didn't have much money, but he knew what little he did have would be stolen in the blink of an eye if he advertised the fact that he was new to the city. As discreetly as he could, he asked a patrolling officer of the watch for directions to the address he wanted, then did his best to appear as though he knew his way around and that the short sword at his hip wasn't merely for decoration.

The officer said the address Gill had given Val was located on the southern bank of the River Vosges, near the Academy of Bannerets. Just the mention of the Academy got Val's heart racing with excitement. He had dreamed of going there from the moment he had first learned of it, and now it seemed he was about to realise that dream.

He kept his excitement contained as he rode along the dirt street at a modest pace, one that he thought befit a young gentleman. What little he knew about the nobility came from watching those who had passed through the Black Drake inn at Trelain, where Val had been employed before convincing Gill to take him on as a squire.

Despite his high spirits, Val couldn't help but detect an air of tension in the city. People glanced about furtively, as though they were on the lookout for someone, or something. Val presumed it was the dragon and wanted to laugh out loud at their cowardly behaviour. Although he was not too proud to admit the beasts terrified him— especially the ones he had seen up close—the nearest one was miles and miles away. Even flying, it would take at least a day to reach Mira- bay from the mountains—perhaps longer; Val wasn't certain how fast they could fly, or for how long. Even then, there were plenty of farms and villages to keep it interested along the way. He reckoned it would be weeks before a dragon had cause to be within a hundred miles of the city, assuming it still lived.

The houses lining the street were fine—far grander than anything in Trelain. Val started to wonder about the man Gill had sent him to. He was obviously very wealthy if he could afford to live in a neigh- bourhood like this, but then again, Gill was a lord, and everyone knew lords were wealthy, and only hung around with other lords.

Eventually Val found the house he was looking for, a pale, stone edifice pocked with ornately framed windows. Large, slate-grey dou- ble doors sat at the centre of the façade, with a smaller wicket door set in one of them. He dismounted and rapped the heavy bronze knocker, then stood back to wait. His heart was racing, and his mouth was dry. He had no idea what to expect. How would this man react to his ar- rival? Would he do as Gill had asked? There was always the possibility that he would refuse, a thought that Val had not allowed himself to entertain up until now, but that dominated his mind as he counted the seconds.

He heard a latch scraping on the far side of the doors, and the wicket door opened. A slim man with lank hair hanging down to his shoulders—less well dressed than Val would have expected for a house such as this—filled the breach. He regarded Val with a hostile stare.

"What do you want?"

"I've a letter here for the master of the house." Val held it up, but out of reach.

The man scrutinised the address, written in Gill's neat hand, and frowned. Val wasn't convinced he was able to read, but he certainly wanted to give the impression that he could. Val couldn't manage more than a few words himself, so he didn't condemn the inability, only the desire to mislead.

"Hand it over. I'll see that he gets it."

"It's to be delivered in person," Val said.

The man took a moment to consider. "Wait here." He shut the door behind him, leaving Val standing on the cobbled street to further consider the neighbourhood. It was quiet, and the day was heading into early evening. Val hadn't given any thought to where he would stay for the night. On some level, he expected to be whisked straight to the Academy and shown to his dormitory, but he realised that wasn't very likely.

He waited there for some time, like the unwelcome caller he was beginning to suspect he was, before the latch scraped again and another man appeared at the door—this one bespectacled and better dressed, but with an equally hard face.

"I understand you have a letter for Maestro dal Volenne?" the man said.

"I do," Val said, once again showing the letter. It was all he had to prove his credentials, and there was no way he was handing it to anyone but the master of the Academy.

"My name is Burgess Prenneau, Crown Solicitor. I represent the Crown in the matter of Maestro dal Volenne's estate, and am officially authorised to receive all correspondence addressed to him."

"I don't understand," Val said.

"Are you claiming relation, blood or otherwise?" Prenneau said, ignoring Val's question.

"No, I . . . What's going on here? May I see Maestro dal Volenne? I was instructed to hand this letter to him personally."

Prenneau seemed to relax when Val said he wasn't a relative. "I apologise," he said. "Maestro dal Volenne is deceased. He died intestate, with no known successors, so his estate is reverting to the Crown. I was appointed to deal with the matter. I can accept the letter and add it to his documents, but I'm afraid there will be no reply."

Val's heart sank. He had no idea what to do or say.

"If you knew the Maestro," Prenneau said, "I commiserate for your loss, but I'm afraid I'm extremely busy. The Maestro was not the most fastidious in managing his affairs and there's a great deal to do."

The awkward silence that followed made it clear that it was time to go. Val doffed his hat and turned to lead his horse back the way he had come. Only moments before, he had been on his way to fulfilling a lifelong dream. Now he was alone and adrift in a great city, with no idea of where to turn.

CHAPTER

2

Trelain might have only been a town, not a great city like Mirabay, but it was big enough to teach Val many important lessons about life, and how dangerous people could be when you were at the bottom of the food chain. Though he had no idea where to go next, he knew better than to start asking passers-by for suggestions of places to stay. Before he knew it, he'd be lying in the gutter with a cracked head, an empty purse, and no horse. Probably no boots, either.

He'd seen it happen, and pitied the unfortunate victims, but felt a measure of contempt for them too—as often as not, they had invited their misfortune on themselves. People could be vicious, and for many, an easy target was hard to pass up. There was no way he was going to make that mistake. Gill had sent him here to start his journey to becoming a banneret, and Val was damned if he was going to fall at the first obstacle.

He had a decent amount of coin in his purse, given he'd been a mere stable boy until a couple of weeks earlier. He'd always been a saver, and at an establishment like the Black Drake, clients tipped well, not to mention the tidy sum he'd made charging a penny a peek to see the head of the first dragon Gill had killed. When it came time to fly the nest, he'd had enough for travelling clothes and a horse. How many lads his age could say the same? He'd be damned if he let someone take a single stitch of it from him.

Coin he might have, but in a city like Mirabay, and an area like the one he was currently in, it wouldn't last long. He needed a day or two to think through his options, and didn't need anywhere fancy.

He ambled through the city in as casual and familiar a fashion as he could muster, carefully surveying his surroundings without, he hoped, looking like he was lost.

The amount of gilt work on the signs of shops, taverns, and inns gradually decreased as he wandered; clearly he was reaching more affordable areas. He'd been working his way along a great limestone block wall when he came to the gate and archway and stopped.

The carved lettering atop the arch read, ACADEMY OF BANNERETS.

Val allowed himself a wry smile at this long-dreamed-of sight. He was finally there, but he wouldn't be passing through the gates as a student. Perhaps it had been too great a dream. The opportunity to throw himself on Gill's good nature had been too good to pass up, but he had expected too much to come from it. Still, how many of those who would pass into those hallowed halls could say they had hunted and slain dragons? Nothing and no one could ever take that away from him.

He urged his horse on. There was nothing to be gained by tarrying there, and he wanted to find a bed for the night before it got dark. He'd spent long enough on the road, and after his disappointment, reckoned he deserved a little comfort. He took the next bridge over to the island in the centre of the river. The street led along the side of the cathedral and out onto a square. There was an inn directly opposite, called "the Little Palace," that had all the earthy charm of the type of place he liked, and had least expected to find in the centre of a great city like Mirabay.

He rode across the square, where market vendors were packing up their stalls for the evening, through the small archway at the side of the inn, and into its stable yard. He whistled for attendance, then felt awkward when a lad around his own age appeared.

"I plan on taking a room for the night. See to my horse, if you would," Val said, realising he'd put on a deeper voice than his usual one. He tossed the stable hand a penny and took his bags from the saddle before heading inside, feeling like an idiot with every step for attempting to sound older than he was.

The interior met his expectations; he could only hope that the price did likewise. A group of men were gathered around a table in the centre of the taproom. There were enough of them to have claimed every stool in the place, leaving all other tables without seats. The bar was empty but for the keeper, who leaned against the shelving behind it, his arms crossed.

"A room, if you've any," Val said, doing his best not to slip into a deep voice again, but only partially succeeding.

The innkeeper gave him a suspicious look, then nodded. "A florin a night, and you'll have the room to yourself. For tonight, at least. Breakfast too. You'll have that to yourself for as long as you're here."

He chuckled and Val did his best to laugh with him, as he felt men of the world did. He had the uncomfortable feeling he wasn't fooling anyone, however. The hair on his chin and upper lip was darkening in a satisfying way, but it was still too light and sparse to be proud of.

"I'll take it," Val said. "Could do with some food now, too."

"Three pennies for stew. Five for beef."

"The stew will be fine."

"Since those lads is having a private conversation," the innkeeper said, pointing to the large group of men, "best you sit up here at the bar."

Val glanced at the men and realised several of them were staring at him. He didn't allow his gaze to dwell long, but saw nothing untoward about the men. One or two had the hardened look of fellows who made their livings with violence, but the rest looked perfectly respectable. Whatever they might be up to, Val had no reason to stick his nose in, so turned his back and waited for his stew. He had plenty to occupy his thoughts.

His route into the Academy had been blocked by the death of its master, but that didn't necessarily change anything. He still had Guillot's recommendation, and every lad who knew anything about the Academy knew being nominated by a Banneret of the White was the surest way in. All he was lacking was someone who could train him up to the standard of the place.

As Val ate, his spirits rose. There was a chance his dream of attending the Academy was not dead just yet. How to keep moving toward it was another question entirely. He would need a skilled banneret to train him and Gill had said it would take him a year at least to be ready to take the entrance exam. Maestro dal Volenne was supposed to have been the answer to that, but there were sure to be other sword-masters in the city looking for pupils.

He wondered how much lessons would cost, and how much money he would need to survive on. That was all he needed to do—survive long enough to reach the skill level he needed. Once he was in the Academy, everything would be taken care of; he simply had to get there.

Val knew how much money was in his purse, down to the last penny, and at the rate of a florin a day for bed and breakfast, he would be broke by the end of the month. He could get a job—he had never been shy of hard work—but going back to mucking out stables seemed like a step in the wrong direction. As he munched his way through three pennies that he would probably have been better off saving, he tried to make a plan.

The first thing he would do was sell his horse. It was true that she had faced down dragons with him, and that had created a bond be-tween them. He didn't like the idea of selling her, but stabling a horse was expensive and he needed every penny he had to support himself. Not to mention that whatever he got for her would lengthen his stay in Mirabay.

He also had to find a cheaper place to live. Then, he needed to find a fencing master who would take him on as a pupil, at a modest fee. After that, he would likely need to find a job. When he laid out each step, it didn't seem like so great a task. However, the city was large and he was a stranger. Nothing would come easily to him, but then again, nothing ever had.

⁂

That morning, after breakfast, he'd taken his horse to a livery near the south gate. The few pennies he got for her would help stave off penury for a few more days. It was a sad parting but a necessary one. That done, salon hunting was next on his to-do list.

It wasn't too difficult for Val to find the addresses of a few fenc-ing salons in the city. Most wealthy men, and some women, practised fencing to varying degrees, so there were plenty of salons to choose from. What would be difficult was finding one who would take him on. He hoped the fact that he had a recommendation from a Banneret of the White would help, but despite the countless hours he had spent shadow-fencing in the Black Drake's stable yard and studying the fencers competing in Trelain's small arena, he had no formal training.

With luck, Gill's letter would convince someone to take Val on. He didn't have the luxury of being able to offer more than their usual rates—in fact, he was hoping he might be able to get a discount if he helped clean up the salon in the evenings. Difficult or not, he hadn't come this far to turn away now.

He made his first attempt on a street that housed four salons. Picking one at random, he let himself in and was greeted by the sounds of activity—the clatter of blades, shouts, and the stamping of boots. Above it all rose a single voice, and it didn't take long to separate the man to whom it belonged from the sparring couples around him. He prowled up and down the salon with a rapier in his hand, using it to correct the positions of his students.

Val watched in silence, wondering how to approach the maestro. His quandary was taken care of when the man's intense stare fell on Val.

"Who are you?"

"I, uh . . ."

The sparring fencers stopped to see who the maestro was speaking to.

"I didn't tell you to stop," the maestro barked. The stamping and clattering resumed. "Now, who are you?"

"My name's Val. I'm looking for instruction."

The maestro approached and looked Val over, including the crude short sword he wore at his waist. Val cringed, wishing he hadn't worn it. Having had it at his side every day since Gill had instructed him to have it made, he felt naked without it, particularly in a big and dangerous city. He'd strapped it on as usual that morning, without giving it a second thought.

"Who have you trained with?"

"Guillot dal Villerauvais," Val said. "I was his squire for a short time. He gave me his recommendation for the Acad—"

"I know of him," the maestro said. "If he trained you, why do you carry that?" He pointed to the short sword.

"It's all I have."

"Guillot dal Villerauvais was a master of masters until he threw it all away. It's sad to see he's lowered himself to instructing youths in how to fight with . . ." He gestured with his free hand as he searched for the word. ". . . farm implements. I do not, and can't assist you. Good day."

He returned to prowling amongst his students, leaving Val red-faced. There was nothing to be gained by responding to the insult, nor by remaining there, so he left, angry and ashamed. Was this the treatment he could expect everywhere? He had been so proud of his short sword, but now it felt like a badge of shame. He stared at the signs for the other fencing salons and asked himself if he wanted to go through that experience all over again.

Val received much the same response at the next two salons he tried. One was a little more polite, but the meaning was the same. He wandered through the warren of alleys behind the cathedral until he felt his resolve build enough for another try. Spotting another sign with the familiar crossed swords on it, he took a deep breath and reminded himself of how Gill took every blow, then picked himself up, and got on with his business.

This premises was in a smaller building on a narrower, quieter street than the others. The inside proved to be as quiet as the exterior, with none of the frantic activity that Val had encountered at the other salons. Not seeing anyone, he turned to leave—and walked right into someone. Val looked into the taller man's face and excused himself. They each stepped to the side to allow the other to pass.

"Wait," the man said as Val headed out the door, "I know you."

Val looked back and frowned. "I don't think so."

"The Little Palace. You were there last night."

Val nodded, finally placing him as one of the men gathered around the table. "I, yes. I needed a room for the night." He'd slipped into his deeper than normal voice again.

"What brings you to my salon?"

"I'm looking for instruction."

"Have you studied with anyone before?"

"A little," Val said. "I squired for Guillot dal Villerauvais for a time."

"Dal Villerauvais . . ." the man said, with a slight smile.

"You know him?"

"We met on a few occasions. But I forget my manners," the man said. "Banneret of the White Hugo dal Ruisseau Noir, at your service."

"Val, at yours. Just Val."

"A pleasure, although I have to admit some surprise at your choice of sword."

Val felt his hackles rise. "It's far more useful than that stick you have when you've a dragon to face."

Dal Ruisseau Noir's eyes widened and he smiled. "You were with him when he faced the dragons?"

"Some of them," Val said, with as much solemnity as he could muster. His indignation began to fade in the face of dal Ruisseau Noir's curiosity.

"And you've come to the city to seek instruction? With what purpose?"

"Gill gave me his recommendation for the Academy," Val said. "But I've still to—"

"Pass the entrance examinations," dal Ruisseau Noir said, nodding. "Easier said than done. The next set of exams aren't until the summer. Two terms away, so there is time. With hard work . . ."

"You'll take me on?" Val said. Now that it seemed he might have found a willing instructor, he was starting to have doubts. Was dal Ruisseau Noir any good? Would he be able to help Val reach the standard in the time they had available? Why was his salon so quiet, when all the others were so busy? He supposed there was only one way to find out.

"There is the matter of payment," dal Ruisseau Noir said.

Val shifted from one foot to the other, trying to work out what kind of deal he could offer. He had enough to pay for a few weeks, but not enough for two full terms of tuition.

Dal Ruisseau Noir smiled. "An impecunious student." Arms akimbo, he looked about the studio. "As it happens, my apprentice has returned to his home in the country to get away from the current unrest in the city. How does this sound. Four hours' tuition per day for four hours' work?"

"What type of work?" Val said. He instantly regretted the question; he should have just taken the man up on the offer. He didn't think it very likely he'd get another as good.

"Keeping the place clean, sharpening and oiling swords, fetching my lunch, delivering messages, all the things that I have neither the time for nor the interest in doing. Do we have a deal?"

Val nodded eagerly.

"Excellent. You can start with my lunch. The Wounded Lion is two streets over. You can't miss it. A slice of pie and a flagon of small beer."

He tossed Val a coin, which Val caught with as much ease as he could muster.

"Try not to let the pie go cold."

CHAPTER

3

The Duke of Trelain would like to see you, your Grace. The Dukes of Bonmille and Castelneuve also."

Amaury smiled at his secretary. "Tell them I'll make appointments with them all at my earliest convenience."

Dealing with them would never be a convenience, but there was only so long he could put off the magnates of the realm. His only surprise was that just three dukes had asked to see him. The rest would likely follow in due course. Power, wealth, and position were up for grabs, and everyone would want their slice. The ones he gave a piece to would be his staunchest allies as long as he kept giving them what they wanted, while the rest would hate him for being shut out in the cold.

Despite Amaury's best efforts, news of the king's incapacity spread through the city quickly. At first he had been furious, determined to root out how word had slipped beyond the palace walls. However, it seemed as though it had been a stroke of good fortune. The unrest that had been simmering toward the boiling point since he'd announced the Order's magical dabbling had calmed considerably. He wasn't sure why, and wouldn't have cared, were it not for the fact that it might be something he could manipulate and exploit going forward.

What mattered for the time being was that it had bought him breathing space. People weren't thinking about the scourge of magic being within their city walls, they were thinking about their young king, who was said to be at death's door. The truth was, Amaury wasn't sure what the king's condition was, and neither were his physicians. Amaury didn't know exactly what he had done to the king, and doubted if he could repeat the act even if he wanted to. It had left him with an equal portion of opportunity and mess.

The opportunity was that he now had the potential freedom to direct the kingdom in keeping with her best interests, meaning he could integrate the Order into Mirabayan society, further invest in study and training, and make sure that Mirabaya was at the cutting edge of magical ability. If any of her neighbours sought to challenge her, they would need to think twice, and when it came to negotiation, they would have a strong bargaining chip to make sure the terms were always favourable.

Mirabay had been primed as the natural successor to the empire—home to the church, and a great centre of science and culture. Were it not for the piratical Ventish and Humberlanders, and the haughty Estranzans, that would have been the case. As it was, with her powerful trading fleets and enormous resultant wealth, even Amaury had to concede that Ostia held that mantle, and it seemed she had been dabbling in magic for some time. He only hoped he was not too late.

Still, Mirabay had advantages peculiar to her history. If his agents managed to find the Temple of the Enlightened, and with it a way to prolong or make permanent the effects of the Amatus Cup, there would be no stopping him. How to use it to the greatest advantage was a matter that often occupied his thoughts, but he rarely had more than a minute or two to devote any attention to it. The king's ailment, and Amaury's de facto appointment as regent, had changed everything.

The more he thought about it, the more liberated he felt. In the past, he had preferred to wield power from the shadows. He had seen too many assassination attempts, successful and otherwise, to desire a public mantle of leadership. He had been happy to use a proxy—the previous bishop, the former king once Amaury had ascended the episcopal throne—but now that he seriously thought through the possibilities, having found himself thrust into the open, he could feel the attraction. It was like having shackles removed, or being told that you can do whatever you choose.

Of course, he was not so great a fool as to think that there were no constraints whatsoever. There were the ever-present nobles who would whine and grate at any changes that took coin from their purses or restricted their privileges. Then there was the public. The citizens of Mirabay had an inconvenient but well-deserved reputation for agitation when they didn't like something. One only had to open a history book to see evidence of the numerous riots and assassinations that had been carried out on waves of popular discontent. Finally, there were economics to consider. To achieve his aims, he needed coin, which meant taxes, which meant all of the above problems, if they were applied too heavily.

As he allowed his mind to drift down this avenue of thought, it felt as though the shackles were going back on. He tried to focus on the positives. To do otherwise would have meant admitting just how alone he was. Before, he had always had adversaries in the battle to win the king's attention and favour. He had almost always prevailed, but sparring with his opponents allowed him to sharpen his thoughts and strategies. Now, all that was gone, leaving him with an empty sensation that bordered on nausea.

Although as regent he assumed all the powers of the incapacitated king, his regency was a temporary measure. It would last only until a valid successor could be found. Since Boudain had no children, that successor would have to come from elsewhere in the family, and would have to be determined by studying genealogies and other documents.

He reckoned setting the wheels in motion to prevent that should be his first order of business. After all he had done to get power, there was no way he was going to step aside for the first inbred aristocrat who could open a vein and spill some blue blood on the ground. However, he remained open to the possibility that there might be an eligible candidate who would be happy to occupy the throne while allowing Amaury to continue his machinations behind the scenes. The last thing he needed was to install an idle fop and find out they had ideas of their own—as he had discovered with the current, and soon to be former, king.

One way or the other, the king's cousins were going to be a problem. Off the top of his head, there was no clear successor. While this gave the Prince Bishop the freedom to choose, it was likely that those who were shut out would raise arms in rebellion. He would love to unleash the Order on them, but his forces had been crippled by casualties since the dragon problem arose. There were enough brothers and sisters to carry out the day-to-day activities he had in mind for them, but not until he had fully unlocked the Cup's potential would he be able to wield them to full effect. Hopefully that matter would be soon settled.

So many problems—so many balls to keep in the air.

He stood and walked to the window of his office, massaging his temples as he went. The garden below was empty, but even its serene setting was not enough to quell his growing agitation. *One task at a time,* he told himself. The Order, the king, the dragons, the successors. That didn't even take into account the usual running of the kingdom. If he didn't find a way to make the Cup's effect permanent, he would end up drinking from it constantly, like one of the drunks who littered the city streets.

If that was what he had to do, then that was what he would do, but he didn't like it. Soon enough, people would realise what the Cup did and would covet it for themselves. Pulling the strings from the shadows was starting to look like a much more attractive option again.

He returned to his desk and wrote instructions for the court genealogists to draw up a list of potential successors for Boudain. That could be compiled quickly, and he could have his agents investigate each one to help him identify which might be potential candidates, and which potential threats.

That done, he signed documents to provide the funds to pay Luther for the mercenaries he had hired for the Order. He didn't like bringing in people he hadn't had time to screen for the qualities he wanted, but for the time being, he needed to replace the dead to give the Order the appearance of being an effective force.

Anyone who was any use had been sent out with the new marshall, Vachon, to deal with the dragon crisis once and for all. That left only a couple of dozen novices at the Priory who could shape any magic. If the sentiment in the city turned bad again—which Amaury fully expected it would—the Priory could easily be overrun and its occupants slaughtered. If he lost them, he would have to restart the Order from scratch, which would set them back years.

A stack of outstanding execution warrants were sitting on the corner of his desk, waiting for his signature. Chief amongst them were the king's former privy councillors, Canet, Marchant, and Renaud. Amaury drummed his fingers on his desk as he considered them. To kill them off now might be too great a shock, and hint that there were mala fides involved in the king's incapacitation, which at present was not suspected—a state of affairs he wished to continue. He didn't like the idea of letting the three men draw breath any longer than was absolutely necessary, but having them discreetly killed at a later time might make more sense. There had been enough upheaval already, without starting a campaign against the king's supporters.

The people he'd chosen as replacements for the privy council needed to be briefed on their duties—another task to add to his ever-growing list. He felt a flutter of panic. What had he gotten himself into? For a moment, he wondered if there was any way out of it, if he could undo what he had done to the king and put him back on his throne. Get everything back to the way it was, where he could plan and wield influence from the shadows.

He took a deep breath. The Cup would see him through. If he could make its effects permanent, all his problems would be easily dealt with. If. One problem at a time. Just deal with one problem at a time, and all would be well. The results would be worth it, and when the day finally came that Mirabay's authority was questioned, the people would thank him. If he wasn't pulled from the palace and burned at the stake first.

Gill stared across the grassland and distant forest in the direction of Mirabay. He, Solène, and Pharadon had taken a short break from their frenzied pursuit of the person who had stolen the Cup from the Temple of the Enlightened to allow Solène to work her magic to refresh their horses. Gill was tempted to ask for a dose of whatever it was she did for himself, but could see how tired she already was, and how much of a strain it seemed to be placing on her.

He was tired also, and hoped the mug of coffee he had brewed over the small, hastily built fire would invigorate him a little. The coffee had been stolen from Vachon's supplies before they'd departed the temple. Between dragons and the Prince Bishop's henchmen, the past weeks had exacted a toll on Gill's body, and age dictated that it was taking far longer to recover than once it had.

Raising his gaze to the sky, Guillot tried to search Pharadon out. He had headed out in dragon form to see if he could locate their quarry. It was bizarre to be allied with a dragon, equal parts terrifying and intriguing. Pharadon had lived during times that had drifted from history into legend. That he had proved to be anything but the mindless beast of terror described by the stories that had been passed down from that time was a jarring concept that was going to take a while to get used to.

"Do you think we'll catch her?" Solène said.

Gill shrugged. The reality was, they had to. The alternative was not one he could bear thinking about. If Amaury managed to get the unused Cup—what Pharadon referred to as a vessel of enlightenment—he would be able to tap into a level of power that no person had been able to wield in nearly a thousand years. Back then, many people had been capable of wielding powerful magic, a fact that kept them all in check.

If Amaury became that powerful, there wasn't a person alive who could stop him. Solène might be able to, if what was said about her was true, but at times she seemed afraid of her ability, and was particularly opposed to the idea of using it as a weapon, even in a good cause.

"I hope so." A growing speck in the sky caught his attention. "Looks like our new friend is on his way back. I hope he's got good news."

Solène followed his gaze before returning her attention to the horses. She looked even more tired than she had only moments before, and Gill worried. Unless Pharadon had the thief clutched in his talons, they had plenty of hard riding ahead of them, and very possibly a hard fight at the end of it. If Solène kept working herself to the limit, she'd be lucky to last that long.

Pharadon drew closer at an alarming rate, then cast them both in shadow as he spread his great wings to arrest his flight and drop to the ground, touching down as nimbly as a cat. There was no body in his talons.

"No joy?" Gill said.

Pharadon shook his head, the expressiveness of his reptilian face still coming as a jolt every time Gill saw it.

"I've detected traces," Pharadon said in a sonorous bass voice. "Places where she delayed a moment and her magic was unable to completely hide her scent. It's not powerful magic, but it's very skilfully worked. I'm unable to see through it."

"So unless we find her the old-fashioned way . . ." Gill said.

Pharadon nodded. "I'm afraid so."

As unappealing a prospect as Gill found Amaury getting his hands on this last unused Cup, he realised it was far more devastating to Pharadon, if he hoped to help the other remaining dragon to enlightenment.

"We can set off as soon as you're ready," Gill said. They couldn't travel through the countryside with a dragon lumbering along beside them, so Pharadon had to transform himself into a surprisingly innocuous-looking human, using magical means that were nauseating to watch and that Gill had no desire to attempt to understand.

"I'll be as quick as I can," Pharadon said, prowling lithely off to obtain some privacy behind the tree where he had left his human clothes.

Gill forced himself not to laugh at the comedy of an enormous dragon hiding his modesty behind a twig of a tree, but he supposed it was large enough to conceal Pharadon while he was in human form, which was when it mattered.

He cast an eye at Valdamar's old armour, bundled on a horse's back. He'd recovered it from one of Vachon's packhorses, along with his swords. He wondered if he should get into the armour in preparation for trouble, but it would make a hard ride pretty unpleasant, comfortable though the armour was.

"Are you ready to go?" he asked Solène.

She gave him a tired smile and nodded. "As soon as Pharadon is."

He mirrored her smile and checked his horse. It looked far fresher than he felt, but it would do no one any good if the horses carried them to their destination with legs to spare, and he didn't have the strength to lift a blade. Pharadon returned, looking tired. Drained. He had said the process of transforming was incredibly taxing, and it was showing on his face. They mounted in silence and got moving. The tender spots, rubbed raw by his saddle, complained instantly, but Gill did his best to ignore them.

Their quarry continued to elude them, no matter how hard they pushed their horses. Their only advantage was that they were pretty certain where she was headed: to Mirabay and the Prince Bishop. Equally, that meant Gill was all too well aware that they were running out of road. Their best chance of getting the Cup back was before the thief reached the city. After that, she would be sheltered by the Prince Bishop and all the resources he could bring to bear.

The evening drew in faster than Gill expected, the changing of the season into winter having caught him off guard thanks to the distractions of the past couple of months. Dusk had taken hold when Gill spotted a rider ahead, moving more quickly than any ordinary traveller. He squinted to make sure his sleep-addled mind and dry eyes weren't imagining it, but the figure was definitely there, cloak billowing out, and he thought he saw them cast a furtive look behind. That was enough to give him hope they had their prey.

"Rider ahead," he shouted, above the thumping of their horses' hoofs on the soft ground of the road.

"You think it's her?" Solène shouted back. "I can barely see from here."

"That person has the Cup," Pharadon said, his voice no different from the way he usually spoke, yet perfectly audible.

"Come on then!" Gill urged his horse on for all it was worth, the excitement of finally being on the thief's tail giving his energy level a boost.

The others followed suit, and the horses thundered down the road. The exhilarating sensation reminded Gill of the joy of the hunt, something he hadn't done—dragon hunting aside—in many years. But the pleasure started to quickly leak away as he realised they weren't making up any ground.

"How long can she keep up this pace?" Solène shouted.

"How long can *we* keep up this pace?" Gill shouted back. Magical intervention or not, Gill knew there was no way their horses would be able to run this fast for long. In the distance, he could make out details he had been dreading. Mirabay was in sight.

He tried to push his horse on harder, but it was already running at its limit and he still grew no closer to the woman ahead. He wondered how she kept her horse moving. They knew she could use magic, so perhaps she was constantly feeding it benefits similar to those Solène provided during their rest stops. If so, there was no way they could catch her. There had to be a way he could slow her.

"Might she be using magic on her horse?" Gill shouted.

"Perhaps," Pharadon said. "It seems likely."

"Can you do the same for mine?" Gill asked. "I know dragons have powerful magic. Cast something on me so I can catch her."

"I can't in human form," the dragon said. "If I change, it will take time before I can shape it again. I was only able to in the temple because the Fount was so strong there. Almost limitless."

Gill looked over at Solène, head and heart railing against one another. Her face was pale and she had dark shadows under her eyes. How could he ask her for more? Was there another way? If there was, he couldn't think of it. There was so much about magic he didn't understand, but he could never forgive himself if he demanded more from her than she was able to give.

Before he could say anything, he saw her brow furrow and his horse surged forward. Rather than argue, he tucked down and encouraged it. Immediately, the distance between him and the thief started to fall away. He could see the woman more clearly now—she looked back every few moments and knew as well as he did that he was catching up.

The walls and towers of Mirabay were growing ever larger and more distinct.

He saw her throw her hand out behind. It took him a second to realise what that meant, and at the speed he was galloping, he barely had time to swerve to the side to clear the caltrops she had thrown on the road. He hoped the others would realise the danger, but was riding at such breakneck speed he wasn't able to look back to see.

Mirabay's walls loomed up, and he could make out the gates now, as well as people standing around them. He was close enough that the muck thrown up by her horse's hoofs was hitting his face. He was close enough to move over in preparation for coming alongside her. The walls were racing toward them and her horse was showing no signs of slowing. He could make out her features now, when she looked back. Dark curls framed a pale face with large eyes and dark lips. Something about her seemed oddly familiar, but Gill didn't have the time to dwell on the thought.

"I'm an agent of the Crown! Let me pass!" she shouted. "Stop my pursuers!"

There was a momentary hesitation before the duty guards burst into a flurry of activity. More of them appeared from the guardhouse, spears at the ready. They moved forward to create a spear wall, and Gill knew the game was almost up. Standing in his stirrups, he leaned forward as far as he could, reaching for the thief. Arm outstretched, he felt the end of her cloak flutter against his fingertips. He made one last desperate grab, nearly throwing himself from his horse, but seized nothing but air.

His horse stumbled a step, not enough to fall, but sufficient to break its rhythm and slow it. The thief sped on; the spear wall opened to allow her through, then closed again to prevent Gill from following. He brought his horse to a halt and wheeled around, spotting his companions some distance away. His horse was anxious and breathing hard—as was its rider.

Gill looked back at the guards, steadfast in their determination to not let him pass, and swore. There was nothing to be gained by trying to force his way in. He would be swamped by the guards' greater numbers and killed, and that would be the end of it.

He turned his horse and rode back the way he had come. They would have to find another way.

CHAPTER
5

Ysabeau trotted her horse toward the palace, through streets far quieter than she would have expected even at that hour. The City Watch were a stronger presence than normal and there was an uncomfortable atmosphere about the city. It wasn't something she could put her finger on, but things were definitely not right in the city of Mirabay. It felt like a black cloud had descended, which at any moment would burst into rain.

If the increased numbers of patrolling watchmen had imbued the city with a foreboding attitude, the number of guards at the palace gates made her suspect something very serious was going on. She was not accustomed to be stopped, so when the guards made her wait for her identity to be confirmed by the palace before allowing her through, she was convinced that there was trouble.

She had to wait for over an hour, glaring at the guards impatiently all the while, until a clerk from the Prince Bishop's office came down in person to escort her. They rattled up the cliffside in the elevator, its creaky nature barely disguised by the plush cushioning on the benches. The winch-operated platform generally accommodated those aristocrats and merchant potentates who lacked either the ability or the desire to make their way up the long, winding, tree-lined avenue that led to the main palace building.

As she quickly swept through the palace, she passed clusters of whispering courtiers, all of whom fell silent once they became aware of her presence, probably not wanting to be overheard by someone not a member of their inner circles.

The Prince Bishop's offices were in the same part of the palace as the king's—close to the centre of power, but hidden behind its majesty. Ysabeau wondered if she got her preference for operating from the shadows from him. Having been without a father for the greater part of her life, she felt odd referring to anyone by that title, let alone the Prince Bishop of Mirabaya, one of the most powerful men in the world.

He wasn't there when she arrived. His clerk showed her into his office to wait. Dominated by a large desk, the office wasn't much to look at. It was very much a place to work, rather than a statement of wealth or power, unlike many of the offices she had been in—usually to assassinate their occupants. The clerk was one of the few who knew who she was—knew the reason she was the only person the Prince Bishop completely trusted—so she was left alone to wait where others would be closely watched.

She wondered if the Prince Bishop was smart to have so much faith in her. She was his daughter, and blood was thicker than water, but after her mother died, she had sworn to always look out for her own interests, to hells with anyone else. Should her long-absent father be exempted from that? Sometimes she wasn't sure if he should, although for the most part he seemed to be trying to make amends for the years he wasn't around. Which, to be fair, was because he hadn't known about her.

Also, he had saved her from the Intelligenciers. That was a big debt, and one she felt would never be completely settled, no matter what she did. Perhaps giving him this Cup would do that, and finally show him how much she was worth. Nevertheless, she wondered if his seeming absolute confidence in her fidelity led him to take her for granted.

The door opened and she stood. Her father, the Prince Bishop, walked in, giving off that air of authority that so many men desire, but few manage to achieve. He was dressed in his usual powder-blue vestments, the uniform of his religious office, even if his temporal one of first minister occupied most of his time. He looked tired, even more than when she'd departed on her last mission, and he had looked exhausted then.

"Please tell me you bring good news," the Prince Bishop said.

No "hello." No "how was your journey." No "good to see you." Ysabeau forced a smile. She'd make him wait for what he really wanted to hear.

"I bring mixed news," she said, deciding that he deserved the bad news first. "Your detachment of Spurriers arrived at the temple with a prisoner. That woman you sent, the one who's good at magic? She allied with him and they killed most of your men, the commander included. Oh, and there were dragons. Two of them. Both still alive when I left, so they're still a problem."

The Prince Bishop turned puce and let out a breath like a hiss. "That doesn't sound like 'mixed' news." He took a moment to consider the information, the veins in his temples throbbing. "Is there anything else?" he said between gritted teeth.

She chewed her lip and thought for a moment. "Oh, yes. The big dragon. It turned into a man."

"It turned into a man?" the Prince Bishop said, his voice laden with disbelief.

"Yes," she said, nodding. "Really was something to see. Can't say I expected it at all." She paused for a moment. "Rather gruesome to watch, though. Not sure I'd want to again." She was enjoying toying with him, no matter how childish it might have been. Still, it was time to get on with things.

Taking her purse from her belt, she hefted it in her hand. "I also bring a gift, which I think will improve your day substantially." Ysabeau pulled open the purse and spilled the Cup into the palm of her hand. The Prince Bishop's eyes widened as soon as he saw it.

The Cup was a curious little thing. Round and with an engraved lip, it bore a resemblance to a sugar bowl. It was made from Telastrian steel, a rare and expensive metal found mainly in the Telastrian Mountains, on the other side of the Middle Sea—hence its name—although small deposits could be found elsewhere, such as in the mountains on Mirabaya's southeastern border. Delicate, swirling blue patterns ran through the metal's dark grey substance. The Cup was beautiful in its own simple way, but there was little to make it remarkable.

"You found another Cup," the Prince Bishop said. He took his from a pocket in his cloak, and looked at it, then at the one Ysabeau held. They were identical. "It was at the temple?"

She nodded. Although he had a Cup already, he had confided in her that he didn't understand it, and only seemed able to use a fraction of its reputed power. He had hoped the Temple of the Enlightened, another of the discoveries from the trove of ancient, forbidden knowledge he kept secreted away under the city's cathedral, would teach him how to properly use the Cup, so he'd sent her to find out. She hadn't—things there had gotten too dangerous, very quickly—but hoped this new Cup, and what she did know about it, might make up for that fact.

"What good is another Cup if I don't know how to make them give me the permanent power they are reputed to?" he said. "I presume you were successful in finding that out?"

She shook her head, knowing that her response would frustrate him, and that soon enough he would vent his frustration at her, if she allowed it to build too much. She hoped to alleviate that.

"The reason the one you have doesn't work the way you think it should is because it's already been used, and they only imbue their full power once."

"This one hasn't been used?" His voice changed instantly from growling malevolence to something brighter, hopeful. Desperate.

She smiled and nodded. "Untouched. The last of its kind. Other than that, as best as I was able to tell, it works the way you think it does. You just have to drink from it. And all your dreams become reality."

The Prince Bishop's eyes widened in delight, then narrowed. "You're certain? Certain that this is how it works?"

The intensity of his delivery made her doubt herself. She shrugged. "I think so."

"That's not good enough," he said. "This is the last one? You said this is the last one."

She nodded. "That's what the dragon said in the temple."

"It spoke?"

"Well, yes. It was in human form at that point."

"Astonishing," the Prince Bishop said. "But if this is the last one, I can't take the risk of wasting it." His voice rose. "I need to know for certain. I need to know the correct way to use it. This Cup might be the answer to everything. I can't waste it."

He paced across the office to the window and stared out into the darkness, tugging at his goatee in agitation. After a moment he turned back to her. "Tell me about the temple. What did you see?"

"It was incredible. Ancient, yet perfectly preserved. That would be because of the magic, I suppose. The whole place was filled with sculptures and covered with inscriptions."

"Inscriptions. Were you able to read any of them?"

"Of course not. I couldn't even tell you what language they were in."

"Couldn't you use your limited magical ability to decipher them?"

She smiled wryly, the dig at her disappointing magical talents not going unnoticed. She wondered if he would ever get over it, but supposed the wound must be particularly sore now, after she had delivered the news of his new protégé's betrayal. It seemed that he was to be ever disappointed by those he placed his hopes in.

"No," she said. "I've always directed my 'limited magical ability' toward things that are useful to me. I've never included millennia-dead languages on that list."

The Prince Bishop let out a breath with a deep sigh, then walked over to his desk and slumped into the chair. In that moment, Ysabeau regretted the attitude she had adopted, and wanted nothing more than to console her father. It felt as though there was a gulf between them, one she could never hope to cross. In any event, she knew that consolation was not what he desired.

"It's possible that there was more detailed information there on how the cups were used. Probable."

He fixed his gaze on her. "I need you to go back. Right away. I'm sure the danger has passed by now, so you'll be free to carry out a more thorough investigation. I'll have some scribes and linguists from the university accompany you, to copy the inscriptions and start working on translations."

Ysabeau gritted her teeth. She hadn't even taken the time to have a drink of water, let alone the lavish meal, hot bath, and ten hours of sleep she'd promised herself during the exhausting ride back from the temple. She'd been running on empty for hours, and it was only having the end in sight that had kept her going.

"Take a room at Bauchard's and get some rest," the Prince Bishop said. "I'll need a little time to get the team I have in mind organised. Naturally you can put it on my tab."

"Naturally," she repeated. There was no asking. He gave his command, and expected it to be followed. No other man alive spoke to her like that, treated her like that. Still, he was her father, and had been there for her when she had most needed him. She smiled and tried to relax. He was ordering her to Bauchard's, a place of luxury, and she was so tired.

"I'll send word when I have everything in place." He stared at her with that expectant look he used to indicate that it was time to leave. Obedient, Ysabeau stood and headed for the door.

"Aren't you forgetting something?" he said.

She realised she was still holding the Cup. She lifted it and allowed her tired gaze to dwell on it a moment.

"I think you should leave it here," the Prince Bishop said. "For safekeeping."

"Of course, Father," Ysabeau said. She placed the Cup on his desk, rather than into his outstretched hand, and left. As soon as the door closed behind her, she realised she had forgotten to ask him about the odd mood in the city. Conversations with the Prince Bishop were usually like that—dealing only with the things he wanted to deal with. At this point, she was so tired she didn't really care anymore.

CHAPTER
6

Gill led his little band around the city walls to St. Boudain's Gate, on the western side of the city, named after a king who was more interested in matters spiritual than temporal. As poor a reputation as he had as a ruler, the funds he diverted into the church were sufficient for his beatification, and he would be remembered as St. Boudain, rather than Boudain the Feckless, which was perhaps more appropriate. Gill had always taken odd pleasure in looking behind the reputations of the great and good of Mirabaya, as though to confirm to himself over and over that his cynicism was justified.

"Think we'll have any problems?" Solène said, as they approached the guarded gateway.

"No," Gill said. "I doubt it. Maybe be ready to gallop for safety, just in case."

"Confident then," Solène said.

He shrugged. "You never can tell. The last lot looked a bit jumpy. If they're on alert, it's possible word will have spread and these guards will be looking for us. I doubt it, though."

"What do we do when we get in?" Solène said.

"Let's cross one bridge at a time, shall we?" Gill said. The truth was, he had no idea. Loath though he was to admit it, he reckoned they'd lost the Cup as soon as their quarry reached the city gate. In all likelihood, it was already in Amaury's possession. He didn't want to say so, though. He knew how important the Cup was to their dragon-in-human-clothing comrade. Best let him find out they had failed by himself, so any anger could be directed elsewhere. Angry dragons were something Gill had had his fill of. He much preferred them when they were playing nice.

He studied Pharadon as surreptitiously as he could. Though the dragon's human disguise appeared perfect—apart from when he tried a challenging facial expression, like smiling—Gill worried that there was a flaw somewhere. An errant horn or a patch of scales that a particularly vigilant guard would spot. He supposed that the phrase "vigilant guard" was something of an oxymoron. Most of them were bored witless and counting the minutes until they could go back to barracks or home to their families. Nevertheless, every so often you got one who was eager to impress, new to the job or looking to make rank.

They reached the gate. On the scale of attentiveness, these guards seemed to be at the lower middle. They were stopping people, but only asking where they had come from. They were paying a little more than lip service to their duty, but not much.

"Where from?" the guard said.

"Trelain," Gill said, immediately wondering if he should have said somewhere else.

"See any dragons?"

Gill chuckled. "No. Not a one."

"Move on."

Gill gave a salute of thanks and urged his horse forward. He wondered how the guard would have reacted had he learned that he was staring at a dragon even as he asked the question.

They passed through the gate without further interruption, and Gill was immediately hit by the sensation of foreboding he had every time he entered the city. His best and worst memories were here. Courting Auroré in the palace gardens and theatres, losing her in childbirth in the townhouse they had owned near the palace. Fighting for his life in the judicial arena. Having his banner torn to shreds and handed to him as the mark of ultimate disgrace. As he thought on it, it became impossible to see the best memories for the worst. He hated Mirabay, and every visit was one too many.

Worse, this time it felt as though the entire city was in mourning.

Mourning with every city watchman out on duty. They were everywhere; he hadn't even realised there were so many members of the Watch.

"Something strange is going on," Gill said. "I've never seen the city like this."

"What do you mean?" Solène said.

"I'm not sure." Gill turned to a passer-by. "Excuse me, has something happened?"

"Piss off." The person kept going without missing a step.

"Not very friendly," Pharadon said.

"Welcome to Mirabay," Gill said. "Perhaps everyone would be better off if your kind burned this place to the ground."

"Except the people that got burned to death," Solène said.

Gill instantly felt ashamed. Considering that that was exactly what had happened to his villagers in Villerauvais, the flippant remark had been tasteless. "I shouldn't have said that. Let's try to find that Cup. Pharadon, can you sense it?"

"I can, but barely. There's so much energy here. All the people. Quite amazing. Not nearly as strong as at the temple, but still. The Cup is some distance away, in that direction." He pointed.

"The palace," Gill said grimly.

"That is bad?" Pharadon said.

"It's not good."

"It's been delivered to the man who covets it?"

"Possibly," Gill said, unsure how the dragon would take the news. "But he might not have used it."

"He hasn't. Even against all the background noise, I can tell that much."

"Then there's still time," Solène said.

Getting into the palace would be nearly impossible. Getting their hands on something as important as the Cup? It might as well not even exist. Was he being too pessimistic? "You know more about all of this than I do, Solène. What are our chances here?"

"The Prince Bishop has placed a lot of importance on this. I'm not sure he'll want to use it until he's certain he knows how."

"When will that be?"

She grimaced. "Probably now. I think the thief might have heard Pharadon and me talking. That would have told her all he needs to know."

Gill took a deep breath and started to think about their next steps. As pessimistic as he was, there was something in him that wouldn't allow him to give up. He wasn't sure if it was some sort of innate desire for justice, or if he simply didn't want Amaury possessing the power the Cup could confer.

"It's no good, sitting here on our horses trying to work things out. Let's find somewhere warm with decent food so we can rest up a little. I don't know about you, but I'm exhausted and starving. If Amaury hasn't used the Cup by now, we might have a little breathing space. In any event, trying to rush into the palace to take it back will just get us all killed."

▲▲▲▲▲

Without the unlimited funds he'd had during his last visit to Mirabay, when he'd been on the Prince Bishop's tab, staying at Bauchard's again wasn't an option. There were a number of other reputable inns about the city, however.

The Wounded Lion was tucked away on a quiet street near the Academy. Nondescript, clean and cheap, it was popular with young men coming to the city to take the Academy entrance examinations. Gill had stayed there many years before for that very purpose; when they entered, not only did the warmth of the fire and the smell of baking greet him, so too did a wave of nostalgia. Everything about the place reminded him of a time when life had seemed like a great adventure and the future had offered nothing but opportunity.

For a moment he was taken back to that time. This was where he'd first met Amaury. They'd both dreamed of getting into the Academy. Amaury had been the best blade Gill had encountered up to that point, and they'd quickly identified their usefulness to one another as training partners. Their first sparring session had been in the Wounded Lion's stable yard. Their last had been in the city's main duelling arena, during the Competition.

That fateful day, he felt certain now, had set in motion the chain of events that had brought Gill most of his misfortune. Of course, he had still been required to make a great number of bad decisions along the way. *Why do I have to have so many bloody memories of this shitty city,* he thought.

"Are you all right?" Solène said.

"Yes, fine. Just a few old memories rearing their ugly heads. Probably should have picked somewhere else to stay, but we're here now. I'll see to rooms and have some food sent over, if you and Pharadon want to relax by the fire."

The young woman nodded gratefully, leaving Gill to try and chase the demons from his head as he went to the innkeeper's desk.

"Three rooms, please," Gill said. "My friends and I would like some food and drink."

The innkeeper nodded and smiled. "Your name, sir?" he asked, preparing to make notes in his ledger.

"Richard dal Bereau," Guillot said, borrowing the name of a nobleman two seigneuries over from Villerauvais. All things considered, there was no way Gill was comfortable giving his real name, but given the odd mood in the city, he wanted his lie to be plausible. Hopefully this would withstand any scrutiny for as long as he needed. It was only then that Gill noticed how quiet the inn was. Even though it wasn't the right time of year for the Academy exams, usually plenty of people would stay at the Wounded Lion, many of them Academy hopefuls, in the city to train with one of Mirabay's many fencing masters.

"Not many people around," Gill said as casually as he could. "I have to admit I picked up on a bit of a strange atmosphere when we got to the city. Has something happened?"

"Oh," the innkeeper said. "I'm surprised you haven't heard. The king was taken seriously ill about a week ago. The news has only just gotten out. The Prince Bishop has stepped in as regent. It's all very peculiar, particularly coming so soon after his announcement about this magical order—" He fell silent, looking suddenly concerned.

"Don't worry," Gill said. "I assure you, we're strangers to the city, only just arrived."

The innkeeper smiled genially. "All I'll say is, I recommend you keep to yourself during your visit. I suspect turbulent times lie in store, so you'd be best completing your business and getting home. It's not a welcoming place for those who don't know their way around."

Gill raised his eyebrows. "Thanks for the warning. We'll be careful. Any *word* on the king's health?"

"I really don't know very much, sir. Only that he was taken very gravely ill. The citizens were already discontented with the Prince Bishop's announcement, but for their king to be at death's door, and so young? It's not the type of instability the city needs right now."

"No city ever reacts well to the illness of a monarch," Gill said. He could remember hearing news of all the riots during the final couple of years of the old king's rule. At the time, it had felt like justice. In truth, it still did. The old bastard had treated Gill abominably, no doubt with Amaury's encouragement.

He returned to the others, who had taken a table by the fire, and relayed the news.

"What does that mean for us?" Solène said.

Worry was clear on her face. Considering all she had seen and done over the past weeks, the fact that the Prince Bishop frightened her said a lot. He frightened Gill, too.

"Opportunities and problems," Gill said. "On the one hand, there's no longer anyone to veto what Amaury does. Without the king keeping him in check, he's free to do as he likes. That could cause us problems, if we get caught.

"On the other hand, such a huge disturbance means things will be pretty chaotic up at the palace, and that represents our opportunity. There'll never be a more dangerous time for us to do what we need to do, but I doubt we'll ever have a better chance at success. I'll head out in the morning to take a look at the lay of the land. Until then, I think we could all do with a good night's sleep."

CHAPTER

7

Val had to quickly learn the routine of life at Maestro dal Ruisseau Noir's salon. His hours of tuition were intermingled with the classes taken by the Maestro's paying clients, and his day was always split by a short trip to the Wounded Lion to fetch a pie and flagon of small beer for the Maestro.

He mopped the floors between clients, and after even a few days his hands had become permanently scented by the fine oil the training blades were coated with after every use. Dal Ruisseau Noir appeared to be happy with his service, rarely commenting on any shortcomings in Val's work, and was proving to be an excellent swordsman and tutor.

The Maestro struck Val as being very much what Gill would have referred to as a "peacock" and seemed cut from the same cloth as the last peacock Val had met, Didier dal Beausoleil. Beausoleil had proved to be made from a much higher grade of cloth than most men Val had encountered and he hoped dal Ruisseau Noir would be the same. The man was a fine swordsman, with a muscular and athletic physique, something he chose to hide underneath the clothing of a dandy. Val saw similarly dressed men all about the city; they appeared to think that swords were a decorative accessory, rather than a tool by which a man might make his living. Val wasn't sure why dal Ruisseau Noir did this—perhaps to affect an air of affluence in front of prospective clients.

Val's skills had notably improved in his three days at the salon; he felt that he had a natural talent for the discipline, even if he did say so himself. One of the benefits of watching other students was comparing himself to them. Like him, most of dal Ruisseau Noir's clients were young men training for their entrance exam, and despite the fact that he had far less training and tuition under his belt, he wasn't all that far behind them, and was gaining with each day.

He reckoned it was all about determination. Most of the other students were rich boys; the sons of aristocrats and wealthy merchants. Val had no family. While they all realised that entry to the Academy wasn't a given, that they had to work hard for it, none of them had quite the edge that Val had. They'd never been hungry for anything in their lives. None of them had spent days on end shovelling horse shit and sleeping in a stable. He reckoned the threat of going back to that pushed him to succeed.

Those boys were sent here by their fathers. Val had worked for years toward getting to this position because he wanted it, not because someone else told him it was what he should do. He was champing at the bit for dal Ruisseau Noir to allow him to spar with one of the other students. Until he tested himself, he wouldn't really know for sure.

Until then, all he could do was work as diligently as he could, and practise in every spare moment. He still had a long way to go, and a finite amount of time to get there. At moments it seemed like a monumental, nearly overwhelming, task, but he supposed it was no different from a huge pile of horse manure—you could only clear it one shovel-load at a time.

Not that he'd touched a shovel in weeks. Now it was a mop—which he was using at that moment to wipe the sweat off the salon's mirror-polished wooden floor—or a lunch pail. His reward was that he got to hold a sword. Even if it all went wrong, that experience could never be taken away from him. It was enough to bring a smile to his face.

"What's got you so cheerful?" dal Ruisseau Noir said, appearing out of the changing room at the rear of the salon. "Menial labour is supposed to drain the soul."

"Might be menial," Val said. "But it's better than shovelling shit."

Dal Ruisseau Noir raised his eyebrows and nodded. "That it is. A fine way to look at it. Anyhow, no time to discuss philosophy, I've some errands to attend. I'll be back late, so lock up when you leave.

Unless, of course, you're planning on staying here tonight. Again." He gave Val a knowing smile.

Val had been staying there for a few days now. Although he wasn't even close, yet, to running out of money, he reckoned it was foolish to keep spending it on an inn if he didn't have to. After the first day of their agreement, dal Ruisseau Noir had given Val a key so he could lock up if leaving after the Maestro. The idea of sleeping there to save a few coins had occurred to Val almost immediately.

He'd been careful. Each morning he rose early, washed in the small dressing room at the back of the hall, packed up his few belongings and spare clothes, and left the salon before the Maestro arrived. He'd take a slow walk around the block, and arrive shortly before his appointed hour, to demonstrate his diligence. Dal Ruisseau Noir hadn't shown any inkling that he knew what Val was up to before now, and Val wondered what had given him away. Had the gift of the key been a veiled invitation? Swordsmen were supposed to be proud and haughty, and the offer of charity was not something an aspiring banneret should ever contemplate.

"I . . ." Val said.

"Good thinking, if you ask me," dal Ruisseau Noir said. "Wish I'd thought of it myself. Better to have someone here at night to keep the burglars away. What with the city in such a miasma, the ne'er-do-wells are out in force." He doffed his hat at Val. "I'll see you in the morning, then."

He left before Val had the opportunity to respond. The young man stood there for a moment, not quite believing that his worry about discovery had been so easily dealt with, then shrugged and got back to his mopping.

Val woke with a start and looked around. There was nothing to see in the pitch-dark salon. None of the light from the magelamps in the street reached the salon's windows, so the darkness was total. There was a thud on the door and Val was instantly reminded of what dal Ruisseau Noir had said about having someone there to deter burglars.

There was another thud. He lay deathly still in his bedroll on the wooden floor, and tried to decide what to do. Should he make noise in the hope of scaring whoever it was away? Should he sneak over to the weapons locker as quietly as possible, arm himself, and surprise the intruder?

Another thud was followed by a whisper. "Let me in."

It was dal Ruisseau Noir. Despite the darkness, Val easily found the door and opened it. The Maestro stumbled in. Was he drunk? Dal Ruisseau Noir turned and shut the door, gasping as he locked it again. There was pain in the sound.

"Are you all right?" Val said.

"Be a good lad and fetch the medicines chest from the closet," dal Ruisseau Noir said.

It was too dark and his surroundings too unfamiliar for Val to do that without light, so he bumbled around for a moment until he found and lit the lamp he kept by his bed.

"Shield the light," dal Ruisseau Noir said. "Keep it from the windows."

Val obeyed the odd command, pulling down the small shutter on the lamp so only a narrow beam of light escaped. He hurried to the closet and searched out the medicines chest. Injuries were an occupational hazard in a fencing salon, so dal Ruisseau Noir kept a selection of the handiest supplies available, from bandages of various shapes and sizes to numbing ointments. There was even needle and gut to stitch deeper wounds shut.

He pulled the chest out, balanced the lamp on top, and carried the lot to where dal Ruisseau Noir leaned against the wall. The light flashed across him for a second, long enough for Val to notice that the Maestro was wearing different clothes than those he had gone out in.

"What's happened?" Val said, as dal Ruisseau Noir bent down stiffly and opened the chest. "Were you attacked?"

"In a manner of speaking." He took a swath of bandage out, then rummaged through the jars of ointment. "Shine that light over here a moment."

Val did as he was asked.

"Ah, here we are." He took out the jar and made to open it, but could not grip the lid tightly. He seemed weak on one side. "You wouldn't mind, would you?" he said, holding out the jar.

Taking it, Val opened the jar with ease, then offered it to his employer. Dal Ruisseau Noir tore open the left side of his tunic before scooping a daub of ointment from the jar. Val strained to see what lay beneath the torn-open tunic but glimpsed only the glisten of blood in the meagre lamplight. His eyes widened; was dal Ruisseau Noir moonlighting on the Black Carpet?

The Black Carpet was the name given to illegal duelling, where the combat was carried out on a black mat, or black-painted floor. Regular competitive duels were fought with blunted blades, and scored by "touches." On the Black Carpet, sharp blades were used, and duels were scored by blood-letting cuts. They often ended with the death of one of the duellists. The black floor was intended to hide the stains of spilled blood.

Val wondered what might have drawn dal Ruisseau Noir to the Black Carpet. For some men, it signalled that they'd hit rock bottom. Fortunes were gambled on the Black Carpet, and it was an easy way to make serious money if you were good enough, or lucky enough. But there was another reason to duel on the Black Carpet: for the excitement of it. For some, sport duelling could never match the thrill of the real thing. It was said to be addictive, but Val wasn't sure that would ever make sense to him. He'd seen men die and be badly injured, and there was nothing about the experience he would choose to repeat without very good reason. A bit of excitement wasn't nearly enough.

Unable to contain his curiosity any longer, Val asked, "What *actually* happened?"

"Do you really want to know?"

Val shrugged, but realised dal Ruisseau Noir probably couldn't see the gesture. "I think so."

"A man cut me. It happens from time to time. Comes with the job."

Val frowned, then uttered the dirty words. "The Black Carpet?"

Dal Ruisseau Noir let out a laugh, then gasped in pain. "No, not the Black Carpet. Nothing like that. I'll tell you someday, I promise, but now's not the best time."

He turned his attention back to dabbing ointment on the wound. There was a hammering on the salon's door and dal Ruisseau Noir hissed a curse.

"Shall I answer that?" Val said.

Dal Ruisseau Noir shook his head, then reached over and doused the lamp. There was more pounding on the door, then a shout.

"It's the Watch. We've seen the light. We know someone's in there. Open up."

Dal Ruisseau Noir swore again. He grabbed Val by the shoulder. "Answer it," he whispered. "Pretend you were asleep. You're here alone. There's been no one else here since the end of classes yesterday. Understand?"

"Yes."

"Good lad. Tell them you're coming, then count to thirty."

"Just a moment!" Val said, then started his count in a whisper.

Dal Ruisseau Noir stole away into the darkness, moving with such remarkable silence that after he had gone a few paces, it was as though he was no longer there.

Val finished his count and made a theatrical amount of noise as he went to the door so that dal Ruisseau Noir knew he was moving. He unlocked the door and cracked it open.

"Who's there?" he said.

"City Watch, and we'd ask you the same thing?"

Two men in the jerkins and steel helmets of the City Watch stood in the doorway, holding a large watchman's lamp that filled the little alcove of the door with harsh yellow light.

"I'm the caretaker," Val said.

"Has anyone come in here?"

"People come in here all the time," Val said. "It's a fencing salon."

"Don't get smart with me, lad, or I'll tan the hide on your arse. Has anyone come in here in the last few minutes?"

"No, of course not," Val said. "It's the middle of the night."

"You're sure?"

"Yes, I'm sure. I was asleep, but the door was locked, and all the windows are bolted shut."

The watchman held up his lantern, allowing the light to flood into the salon. Val's heart leapt into his throat as he looked over his shoulder to see what the illumination had revealed. But for the medicine chest and Val's small lamp, the salon was empty. Dal Ruisseau Noir was nowhere to be seen.

"See," Val said. "I'm here on my own."

The watchman surveyed the room a moment longer, then nodded his head. "Make sure the door is locked after we leave. The streets aren't safe at the moment."

"Thanks," Val said.

"Sorry to have disturbed you," the watchman said grudgingly.

Val shut the door, locked it, then returned to his lamp and turned it up enough to see the whole salon. There was indeed no trace of dal Ruisseau Noir—not even a drop of blood. He wasn't so gullible as to call out for dal Ruisseau Noir, and from the stealthy way he had disappeared into the night, Val reckoned his tutor was well versed in how long he needed to delay before it was safe to reveal himself again.

When dal Ruisseau Noir walked into the salon the next morning, it was as though the events of the previous night had not happened. Val waited awhile for him to bring it up, but when it was clear he intended to let the matter lie, Val approached him at the end of one of their hour-long sessions.

"Is now a good time to tell me what happened last night?" Val said. He knew he was pushing the boundaries of their short-lived association, but he had lied to the City Watch for this man, so felt that dal Ruisseau Noir owed him an answer.

"I'd prefer not to," dal Ruisseau Noir said, "but I suppose you're involved now. I'm sure you've heard about the king taking ill, and the Prince Bishop's announcement a bit before that?"

Val nodded his head. It was a strange thing—everyone knew about it, but no one seemed to want to talk about it.

"Well, there are those who think it all a little convenient that the Prince Bishop announces something so profound as the use of magic, and then the king—a fit and healthy young man—falls ill, leaving the

Prince Bishop to take over control of the state as regent. I happen to be one of those people."

"That doesn't explain why you stumbled in here in the middle of the night with a wound."

"No. No, I suppose it doesn't, does it." Dal Ruisseau Noir scratched his clean-shaven chin. "I reckon if you were working for him, you'd already have enough on me by now to put me on the headsman's block."

"Working for who?"

"The Prince Bishop, of course."

Val couldn't help but laugh. It struck him as ridiculous that he might be thought a spy. It was flattering, though. "I don't work for him. I've never even seen him."

"Well, like I said. Anyway, I don't believe the king has taken ill. I think the Prince Bishop arrested him, threw him in a cell, and is in the process of stealing his throne. I went up to the palace last night to take a look for myself." He gestured to his waist, where his wound was concealed by his tunic. "As I'm sure you've worked out, I got caught."

Even to Val, undertaking such an action alone seemed foolishly dangerous. What could dal Ruisseau Noir hope to achieve against the might of the most powerful man in Mirabaya?

"I know what you're thinking," dal Ruisseau Noir said, with that affected, casual wave of his hand that made him look like an idle dandy. "What can one man hope to achieve in the face of such opposition?"

Val nodded and dal Ruisseau Noir laughed.

"I wasn't alone last night. I'm afraid that I'm not going to tell you any more than that, however. Still, seeing as you're in on part of the secret, I'm going to ask you to do something for me."

He took a scroll from his tunic and handed it to Val. A small blob of black wax sealed it shut, but there was no crest impression on the seal, as Val would have expected. "Will you deliver this for me?"

"Where do I need to take it?"

CHAPTER
8

Gill got up early the next morning, eager to take a look around on his own and get a better sense of the mood in the city. For the most part he was hoping for inspiration as to how they could get into the palace. He had spent plenty of time there as an active member of the Silver Circle, and hoped a stroll around some familiar landmarks might jog his memory of some of the palace's secrets. With his hood pulled up to minimise the unlikely chance he would be recognised after five years in the provinces, he wandered toward the palace.

It was an old building, and old buildings always had entrances and passageways that had been forgotten, or were known only to a few. He had spent enough time sneaking women in to see the old king behind his wife's back, not to mention the legion of mistresses who were marched in and out of the quarters of his Silver Circle comrades, to know this. The hidden doors he knew of were out of sight, rather than secret. If the head of the palace guard was worth his pay, they'd all be patrolled pretty regularly.

The old quarry shaft left over from the palace's construction was the obvious way to try to sneak in, but it had been pretty comprehensively sealed up not long before Gill's departure from Mirabay in disgrace. He recalled the engineers saying there was no way it could be breached. Of course, they hadn't had access to the most powerful natural mage seen in centuries. He wondered if Solène would be able to do anything with it, and added the idea to his mental list.

Even if he could get into the palace and as far as Amaury's office, he still had to take the Cup from the Prince Bishop. Both Cups, in fact. He didn't have a problem with that—a reckoning between Gill and Amaury was long overdue and he relished the prospect. If he had to kill Amaury to get the Cup away from him, all the better.

He reckoned something of such importance would be with the Prince Bishop at all times. All he had to do was get to Amaury before the man finally decided to use the Cup. Ordinarily, the easiest thing to do would be wait for him to be out and about, somewhere Gill could get to him without too much security. A few sell-swords, or a little magical distraction from Solène, and Gill would have the singular pleasure of prising the Cup from Amaury's cooling dead fingers.

Sadly, from the look of the palace, that plan didn't have a chance. In all his time there—even after the many attempts on the old king's life—Gill had never seen such a heavy, visible presence of the palace guard. If Amaury had locked his gates so securely, there was no way he planned to come out any time soon. Certainly not before he'd used the Cup. While he was holed up safe in there, sending his underlings out into danger, he could take his time. Amaury was many things, but he wasn't stupid. If they wanted the Cup, they'd have to go in and take it. That was going to bring with it a whole world of problems.

Determination was all well and good, but it didn't get him into the palace, or to Amaury. He wondered if there was anyone in the city he could call on for help. No one sprang to mind, although it did remind him that Val was in the city somewhere. He wondered how the lad was progressing. Perhaps, if things went well, when all this was over, he could call on the youngster.

As he walked back to the Wounded Lion, he racked his brains for any old associate, legitimate or otherwise, who might be of use. There were sell-swords, smugglers, and thieves who had crossed his path over the years, whose services could be had for coin, but after Barnot's betrayal, he felt it prudent to avoid them.

By the time he got back, the only idea he'd come up with was to have Pharadon turn into a dragon and torch something to draw troops away. He paused in the doorway and thought about it more. He'd have to move fast while Pharadon was doing his thing. An attack like that would only encourage Amaury to use the Cup. Gill shook his head and he was filing that away as a last resort when he realised there was someone behind him trying to get in.

He stepped into the Wounded Lion, apologised to the person he'd blocked, and only then looked to see who it was. Val. He did a double take, to confirm it really was who he thought it was.

"Val?" The worried look on the boy's face added years to him. It wasn't what he expected if Val was living and studying with Hubert dal Volenne, and Gill wondered what had happened.

Val looked at Gill with suspicion. For an instant his face hardened, but as soon as recognition reached his brain, he smiled.

"Gill?"

"Not too loud, lad," Gill said. What happened next came as a complete surprise. Val threw his arms around the older man and gave him a hug. Guillot didn't know how to react. He gave Val an awkward pat on the back. "It's good to see you too."

"I didn't know if you were alive or dead," Val said. "I didn't even know how I'd find out."

"I was going to call on you as soon as I got the chance. How's life with old Hubert? He's a good sort, if a bit old-fashioned. I learned so much from him back in the day."

"He's dead," Val blurted out.

"Come again?"

"He died some weeks ago."

Gill frowned with confusion. "What did you do?" He realised they were still standing at the doorway. "Come, let's get a seat. Innkeep! Two mugs of your morning-brew coffee!"

"I'm here on an errand," Val said. "It won't take a second."

"Of course," Gill said. He wasn't entirely surprised that Val had found himself a job. He was an enterprising and determined lad, as his getting Gill to take him on as his squire had shown. "I'll wait for you at the table. Come join me when you're done."

Val nodded eagerly and Gill took a seat. He allowed his mind to return to his problem and watched Val approach the bar while anticipating the invigorating effects of the Wounded Lion's morning brew. It gave a kick to the system that would enliven even the most tired mind and was the saviour of many an Academy student in the run-up to exam time. Hopefully it would provide him the focus he needed to come up with a workable solution.

There was something decidedly odd about the way Val was behaving, almost as though he was acting out a pantomime of carrying on in as suspicious a manner as he could manage. At first Gill didn't think too much of it; after all, the lad had come from the stable at the Black Drake and had been squire to someone who rarely observed the niceties. Gill reckoned it would take Val a while to feel comfortable on the inside looking out, rather than on the outside looking in. When he saw the lad pass the innkeeper a small scroll sealed in the anonymous black wax of the Intelligenciers, Gill nearly threw up.

He drummed his fingers with agitation as he did his best to pretend he wasn't watching Val conclude his exchange. What had the lad gotten himself into? Once the scroll was handed over, Val visibly relaxed, then came to join Gill. The coffees arrived a moment later, and Gill took as much of the hot liquid into his mouth in one go as he could manage. The warmth coursed through him and helped him relax.

"So," Gill said, "if old Hubert has gone to the gods, what have you been doing?"

"I found myself a new tutor," Val said proudly. "Hugo dal Ruisseau Noir."

He explained what had happened since he had reached Mirabay; nothing about the story even hinted at where the note sealed with black wax had come from. Other than this new fencing tutor, dal Ruisseau Noir, Val didn't seem to have had any worthwhile interactions with anyone in the city. How did a lad like him get caught up in Intelligencier business after such a short time in the city? In the end, he was left with no option but to ask.

"Val, I couldn't help but notice you passing a note to the innkeeper."

"Oh, that?" Val said, blushing enough to confirm that he was about to lie. "I deliver messages for a few businessmen. It doesn't pay much, but it's enough to keep me going."

"The black wax the note was sealed with. Do you know what that signifies?"

Val narrowed his eyes, then shook his head.

"That's the Intelligencier seal," Gill said. "Interfering or tampering with it is an instant death sentence. Only the intended recipient is allowed to open it. Even handling it without proper authority can get you killed. Where did you get it?"

"I . . . I really can't say."

Gill nodded slowly. The truth was, it was none of his business, but he didn't like to think the lad had gotten into something over his head. "If you're in trouble, I'll do my best to help you. I'd like to think you can trust me. Not many men can say they've faced down dragons together."

Val chewed his lip for a moment. "There are people in the city who are concerned for the king."

"I heard he was taken ill."

Val shook his head. "That's not what I heard," he said, dropping his voice to a whisper. "I've heard that there's nothing wrong with the king, that the Prince Bishop is behind this whole magic thing, and threw the king into the dungeons when Boudain tried to stop him. There are people looking into it." He smiled with conspiratorial glee. "I'm helping."

Gill leaned back into his chair and thought for a moment. "And these people plan to do what, exactly?"

Val shrugged. "I don't know that. Not yet. But I suppose they're going to free the king, and put him back on his rightful throne."

"Easier said than done," Gill said. "That's a dangerous business to be in. Are you sure you know what you're getting yourself into?"

Val looked sheepish. "No. No, I don't, but I'm in it now, and it feels like the right thing to do. If the Prince Bishop has overthrown the king, someone has to stop him. What right do I have to expect someone else to do that for me? I'm here. I'm involved. What other option is there?"

Gill nodded slowly. It was a noble sentiment, and he could see some of his own youthful attitude in Val. However, he'd learned the hard way that noble sentiments were often a slippery path to disaster. However, this might be the opportunity Gill had been looking for.

"Can I ask how you got into this?"

"It's a long story," Val said. "One that I'd rather not go into."

Gill took another mouthful of coffee and wiped his moustache. If these people Val had taken up with were trying to get at Amaury, they might prove useful allies. He couldn't trust anyone without a vested interest in this, and if they were trying to restore the king to his rightful place, perhaps he could tag along for the ride and snatch the Cups when the time was right. Assuming they were in any way competent. The few conspiracy groups he'd helped stamp out when in the Royal Guard were little more than drinking clubs of idiots with grand ideas, big mouths, and no ability. At the very least, they might provide a more subtle distraction than having Pharadon torch part of the city.

"I'd like to meet this group," Gill said.

Val looked panicked.

"It's nothing untoward," Gill said. "I think that our interests could be aligned, and we might be of assistance to one another."

His words did little to settle the lad. Gill knew that Val had said far more than his new friends would be happy with, and it would be difficult to progress along this avenue without him suffering some loss of esteem. Still, perhaps it would show what a forward-thinking good judge of character he was. Gill smiled to himself. Unlikely.

Solène walked in and Pharadon appeared a moment later. Each day that went by, his human appearance became more and more natural; Gill couldn't see any flaws in his appearance. There might be hundreds, thousands of dragons living amongst people, without anyone knowing. It was a sobering thought, but at least if they could turn into human form, they were enlightened, and unlikely to go on a rampage of flame and slaughter.

"You might remember Solène," Gill said, as his companions approached. "She stayed at the Black Drake with me. This other handsome fellow is our new comrade, Pharadon." For a moment Gill considered going into greater detail, then thought better of it. "Everyone, this is Val, my erstwhile squire. I think he may be able to help us."

CHAPTER
9

Val refused to take all three of them to meet his contact, and was clearly uncomfortable having Gill with him without having first discussed it with his mysterious confederates. Gill didn't like pressuring him into it, but he reckoned it would be for the best in the long run. He didn't want to hang about.

The walk from the Wounded Lion was shorter than Guillot expected; despite what Val had told him about his new tutor, Gill was surprised to find that their destination was a fencing salon. In Guillot's experience, political agitators tended to be of a more cerebral nature, frequenting coffeehouses and reading rooms more often than training venues. However, it appeared that Val's new fencing master was one of the conspirators. Judging by that wax seal, he was also likely an Intelligencier. *Dangerous men to be involved with,* Gill thought, *but needs must.*

An Intelligencier wasn't likely to support a ruler who was trying to reinstitute magic, given that their primary purpose was to prevent the scourge of sorcery from ever rearing its head again. Access to their network was exactly what Gill needed, but he'd have to play his hand very carefully. They were likely to turn on him, Solène, and Pharadon if they learned the truth.

In the salon, he was presented with one man overseeing two students working their way through the positions—the series of guards that all trainee swordsmen practised daily until they were perfect in form and had become second nature.

The maestro, whom Gill took to be dal Ruisseau Noir, frowned as soon as his gaze fell on Gill. He drew himself up and immediately dismissed his students. "That will be enough for today, boys. I'll see you at the same time tomorrow."

Awkward silence prevailed while the two young men packed up their practice blades and left the salon. All the while, their instructor watched Guillot carefully. Gill returned his gaze steadily, but the man was inscrutable. When the door finally closed behind the two students, the man spoke. To Val.

"Who is this?" he asked.

"This is my former lord, Guillot dal Villerauvais."

"Why did you bring him here?" The lean, somewhat foppish-looking man studied Gill. "I've heard of you, sir. I can't imagine you've come for instruction."

"Do I get an introduction?" Gill said, his temper tickled by the man's condescending tone.

"Of course. Banneret of the White Hugo dal Ruisseau Noir," he said, confirming Gill's assumption of his identity. He gave a curt banneret's salute, which Gill returned.

"I'm not here for instruction," Gill said. "I'm here to make a proposal. I think we may be able to help one another."

Dal Ruisseau Noir cast Val a filthy look, but the lad just shrugged. Gill hoped his new tutor wasn't one to bear a grudge.

"Really?" he said, then turned a hard gaze on Val. "I worried that I'd made a mistake telling you anything. Who else have you spoken with?"

"I've not spoken with anyone," Val said. "Anyone else."

"He's a good lad," Gill said. "He didn't tell me anything that would get you in trouble, and spoke only because he knows he can trust me. I'm no friend to the Prince Bishop. You'd not have to ask many questions to find that out."

Dal Ruisseau Noir nodded slowly. "Your proposal?"

"We both want the same thing. The king back on the throne, and the Prince Bishop gone. I suggest we join forces."

"Tired of slaying dragons?"

"You've heard of me?"

"Everyone has. I'd also heard you were dead."

"Wishful thinking on the Prince Bishop's part, I expect," Gill said.

"Where are you staying?"

"The Wounded Lion."

Dal Ruisseau Noir smiled at the name. It seemed most Academy graduates had fond memories of the place.

"How many people do you bring to the equation?"

"There are three of us. All competent. A mix of useful skills and knowledge. I'm not going to be any more specific than that for now."

"That's reasonable," dal Ruisseau Noir said. "I'll take your proposal to my friends. We'll be in touch."

◆◆◆◆◆◆

The city's atmosphere felt even more oppressive to Gill, now that he was entering into a conspiracy against the country's current ruler. Gill had to hand it to Amaury—if the king hadn't really fallen ill, the Prince Bishop had a lot of nerve. And even more ambition. Perhaps he thought that with the Cup's power, he could do whatever he liked. It was a frightening thought. Guillot could only hope dal Ruisseau Noir's people could bring something useful to the party.

When he got back to the Wounded Lion, he updated the others on what had happened. Since he wasn't sure what to make of dal Ruisseau Noir, he painted as neutral a picture as he could. He'd shown himself to be a poor judge of character before—tending to assume the worst—so he reckoned it was likely that any opinion he formed now would be wrong.

They didn't have to wait long for an answer. One of the inn's errand boys knocked on Guillot's door to let him know he had a visitor. There was always the danger that they had been found out, that the "visitor" was a detachment of the City Watch or, worst-case scenario, a unit of Intelligenciers. Gill didn't think either was likely, but put his sword belt on before going down, nonetheless.

Dal Ruisseau Noir was waiting for him in the inn's taproom, alone, when Gill got downstairs. The familiarity of the Wounded Lion was comforting, but today he knew he couldn't lower his guard.

"I didn't expect to see you so soon," Gill said.

Dal Ruisseau Noir gave the innkeeper a knowing nod, and gestured to a table in the corner of the otherwise empty room.

"This is an urgent situation, so my friends made themselves available immediately to discuss your proposal."

Gill nodded and sat.

"One of my friends was able to fill me in a little more on your history, and also gave me some information on one of your friends, Solène of Bastelle-Loiron. She was in the Prince Bishop's Order of the Golden Spur for a time, was she not?"

Gill nodded. There was no point in lying—dal Ruisseau Noir already knew the answer.

"Do you know what her role there was?"

That sounded like a genuine question—after all, not all the Spurriers were mages. Gill was glad he had his sword. Dal Ruisseau Noir had introduced himself as a Banneret of the White—if it came to a fight, it wouldn't be an easy one. "Researcher, I believe. She wasn't there long."

"A researcher?"

"To the best of my knowledge. You'd have to ask her for the specifics."

"I'll be sure to," dal Ruisseau Noir said. "The other member of your party, Pharadon—I could find out nothing about him, which is unusual, but no matter."

Gill shrugged. If confirmation was needed, he now had it. Dal Ruisseau Noir was an Intelligencier. There had always been rumours that the Intelligenciers maintained a network of agents and spies in undercover roles throughout Mirabay, in an effort to spot and head off trouble before it got started. Magic wasn't the only thing they kept an eye on.

"Pharadon is handy in a fight and has brains to burn. We fought dragons together in the provinces. I trust him in this implicitly."

Dal Ruisseau Noir looked at him suspiciously.

"I'll have to take your word on that, for now," he finally said.

"How very kind of you," Gill said.

"The king is being confined within the palace at the Prince Bishop's order, but that's all we know," dal Ruisseau Noir said. "The place is locked up pretty tight and our attempts to get in have been rebuffed. If all is as we fear, then I suspect the king will be put to death as soon as the Prince Bishop has things in the palace under control."

"Do you've reason to believe he doesn't?"

Dal Ruisseau Noir shrugged. "There are a lot of competing factions among the nobility. No man is safe on the throne, tyrant or not. It'll take him time to pull his supporters into line and put enough of a fright into the rest to keep quiet for the time being."

"So we need to move fast," Gill said, glad that the conspirators' plans were in line with his needs. He wanted to hear the extent of their aims before revealing his own, however, particularly as he was wondering why the Intelligenciers were so willing to ally themselves with relative unknowns. As flattering as it was to consider, Gill very much doubted it was due to his reputation.

"Ideally, yes. I don't think the king has long to live."

"And the Prince Bishop? What do you intend for him?"

"For the time being, we couldn't care less. I'm confident the Prince Bishop will get what's coming to him. My priority is to get the king to safety, where plans to restore him to the throne can be put into place."

"Might this not offer the perfect opportunity to kill two birds with one stone?"

"If the chance presents itself, we'd be fools not to take it, but the priority remains to rescue the king. We do not take any risks with his life."

"Agreed," Gill said, meaning it. At heart, he was and always would be a servant of the Crown. "What's your plan to get the king out?"

"We have people in the palace now, trying to determine His Majesty's location. It's tricky, as the Prince Bishop has long maintained a network of spies there, but we've made progress. I hope to have a location by nightfall. We'll have to be ready to move quickly."

Gill nodded. Dal Ruisseau Noir wasn't messing around. It was fast, assertive action, but there wouldn't be much time to prepare. High risk. High rewards.

"I'll make sure my people are ready. Have you worked out how we'll be getting into the palace?"

"We have people looking into options in that regard also."

"I might be of help in that regard. An old quarry shaft runs down through the hill to the river's edge. It's been there since before the palace was built."

"It was sealed shut with steel panelling a number of years ago," dal Ruisseau Noir said.

"I was still there when that happened. Some of the Silver Circle used it to bring women into the palace. One of the ladies—I think she was a friend of Charlot's—got a little familiar with the Duke of Fontonoy in front of his wife, the old king's sister. The princess kicked up a stink. Everyone at the palace knew about the passageway, guards included. They'd been using it to sneak stuff in for years too, but the old king needed to keep his sister happy, hence the steel barrier bedded in concrete, and the instant drop in pox and drunkenness amongst the palace guard."

"I've heard the story. I didn't think it was true."

"Oh, it's true all right." Gill smiled, realising that was the first time he had entertained a fond thought of his time in the Silver Circle in quite some time.

"I don't see how that solves our problem. Getting through that door is impossible."

Bringing up the topic of magic in front of an Intelligencier was not something a smart person did. When there was likely a second Intelligencier tending a bar close by, it was an even worse idea. Nonetheless, he couldn't think of any other way to get through six feet of engineered steel.

"I think I may have a way for us to deal with that."

Dal Ruisseau Noir looked at him quizzically for a moment, but evidently decided not to pursue the thought, for he said, "And you? What do you hope to gain out of all of this?"

Gill had thought about this since they'd first met. There was no need for dal Ruisseau Noir to know about the Cups. "I have an old score with Amaury, and the time has come to settle it. We'll likely provide perfect distractions for one another."

Dal Ruisseau Noir nodded slowly. "Yes, I can see how that might work." He held out his hand.

Gill shook it.

Ysabeau never questioned her employers' desires, so long as she was free to determine the most effective method of bringing them about. She wouldn't tell them how to negotiate trade deals or manage their estates, so never expected them to tell her how to disappear a person who was vexing them. That her father felt the need to instruct her on every minute detail was tedious, and insulting. She'd survived, and thrived, on her own for years, both before and after they had discovered one another.

The team he had cobbled together for her was motley to say the least. It was composed of three academics who looked like they had never been on horseback before and three members of the Spurriers for security. The scholars were clearly not thrilled by having to venture into the wilds of the provinces, and the Spurriers were clearly new inductees—only one had an actual uniform.

That one had some magical talent, which might be needed to decipher the inscriptions, but Ysabeau didn't have too much confidence in his powers, given his appearance.

He was tall and skinny, with a nose too large for his face, and was topped with lank, mousy hair. He had a hangdog look about him, and Ysabeau could only hope that her father hadn't been scraping the bottom of the barrel when he recruited him. If she wanted to get through this mission quickly, effectively, and without burning herself out playing with types of magic she knew nothing about, she'd need him.

The Spurrier her father sent to Bauchard's with them to collect her had made introductions, but she had not been long out of a very deep sleep and now couldn't claim to remember any of them. As they rode away from the city, she called to Hangdog.

"You," she said. "Can you shape rejuvenation spells?"

He looked back at her. "I am Sergeant Pur—"

"I don't care. Answer my question."

"Yes. I can."

She could tell her attitude had put him out, but she didn't care about his name. She wanted to get this job done and dusted as quickly as she could, so she could get her very worthwhile reward. "I don't plan on stopping until we get there. I want you to keep all our horses fit and rested. Us too, if anyone needs it. I doubt our three learned friends over there will last the distance without a little help."

"When should I start?"

"I just told you to," she said, but knew her anger was partly with herself. She should never have come back to Mirabay. She had plenty of money and could have set herself up nicely in any number of places. Instead she was racing to an ancient temple on virtually no sleep. For the second time in just a few days.

There was no sign that her pursuers were waiting for her outside the city, although she hadn't expected there to be. They were after the Cup. It occurred to her that in her tiredness, and because she resented the way her father had controlled her for the short time she was in the city, she hadn't thought to tell him that she had been actively pursued. It was an oversight, but she was sure that with all his power, three people wouldn't pose him much of a problem.

◆◆◆◆◆◆

"The Counts of Aubin and Chabris have both declared against your regency. They're in the process of raising their levies and calling in whatever favours they can."

Amaury stood at the window in his office, listening to the report from his minister of state and looking down on the empty garden. It had been some time since he had seen anyone other than the gardeners in it, and he suspected that word had finally spread that he had a vantage point on what most had hitherto considered a secret getaway within the palace. It seemed his watchful gaze could make the serene beauty of the garden toxic. He didn't know if he should be disappointed or proud. He turned to face the minister, a man substantially older than Amaury who had given his entire life to service of the Crown. He still possessed razor-sharp faculties and had done nothing to make Amaury question his loyalty. He seemed to have swallowed the story Amaury had offered to explain the king's condition, and had received advancement as a result.

"How many men are they likely to be able to raise?"

"I can't say for certain. It's been many years since either of them mustered their levies."

Amaury took a deep breath and let it out slowly. "And the likelihood of them uniting against me?"

"There's no love lost between them, and I expect their rival claims will only drive the wedge between them deeper. The Count of Savin remains an unknown and could tip the scales one way or the other."

"Tell me about Savin, then," Amaury said. Might it be too much to hope that the extended royal family hated one another so much they'd destroy their armies fighting for prominence before ever reaching his walls? It wouldn't be the first time in Mirabaya's history.

"He's something of an unknown," the minister said. "He's never been to court and has shown no interest in politics."

"What does he do with his time?" Amaury said.

"Hawking, hunting, managing his estates. He soldiered for a while, but he gave that up about a decade ago."

Amaury nodded thoughtfully. There wasn't enough to worry about. Yet. He had plenty of more pressing problems and couldn't shake off the feeling that he had his hands tied behind his back. He had the object he had coveted for so long, yet felt he couldn't use it.

Why was that? He had a strong indication of how it worked, and what he needed to do, but still couldn't bring himself to drink from it. He was worried—would he ever have enough information?

He made a resolution with himself that he would use it once Ysabeau got back, irrespective of what new information she brought him. It was as much use to him sitting in his pocket as if he wasted it. He couldn't live much longer on the promise of a better future. Amaury wanted it now.

"What of the city? I'm sure all the little schemers in the coffee-houses are delighting in the current situation."

"There are reports of unrest, but the increased presence of the City Watch has kept any trouble off the streets. In that regard, Watch Commander Mensiac is taking to his new role well, but has asked that you bolster some of his patrols with members of the Order."

"Out of the question," Amaury said. "I don't want the Order to be seen as an instrument of social control. That's our absolute last resort."

"I think that's a wise move, your Grace," the minister said.

Amaury nodded, quenching his irritated frustration. Of course it was a wise move. That was why he made it. He wasn't fool enough to think people would accept magic if the wielders of it were seen as a force of oppression. Sick children cured, injuries healed, the reduction of the pain, suffering, and misery that life in a city like Mirabay brought those at its lower levels—that was what would make the mobs of Mirabay see the value in magic. People were motivated by self-interest. He would make sure everyone knew magic was in their best interest.

"That will be all for this morning," Amaury said. "Tell my clerk to send in my next appointment."

Amaury returned to the seat behind his desk. There was nothing worth seeing out that window anymore. His next appointment was dressed in the cream robes of the Order, although she wore a black, hooded cloak over them. Travelling the streets in Spurrier cream was not the thing to do these days.

This was Zehra Kargha, the Order's new marshall. Amaury was coming dangerously close to losing count of how many of the Order's senior officers had been replaced in the last few months. Dal Drezony, Leverre, Vachon, among others. It was surprising how much the rapid changes in personnel had altered the Order's character.

The new marshall was something of an interesting proposition. A Darvarosian mercenary, she'd impressed the Prince Bishop during their few previous dealings, and when the position became available, once Ysabeau reported that Gustav Vachon had met an untimely end, Amaury had decided to offer her the job.

Kargha wasn't one for talking, so sat there silently, glowering in that foreign way of hers. Amaury wasn't used to that, and as amusing as the novelty was, he felt as though it put him on the back foot in a way he didn't usually experience.

"I know the soft approach isn't your normal one," Amaury said when he was unable to bear the silence any longer. "But that is what I need you to do, for now. I will be appointing a new seneschal and chancellor in due course, and they will take care of the Order's charitable and social functions, but for now you are the only command-level officer of the Order. I need you to organise and manage clinics throughout the city, for the treatment of the sick and injured. The Order's corps of magical physicians has lost many of its more talented and experienced personnel recently, but those who remain are more than capable of dealing with non-life-threatening cases."

She eyed him suspiciously but said nothing. If she hadn't spoken Imperial to him in the past, he would have wondered if she could understand him.

Eventually she shifted in her chair and spoke, her accent rich and her voice sonorous. "This is not a task I expected to be given."

"And it's not one I expect you to carry out for long. Merely until I've had the chance to replace the other command-level roles. That of marshall is most important, so was the one I sought to fill first."

"Clinics for the sick?" she said.

She had a hard face, and Amaury didn't reckon a good bedside manner was one of her talents. Still, needs must. "Clinics for the sick," he said.

"How many?"

"As many as the Order can accommodate. This is a campaign to win the support of the people."

She nodded. "Fine. I'll do it . . . until you find someone more suited."

"There are other projects I need you to oversee for the time being. Water treatment, food preservation, things like that. The Order's remaining mages all know what to do, they just need direction. The details are all in this file." He slid a purple folder across his desk to her.

Kargha picked it up, gave him a nod, and left. Amaury couldn't quite believe it. He couldn't remember the last time he had been treated with such casualness—no bows, no flattery, no obsequiousness. Luther, the mercenary fixer who had originally put them in contact, had said she was a princess. Although Darvarosian royalty was almost as common as Mirabayan aristocracy, they had an attitude, particularly toward those they viewed as being of a lower social rank. She'd need to be good at her intended role, when the time came. If not ... He shook his head. He'd lost enough commanders already. Killing another one who was making his life difficult wasn't going to aid his cause. Not for the time being, at least.

CHAPTER

11

Six of them stood over a roughly drawn map of the palace that had been laid out on the floor of dal Ruisseau Noir's salon: Gill, Solène, Pharadon, the salon master, Val, and another man—who had the intimidating and mysterious look of an Intelligencier who wanted to look intimidating and mysterious, rather than utterly anonymous, as Intelligenciers usually did.

Gill's initial reaction to the small, and not at all merry, band was "Is that it?," but he kept the thought to himself. It quickly became obvious the Intelligenciers had suffered badly in the days following the coup. Their official structure had been all but wiped out—all that remained were some clandestine elements that had already been operating in the city. He had to admire their resolve. There were few groups who would remain true to their mission after the beating they'd taken.

Dal Ruisseau Noir knelt and pointed to what Gill recognised as the Tower of Forgetting, where high-level nobles were imprisoned—and forgotten about. The only one Gill had ever seen leave was carried out in a nondescript wooden crate.

"This is where the king is being held," dal Ruisseau Noir said. "We've confirmed that he is indeed taken ill, so that wasn't simply propaganda on the Prince Bishop's part. Quite severely ill by all accounts, perhaps to the point of being completely incapacitated, but he's still alive.

"The main advantage we have is that we're infiltrating a palace rather than a fortress. If the king were being held in the castle, our chances of success would be nonexistent. As it is, we have only two options for gaining access to the palace," dal Ruisseau Noir continued. "Our man on the inside can do his best to get us into the complex through the front gate and into the palace itself through one of the service entrances.

"We can try this as a group or individually. While moving as a group might on its face attract more attention, staff enter the palace in this fashion several times a day, and it reduces the number of opportunities for discovery at checkpoints."

"Makes sense," Gill said. He kept casting obvious sidelong glances at the other man, hoping he might get an introduction. During the wars, he had sometimes been infiltrated behind enemy lines for whatever purpose, but he had always at least known who the men he was fighting next to were. All the cloak-and-dagger stuff the Intelligenciers went on with seemed like a little much. Still, they were moving forward with such a pace, they were going to be ahead of any information of their plans, which was reassuring.

"The alternative," dal Ruisseau Noir said, "is here." He pointed to the quarry shaft. "Until now, we thought this access point to be impassable. That no longer seems to be the case." He looked up at Gill.

"Ah, yes. It's a steel panel that was concreted into the passage shaft. It's thick—at least three feet, I think. The engineers said at the time there was no military technology that could breach it. They said it was more impenetrable than the city walls." He admitted, "Perhaps I was being hasty in saying it was an option."

Dal Ruisseau Noir looked at Solène, then at Gill. "We know what she is, and we also know that the magic jar has been opened, and the lid lost. There will be much discussion amongst my superiors about how we interact with magic in future." He turned his attention back to Solène. "But for now, our sole remit is to rescue the king. On another day, perhaps we will be adversaries, but not today. I would be grateful for whatever assistance you can provide."

Solène chewed her lip for a moment. "Do we only get one shot at this, or can we try your plan if I can't get through the barrier?"

Dal Ruisseau Noir shrugged. "That depends. How much noise will you make trying to get through the barrier?"

Watching carefully, Gill could see a determined look come over her face. He knew that she didn't like to back down from a challenge, and now that he had placed the idea, she was trying to work out if she could actually pull it off.

"Possibly none," she said. "Magic doesn't tend to make any noise. The effect it causes does sometimes, but not the magic itself." She nodded. "Probably none."

"There's no reason we'd be seen from the palace getting to the shaft's entrance," Gill said. "We can take punts up the river and disguise ourselves as fishermen. There'll be plenty of other people out on the river. If it goes wrong, we can jump back in our boats and try the other way."

"That could work," dal Ruisseau Noir said. "We'll need to organise boats and clothes." He took a notepad and pencil from his tunic pocket and scribbled something down. He tore it off and handed it to Val. "Go to this address and speak to Louis. He'll deliver the clothing we'll need to look the part. Then go to the south docks, pier four, and ask for Gaston the Hook. You'll know why he's called that when you see him. He'll arrange the boat. Then back here right away. Understand?"

Val nodded and was gone. It felt odd to Gill, watching someone else give orders to his former squire. Val hadn't been in his service long, but long enough that Gill felt a proprietary interest. He felt bad, seeing the lad still in a position of danger, all the while trying to do his best and what he thought was right. If there was any justice in the world, Val would be studying under a solid swordmaster, working his way toward his Academy entrance examinations. Instead he was way in over his head in matters a lad his age should barely be able to dream up, let alone take part in. There was no getting away from it now, though.

"We've covered the getting-in-the-door part," Gill said. "What comes next? How do you propose we move through the palace and get to the Tower of Forgetting?"

"By the time we're inside, it will be close to eight bells in the morning. The servants change shift then, having served breakfast. There'll be a lot of people moving around, and it will be easy for us to get lost in the crowd. Our man inside indicates the king is pretty popular with the staff, the Prince Bishop considerably less so. He's had senior people in the household arrested, and everyone's scared. They're keeping their heads down and looking out for themselves. We should be able to get by without too much trouble."

"Unless some little rat who wants to win the Prince Bishop's favour spots us," Gill said.

Dal Ruisseau Noir smiled. "There are nearly five thousand people working up at the palace."

Gill raised his eyebrows. "Really?" In all his time at the palace, both in the Royal Guard and in the Silver Circle, he'd never known that. Good servants were invisible, and the ones close to the king were very good.

"Indeed. The palace employs more people than anything else in the realm. A few unfamiliar faces aren't going to be noticed or re-marked upon.

"I have appropriate clothing for that part of the job already, so we'll be able to move through the palace via the servants' passages until we get to the Tower of Forgetting. That's where our ruse will have to be abandoned. Access to the king has been severely restricted, so at that point we'll likely have to fight our way past the guards, then get the king out and back to the quarry shaft as quickly as we can. From there it's back to the boats, and to a safe house until we can get the king out of the city."

The plan was streamlined, and Gill didn't see any opportunity for him to get to Amaury and the Cup. Amaury's offices were on the other side of the palace from the Tower of Forgetting, so they'd have to split up at an early stage.

They were going into a very dangerous situation, and would be stirring up not one but two hornets' nests. There was a chance trouble in two different parts of the palace would cause enough confusion to work to their favour, but it would also separate them, and might bring down on their heads every soldier Amaury had at his disposal. If he was going to ask someone to face additional danger on his account, Gill was at least going to be honest about it.

"There's something else we have to do when we're there," Gill said, his decision made.

"What do you mean?" dal Ruisseau Noir said, his face turning dark.

"The Prince Bishop is in possession of something that could give him a great deal of power. He hasn't used it yet, so far as we kn—"

"He has not," Pharadon said.

"Thanks," Gill said. "He hasn't used it yet, but when he does, he'll be all but untouchable."

"What is it?"

"It's something ancient that doesn't belong to him. A cup. We need to take it from him before he uses it."

"And what do you plan on doing with it?" dal Ruisseau Noir said.

"Return it to where it belongs, and make sure it isn't used by any man or woman. Then kill him."

"Not tempted yourself?"

"Not even remotely," Gill said. He could feel Pharadon's gaze burn into him. He'd happily forego the Cup's wonders if it meant not having to fight another dragon. Truth be told, it hadn't even occurred to him to try taking the Cup for himself. Considering all the bad choices he'd made in life, he liked to think he'd become adept at spotting them. It didn't always mean he had the presence of mind to avoid them, but in this instance, he wasn't even tempted. The sooner it was out of the hands of the human race, the better.

"This is why you really came to me, isn't it? Not simply to kill the Prince Bishop."

"Yes, it's what we're here in the city to do. I thought if our objectives were aligned enough, we could help one another."

Dal Ruisseau Noir stood up and sighed. For a moment, the strain that was on the man showed, but his inscrutable mask returned as quickly as it had disappeared. Gill reckoned he felt that the fate of the king, and the entire kingdom, was resting on his shoulders. For all his sinister Intelligencier ways, he was quite a young man, less than thirty years old, and he had a lot to deal with now that Amaury had destroyed his chain of command.

"You're telling me the truth?" dal Ruisseau Noir said, then answered before Gill could. "Yes, I think you are. Why hasn't he used it, though? Why is he delaying? If it can give him that much power, all the problems he faces now will be like chaff on the wind."

"We're not sure," Solène said, "but probably because this is a onetime opportunity for him. If he gets something wrong, there won't be another chance. I'm sure he's tempted, but he's being prudent. We have no idea when he'll take that step, though. It could be tomorrow. It could be a week from now."

"Well, he has to be stopped," dal Ruisseau Noir said. "That much is clear, and all things considered, it falls to us to do it."

"There's no one else," Gill said. "No one else even knows he has it."

"We'll need to work the details out carefully," dal Ruisseau Noir said. "Ideally, we'll take the king and you'll deal with the Prince Bishop and the cup at the same moment. I presume this item will be with the Prince Bishop, or close to him?"

"I expect so," Gill said. "The truth is, we don't know exactly where it is, but it can be sensed, and we'll be able to pinpoint it once we get closer."

"Within a hundred paces, I should be able to determine exactly where it is," Solène said.

"That means you're going with Gill," dal Ruisseau Noir said. "And what about you, my silent friend? What unique skill do you bring, and where might it be most usefully employed?"

"My interests lie with the Cup," Pharadon said. "I will accompany Gill."

"I thought that might be the case," dal Ruisseau Noir said. "So, we gain entry together, then your party proceeds to take the cup and kill the Prince Bishop, while mine goes to rescue the king."

"Agreed," Gill said.

"Good," dal Ruisseau Noir said. "We'll be ready to go at first light. We'll meet at pier four on the south docks at dawn."

CHAPTER

12

It had been a long time since Gill was last in a boat. Pharadon had never been in one. They had both stepped into it at the same time, and very nearly gave their mission a wet start. Considering the citizens of Mirabay used the river for waste disposal, it wouldn't have been a particularly pleasant one either. As though the gods favoured their endeavour, a mist had descended on the river and spilled out over the banks. As propitious as it was, river fogs were common in Mirabaya, as the water, chilled in the distant mountains, met the warmer air of the lowlands.

A boatman—another undercover Intelligencier, it seemed—rowed them up the river, dodging the traffic of other fishing boats and ferries, which was heavy even at that early hour. The current wasn't strong at that time of year, the spring thaws being long past and the winter rains not yet come, which meant the water was fouler than at any other time of the year. As various pieces of flotsam and jetsam floated by, Gill felt doubly glad he hadn't ended up in the water. It was heartening to see the water get clearer and fresher as they put more of the city behind them, until they were in the veritable wilds of the upper reach, with the Isle behind them, open ground and fields on the left bank, and the forested slopes and cliffs of the hill on the right.

While dal Ruisseau Noir stood at the back of the boat with a fishing rod, seemingly unperturbed by the boat's rocking, Gill scanned the shore for the quarry shaft's entrance. He'd never seen it from this vantage point—he'd always been on the inside, letting people through the gate. He expected that the entrance had become heavily overgrown, and the task of spotting it was made even more difficult by the fog.

Pharadon personified discomfort. He sat on the narrow wooden bench beside Solène, gripping the bulwark with both hands. It made Gill wonder how vulnerable the dragon was while in human form. He certainly looked far frailer as a human, and he had already alluded to the fact that he could only shape very limited magic while in this form. Like as not, he would be no easier or harder to kill than anyone, but for a creature as ancient and mighty as him, the vulnerability everyone else took for granted must be a shocking proposition.

"I think that's it," dal Ruisseau Noir said.

Gill tried to follow his gaze and eventually spotted a shadow on the cliff face, partly concealed by bushes. He looked up the cliff, trying to get a sense of the location by checking the position of the palace walls and towers, but the structure was completely obscured by fog.

"Looks like it," Gill said, shrugging.

Without needing instruction, the oarsman turned the boat toward shore, and continued his rhythmical movements, accompanied by the gentle creaking of the rowlocks and the splashing of the oars. The day was wearing on, and Gill hoped the fog wouldn't burn off under the day's sun—it would be a gift when it was time to make their escape. Still, he had long since learned not to rely on the things he couldn't control. *Which is pretty much everything.*

The boat juddered and there was a crunching noise as the oarsman drove the craft onto the shore, far enough out of the water that they could hop out without getting their boots wet. *Best not to leave a trail of wet footprints through the palace,* Gill thought.

They got out quickly and hurried to the shelter of the cliff, where they would be out of sight of anyone up on the walls. Dal Ruisseau Noir delayed, shoving the boat back out into the river and giving the oarsman a salute before joining them. Returning the gesture, the boatman then resumed his steady motion, heading for the left bank, where he would wait out of sight.

Pushing aside some of the overgrowth revealed a passageway that sloped upward for a few paces before terminating at the impassable seal. Gill wondered for a moment if the engineer was still alive, and in a flare of twisted humour, considered sending the man a note letting him know they'd gotten through. Assuming they managed it, of course.

Enough light made it in to show that the surface of the steel had taken on a rough, rusty quality, but it still looked impenetrable. He placed his hand on the cold, damp, and gritty metal and gave it a push, just to be sure, but there was no movement. It was as solid as the rock that surrounded it. To be fair to the engineer, Gill didn't think there was any way through it without magic, and even then, seeing and feeling it, he wasn't entirely sure magic would be enough.

"What do you think?" he asked Solène.

She shrugged and gave him a hopeful smile.

Val, Pharadon, and the unnamed Intelligencier remained outside the passage, but dal Ruisseau Noir joined them.

"How does this work?" he said. "In truth, if it's not going to then we can't afford to waste much time on it."

"I don't know yet," Solène said. "I have to decide what result I want, then work out a method of achieving it. That's the starting point. It'll require a little time and a lot of concentration . . ."

"Understood," Gill said. "We'll leave you to it."

He placed a guiding hand on dal Ruisseau Noir's shoulder and led him back to where the others waited. Making small talk was not something Gill was usually inclined toward, but he could see how pale Val had gone, and he felt sorry for Pharadon, who was likely wondering why the hell he'd agreed to this instead of flying in, burning the place to the ground, and picking the Cup out of the ashes.

It spoke well of Pharadon's character, and to the quality of being enlightened, that he was willing to risk death to minimise the death and destruction caused in retrieving the Cup. Gill found himself in quiet admiration.

"Stay close to dal Ruisseau Noir," Gill said to Val. "I'd have you with me, but he'll need the help. You understand?"

Val nodded.

"Don't worry. Dal Ruisseau Noir's a Banneret of the White. I'm sure you'll be in safe hands. Just keep your wits about you and don't try to be a hero."

The lad gave a forced smile and didn't say anything. He looked more nervous than he had before the dragons, but Gill knew that was often the way of it. Your first battle, you don't know what to expect. You're too ignorant to be afraid. Once you've seen all that death and misery, had a taste of it, that changes. Your second battle, you're scared witless. You've seen friends you've known since childhood die in the mud, holding their guts in their hands and calling for their mothers, and you know it could just as easily be you this time.

It was the best argument for being a farmer or a merchant that he could think of. There was an academy full of headstrong young men who'd sneer at that attitude—Gill had been one of them, once upon a time—but he wondered how many of them still would in a decade, after they'd seen some of what it meant to be a banneret and a soldier.

"Where's this safe house of yours?" Gill said to dal Ruisseau Noir.

"Better you don't know," he said. "If you get captured . . ."

"Of course," Gill said. "I'm new to this type of thing."

Dal Ruisseau Noir gave him a sympathetic smile. "I don't think any of us expected ever having to do anything like this."

"Can't say I did," Gill said. He peered into the passageway to take a look at Solène's progress. She was standing with her back to him, staring at the steel barrier. He wondered if she had given up and was simply making a show of things. It was a big ask of her. Powerful or not, she'd only been learning to properly wield that talent for a short time. He felt bad putting so much pressure on her, but he reckoned the circumstances justified it.

▲▲▲▲▲▲

Solène stared at the steel, feeling daunted. Surrounded by rock, she had access to far less magical energy than she'd had only a few paces back. *The Fount is such a curious thing,* she thought, knowing that she was distracting herself from doing something people claimed could not be done.

Magic was no longer something she feared the way she once had. She knew its dangers were ever-present, but since encountering the storm surge of Fount energy at the temple, she had come to realise that even at its most potent, raging force, it was usually completely benign. It was a dichotomy that she'd never have been able to wrap her head around had she not experienced it firsthand.

The thought that she found most unsettling was that she was doing this in plain view of two Intelligenciers. While she was not especially worried about them, the experience brought on an odd feeling, like stealing in front of a watchman, or picking her nose as a child in front of her father, after he'd just told her to stop.

She cast a furtive glance back down the tunnel; the men standing there abruptly turned around, as though caught in the act of trying to sneak a glimpse of her doing magic. It made her want to laugh.

Turning her mind to her problem, Solène studied the door. It was an incredibly thick barrier and there wasn't much Fount present for her to draw on. It felt similar to the way the Fount was choked off by the rock surrounding the archive beneath the cathedral. Although she could see glowing blue tendrils of Fount energy tease around the entrance to the tunnel, very little made it in.

She stared at the lightly rusted steel and chewed on her lip before realising she was looking at the problem from completely the wrong side. She'd allowed one aspect to dominate her thinking to the exclusion of the other possibilities, and chastised herself before walking outside.

"Is there a problem?" Gill said.

"No, just considering the options," she said.

"We really need to get a move on," said dal Ruisseau Noir. "We can't spend too long here or we'll be seen. Do your thing, and please do it quickly."

Solène smiled. "Last time I checked, incitement to do magic was as serious a crime as the doing itself. Being seen isn't the only thing you have to worry about now."

Dal Ruisseau Noir smiled, nodded, and mimed tipping a hat he was not wearing.

"You might want to step back a pace or two." She took a deep breath. Out in the open, there was Fount aplenty, and she could still see the barrier. She focussed her thoughts and pushed everything else—the magnitude of the challenge, the Intelligenciers watching, the task that awaited them once she'd bored through—out of her head. She couldn't simply wish the barrier away—she needed to decide on an approach that would work, and shape the magic to that end. A blow large enough to smash through would likely bring down half the cliff, and perhaps a section of the palace. Even if it didn't, it would alert everyone in the city, possibly the whole county.

She needed to be more subtle. She didn't know of any magical way to drill through a barrier. It was too complex an idea to shape without instruction, or a huge amount of incremental experimentation to get right. Then it occurred to her: all metal melts.

The idea of heating the steel wasn't difficult to hold in her mind—it was no different from the process of creating a flame or a light. It was only the power required that was different. Very different. She channelled the Fount through herself, drawing in the raw, formless energy and converting it to the shape of her desire.

Something inside the tunnel started to glow, illuminating the dark maw of the entrance. It grew ever brighter, until it felt like she was staring at the sun. Hot air billowed out, at first a warm caress, then a constant blast of roasting heat. All the while she fought to hold on to one single thought—the focus of the magic she desired.

This was among the most powerful magics she had shaped. It was not the most complicated—healing would always take that accolade—but the sheer energy she was using was tremendous, daunting. The intense heat and light made it so hard. Solène wanted to shut her eyes, to step away, but knew she couldn't. Even acknowledging the discomfort was straying into dangerous territory, so she shut it out.

She forced herself to ignore the searing heat and blinding brightness, until finally she felt the resistance to her magic give way. Solène released the Fount, and then her focus. The relief was tremendous, and she took a step to steady herself. She felt drained and light-headed, and as though she'd been standing in a gale-force wind, but took satisfaction in her success. Even a few weeks earlier, she wouldn't have been able to shape so powerful a piece of magic. She also knew that had she tried, the effort would certainly have killed her.

"The way is clear," she said.

▲▲▲▲▲▲

He'd shied away from the overpowering heat and light, until it all ended abruptly. Gill walked up to Solène as she staggered sideways one step.

"Are you all right?" he said.

"Fine," she said. "A little tired, but that's to be expected."

Gill looked into the tunnel and saw a large oval hole in the metal plate; the edges were melted and smeared like warm butter. A stream of hardened metal on the ground looked like it had been flowing toward the entrance to the passageway, but had cooled back to solid before it had gotten far.

"Impressive," Gill said, stepping forward. As he approached the former barrier, he could feel the heat of the metal, which he reckoned was still enough to fry an egg. He stepped through, careful not to make contact with any of it; he knew it would burn through his clothes and sear his flesh.

The far side of the shaft bore all the hallmarks of somewhere that no one had been for many years. It was cold, dark, and damp, filled with cobwebs and the sound of dripping water. The thought popped into his head that it must make Pharadon feel right at home. In the next instant, he felt ashamed of the idea. He still had trouble separating the enlightened dragon from his more savage brethren, and from Gill's own preconceptions.

"It's safe to come through," he said.

Dal Ruisseau Noir lit a narrow-beam lamp and shone it up the passage. "Looks to be clear the whole way up. Let's get moving."

They all knew what they had to do, and now that they were getting closer to the palace, silence was essential. They discarded the oilskins they had worn on the fishing boat to complete their first disguise, revealing their second—the palace's service livery of white with gold embroidery.

They moved off at a brisk pace. Gill felt naked without a sword strapped to his waist, but there was a balance to be struck between getting into the palace without drawing attention to themselves, and being able to handle a fight. Dal Ruisseau Noir assured him that their operative in the palace had left a stash of weapons for them near their objectives. Gill thought it an empty gesture. If they found themselves in need, it would be too late to seek out their arms. Claim them too early and they revealed themselves.

Guardsmen's uniforms would have made more sense and allowed

them to carry weapons, but were a far more complicated disguise to put together in the short time dal Ruisseau Noir had had to prepare. There was also the fact that the nature of a royal regiment was such that any mistakes or omissions would have been noticed by sergeants and officers straightaway. Gill had hidden a dagger in his tunic. It wouldn't be much use against a guardsman with a broadsword, but it was better than nothing, and Amaury's powder-blue vestments wouldn't pose much trouble for its point.

The shaft was dead straight for the most part, occasionally turning back on itself as it worked its way up through the heart of the hill. There were larger open spaces at irregular intervals—some were natural formations, while others had been cut by men harvesting some of the dazzlingly pure white limestone used in the palace's construction. He wondered at the backbreaking labour required to cut their way down here, and at the hubris of the king who had commanded it, all to find stone that was perfectly white enough for his new palace. The end result was magnificent, but at what cost? Years of chiselling stone in the darkened bowels of the hill.

Finally they reached something Gill recognised—the double doors leading into the palace. Dal Ruisseau Noir extinguished his lamp and turned to the group, illuminated only by the light coming in through the cracks around the door.

"Everyone ready?"

The door provided a little resistance—mainly from long lack of use. Dal Ruisseau Noir listened by it for a moment, then pushed it open with a gentle squeal of protest from the dry hinges. The door led out into an old storeroom at the back of the palace, deep in the heart of the service area, and somewhere the building's aristocratic inhabitants ventured only for an illicit liaison.

The room didn't appear to be in regular use—other than some stacked furniture covered in dust sheets, it was empty.

"I suppose this is where we go our separate ways," dal Ruisseau Noir said.

Gill felt the first flutter of nerves in his stomach. Events had been unfolding so quickly he hadn't had the time to consider them properly. He preferred it like that—the waiting was always worse than the doing. What made him concerned was that while dal Ruisseau Noir seemed to have a clear plan of action, he himself only had a vague notion of the result he sought, with no real idea of how he was going to effect it. Getting into the palace had been such a dominating obstacle that he didn't know what to do next. Should he simply walk up to Amaury's suite of offices and make an appointment with his secretary?

"Good luck," Gill said.

"All being well," dal Ruisseau Noir said, "I'll see you here within the hour."

It sounded optimistic to Gill, but he supposed if it took them any longer than that, their mission was going to a hell in a handcart.

Dal Ruisseau Noir gave Val and his anonymous, silent colleague a nod, and they were off, leaving Gill in the storeroom, with Solène and Pharadon staring at him expectantly.

Gill thought hard. It was early, so if he was keeping true to form, Amaury would be in his office doing administrative work. He almost certainly had the Cup with him. Now that they were inside the palace, getting there shouldn't be too difficult. Pretty much every guard the palace had seemed to be stationed at the gates and on the walls when Gill had gone on his walk the previous morning. Even if there were roving patrols, he didn't think three random servants would garner too much notice as long as they didn't do anything stupid.

"Let's head for Amaury's offices," Gill said, leading the way.

He had to fight the impulse to run. He wanted to get there as quickly as he could and get the whole thing over with, but palace servants didn't rush—it was a rule. Gill wasn't sure if there was a practical reason for it, or if one of the old kings had simply found running unseemly. Nevertheless, a decorous walk was all that was allowed.

They had not gone far before they encountered another servant, dressed in the same white and gold they were wearing. Gill's heart was in his throat as the man drew closer, but the stranger just passed them with a nod and a friendly "Morning," which Gill had to remind himself to return. Safely past, he wanted to let out a deep sigh, but restrained himself—*so long as we do nothing out of the ordinary, we'll blend in, just like the furniture.*

They continued their slow progress through the palace. There was nothing about the experience Gill was enjoying. He was looking forward to getting into Amaury's office and having a fight—this cloak-and-dagger stuff was too much for him. Far better to rush a bridge filled with hundreds of men who want to kill you, than to sneak around risking heart failure like this.

Even so, as their journey through the palace's service passages went unhindered, Gill gradually relaxed. The passages themselves were a stark reminder of the polarised life of people in Mirabay. Here, the walls were roughly rendered and whitewashed. They had perhaps been touched up over the years, but not often, and they bore all the scuffs and marks of long use. Inches away, on the other side of the wall, there would be wood panelling, plaster mouldings, gilt work, and paintings and frescoes worth thousands of crowns, if a price could be put on them at all. Rich opulence everywhere you looked, hiding a world of whitewashed plaster.

While he was not familiar with the palace's service passages generally, he had used the route down to the quarry shaft a great number of times over the years, and knew the general direction of the Prince Bishop's office. As he led the way, the trio passed numerous servants, all too busy to care about another unfamiliar face amongst many.

Finally, it was time to exit the hidden world of service and enter the opulent world of the rich and titled. Gill took his bearings and set off. His shoes squeaked on the polished parquet floor, a marked contrast to the austere stone flags in the corridors they had just left.

There were more people out here—guards standing sentry duty at various doorways leading to important parts of the palace, groups of nobles discussing matters that were probably far less consequential than the aristocrats were making them out to be, with their hushed voices and severe expressions. Other courtiers moved about too, the "dandies" as they were usually known—those who participated in society for society's sake, rather than for any political or career motivation. Lastly, there were the unnoticed, like Gill, Solène, and Pharadon.

No one even spared them a glance as they passed. Despite Guillot's earlier fears, being dressed as servants seemed to be the perfect disguise. Why would you need a weapon when you don't exist?

There was only one clerk in the antechamber of Amaury's office suite. He looked tired, a harried expression on his face. Amaury had never been easy on his staff, and that didn't seem to have changed. Gill felt bad—what he was about to do wasn't going to be pleasant for the clerk, but at least it wouldn't be fatal. A chokehold would have the man out cold in only a moment, and aside from a wicked headache bad enough to rival the most malignant of hangovers, he would be none the worse for it when he woke up.

"Can I help you?" the clerk said as Gill moved toward him swiftly.

Before Gill reached him, the aide twitched suddenly, then slumped in his seat, chin on his chest, mouth open and eyes shut. He started to snore. Gill cast Solène a glance and she shrugged. He hadn't seen her do that since the highwaymen had tried their luck with him and dal Sason after they'd rescued Solène from a witch hunt in Trelain. It seemed like a lifetime ago and he'd all but forgotten that she was capable of such feats. Probably far more now, after the training and practice she'd had.

"The Cup is yours, Pharadon, but Amaury is mine," Gill said. "I'll be the one to kill him. Understand?"

Both Pharadon and Solène nodded. Guillot opened the door, revealing Amaury dal Richeau, Prince Bishop of the Unified Church, First Minister of Mirabaya, and now Regent. Despite all the grand titles he'd amassed, he was still the puffed-up prick Gill knew him to be.

Clad in his usual powder blue, the Prince Bishop looked up from a pile of paperwork, pen in hand. His face twisted with irritation at the disturbance, and it took him a moment to recognise Gill. Surprisingly, his reaction was to smile.

"I'd rather hoped you'd be dead by now," the Prince Bishop said. "Life seems to be full of disappointments."

"That's funny," Gill said. "I was going to say exactly the same thing."

"And you," the Prince Bishop said, turning his gaze on Solène. "After all I offered you, you chose to betray me."

"Everything you offered came with a price I wasn't willing to pay," she said.

He shrugged, then looked at Pharadon. "You, I don't know. While I can speculate with reasonable authority on what brings Gill and Solène to my office on this fine autumn morning, I'm at a loss when it comes to you. Have I caused you injury at any point, or are you simply in Gill's employ?"

"I've come to retrieve something that doesn't belong to you," Pharadon said calmly.

"Ah," the Prince Bishop said. "The new Cup? Is it yours?"

"After a fashion," Pharadon said.

"After a fashion," the Prince Bishop repeated. He moved a bundle of papers to one side, revealing the Cup sitting on the table.

It was exactly like the one Gill had found, and he couldn't be certain it was the one they were after—the unused Cup that Pharadon needed to ensure the goldscale dragon reached enlightenment.

"Is that it?" Gill whispered to Pharadon.

"That is it," Pharadon said.

"You're sure. He has two of them now."

"That is the unused Cup."

"I'm sorry," the Prince Bishop said. "I hate to interrupt, but I'm very busy, so can we move along? You're here to take the Cup from me, so come and take it."

Gill studied him. He was very confident for a man facing three opponents. It wouldn't be beyond Amaury to try bluffing them, to stall for time until help could arrive. He probably had a bellpull under his desk, connected to the nearest guardroom. Then again, he might have something up his sleeve, and Gill didn't have a sword to dig his way out of trouble with, only a dagger. It would be enough to deal with this ponce, though. Gill didn't expect Amaury to have a sword—it wouldn't look right with his church vestments.

"Give us the Cup and this doesn't need to get unpleasant," Gill said, oddly feeling bad for the lie.

The Prince Bishop laughed. "How very sporting an offer. However, I'm afraid I must decline. Perhaps I can offer you something else? After all our history, I won't lie to you, offer you a role in my government, titles, and a happy-ever-after in Mirabaya, but I can offer you a large sum of gold on the understanding you leave the country on the first ship and never come back."

He scanned the others. "I can offer you all the same deal. Ordinarily I wouldn't even be this generous, and as much as I'd like to see your head on a spike, Gill, I've far bigger matters to deal with, and swatting mosquitoes is something I simply don't have the time for."

"You say the sweetest things, Amaury," Gill said. "Shame you couldn't have been so generous when you were convincing old Boudain to have me done for treason." He knew he didn't have time for verbal sparring, but if he was going to kill Amaury, Gill wanted him to know that he knew all the wrongs done against him.

"Ah, you know about that?"

"I suspected, but now I do. Like you said, we've a lot of history. A turd that big won't make it under the bridge with the water. Give me the Cup and I'll end you fast and painlessly."

The Prince Bishop gasped in mock indignation. "Well, when you put it like that."

He reached for the Cup and Gill moved to cut him off, drawing his dagger. He was too slow—the Prince Bishop lifted the Cup, put it to his lips, and tipped it back.

Pharadon roared. Solène blasted the Prince Bishop into the back wall of his office. He sat there a moment, dazed, shaking his head. Gill grabbed him by the neck and hauled him to his feet.

"You greedy bastard," Gill said, holding his dagger to Amaury's neck. "There'll never be enough for you, will there? You'll always want more. I wonder which hell you'll end up in." Before he could cut Amaury, he found himself flying back across the room and slamming into the wall with a brain-rattling impact. Groaning, Gill did his best to get back to his feet while trying to stop the room from spinning around him.

"Well, I've definitely never managed anything like that before," the Prince Bishop said, "so I'd say it's worked. To think, it's been sitting on my desk, full to the brim, for a couple of days now, and I was too afraid to drink from it."

Gill looked up at Pharadon and was pained by the distraught look on the old dragon's face. He stared dumbfounded at the Cup, lying on the floor. It was Gill's fault. If he hadn't insisted on being the one to kill the Prince Bishop, the bastard would be dead and they'd be on their way out of the palace with the king, the Cup, and the realm saved. He was a fool. Such a bloody fool.

"I have to thank you, Gill," Amaury said. "You're the perfect cure for the paralysis of indecision. Do I know enough to make it work? Should I take the chance? You forced my hand. All that wasted emotional energy. Not good for the heart. Still, all's well that ends well. You won't, of course. End well, that is."

The Prince Bishop smashed him into the wall again. It was an odd sensation. Not initially painful, it was like being hit by a wave. The impact was the thing, and that knocked the air from his lungs and filled his vision with stars.

"This really is something special," the Prince Bishop said. "And to think, Solène, that you've had nearly this much power all along, and done what with it? Bake nice bread in Trelain until you were nearly burned at the stake? You could have flattened that mob and taken the whole town as your own. What a wast—"

The Prince Bishop's words stopped abruptly. Gill looked at Solène, who had a look of furious concentration on her face.

"Get out now," Solène said. "I'll. Hold. Him. As. Long. As. I. Can."

"I can't leave you here," Gill said.

"Go!" she hissed through clenched teeth. "I'll follow when I can."

Pharadon grabbed him by the shoulder and pulled him out the door. They started to run.

sible for their failure, there was no telling what the dragon's n would be. Likely it would be fatal.

an't believe I let Amaury get the better of me again," Gill said, to bear the silence any longer; Pharadon remained standing, g out into the mist. "He pulled my strings perfectly. I should have n my dagger into his eye the moment I walked through the door."

hough, perhaps, it isn't," Pharadon said, his voice back to nor-ompletely ignoring Gill. "There's no way to know, and no way to ge what has happened. It was merely luck that the Prince Bishop t use the Cup as soon as it came into his possession. We were lost noment his agent managed to sneak it from the temple."

What do we do now?" Gill said. "Is there any hope for the gold-?"

haradon shrugged. "So long as we draw breath, there is always e. It's said goldscales can reach enlightenment by themselves, but might be legend. I wasn't willing to take that risk—she might be last of my kind. I can't claim to know all the secrets of my race, so return to the temple, and read from the inscriptions. Perhaps there l be an answer there. Perhaps fate will be more discerning, than to my kind vanish from the world."

"I'll help you," Gill said. "However I can."

Pharadon turned to him and smiled. "Thank you."

Noise in the passageway drew their attention. The commotion grew oser, and Gill swore in frustration. Why had he not left some swords n the riverbank? They had moved from plan to action so quickly that e had not had time to think through every potential problem.

Dal Ruisseau Noir emerged from the tunnel, a man-sized bundle n his shoulder. He was breathing hard.

"We got the king," he said, but there was no triumph in his voice.

His silent comrade emerged from the gloom of the passageway a moment later, also carrying someone over his shoulder. Gill felt his stomach turn at the sight. It was Val.

The Intelligencier set his burden down on the shore. Val's face was deathly pale and there was a trickle of blood coming out of the side of his mouth.

"What happened?" Gill said.

CHAPTER

14

G ill slumped down on the riverbank, exh
through the palace corridors. He and Ph
a number of disapproving looks from ser
possibly one or two admiring glances from youn
yet fully given in to the rules. The boat wasn't w
neither were dal Ruisseau Noir and his party. Ei
left—and Gill reckoned dal Ruisseau Noir's dev
would have allowed him to make that call with li
they had not yet returned.

Hopefully their mission had gone better than his
Pharadon in the eye. His desire for revenge, to sett
Amaury, had cost them everything. How could he l
fool? How could he have allowed himself to grow so
A little luck against one deranged adult dragon and a c
ture, unenlightened juveniles, and he had behaved like
his prime. Was he doomed to never learn from his mis

"We were so close," Gill said. "Pharadon, I'm so so
fault."

"Perhaps it is," Pharadon growled.

His voice held that low rumble that Gill had only hear
ons in their natural form. It seemed completely unnatu
from a man and made the hairs on the back of Gill's nec
Feeling naked without a sword at his waist, Gill looked at
in human form, but it was impossible to judge what Pha
thinking or feeling. Every expression on his face was ai
tended to make him look like a normal person. If he believe

respon
reactio
"I c
unable
starin
throw
"T
mal,
chan
didn
the r
"
scal
l
hop
tha
the
I'll
wi
se

cl
o
h

"There was a small skirmish," dal Ruisseau Noir said. "Val did well. Very well." He paused, then said, "They wounded him."

That much, Gill could see. "How do you feel, lad?" He took Val's hand. It was cold.

"Sore," Val said. He tried to smile, but his face was too twisted with pain. "We saved the king, didn't we?"

"We did," dal Ruisseau Noir said. "We have him here. He's safe."

Gill feared anguish would overcome him. Where was Solène? Had she managed to get away from Amaury? If she was here, she'd be able to do something for Val. He should have stayed back in the office to allow the others to escape. They were all of more use than he was. Another mistake.

Val coughed wetly, splattering blood over his ghostly white face.

"Rest easy, Val," Gill said. "Solène will be here soon. She'll be able to help you." He looked up to Pharadon. "Is there anything you can do?"

Pharadon shook his head sadly. "I'm sorry, Gill. I can't shape magic like that on anything but my own kind."

Full of despair, Guillot squeezed Val's hand and felt the lad's feeble effort in response.

"I didn't get to be a banneret, Gill," Val said.

"It's a silly thing, Val, just a name, nothing more."

"Still," Val said, his voice fading, "I slew dragons and saved the king. That's not bad, is it?"

Gill felt tears stream down his face. "It's more than most bannerets can ever dream of."

"I liked being your squire," Val said. And then he was gone.

"No, no, no," Gill said, balling his hands into fists and pressing them against his eyes. "No more. I'm going back in to get Solène. I can't lose anyone else."

He stood and made for the entrance to the passageway, but Pharadon grabbed him, then embraced him. Gill let out three great, wracking sobs. He had no more fight left in him. Every time he tried, it ended in disaster. He was a disaster.

"There's nothing to be gained by going back," Pharadon said. "You'll die. Only Solène had the power to delay the Prince Bishop and get away. She knew that, and that's why she did what she did."

"I'm sorry about the boy," dal Ruisseau Noir said. "It was damned bad luck."

Gill nodded mournfully. "How is the king?"

Kneeling beside Boudain, dal Ruisseau Noir shook his head. "Not good. I don't know what the Prince Bishop did to him and I don't know if it can be undone."

"Where's your boat?" Gill said.

Dal Ruisseau Noir got to his feet and looked across the river, seeming worried. "I don't know. It should have been here by now."

There was more noise in the passageway. They all turned, and drew whatever weapons they had on them. Solène emerged, looking utterly drained.

"Where's the boat?" she asked, seeming surprised to see them all standing around.

"Not here yet," Gill said.

"I'm being chased," she said. "There's no time to wait."

"We'll have to swim for it," Gill said, bending down to pull off a boot.

"What about the king?" dal Ruisseau Noir said. "He'll drown."

"Maybe," Gill said. "But if Amaury gets him back, he'll be dead before sunrise."

"There's another way," Pharadon said.

When Gill looked at him, he saw that Pharadon's human form was already starting to break down at the edges; he looked like a person who had started to melt. The shape beneath the malleable flesh began to change and grow larger. His skin grew dusky, then took on a rose tinge. Gill could see individual scales starting to form. For a moment Pharadon looked like some strange human lizard being, having the general form of a man, but covered in lustrous red scales.

"What in the name of the gods?" dal Ruisseau Noir said.

"There's no need to worry," Gill said. "I assure you, he's on our side."

There was something stomach-churning about watching the transformation—seeing a person come apart like putty and become something else. At the same time, there was something intimate about the act, and Gill felt that continuing to watch was in some way an invasion of Pharadon's privacy. He turned and looked out over the mist-laden river, pretending to look for the boat, which he was beginning to realise was never going to come.

Solène placed a comforting hand on Gill's back. He looked up at her. She was staring down at Val's body.

"Is there nothing you can do for Val?" he said.

"I'm sorry, Gill; he's dead. Even if I'd made it back earlier, I don't think I could have helped—it was too great a wound. I only seem to be able to heal injuries that would mend on their own, given time. A mortal wound is beyond any skill I have. Moreso when I'm as drained as I am now."

"How did you get away?"

"The Prince Bishop doesn't know how to wield his power yet. He overreached. I was able to take advantage of that and get away from him, then mask myself from others. It took nearly everything I had. We need to get out of here. Before it's too late."

He nodded. "Can you swim?"

"A little."

"Good, you might have to rescue me," Gill said. To his surprise, he laughed, and after a moment, so did she. When he turned back to Pharadon, the ancient creature was now the size of a small house and fully returned to his dragon form. He continued to expand, albeit more slowly, until he reached his normal dimensions—and just in time. Gill could hear noise coming down the passageway. Someone must have finally figured out that the quarry shaft's impenetrable barrier was no more.

Dal Ruisseau Noir and his colleague were both staring at Pharadon with dropped jaws. It struck Gill as odd that the sight of a dragon was no longer astonishing to him; it seemed that even the most fantastic act could become mundane, given enough time.

"Will you take Val also?" Gill asked. "I want to make sure the boy gets a proper burial."

"I will," Pharadon said.

"There's a village a full day's ride east of here," dal Ruisseau Noir said. "Castandres. I'm told that one of the king's cousins has established a garrison there to maintain the peace. We should regroup there."

Pharadon's mouth curved into a smile. "If there are a large number of soldiers there, landing a few miles away might be better for me. I'll revert to your form, then fetch you to your king."

The noise in the passageway resolved into the sound of men running in armour, a noise which was ever the signal that it was past time to leave. Pharadon stretched his wings, casting them all into shadow.

"Time for us all to depart, I think," the dragon said, his voice rumbling from his massive chest.

He sprang into the air, showering them all in dust and gravel. Gill didn't need to be told twice. He plunged into the river, which was as cold as he had feared. He gasped for breath as he turned to look back. The others were following him into the river, while Pharadon, hovering, had taken the king in one claw and Val in the other.

As Gill floated downstream, he watched Pharadon rise in the air as effortlessly as smoke, then turn and disappear from sight. He wondered how many people would see the dragon and what panic that might cause.

He couldn't shake the thought of Val's lifeless face from his mind. It wounded Gill to the core of his heart to see a fine young man dead. He tried to console himself with the warning he had given Val when the lad had first asked to be his squire. Val had chosen this life, and the risks it entailed, as did every young man dreaming of being a banneret.

None of them expected it to end badly, though. They all thought they were invincible—that belief was vital to the dream. If they knew the reality, if their fathers had taken them to see a battlefield rather than to the parade of an army marching out of the city, he suspected the Academy's dormitories would be far less crowded.

It was said that the sons of Mirabaya died cheaply for a priceless dream. Guillot had seen that more times than he cared to dwell on. He rolled over and started to stroke downriver as shouts erupted from the mouth of the passageway. Amaury might have won today, but they weren't done. The debt had grown ever greater, and so long as Gill drew breath, he was determined to see it settled.

CHAPTER
15

Ysabeau surveyed the temple site from a distance, and maintained her watch for at least an hour. Only when she was sure there was no movement did she approach—alone—to take a closer look. She peered down into the hole and was relieved to see no signs of activity. The temple itself looked exactly as she remembered it, magnificent and ancient. The academics would wet their britches when they saw it. Still, she had to be certain it was safe before she let anyone else enter. Enough people had been lost down there already. She doubted her father would be happy with her if she lost more.

She used a touch of magic to conceal herself—there was an enormous amount of energy to draw on down there, so she had no trouble making herself all but invisible. The hardest part was keeping all that power out. She shuddered at the thought of what might happen to her if she let its full force flow through her.

When she entered the second, lower chamber, Ysabeau stopped dead in her tracks. She even held her breath, so terrified was she of making a sound. One of the dragons was still there. It took her a moment to push the initial fear aside and get her mind working again. The creature seemed to be sleeping, and had not been disturbed by her presence. The temptation to go over to it for a closer look was almost overwhelming. How many people could say they had seen a dragon from so close, and lived to tell the tale?

What should she do? If she brought her people down to do their job, they would certainly wake the creature, and it would kill them all. Likewise, she had no great desire to return to Mirabay and explain to her father why she had failed. Might they slay it while it slumbered? She had heard the stories of how many men her father had sent to kill dragons, and knew how many of them still lived, so didn't think for a second it would be an easy job, but perhaps, if they were fast, and silent?

She returned to the surface and called the Spurriers to her. The academics looked annoyed that they weren't being made privy to the conversation, but after the long and unrelenting ride, they had learned better than to complain. She would have told them, but didn't reckon their bowels would hold up to the prospect of a dragon slumbering beneath their feet.

"There's something down there I wasn't expecting," she said quietly to the three Spurriers.

"What?" Hangdog said.

It was no surprise that he was the only one to speak. The other two were professional soldiers, happy to follow orders. Likely they would voice an opinion only when dealing with a matter of a military nature.

"There's a dragon down there."

"What in hells?" one of the soldiers said.

"Sergeant Tresonne, isn't it?" He nodded. Ysabeau smiled thinly. "It's sleeping."

"Great," Hangdog said. "Let's get out of here before it wakes up."

"Would you like to be the one to tell the Prince Bishop why we've failed our mission?"

Hangdog shook his head.

"Didn't think so. I've no more desire to die here than any of you, but if we can complete this mission, we will. Now, the dragon seems to be very deeply asleep. Hibernating maybe, I don't know. It didn't react to me being down there at all. We might be able to do what we need to do and get out of here before it wakes." A thought occurred to her: just how deeply did this creature sleep?

"We'll need to be careful," Hangdog said.

"Of course," Ysabeau said, not bothering to hide the contempt in her voice. "Why don't you go and explain the situation to our learned friends? Try not to scare three hells out of them. There's a good chap."

⋀⋀⋀⋀⋀

Ysabeau needed to give everyone a few minutes to come to terms with the fact that they were standing next to a real, live dragon. It wasn't as large as the other one she had seen, but its lustrous golden scales made it far more magnificent. It had to be one of the ones that had reached the temple when she had been there the last time, so it had been awake recently, and that made her wonder if it might awaken again soon. Was her intention to push forward worth the risk?

Every one of them had heard tales as a child, of slumbering dragons in dark, forgotten places, keeping an ages-long vigil over their hoards of treasure. She supposed the treasure in this instance was the forgotten knowledge the temple contained. That might disappoint an ordinary person, but for those who already had money and power, this was the true treasure.

No one dared let out even an overly loud breath, let alone speak. They were all in awe, even Ysabeau, who had seen the creature before. It truly was incredible, and she reckoned she could stare at it for hours.

Recalling the violence that had taken place during her previous visit to the temple, she looked around. There was nothing to mark that incident—not even patches of blood on the floor. Of the bodies, or the Spurriers who had still been alive when she left, there was no sign. It was curious, but then again, the temple was a curious place.

The magic here was potent beyond belief—there was no dust, no deterioration, nothing at all to indicate how old the place was. The reliefs were crisp and pristine, as though they'd been created only yesterday; the inscriptions were sharp and distinct. The statuary, mainly of dragons, was vibrant and lifelike. There was no moss, no muck, nothing but what the creators of the place had intended. Perhaps there was an enchantment that kept it clean. She hoped that it was included in what was inscribed on the walls—she could certainly do with it for her apartment in Mirabay.

"All right," she whispered. "Time to get to work."

The academics reluctantly pulled themselves away from the spectacle of the slumbering creature. The temple was surely an incredible place for them, the type of thing archaeologists and linguists must dream of. That the three of them had barely noticed the wonders on the walls spoke volumes about how breathtaking the dragon was. As they walked by, she couldn't help but glance at their britches. None of them had pissed themselves, which impressed her. Perhaps they were made of sterner stuff than she had given them credit for.

Now that their attention was turned to the wealth of material all around them, they whispered excitedly, dividing tasks up amongst themselves. That done, they unpacked materials from their satchels and moved to their designated sections of wall. They were in their element now, exploring knowledge being their comfort zone. Gone were the quiet, sullen countenances, replaced instead with excited faces full of youthful energy. She supposed if you matched someone to their interest, anyone could display passion.

"I suppose we just need to wait and let them do their thing," Hangdog said. "How long do you think they'll take?"

Ysabeau shrugged. "As long as it takes. I want to be out of here in no more than three days, though. If they're done before then, great. If not, best make yourself comfortable. And useful, if they need any of your 'special' help." She turned to the soldiers. "Let's keep an eye on that dragon, be ready if it wakes up."

They both visibly paled.

"Don't worry," she said. "I'm not trying to make a bunch of dragon-slayers out of you. We just need to hold it at bay long enough for that lot to get away with whatever information they've gathered. That's the mission goal, that's what we have to make sure happens."

"We could build a picket of some sort," Tresonne said. "I doubt it'd last long, but it might buy us the time we need if that thing wakes up."

"Get on it," Ysabeau said. "But do it quietly."

No sooner had the words left her mouth than there was a clatter behind her. She turned to see what had happened. One of the academics stood sheepishly over a portable easel that lay flat on the ground.

Fear surged through her as she turned back to the dragon, but the beast slumbered soundly. She breathed a sigh of relief.

The noise had been loud—certainly loud enough to have woken the beast. Perhaps this dragon was in one of the thousand-year sleeps the old children's tales spoke of. The thought she'd had earlier returned. What was more impressive a feat—slaying a dragon, or capturing a live one?

She clapped her hands hard, then again. The sound rang sharply through the temple and everyone flinched, even the soldiers.

"What in hells are you doing?" Hangdog said.

"It's out cold," Ysabeau said, clapping again. "It must be some kind of hibernation." She clapped one last time, then shouted as loud as she could, then laughed.

"Tresonne, that last town we passed through. Get back there fast and have the smith build us a cage. I think you know how big it needs to be!"

"You want to capture it?" Hangdog said.

"Why not? Better than leaving it here, don't you think?" If this didn't impress her father, nothing she ever did would. Bringing home a live dragon . . . The thought brought a smile to her face. She walked forward and reached out. Ysabeau hesitated for a moment—was this the most foolish thing she'd ever tried?—then placed her hand on the dragon's snout.

It didn't feel how she expected it to, but then again, she had no idea of what to expect. She'd seen snakes in menageries, but never touched one. The dragon's scales were hard, but not like pieces of slate—more like a boiled leather cuirass, but thicker. They were warmer and softer to the touch than metal or stone, but looked like they were made from beaten gold. She wondered if there was any actual gold in the scales. If there was, the scales on this creature would be worth more than the king's fortune.

The beast was breathing, albeit very slowly. Ysabeau counted twenty of her breaths for one of its, although she was breathing faster than normal. Her heart was racing, too. It would take far more than a gentle touch on the nose to get the dragon into a cage. She tapped it and immediately sprang back, but it didn't react. She moved forward and tried twice more. Still nothing.

"We're capturing this creature, and we're bringing it back to Mirabay with us." It might have been taking a risk, but the reward? The prestige of possessing a captured dragon would far outweigh any power that silly little cup could give him. Magic had too many limitations—far more than her father seemed to realise. Reputation didn't.

She wanted it, but it was a big task and they had to move fast. Who knew when the creature might awaken? They'd all be in serious trouble if it wasn't constrained by then.

"You go with them," she said, pointing at Hangdog. After the way she'd shut him down when he'd tried to tell her his name, she didn't want to have to ask it now. "Do whatever it takes to speed the process up. I don't know how long it takes to make a cage, but I want one here tomorrow. Understand? Magic, manpower. Whatever. It. Takes."

He looked at her with an expression of disdain. Clearly her time frame was unrealistic, but that was why she was sending him. During her time at the Priory, she'd seen impressive feats that would have taken a team of people days to complete, carried out in only a few hours. That was what she needed from Hangdog and the village's smith.

"A wagon also," she said. "The biggest one you can find, and a team of oxen to haul it." She moved around to the dragon's side and wondered if she was biting off more than she could chew. It was large, but it was far smaller than the other one she had seen. The wagon would still need to be big, though, to support the weight of the cage as well as the creature. As she thought on it, they might need more than one.

"Tresonne, judge for yourself if we'll need more than one wagon and team to move it when you see the finished cage. It'll be best to assemble the cage around it, so have the smith make it in parts that we can assemble here. Bring him back with you to finish the work. Also a team of men with blocks, tackle, and line, and struts to get the whole thing out of here."

"Yes, ma'am," Tresonne said. "I'll rustle up as much help as I can. Better to have more than we need than not enough."

She was fast coming to appreciate Tresonne. He didn't say much, but when he did, he was worth listening to. The academics had huddled and were watching the exchange.

"Have you completed your task?" she said.

One of them shook his head.

"Then I suggest you get back to it. Tresonne, as fast as you can, please."

"Ma'am."

She turned her attention back to the sleeping dragon as Tresonne and Hangdog left the chamber. This wasn't going to be easy. Then again, the things worth doing never were.

PART TWO

CHAPTER
16

Ysabeau didn't sleep, and barely took her eyes off the dragon for a day, a night, and another day, as she waited for Tresonne and Hangdog to get back. Magic kept her alert and functioning, but there was only so long she could burn that particular flame before she paid the price. With luck, she'd be long gone before it came to that.

The academics worked industriously, making sketches, taking rubbings, and copying inscriptions. They had decided their time in the temple was best spent acquiring as much information as they could. They could take the time to study and interpret it when they were back in the comfort of their university buildings. She reckoned it was the right decision—it was always best to make hay when the sun shone. You never knew when the clouds would close in. Nonetheless, she was intrigued—what secrets were hidden in those indecipherable-to-her carvings?

She felt sorry for the scholars when they chattered excitedly about the books they would write about their discoveries. Each expected his name to go down in academic history. Solène suspected none of the knowledge discovered in this chamber would get far beyond her father's office, and there was a distinct chance these three men would end up floating down the Vosges when their usefulness had passed. Knowledge had value only so long as it was controlled. When everyone had it, its power was gone. Her father, who knew that well, was not a man to give to others what he could hold on to himself.

Noise at the entrance to the temple came as a huge relief. She had been on edge for a long time now, and her heavy use of magic was making her jittery. She walked up the ramp from the main chamber to the open-topped room that served as the entrance.

Tresonne peered over the edge.

"I think we've got everything we need," he said. "We'll start lowering it down."

The cage came down in six sections; bolt clamps around the edges would affix each section to the next. Ysabeau inspected the work, hoping it would be strong enough if the dragon woke up. The bars looked like good-quality steel, and the welds all appeared to be sound to her inexpert eye. It was as much as they could do, but might still count for naught if the dragon was strong enough to smash its way through. It would be best for all involved if it remained in hibernation, but that seemed like too much to hope for.

True to his word, Tresonne had brought help—half the village, it seemed. Ysabeau was ambivalent about letting any of them see what was down here. There was enough gold in the statuary and reliefs to make them all wealthy, and certainly more than enough to tempt even the most honest to theft. There was an easy solution to that, once they had finished their work, but killing most of a village's able-bodied men seemed excessive, even to her.

There was another solution available, but she wasn't sure it was wise, considering how much magic she was already using. Still, short of murdering a great many innocent men, she couldn't think of a better way. They were coming down here to pull a dragon out from what they probably assumed was a cave. With their minds already open to the idea, creating the necessary illusion to feed that belief required far less magic than it might have otherwise. Still, shaping that magic would be a test of her skill at the best of times, and now, tired as she was, it would be a true challenge. She had never backed down from one before, though, and didn't plan on starting now. She explained to Tresonne and Hangdog what she planned to do with her illusion, and instructed them not to mention anything about the temple's true appearance, and to act as though it was a plain cave.

The men looked about themselves nervously as they carried the sections of cage down the ramp and into the main chamber. To their eyes, thanks to Ysabeau's work, it appeared to be a natural chamber in the rock, complete with stalactites, stalagmites, and echoing drips of water. Their shocked reaction to the sleeping dragon was so strong that she was amazed they didn't drop their burdens or pass out. Once the cage sections were in, they brought down a number of logs to use as rollers under the assembled cage. It was going to be a big job, but she could see it all coming together.

The men needed some encouragement, and then threats, from Tresonne, to get them to bring their sections of cage right up to the creature, but their fear of him seemed to win out over a sleeping dragon. All the while, Ysabeau stood aloof, pretending to be foreboding, but really doing her best to maintain the illusion.

Tresonne joined her to watch the growing accumulation of equipment and tools.

"What else do you have up there?" Ysabeau asked.

"Two of the biggest ox wagons I've ever seen, and two teams of eight. I've left some men up there to rig up a pulley to lift the caged beast. Most of it has to be made from scratch, but it's just a bigger version of the ones they use to haul bales of hay into the barn lofts, so they know what they have to do."

"Excellent," she said.

"We can use the oxen to pull it out and onto the wagons."

Ysabeau nodded, wondering if even that many oxen would be enough to hoist the dragon and the cage. They might need magical assistance. Unfortunately, while she could leave the cave illusion to its own devices for short periods, she could not afford to neglect it for long, nor could she divert much of her focus or energy from it.

She wondered if Hangdog might be able to help with the heavy lifting. The last thing she needed was for a line or pole to break, and dump the caged dragon back to the chamber floor. So much could go wrong and everything hinged on the beast remaining asleep. It was a pretty precarious task, but the rewards would be huge. It was unthinkable, to possess a living dragon. The prestige it would bring . . .

The first challenge was to work out how to get the dragon onto the bottom piece of cage, or it underneath the dragon. This was the part of the process she reckoned presented the greatest danger. If it was going to wake, this was when it would happen, and what creature liked waking up to find it was being stuffed into a cage?

"Bind its snout," she said, not sure why the thought hadn't occurred to her earlier. She was certain it could do plenty of damage with its horns, claws, and barbed tail, but it was the thought of being eaten, or having parts of her body bitten off, that inspired the greatest terror in her.

She waited, and waited, but no one stepped forward to do as she ordered. "Bloody cowards," she muttered, then picked up a coil of rope the village labourers had brought in. She looked at the three-strand rope—simple hempen fibres—and wondered if it could possibly be strong enough to keep the beast's jaws locked shut. Still, it was the smart thing to do, no matter how close to danger it put her.

She looped the rope over the top of the dragon's snout, then tried to shimmy it underneath. With each gentle tug, her heart jumped into her throat, but the beast remained asleep, no more disturbed than it had been when she had tapped its snout. Satisfied with its position, she tied it off, then repeated the process until there were six wraps. That done, she stepped back and gave all the men who had been too afraid to do the job a filthy look before topping up the cave illusion. Each refresh required less time and energy, but she was tired. More tired than she was willing to admit.

"Now," she said, "how are we going to get it onto the bottom section of cage?"

"We could roll it on," one of the villagers said.

"Roll it?" she said. "You were all just too afraid to put a rope around its snout, and now you want to roll it?"

"Its teeth are tied up now," he said.

He obviously hasn't paid much attention to the claws, she thought. "Anyone else have any other suggestions?" It didn't strike her as the ideal solution, but she couldn't come up with anything herself. If it hadn't woken up so far, maybe they'd get away with it.

"Get the top, bottom, and three sides of the cage assembled beside the creature," she said. "Leave one of the long sides open. Actually, attach it at the top. Someone can climb up there and hold it open until we get the dragon inside, then drop it down so the others can secure it fast."

She gestured for Tresonne and Hangdog to join her.

"I can't think of a better way to do it, can either of you?"

Hangdog shook his head.

"No," Tresonne said. "Trying to rig up a pulley system to lift it would be difficult. This is probably the best way."

"There's a good chance we'll wake it up," Ysabeau said. "I'm not having this mission fail. Gather up the academics as quietly as you can and move them to the entrance chamber. At the first sign of trouble, get them and their work back to Mirabay as fast as you can. After we get the creature caged, we can send them back down to finish up while we're getting it loaded for transport."

"Do you really think it'll stay asleep?" Hangdog said.

She shrugged. "Your guess is as good as mine, but if we return to Mirabay without it, we'll be back here by the end of the week to fetch it. Mark my words. Better we do it now and surprise the Prince Bishop. He can be very generous when he's pleased with you. If we can pull this off, the reward will be immense—for all of us. I can promise you that much. Let's get to it."

The villagers had nearly completed the construction of the cage. Some men had begun to lay out the logs forming a track along which they could roll the cage. The fact that they'd done this suggested they thought the plan would work, which was something. She'd long since learned that when a person believes a thing will happen, they're far more likely to make it so. She wasn't at all sure she shared their confidence, but she knew they had to try.

It was amazing, what a little fear could do to motivate people. The workers all knew that the sooner they had the dragon in the cage, the sooner they would be able to go home to their families—and the more likely it was that they would be alive come morning. To Ysabeau, a faster finish meant she could drop her illusion sooner. She might even be able to find some space on one of the wagons where she could sleep for an hour or two on the way home. That was a very attractive thought.

She walked around the cage, giving each of the bolt clamps a cursory test. It was all for show, really—her strength, even if she enhanced it by magic, could not compare to a dragon's. Still, she reckoned it was good for morale, and it at least confirmed that they'd all been properly fastened. As she surveyed the entire construction once more, she realised she was delaying. It was time to get on with it.

"Do we have poles we can use as levers?" she said, studying the sleeping dragon.

One of the villagers nodded and headed off, presumably to fetch them. It would be difficult work, and not only did she want to keep the dragon asleep, she didn't want to injure it. Perhaps adding some magic to the mix might speed something up. She was about to call for Hangdog, but she'd already run him hard in the last few days and needed what energy he had left to keep the block and tackle secure. She didn't have enough energy of her own left, not if she was to maintain the cave illusion—so it would have to be done the old-fashioned way.

The villager returned, carrying a tied bundle of staves. They looked flimsy, but she hoped the combined force of all of them would be enough. She wished she had something better to go on, as she lined the men up along the dragon's length, each armed with a stave.

"As gently as you can," she said.

They advanced and worked their staves in under the dragon. Realising she was standing a little too near the creature's snout for comfort, Ysabeau took a few steps back. If it woke, she would be the first thing it saw, and possibly ate. That prospect didn't do much for her.

The men began to put strain onto their staves. The dragon remained motionless at first. After what felt like an eternity, its body started to lean with the force, but it remained asleep. The men were red-faced and sweating, putting all their effort into the task. The dragon lifted, then toppled, and as easy as that, it was lying on its side in the cage, still soundly asleep.

There were sighs of relief all around, one of which came from Ysabeau. As soon as everyone had taken a moment to revel in the fact that the beast had not woken and killed them all, they pounced on the cage, closed the open side, and fastened the remaining bolt clamps.

Ysabeau did her best to look calm and collected, when all she wanted to do was let out a cheer of joy. They'd done it. They'd actually done it. Now all they had to do was get the beast out of there and back to the city, but the hard part was done.

17

Gill and Solène reached Castandres, the village dal Ruisseau Noir had chosen, after dark on their second long day of walking. It had taken time for the river to carry them clear of the city and for them to extract themselves from the water. Gill had thought it better not to risk the main roads and any larger settlement. Unable to acquire horses, they had had no option but to walk. For many hours.

While they walked, Gill had plenty of time to ruminate over all the little things he'd neglected while planning their mission into the palace. If only he had had more time to prepare.... Money, horses, and a change of clothes topped his list, but despite the time he spent picking over the details, he could not escape the spectre that was lurking in the back of his mind. He was the one who had messed it all up. Him alone.

He should have killed Amaury straightaway, without so much as a "Remember me?" or a "Prepare to die." But he hadn't been able to leave all the things that boiled around in his head unsaid, and even then he'd not got even half of it off his chest. Because of his delay, the Cup had been used. Pharadon's only hope for his species was lost, and Amaury, who hungered for power like no other, had as much of it as he could handle.

He couldn't even bring himself to think of Val. Why hadn't he refused to allow the lad to come along? He knew the answer—he'd been in battles as a squire himself. Friends of his had been killed in those battles. It was normal for men who desired a life by the sword. It didn't make the loss any easier to bear, though.

By night, Castandres resembled an army encampment, with nu-merous flickering campfires spread across its fields. Gill hoped dal Ruisseau Noir and his Intelligencier comrade had reached it, as planned. They had not seen dal Ruisseau Noir or his comrade since they'd leapt into the river, as the Vosges's fickle currents had sent the two pairs down opposite sides of the Isle.

Gill could see pickets when they drew near. He and Solène looked like a pair of vagrants, but the soldiers were on edge enough to see everything as a threat, particularly at night. That was probably a good idea, Gill thought. Now that Amaury had used the Cup, he was un-likely to tolerate rebellion for long. He was unlikely to tolerate Gill for much longer either, so a rebellious army struck him as a good place to see out his days. It might even give him the chance to cause Amaury a few problems before he met his end. If that was all he could hope for, it would have to be enough.

"Who goes there!" came a challenge from one of the pickets.

"Friends," Gill shouted back. "We've come to meet with someone here."

"Who?"

Gill wasn't sure if dal Ruisseau Noir would appreciate having his name shouted about, but equally, Gill didn't appreciate the thought of being stuck with a crossbow bolt by a trigger-happy guard.

"Hugo dal Ruisseau Noir."

"Wait there."

The pickets consisted of whatever this army could get their hands on at short notice. There were stacked-up sacks of meal, overturned carts, crates, and hastily built palisades. It wouldn't stand up to a de-termined assault, but it probably gave the men inside a little more confidence, which made it worthwhile for that alone.

They were left waiting awhile. Gill suspected they'd sent someone into the village, to find out if anyone knew who Hugo dal Ruisseau Noir was. Eventually someone who looked like an officer appeared.

"I'm here to bring you through. Banneret dal Ruisseau Noir ar-rived this morning."

The soldiers wrestled with a section of the picket to move it out of the way. The design was so hasty it seemed no one had given any thought to making ingress and egress possible. Everyone was in a hurry these days. The officer, a young banneret who looked full of the excitement of his first campaign, greeted them.

"Banneret Guillaume dal Coudray, at your service." He couldn't hide the look of disgust on his face when he caught smell of them.

"Banneret of the White Guillot dal Villerauvais. I'm afraid we had to take a swim in the Vosges. A change of clothes would be very much appreciated."

"I'm sure we can rustle something up," dal Coudray said.

"Whose army is this?" Gill said.

"His Lordship, the Count of Savin, cousin of the king."

Gill nodded. He'd never heard of the man.

The tent camp around the village held all the sights, smells, and sounds of an army—soldiers lounging by their campfires, smoke and cooking, ribald chat and laughter. Gill scanned what he could see and reckoned there were two, perhaps three thousand men mustered there. Whoever was in charge would need quite a few more before facing Amaury's forces, but it was a solid start.

Spotting dal Ruisseau Noir walking toward them, Gill raised a hand in greeting.

"I'm glad you made it out of the city," the former fencing master said, coming up to them. "I lost sight of you once we got to the Isle."

"We ended up going down the other side," Gill said. "Not the nicest spot for a swim. Has Pharadon brought the king?"

"Not yet. I was hoping he'd have arrived by now. I'm starting to get worried. The king needs care that Pharadon can't give him. You definitely trust him?"

Gill nodded, with genuine sentiment. "I dare say Pharadon is a little hesitant to come anywhere near a village packed with soldiers."

"True," dal Ruisseau Noir said. "I wasn't expecting there to be so many."

"Can't say I was either."

"The last I heard, Savin was the only one of the king's cousins who hadn't raised in rebellion, he was only gathering forces to maintain order in his lands. This village is in his county, and it's why I chose it. I thought it would be quiet and safe."

"Well, not anymore. You say all the king's cousins have rebelled?"

"It seems so, but only Aubin and Chabris were serious before. I'm going to ride out to see if I can find Pharadon if you're interested in coming. I can delay a few moments longer if you want to get a quick bite to eat and a change of clothes first."

"At night?" Gill said.

"The king's condition is dire."

It was the last thing Gill wanted. He'd been dreaming about clean clothes and a hot meal for more hours than he could count with his fingers. Still, he could hardly say no.

"Give me a few minutes," Gill said.

"Coudray will sort you out," dal Ruisseau Noir said.

▲▲▲▲▲▲

A quick wash with a damp cloth, a change of clothes, and a few scraps of food had Gill on the way to feeling like a new man, but he knew it would take at least ten hours of sleep and a proper hot meal before he got there. He and Solène rode with dal Ruisseau Noir on horses borrowed from the count's troops. The count himself hadn't arrived yet—the army was being mustered up by a few of his senior noblemen—and in his absence, dal Ruisseau Noir seemed to be able to exert quite a bit of influence. Everyone was scared of Intelligenciers, even now when most of the Mirabayan ones were dead.

"Where are we heading?" Gill said. He'd seen nothing of Pharadon since he flew out of Mirabay with Val and the king. There was no reason to think there was a problem, though. He would have been away from the city far faster than they were—it was only a matter of reuniting with him.

"Back in the direction of the city," dal Ruisseau Noir said. "No one in the village has reported seeing anything out of the ordinary, so I don't think he flew this far. I don't expect it'll take us long to find them."

The countryside was open pastures and farmland. There were pockets of forest, but most of the land in the region had been cleared for generations. The thick oak forests that Mirabaya was famed for were all but gone, this close to the city. As nice a night as it was for a ride, Gill could think of a great many places he would rather be, beginning with being tucked up in the Wounded Lion with all of this nothing more than a bad dream.

"I'm told the Order's healers can accomplish all manner of things that are far beyond the skills of an ordinary physician," dal Ruisseau Noir said after they had gone a short distance.

"I, yes, they can," Solène said. "I didn't have the chance to get any training in healing, though."

Gill could tell where dal Ruisseau Noir was going with this, an odd thing considering he was an Intelligencier, but they blended devotion to their original purpose with patriotism in a way that Gill had often found difficult to get his head around.

"But you have the ability to heal?" dal Ruisseau Noir said.

"The ability, yes. I suppose I do. But I really don't have the skills needed. I can heal a cut, ease the pain of a bruise. I can even take a chance at mending some broken bones, but nothing more complex than that. It's very easy to do more damage than was there to begin with, if you don't know what you're doing. Which I don't."

Gill raised an eyebrow, wishing he could see dal Ruisseau Noir's reaction. Gill reckoned Solène was treading on dangerous ground, making jokes about magic with an Intelligencier. Nonetheless, it was clear he was building up to ask a very big favour of her, so she could probably get away with it.

He already knew what the favour was, and he was sure Solène did as well. He could tell she was getting uncomfortable. She'd tried to heal people only on two prior occasions. Her first patient, Felix Leverre, had died. In great pain, if her description had been anything to go by. The second time, she'd healed Nicholas dal Sason—indeed, she'd made him a bit too healthy for Gill's liking, considering they'd fought a duel to the death a short time after. Dal Sason's injuries had been limited to a fever and some broken ribs. Nothing compared to whatever was wrong with the king.

"We have to find him first," Gill said, hoping to move the conversation on. It seemed to have the desired effect, as they all fell silent. They spent another hour on horseback before a lone figure, leading a mule, emerged from the darkness.

As they grew closer, Gill realised that it was Pharadon, back in human form, and that there were two bodies draped over the mule's back. Gill's heart dropped into his stomach as he wondered where he should bury Val. The lad had never spoken of any family, had given every indication that he was an orphan. The speed with which he departed Trelain suggested he didn't have any great love for the city. Gill decided he'd find a nice churchyard somewhere, perhaps even this village, and make sure he had a plot and headstone to himself.

"I'm glad to see you all alive," Pharadon said.

"Likewise," Gill said.

"I apologise for my delay. It takes some time to recuperate enough from one transformation to carry out another, and I felt I would be safer travelling the countryside in your form."

"It's lucky we happened upon you," Gill said.

Pharadon gave him a curious look. "No, it wasn't. I knew exactly where you were."

Magic, again, Gill thought. He was starting to feel a little inadequate, having to rely on the traditional ways of doing things.

"The king?" dal Ruisseau Noir said. "Is he well?"

"As well as he was when I took him from the city," Pharadon said, "which is to say, not well at all, but he lives. I brought Val, also." He gave Gill a sad look as he handed the mule's reins to dal Ruisseau Noir.

"Where did you get the mule?" Solène said.

Pharadon shrugged. It seemed that was all the answer they were going to get. He returned his attention to Gill. "It's been an interesting experience, Guillot, but I bid you farewell."

"Where will you go?" Gill said.

"Back to the temple and the goldscale. Dragons reached enlightenment before we began using the Cups as a tool to ensure the process was successful. Perhaps I can find a way, some method of the ancients."

"Thank you for helping us," Gill said.

"Likewise," Pharadon said. "I'm only sorry that our respective quests have led us to so much sorrow and disappointment."

There was something tragic about the matter-of-fact way Pharadon delivered this line, as though in his ancient wisdom, he had come to accept such things without question. For someone so short-lived as Gill, such resignation was difficult.

"Wait," dal Ruisseau Noir said. "You might not be able to cast spells on a person, but you do know much about magic?"

Gill had to think for a moment to digest the abrupt change in the conversation's direction.

"Spells aren't cast," Pharadon said. "Magic—actually the energy that allows it, the Fount—is shaped. That shaping of that energy is what affects the physical world. And yes, dragons are creatures of the Fount, and I know as much about it as I suppose anything living at this moment. Even your Prince Bishop."

"So you could instruct Solène on how to heal the king?"

Pharadon hadn't been back in human form for very long, so Gill wasn't sure if his stiff expression stemmed from that, or if he was truly dumbfounded.

"You've learned firsthand what a dangerous threat to the world the Prince Bishop is now that he has all this magical power," dal Ruisseau Noir said. "Do you think he'll rest easily knowing there are dragons in existence, that you might be strong enough to tear down all he's built up? He sees your kind as vermin, and once he is secure, he will have you all hunted until he is certain you are no more."

"His task might be easier than you think," Pharadon said, "considering I am likely the last of my kind. Seeing as this is something he has already tried, I'm inclined to agree with your assessment, however."

Gill felt guilty that his behaviour had contributed to losing the Cup, and more so at prevailing upon the dragon's charity when the only other dragon they knew to be alive was inching ever closer to a descent into savagery. How could they ask him for anything more?

"The temple's intense magical power means the slumber I put the goldscale into should keep her frozen until I release the magic," Pharadon said. "As the situation is so dire, I'm willing to chance a little more time with you if it means your Prince Bishop might meet with justice. I will try to guide you, Solène, if you are willing to attempt a healing. There is only so much I can do, however. I can teach you how to guide the tool with precision, but not necessarily which bolt to

turn. That is a matter for those with knowledge of the human body to instruct you on."

They all gave him an odd look at the use of the idiom.

"We can find a physician to give you guidance in that regard," dal Ruisseau Noir said. His voice was full of energy again, now that he saw a solution to his problem. "Let's return to the village."

Gill cleared his throat and gave dal Ruisseau Noir a look.

"Of course," the Intelligencier said. "Thank you, Pharadon. For your continued help. The kingdom will owe you a great debt."

CHAPTER
18

Daylight, the next morning, gave Gill his first proper look at Castandres. It was a little larger than Venne, but built along similar lines—a rectangular market square surrounded by two-story buildings. The church stood proudly at one end, its belfry towering above all else. There were some stone buildings, and a stretch of arcade across the square at the end opposite the church, but most structures were rendered timber construction, with old, bleached oak beams crisscrossing their façades and lending the place a charming character.

Guillot, Solène, and Pharadon had been put up at the village inn, which was larger than a village this size would have otherwise possessed, were it not on a major road to the west. Gill felt refreshed by a night in a decent bed and a generous breakfast, but his body didn't shake off abuse quite the way it once had, and he couldn't think of anything nicer than a prolonged period of idleness. His gut twisted with unease when his train of thought added "and a few bottles of a fine vintage," thereby ending that dream. That was a road he didn't want to walk down again. Perhaps constant activity was the best thing for him after all.

Every large building in the village had been commandeered for billeting by the army; smaller structures were being used to accommodate officers whose dignity couldn't stretch to sleeping in a tent if there was an alternative. Gill didn't see many villagers moving about, but that was only to be expected. An army of strangers, ostensibly friendly or not, was never something you wanted to see camping next to your home. Everyone had heard horror stories of the actions of unruly armies, and no village wanted to become the source for the next one.

The night before, when Gill and his companions returned to Castandres, they had brought the king to the tavern and gently laid him on a worn, stained oak table at one side of the taproom. The army's physician had assumed responsibility for his care. Despite their conversation about healing, neither dal Ruisseau Noir nor Gill suggested Solène attempt it right away; they could see how exhausted she was.

This morning, however, it could be put off no longer. Gill turned away from the village scene, the cathartic distraction it provided short-lived, and went back into the inn. He'd met Boudain only once before, when the young king had requested Gill's participation in the first dragon hunt; the contrast between then and now made for grim viewing. To Gill's eye, there didn't appear to be anything wrong with him—no wounds, no obvious injuries. But his eyes rolled in their sockets and there was a sheen of drool on his chin. Gill had seen men like this before. Their conditions had been caused by a heavy blow to the head, and none of them had ever recovered. He couldn't claim to understand much about magic, but fixing a man's head seemed like a big ask.

There was quite a gathering that morning, to witness the spectacle of the king being brought back to health by means not used for a millennium. If magic really could achieve such wonders, why had it been outlawed and oppressed for so long? How many lives might have been saved or improved by it? Then again, human beings seemed particularly ill-suited for great power, and there was always someone who would seek to exploit such a gift for personal gain. A fine example of that sat on the throne in Mirabay at that moment. Contrast that to Pharadon, who had enjoyed that power and more for centuries, yet lived contented in a mountaintop cave.

Gill cast Solène a glance; he could tell from her expression that she was thinking more about the gathered crowd than the task before her. She had slept for a time, but much of her night and morning had been spent in discussion with Pharadon, for magical guidance, and the physician, for instruction on the human mind. The physician was the Count of Savin's personal doctor—considering the count's wealth and close relation to the king, Gill hoped he'd attracted a good one.

Still, how much did anyone know about a person's brain? It's not like it beat, like a heart—it just sat there, thinking. Gill reckoned that thanks to battle, he'd seen as many brains as any physician, and he didn't have the first clue how they worked: he only knew that when you drove a blade into one, or bashed it hard enough, it stopped.

Dal Ruisseau Noir was barking orders to the tavern keeper. Water, towels—hot, cold, damp, and dry—seemingly anything he could think of to keep the king comfortable. There was still a continuing discussion on how they were going to proceed, whether the physician would try some conventional treatments first, or if Solène would lead the way. Despite what magic promised, it was proving difficult to convince everyone that it was their best option.

Feeling of little use and keenly aware that while the king was getting all this attention, poor Val was waiting for a send-off that befitted his great courage, Gill left the tavern. He collected the lad's body from the shed they'd stored it in the night before; ignoring the smell that was starting to grow strong, Gill carried him to the church.

A small yard to the side of the church held a dozen or so graves marked with headstones. Rural and urban communities alike tended to cremate their dead, unless the person was of some significance. Most of these stones probably belonged to former seigneurs—those who didn't have a crypt at their manor. There was room for Val, and there were plenty of soldiers idling around who'd be glad of a coin to help dig the hole. Gill pounded on the weathered wooden door and waited for the churchman. In a place this small, the clergyman was likely no more than a deacon.

For a soldier, even a church this modest was a potential target for theft. There was always a bit of silver plate or a gold chalice to be had, so it was no surprise that whoever was inside was reluctant to open the door. Gill pounded on it again but there was still no reply.

"I'm here to buy funeral rites," Gill shouted. "I have coin. I'm not here to cause trouble."

If there was anyone in there, Gill reckoned they'd need a few moments to consider what he'd said. While it didn't appear as though the army was causing any problems, they hadn't been there long, by all accounts, so there was still plenty of time for that. A billeted army was rarely a positive thing for a village's residents. The most they could hope for was that the troops would leave before stealing or destroying too much. He supposed that if he'd already been tarred with that brush, he might as well take advantage of it.

"I'm happy to pay for the rites," he shouted. "But if I have to kick in this door, I'm not paying for repairs."

That seemed to do the trick, as a moment later he heard the scratch of a bolt being drawn. The door creaked open and a man in stained vestments—white, with a powder-blue trim—peered out. He looked at Gill suspiciously, but relaxed when he saw Val's body. *An odd thing to make someone relax,* Gill thought.

"Your son?" the deacon said.

"Squire," Gill said. "I want him buried. There's a nice spot over there."

"We only bury our—"

"Buried," Gill said. "I'll pay you three crowns, three times what the rites should cost. I can have some soldiers dig the hole for you. All I need is space in your yard, and the rites."

They said charity started with the church, but Gill reckoned greed did too. Still, there was no point expecting churchmen to be better than everyone else when they were led by a man like Amaury. The promise of three gold coins was enough to convince the deacon. Gill would have to rustle them up from somewhere. His purse had gone astray at some point, likely while in the river. Considering all that he had done, he reckoned he had more than three crowns owing to him at that point, and he was determined Val's funeral would be properly paid for.

"That spot, you say?" He pointed.

Gill nodded.

"That won't be a problem. You'll have the hole dug?"

"That's what I said."

"Bring your squire in. I'll see that he's prepared and ready."

Gill carried the body inside and laid it on the anointing table. There was nothing more he could do for the lad now. He frowned, thinking, and realised that perhaps there was one more thing.

"Is there a seamstress in the village?" Gill said.

The deacon nodded. "Across the square in the arcade, three doors to the left. The blue one."

Gill forced a smile of gratitude. As he walked out, the deacon called after him.

"Don't forget to see to the hole. And the coin."

Gill smiled wryly to himself. *It's always about the coin.*

▲▲▲▲▲▲

Getting into the seamstress's house proved even more of a challenge than the church. It appeared that the town had played host to an army at some point in living memory, and wasn't going to have the same experience twice. Gill had to borrow some money from dal Coudray, and slide three florins under the door before the seamstress even agreed to open it.

The seamstress was younger than he expected—about the same age as Solène. Gill always imagined seamstresses as grey-haired spinsters, probably because that was what the one in Villerauvais had been. Drawing on his limited creativity, Guillot explained what he wanted in as much detail as he could, then gave her another florin to finish the job before sunrise. He'd paid more than twice what the task should have cost, but had no regrets. Val deserved it.

Everybody had to lie in repose for one passing of the moon—Gill had no idea why—so he had until dawn the next morning to find some men willing to dig the hole. He wandered out toward the tent village, where he found four men willing to dig the grave for three florins apiece—and willing to wait until the job was done to be paid.

His meagre loan now fully accounted for, and then some, Guillot wondered who he should appeal to next. While he was confident he was owed significant back pay, it would have to come from the Crown's coffers, and Amaury was currently in charge of those, which meant Gill was unlikely to see any of that cash any time soon. The king was unlikely to have remembered his purse during the flight from the palace, what with him being completely debilitated at the time.

It occurred to Guillot that he should return to the inn, to see what progress was being made with the king and find someone willing to advance him a few more coins. When he got inside, he saw that a group were clustered around the table where the king lay. He could not approach—two men on guard duty held him back and threatened to forcibly remove him.

"Hugo," Gill shouted. It wasn't polite to use dal Ruisseau Noir's given name, but the whole assemblage was too unwieldy in the midst of an increasingly less polite struggle.

From the king's side, dal Ruisseau Noir looked over. "Let him through!"

The guards released him immediately and Gill joined the group around the table.

"This is Banneret of the White Guillot dal Villerauvais, my Lord Savin," dal Ruisseau Noir said, introducing him to a distinguished-looking gentleman who appeared to be a handful of years older than Gill himself. The Count of Savin had a thick grey moustache and similarly coloured, slicked-back hair that was receding from the temples. He was wearing a white sash, signalling that he was also a Banneret of the White. Gill made the appropriate salute, which the man returned.

"The Dragonslayer?" the count said.

Gill's eyes flicked to Pharadon, who was also at the table, along with Solène, and several men Gill didn't recognise. He did his best not to blush, and wondered what Pharadon thought, hearing him referred to like that.

"Merely a servant of the Crown," Gill said.

The count nodded toward the king. "Why did you bring him here?"

"He's severely injured, and it's our duty to do all we can for him. We thought he'd be safe here."

"You've brought a world of trouble down on us," the count said. "You and your friends. I was hoping to muster my forces here quietly, but now? And this fellow"—he gestured to dal Ruisseau Noir—"says you intend to use magic to heal His Majesty? I'm glad I arrived when I did to inject a little sanity back into the discussion."

Gill narrowed his eyes and wondered what the count was getting at. Naturally, Savin's ambitions would be curtailed by the restoration of the king's health, but having Amaury in charge was a huge danger to him.

"It's my belief it's the only option if we want to return the king to his faculties."

"Magic?" Savin said. "This puts us all in a great deal of danger."

Dal Ruisseau Noir was staring at Gill intently, and Gill realised that this was not what he had expected either.

"As servants of the Crown, it is our duty to protect the king," Gill said. "We've kept good faith with that, and once the king is returned to good health, I'm sure he will agree that we've behaved correctly." *If he's returned to good health,* Gill thought. "As one of royal blood, I think your position is far better served by fidelity to the king than by allegiance to a usurper for whom you represent a rival."

Savin nodded and looked down at the king. There was no sympathy on his face or in his voice. "He's not going to be much use to anyone like this. He's a vegetable."

The expression on the count's face caused Gill to feel a flash of alarm. Savin might be the king's cousin, but he would be a serious contender for the throne if the king were to die. It occurred to Gill that they might have rescued the king from Amaury's clutches only to drop him into the hungry jaws of avarice.

Before Gill could speak, the look was gone.

"I don't like all this talk of magic and whatnot, and I don't like the idea of it being used here." Savin cast a glowering look around the table. "But it seems that everyone here—" He cast a look at his physician, who nodded vigorously. "—my personal physician included, has agreed that magic is indeed what is needed. That doesn't change the fact that the Intelligenciers will be after the lot of us if we stand by while it happens."

"I can assure you the Intelligenciers will overlook this incident as being pursuant to the exigencies of the common good," dal Ruisseau Noir said. "I can provide my credentials, if necessary."

Savin looked at dal Ruisseau Noir and raised an eyebrow, then nodded. "My man will take a look." He gestured with his hand, and one of his aides brought dal Ruisseau Noir away from the group where they spoke for a moment, and dal Ruisseau Noir produced what appeared to be water-stained papers. The aide returned to Savin's side and whispered in his ear.

Savin nodded. "Very well. If this is what it takes to get the king back to himself and back on the throne, then that's what will be done. Do your worst, lady magister," he said, directing his gaze at Solène. "But don't expect any gratitude for exercising your wicked ways. I'll be in my campaign tent. I want regular progress reports. Then we'll go and make sure the Prince Bishop wishes he never set foot outside of his cathedral."

No one in the group spoke until the count, his aides, and his guards had left the tavern.

"Odd fellow, that," Gill said then. "Old-fashioned views on magic, yet willing to let us use it to save the king." He shrugged. "His gratitude was heartwarming, though."

Solène laughed.

"He knows the fight between him and his cousins will hand the throne to the Prince Bishop," dal Ruisseau Noir said. "I don't think the count likes him."

Gill nodded thoughtfully. "Amaury is an easy man to dislike."

Ysabeau's heart was in her throat as she watched the cage containing the still-sleeping dragon lift off the floor. Above, the team of oxen inched forward, hauling the burden out of the chamber. The hoist looked precariously flimsy—slender sticks silhouetted against the light; would they be enough to support the enormous weight of cage and dragon?

Every block, line, and beam in the assemblage creaked and groaned as though on the verge of giving way. The cage hovered a handspan above the ground as the beasts of burden rallied themselves for another effort. The men in the chamber were silent, speaking only in harsh whispers when absolutely necessary. Even though the creature had remained asleep after all the manhandling it had been subjected to, they were terrified of waking it.

Ysabeau had to remind herself to breathe as the oxen pulled again, jerking the cage up to head level. It swung gently from side to side. With each swing, she cringed, waiting for one of the beams to be tugged from true, to snap. What magic kept the beast in slumber? It had to be incredibly powerful, like the torrent of energy that swirled around the temple, invisible to all but her and Hangdog. The Fount was relentless in its efforts to force its way in. It was like having someone banging constantly on your front door, shouting and raging and demanding entry—there was no way to ignore it. She wondered if Hangdog felt it too.

She would be glad to be out of this place. As she grew ever more fatigued, the Fount's energy became increasingly imposing. If she hit her breaking point, she was dead. She had seen some of the Order's initiates burn themselves out, in the early days of magical experimentation, and had no desire to experience it firsthand.

She wondered if she was a fool to try and capture this dragon. It was the type of overreach she'd always been careful to avoid. No matter how smoothly things went, she couldn't shake the sense of impending doom. The creature looked so huge and powerful; the iron bars containing it looked like twigs. If it woke, it could burst out and slaughter them all in an instant. Added to that was the difficulty of continuing to maintain the cave illusion, which had given her a ferocious headache and the sensation that every muscle in her body had been gently broiled for an hour or two. *Still, the rewards of a coup like this,* she thought.

The cage jerked up again. In the distance, she could hear the drover's voice, cussing and goading the oxen forward. If the draft animals saw what they were hauling out of the hole, she reckoned they'd be on the far side of the county before they could be herded up again. Fear was such a wonderful motivator.

She watched a moment longer, then decided there was little to be gained by standing there. If things went wrong, there would be enough noise to alert her to the fact. She wandered back down to the main chamber and had one last look around; since she controlled it, the illusion did not impede her vision. The temple truly was a magnificent place, and she wondered what discoveries the academics would make over the coming weeks as they dug into the material they'd gathered.

Unbeknownst to them, Ysabeau had been giving them gentle top-ups of energy to keep them going, but she didn't have enough left in her to keep that up now. They were going to come down hard when it wore off, but by then, they'd be back in Mirabay and the scholars would be someone else's problem.

She wondered what else might lie hidden in the temple, waiting to be discovered. They'd found several additional passageways, but all stopped after only a few paces, blocked by stone walls that looked no different from the rest of the temple's construction. Still, they hinted that there might be other chambers, patiently waiting to reveal their secrets.

Focussing her mind, Ysabeau tried to view the outline of the Fount to see if she could spot any voids behind it—the Fount usually lined surfaces, a handy fact that had allowed her to discover more than one hidden room over the years. All she could see was the raging swirl of blue energy, and she had to instantly close her mind to it before it overwhelmed her. Holding it back was becoming almost impossible. It was time to go.

She walked around the edge of the room, giving the magnificent art a final viewing. Even if there was no great and important message being passed down through the mists of time, the aesthetic value of them was beyond measure. To think they must have been created so long ago, perhaps even before the Empire had left the shores of Vellin-Ilora, was astonishing.

Something glittered on the ground, catching her eye. She walked over and saw it was a gold coin. Her first thought was that it must have been as ancient as the temple, perhaps bearing the visage of some long-forgotten king. Picking it up, she was disappointed to see none other than the present king's father, making the coin only a few decades old at most. One of the villagers must have dropped it when they were working on the cage. She popped the coin into her purse. *Their loss. My gain.*

She returned to the entrance chamber, hopeful that the most nerve-wracking part of the job was complete.

⁂

Amaury felt like a child in a sweetshop. Anything he put his mind to, he could do. The power was at once both exhilarating and terrifying. He had all Kayte dal Drezony's portents of doom bouncing around in his head: he could burn himself out; too much power, too quickly. All that sort of nonsense. The only problem was, it no longer felt like nonsense. He could feel the power.

To him, the Fount was no longer a trickling stream but a deluge. After he had drunk from the Cup, it had been hours before the world had lost its blue, coruscating glow. There was a time when it had taken every ounce of concentration he had to see it. Now it took effort to ignore.

The magic he'd cast on Gill had taken a lot out of him. His magical grapple with Solène, more still. That was the only thing that had allowed her to get away. When she had released her grip on him, Amaury had been more exhausted than he'd ever felt before. He'd collapsed, lying unconscious for a time. That had been deeply troubling. Dal Drezony's lectures on magical burnout echoed in his mind. Even now, he could feel the aftereffects. His body ached and he had no energy or motivation to do anything. Still, it had been an incredible application of force, and all things considered, he was none the worse for it.

He was sure these were things he could overcome with time, practice, and experience. Like anything else, he was sure, it needed training to develop, but he found himself longing for a guiding hand. It was a shame dal Drezony had become too great a problem to be allowed to live. She had made herself an expert in magical safety and had known more about the dangers of burnout, and the countless other side effects of excessive magic use, than anyone else alive. That was a safety net he would have been very glad of at that moment, but he was an intelligent man. A prudent and careful one, too, if a little impatient at times. He was confident he could work out what his limits were and avoid putting himself in any real danger. Fatigue, plus aches and pains, he could deal with. The reward was more than worth it.

As much as he would have liked to devote every moment to exploring the power this new Cup seemed to have permanently granted him, he still had a kingdom to run and a population to calm. There were reports coming in of a dragon sighting over the city, but they were so few that he wrote them off as hysteria. With so much talk of dragons these days, every misshapen cloud would appear to be the subject of their nightmares for some.

What was more irritating was that Gill and his friends had escaped with the king. Amaury couldn't be sure how big a problem that might be, couldn't determine if it would actually work in his favour. That the king had taken seriously ill would be obvious to everyone who saw him. There could be no accusations that Amaury had deposed and imprisoned a healthy man. It was evidence, if he needed it, that his regency was entirely legal.

It also opened the door to another interesting possibility. He'd long since accepted the fact that, at an opportune moment, King Boudain the Tenth would have to be killed. No matter how effectively he contrived the death to look like a consequence of the man's illness, there would always be those who would accuse him of regicide. Now that the king had been taken from his protective custody, away from the finest physicians in the land? The responsibility for the king's health and safety resided with the misguided fools who had taken him from the palace. If the king were to die now . . .

Amaury smiled at the thought. Ever able to pull opportunity from defeat—save for that time in the Competition. That was the only true defeat he had suffered in life. It was something that he couldn't let go of, no matter how much wealth and how much power he had. Even now, granted all the boons the Cup from the ancients could grant, he was sitting in his office thinking about Gill and getting angry.

Still, his hip was an unpleasant memory he could now erase. A physician would be calling that afternoon, to start instructing him on the anatomy of the hip, which seemed to be a remarkably complex system of joint, muscles, and all the various things that went with them. He knew from the Order's healers that healing was not just about having the magical ability to make the repairs needed, it was about knowing how every element in the body was supposed to be, and returning it to that state.

Amaury didn't have that knowledge and wasn't willing to start experimenting on himself. Until he was confident he could properly execute the healing, his hip would have to wait. He might be impatient, but he wasn't a fool—he had no desire to make the problem worse. Still, now that he knew the fix was at hand, it felt like far less pressing an issue. The man who had caused it, however . . .

He stood and swore, looking at the cracked wooden panelling and damaged plaster, signs of Gill's impact with the wall. The memory of the look of surprise on the clown's face brought a fleeting smile to Amaury's. He should have drunk from the Cup earlier. Then he would have been ready for Gill when the man had had the audacity to come to the office with his cronies. He'd have been able to settle that score once and for all. As it was, all he'd been able to do was leave Gill with some bumps and bruises. The fellow had still managed to get away from the palace and disappear. He continued to be the thorn in Amaury's side. Still, like the Prince Bishop's hip, that was a matter that would not be long in the settling.

Amaury did his best not to dwell on his frustration. To do so caused rage that clouded his mind, a problem since he had many things he needed to focus on. At least he had taken the Cup from Gill. From everyone. They would fear him now, but as tempting as it was, he knew the time wasn't right for a demonstration of what he could do. How he could be the great leader Mirabaya so desperately needed.

The people were afraid. They were angry. They needed the benefits the Order could bring, but they didn't know it yet. He needed to demonstrate the wonders magic offered each and every one of them. Only when they accepted those gifts would he show them what magic could really do. What he could really do. For them, and for Mirabaya. But most of all, for Amaury.

Gill was feeling rather redundant. He didn't have a sword, and even if he had, there was presently no one for him to stick it in. Solène, Pharadon, and the count's physician were in conclave at a corner table, making their final preparations. The count himself continued to absent himself, no doubt hoping not being present would limit his culpability should the use of magic later be questioned. Dal Ruisseau Noir had also vanished, Gill knew not where.

The soldiers Gill had hired to dig the hole did it quickly, eager to get their money and return to lounging by their campfire. They would have to wait a little longer, however. Not until the seamstress finished her part could the deacon conduct the rites . . . and Gill still had to find a few more coins to pay for it all. Now that Savin was around, Gill was tempted to put it to him—he would be bankrolling the activities of the next few weeks, until the king, once he was recovered and restored, had access to his treasury again.

He knew there was only so long he could sit in the inn with all that tension before the temptation to have a drink became too much to resist. It wasn't something that played on his mind much anymore, but the desire still lurked there, offering to help him through troubled times. Considering the disastrous consequences of his last lapse, he wanted to put some distance between himself and alcohol.

Outside, he stared skyward at the early evening stars. He heard some noise behind him, and turned. It was dal Ruisseau Noir.

"Fine evening," the Intelligencier said.

Gill had always thought a fine evening to be one where he could relax on his porch, in that old rocking chair, with a twist of tobacco and not a care in the world. He couldn't imagine being much farther from that state than he was now. The thought of Amaury ruling the realm pushed him to the point of despair.

"Fine enough," Gill said with a nod. He felt unusually talkative, eager to distract himself from dwelling on Amaury, or what might be going on inside the inn. "Tell me, where is Ruisseau Noir? I've not heard of it."

Dal Ruisseau Noir smiled and tapped the side of his head.

"Oh, of course," Gill said, then frowned. "Would you not have picked something a little easier to manage?"

The other man shrugged. "If you're going to tell a lie, it might as well be a big one. They're more likely to be believed. The bigger and more implausible the lie, the harder it is for a person to imagine that anyone is making up something so preposterous.

"Few Intelligenciers keep their real names when they join the service. To do so might endanger family members and such. Besides, I like the way it sounds."

For a moment he reverted back to the foppish persona he had been maintaining when Gill had first met him.

"Makes sense, I suppose. Seems like a harsh thing, though. To have to give up who you were before." Gill thought on it for a moment. "Perhaps not, though."

"What brought you into all of this?" dal Ruisseau Noir said.

"Amaury," Gill said. "The Prince Bishop. Who else? His people woke up the first dragon when they were looking for the Cup. He wanted me to try to kill it. Not sure why—something to do with the Silver Circle having been dragonslayers back in the day, he said, but most likely I expect he saw it as an easy way to get rid of me. Didn't quite work out for him the way he hoped. Which is something, I suppose."

"The people most unsuited for rule are often the ones who reach the top," dal Ruisseau Noir said.

"What inspired you to mount the rescue mission?" Gill said.

"My commander's last order was to oppose the Prince Bishop at every step, and continue carrying out our duty to the Crown. We were all but wiped out during Amaury's takeover. A secret war was waged on the streets, and though we were ready for it, there are only so many ways to fight a power that knows almost everything about us. Only a few undercover groups, like mine, survived. You can't stand by, hoping that someone else will take on the task that's supposed to be yours."

His words reminded Gill of something Val had said. Sentiment like that was a good way to get a man killed, yet it was something he couldn't dismiss. He remembered all too clearly the time when he had lived by similar sentiments. He couldn't decide whether there was nobility in these thoughts, that they were a good guide on how to live, or if it was all nonsense, poured into the heads of impressionable youths. Then they'd willingly march off to lay down their lives so that someone else could become a little wealthier or a little more powerful. Perhaps he was just a cynic. Perhaps he was right. Either way, the thought of Amaury on the throne was one he couldn't stomach.

"What's next for you?" Gill said.

"I need to contact my commander in Humberland. I'm not convinced our last message got through to him."

"Back to mage hunting?"

"Perhaps," dal Ruisseau Noir said. "I think that may be shutting the stable door after the horse has bolted. We'll have to adapt to the new reality and find a worthwhile role within it."

"You'll be telling your commander that?"

"I will. I don't doubt that there will be plenty more like the Prince Bishop who'll abuse magic for all it's worth, but people like Solène can do a lot of good in the world. We could all use a little more of that, I think."

"A fine sentiment," Gill said, "and one I agree with." He took one more reticent look at the stars, then turned. "I'm going to get some sleep. I'm not any use to those inside. Better to be rested for when I will be."

⁂

Solène knew she could put things off no longer. The count's physician had, sadly, not known nearly so much about the human brain as she had wished, while Pharadon knew far more about magic than she could hope to absorb in a lifetime. One thing was clear, however. Without her intervention, the king would continue as he was until his body weakened to the point that he would fall ill and die. She was the only one who could change that future.

She didn't want rumours flying around after this was done with, stories of all sorts of horrible magical goings-on. If she performed the healing behind closed doors, she knew that she would be perpetuating all the old fears of sorcery. If there were witnesses, the reality would have a chance of being known. She didn't like having an audience, but in this case, it was important. Once the king was back on his throne, there might be a chance for her and those like her to play an open, useful role in society. Allowing people to see how innocuous the healing process was could go some way toward helping to create that reality.

The count had called in to get an update from his physician, so the moment seemed ideal. It struck her that it might be important to have someone of his rank present to see what happened.

Solène cleared her throat. "Perhaps, Lord Savin, you might wish to remain for the procedure? Your aides too? Banneret dal Ruisseau Noir, you're welcome to remain also. All I request is that you keep completely silent. The concentration this will require is enormous. Any distraction could prove disastrous."

Savin prevaricated for a moment, but in the end gave a short nod. She knew he was uncomfortable being present when magic was shaped, but she valued her own safety far more than his comfort. Dal Ruisseau Noir gave her a nod. It felt odd knowing an Intelligencier would be watching her, but she knew he was as important an observer as could be had, if there were any future recriminations.

Solène was as daunted by what she had to do as she had ever been. She might want it to appear innocuous to those watching, but it would be far from that. While she had drawn on an enormous amount of energy to melt the barrier beneath the palace, there was no finesse involved in that effort; thus, it was less taxing. Here the situation was reversed. The control required would make needlepoint look like the clumsiest of pastimes.

The physician still looked unhappy that magic was going to be used to restore the king. He had suggested a trepanning—cutting a hole in the king's skull—to let the foul humours out of his head, at which point Solène had ceased to pay attention to him.

Her discussion with Pharadon had been far more enlightening. He told her that magic left a fingerprint and that with time she might become able to identify the shaper of the magic from the traces left behind. For now, though, if she sought out those traces within the king's brain, she would be able to locate where the damage had been done. If the Prince Bishop had caused the injury by magic, as they suspected, this was her best approach. If it was something physical— apoplexy, some other ailment, the result of a blow—she would have to find another way.

It was a start, but it didn't change the fact that once she'd located the problem areas, she had to fix them. Might it be as simple as will- ing them to return to their former state? She could get a sense of that from the areas that weren't damaged, and even by looking within her- self, to develop a picture of what she was trying to achieve. Then there was the precision with which she would have to apply the Fount. It was daunting. Beyond daunting.

Her only comfort was that she really couldn't make the situation any worse. Even if she caused the king pain, he wasn't aware enough to feel it. That magic had caused this wounded her. It proved right any per- son who feared magic, even justified the violence done to her and other mages. If she could heal the king, with others watching, she might be able to change the future for those like her. And she would save the life of a monarch who, in all respects, appeared to be a decent man.

"I'm about to begin," she said. "Please, complete silence from now on, until I tell you I'm finished."

Savin had kept back five men, two of them tough-looking banner- ets who, Solène feared, might be there to deal with her, should her magical ways prove to be too profane for the count.

"So much as a squeak out of any of you," Savin said, "and I'll have the hide off your backs."

He gave her an authoritative nod. It wasn't what she would have done in his place, but so long as the result was what she wanted, there was no harm done. Pharadon and the physician stood at the other end of the table. Pharadon gave Solène an encouraging smile, while the physician stared at the king with a consternated expression on his face. All being well, he was about to watch his profession become obsolete.

She took a deep breath, closed her eyes, and opened her mind to the Fount. She allowed herself to relax as her mind drifted along the lines of beautiful, glowing blue energy. Feeling more at peace with the Fount than she ever had before, Solène began to focus on the king, his form outlined in blue light. She moved into his head and almost let out a gasp when she saw the traces Pharadon had spoken of. Glowing blue scars, but not the sort of narrow, smooth marks created by a sharp knife. They were rough, as though made with a serrated blade, or a clumsy cut.

After a moment's study and thought, Solène chose her approach. Rather than will healing, she decided to will the hideous scars away, using the Fount to gently wash them from the king's flesh, conveying energy into his brain to restore it to its original form.

It was painstaking work. As the tide washes pebbles along the beach, so too did her application of the Fount's energy sweep across the king's brain. The danger was she would wash away something that was supposed to be there. She focussed her will to applying tiny, delicate brushstrokes of energy, like a fine artist painting in a subject's eyelashes. She allowed herself a momentary smile as the first scar began to recede, the edges drawing in, leaving normal flesh behind. She couldn't be sure the end result would be what they were all looking for, but she was certainly removing the damage the Prince Bishop's clumsy magic had caused.

On and on she went, one delicate stroke at a time, narrowing her focus to a pinpoint, and regulating the amount of energy she allowed to flow through her, all the while trying to pretend that there weren't eight other people in the room, watching her stand there with her eyes closed, apparently doing absolutely nothing.

When Gill came down to the taproom the next morning, looking for breakfast, King Boudain was sitting in a chair, wrapped in a blanket, drinking a mug of broth. By himself. He had the distant stare of a man who'd been to all three hells and back. Despite all that, he didn't look too bad, all things considered. A little pale, emaciated, and bedraggled, but nothing that some healthy living wouldn't put to rights in a few weeks. To think of the state he'd been in the previous day . . .

"Highness," Gill said, bowing his head belatedly.

Squinting up at Gill, the king said, "Dal Villerauvais, isn't it? The slayer of dragons."

"The same, Highness," Gill said. The moniker felt awkward, but it seemed to be sticking, so he reckoned he might as well accept it.

"It seems we have one last dragon that needs slaying," Boudain said. "Can I count on you once again?"

"I'm ever a servant of the Crown," Gill said, wondering if he'd ever be able to tell his liege to leave him in peace. Still, it wasn't like he had anywhere to go, and despite his belief that many of the battles he had fought over the years had no worth, this one did.

"Good man, good man," the king said, sounding distant.

"How are you feeling, Highness?" Gill said.

The king's focus, which had drifted, snapped back. "Who are you?" He looked around. "Who is this man? Where am I?"

The physician rushed over—he'd been sitting at the bar. He looked like a man who hadn't had any sleep the previous night.

"Relax, your Highness," he said. "You've had a bad injury to the head. All's well now, but you'll be a bit confused for a while. Breathe easy now."

Boudain looked at the physician with a puzzled expression, but his agitation quickly melted away and he took another sip of his broth.

Gill left him to the physician, and broke his fast at the bar—eggs, sausage, and pancakes. Dal Ruisseau Noir appeared just as Gill was finishing. He looked tired—clearly he, like the physician, had not slept.

"How's Solène?" Gill said.

"Exhausted. Whatever it was she did, it took hours, and she collapsed at the end."

He felt a flash of panic. He knew what that might mean.

"Pharadon is with her," dal Ruisseau Noir said. "He says that she's in no danger, but will take time to recover. The feats she's accomplished in the last few days are really quite breathtaking. The strain they must have placed on her, I can only imagine."

Gill relaxed a little. Pharadon was the right person to be with her, he reckoned, and then wondered if Pharadon could be called a person. "What about the king?"

Dal Ruisseau Noir shrugged. "No one can say for certain. He's certainly better than he was before, and the periods of lucidity seem to be lasting longer between each relapse. We're hopeful that he'll be back to normal before too much longer. It seems Solène's magic has done what we needed."

"How do you feel about that?" Gill said, unable to resist the question.

Dal Ruisseau Noir took a deep breath. "As I said before, magic is back in the world. I'm not sure there's any way of stopping it now. We've been watching developments around the Middle Sea for years, and in the past few, the reports have been the same everywhere. More and more individuals are turning up who can wield real, powerful magic. Far more than the ones we used to chase down, who could, at most, conjure up some sparks and bangs to entertain children, or who could convince adults to part with their money in exchange for some great, never-realised, magical boon. Making sure it's used properly is going to be the challenge now. I'm convinced of that after what I witnessed last night."

Gill didn't know whether or not to be frightened by what dal

Ruisseau Noir said. There was a new age looming and he wasn't sure he could adapt to a new world; he felt a pang of loss at no longer having a home to escape to.

"When do you leave?" Gill said.

"Immediately. Now that I've seen the king is well, I can rest easy, knowing I've done my duty to the Crown. Now I need to do my duty to my brother Intelligenciers and make my report."

"A safe journey to you," Gill said, giving the banneret's salute of clicked heels and a sharp nod. Dal Ruisseau Noir returned the gesture.

"It's been interesting knowing you. I hope I have the chance to raise a glass with you in more settled times."

With that, he left, walking swiftly. Moments later, Gill slipped out of the tavern and went to the seamstress's house. She'd finished her task, and he studied the result, pleased but also bitterly sad: a small white flag, embroidered with a stylised dragon in dark green thread. It was a small gesture, but one that Gill felt compelled to make. A similar banner, each bearing a unique sigil, was given to every student at the Academy on the day they graduated. Val had not made it to the Academy, but in all respects, he exemplified the qualities that institution claimed to espouse.

Gill held the banner tenderly in both hands as he walked to the church, wondering how Val would have reacted had he seen it while he was still alive. Crossing the square, Gill was surprised to see the king walk out of the tavern, closely followed by several concerned-looking barons, lords, and bannerets, who seemed to have become his court away from court. Gill wasn't under any illusion that they were present because of a sense of undying loyalty. These men would likely never have gotten within twenty paces of the king, let alone close enough to have his ear, in the old days. If they managed to get the king back on his throne, they would advance more than they ever could have otherwise.

"I'm glad to see you up and well, Highness," Gill said.

The king nodded and gave Gill a wave. "Still a little shakier than I'd like. A few little ongoing episodes, as Savin's physician likes to call them, but I recover faster after each one, and am hopeful I've seen the last of them. What do you have there?" He pointed at the cloth Gill was clutching with a nod.

"It's for a friend," Gill said. "A dead friend."

"The young man I'm told was killed during my rescue?"

"Yes, Highness. Val—Valdamar was his name. My squire."

"A brave lad by all accounts," Boudain said. "You're burying him?"

"I am, Highness."

"Now?"

Gill nodded.

"I'll attend," Boudain said.

"Highness, you really should rest awhile," the Count of Savin said. "You might feel well, but that doesn't mean you're completely recovered."

"Nonsense. I feel perfectly well, and it's the least I can do. We'll only be over there." He pointed to the church, then looked to Gill for confirmation.

Gill nodded.

They set off, Val's cortège of one dramatically expanded by the king he had died saving, and by a number of men who wouldn't have spared the lad a second glance, so caught up were they in their own self-importance. The walked in silence, Gill and the king leading the way.

The deacon had done his job well; at least, it appeared so to Gill's inexpert eye. The last time he'd attended a funeral, it had been for his wife and child. The body was laid out with coins on the eyes, and Val's hands were folded neatly on his body. In a gesture that was either somewhat touching, or motivated out of their desire to make sure they got paid, the grave-digging soldiers were lined up solemnly on the far side of the grave. Gill stepped forward and tucked the banner under Val's dead hands.

The king gave him an odd look, so Gill explained, saying, "Lad wanted nothing more than to be a banneret."

"Then he'll be one," Boudain said. "Posthumously, at least." He held out his hand and fixed one of his new attendants with his gaze. "Your sword."

The man looked nonplussed, but did as his king commanded and handed over his sword, hilt first. The king took it and strode forward. With little grace, he took the banner from beneath Val's hands and looked at it.

"A fine sigil," Boudain said before tucking it back into place. He did his best to lever the stiff fingers around the sword's grip. "For service to your liege, I invoke my rights as sovereign of Mirabaya, and with this sword and this banner, I name you, Valdamar, Banneret, with all honours, rights, and dignities so entailed."

The man who had handed over his sword looked shocked. Gill hoped the blade wasn't a treasured family heirloom, as its former owner wasn't likely to see it again. Judging by the gemstones encrusting the hilt—an affectation that wasn't to Gill's taste—it was, at the very least, expensive. Still, all being well, the man's advancement in the king's service would more than make up for the loss of the costly weapon.

It was a touching act, even if it was no more substantive than Gill's having the banner made. Still, he would make the king sign a letter giving effect to what he had just said, and send it to the Hall of Bannerets in Mirabay, to ensure that Val's name was added to the register.

Gill did his best to listen to the deacon's short sermon as the gravediggers placed Val in the ground, but his mind was filled with a turmoil of emotion that he struggled to keep at bay. Grief, guilt, loss, thoughts of others he had cared for, who had all ended up in the ground, while he still stumbled from day to day. As the ceremony came to an end, Gill realised there were still some matters outstanding.

Gill cleared his throat and wondered which of the hangers-on would have to reach for his purse. "I hate to trouble you with this, Majesty, but there remains the issue of the bill. . . ."

⁂

After the funeral, Gill paid the gravediggers and parted company with the king, who wished to look over his army, before returning to the inn. He was eager to check on Solène, to see if she was recovering from the strain of her efforts. Before he got there, he spotted a lonely figure walking away from the building. A familiar one. Gill jogged through the village to catch up to him.

"Pharadon!" he called.

The dragon in human form turned to look back at him. He appeared tired to Gill, but Guillot was never sure what was a reflection of the dragon's true feelings and what was a mask.

"You're leaving?" Gill said.

"I'm returning to the temple. It's time I get back to the goldscale. I'll do what I can for her, then we'll get to the mountains, away from all this. I fear hard times are coming to the lands of humankind."

"I think you're right." It occurred to Gill that having a dragon on their side would give them a huge advantage. "I can't convince you to stay? Help us finish this?"

Pharadon shook his head. "People are already terrified of dragons. They only know us in our base and savage form. How do you think seeing a dragon slaughtering swaths of soldiers would appear to them? Enough damage has been done. Best that my kind aren't seen by people again for a very long time."

"I suppose that might be for the best," Gill said. "We owe you for what you've done. Getting the king out of the city. Staying on to show Solène how to heal him."

"Faced with the alternative of the man who had the vessel of enlightenment stolen, helping the king seemed like the right thing to do."

"Hopefully the kingdom will last long enough to thank you. Repay you in some way, perhaps."

Pharadon nodded but said nothing.

"Safe journey," Gill said.

With that, Pharadon turned and continued his lonely journey.

"I believe we should treat with him, Highness," the Count of Savin said. "No one wants civil war."

Gill observed the council of war from the back of the inn's taproom, which had been converted from infirmary to command centre. The Count of Savin's attitude had changed significantly since the king had regained his faculties. Everyone's had. Boudain was a king without a throne, a man who had many enemies. If his side won the coming war—a war that Gill was convinced would take place—those enemies would be dispossessed; many lands and titles would be up for grabs.

"We'll send word to your cousins to announce your recovery, but I wanted your guidance on how to open negotiations with the Prince Bishop," Savin said. "What should we send him?"

"The Usurper?" the king said. "We'll send him nothing. There will be no negotiating with him. I want his neck on the headsman's block. He tried to kill me, and it's only luck, or the fact that he lacked sufficient magical power at that time, that saved me. By all accounts he now has more power than he knows what to do with. He needs to be put down like the rabid dog that he is."

That silenced the gathering for a moment. Gill could see that the king was struggling to contain his anger and worried that too much stress might cause a relapse.

"When can we expect to hear back from my cousins?" Boudain said.

"Two days, Sire," someone said. "They're both camped within a day of Mirabay."

"If it takes longer, that means they're thinking about their response," Boudain said. "They shouldn't need to. I am still the king, the Prince Bishop's actions notwithstanding. Any man who stands against me will be guilty of treason, and treated accordingly. Make sure my cousins are aware of that."

"Yes, Sire."

A man rushed into the tavern. "Soldiers approaching!"

"Friends or foes?" Savin said.

The man shrugged.

"I suppose we best take a look for ourselves," Boudain said.

▲▲▲▲▲▲

Gill and a number of the hangers-on followed the king's party out to the picket, where the guards silently observed the approaching army, which looked to number five, perhaps six thousand men. They outnumbered the king's men by about two to one. If they weren't friendly, things could go very badly, very quickly.

Someone produced a field telescope and handed it to the king, who scanned the approaching force.

"I can just make out some banners," he said, squinting down the eyepiece. "Ah, there's Aubin." He continued to squint. "And Chabris . . . Odd to see my cousins marching together. Here of all places."

"Our scouting network isn't as extensive as I might like," Savin said.

"Apparently not," Boudain said. "The only question that remains is if they are here to join us?"

"I've not had any contact with them," Savin said.

"Best to assume that isn't their intention, then. Get me a horse and form an honour guard. Have everyone else prepare for an attack."

"Highness, are you sure—"

Boudain glared at him. "Now would be a good time for everyone to stop asking if 'I'm sure,' and start doing what I command. Understood?"

"Of course, Highness," Savin said.

The king surveyed the crowd. "Villerauvais, you're with me."

Gill nodded and stepped forward.

"I'll need a horse, too," Gill said, as Savin passed him. "And a sword."

Savin had a face like thunder. "Would mine do?"

Gill shrugged. In truth, the count's weapon was a little fancy for his taste, but with his own swords having been left at the Wounded Lion in Mirabay, it was better than nothing.

"I didn't mean it literally," Savin said, resuming his determined march. "I'll see what I can do. Coudray!"

The junior officer pushed through the crowd and fell in beside his master; they set off to get things organised. Gill realised the king was standing beside him.

"Are they coming here to kill me, do you reckon?" Boudain said.

"I expect so, Sire." Gill had never been one to dress things up to suit the audience.

Boudain laughed. "And my cousin, Savin? What do you think of him? And all the men who are suddenly so eager to serve me?"

"I've always felt the best people to rely on in a time of crisis are the ones who were most reluctant to get involved," Gill said. "It's the ones who are too eager to please that you need to look out for. Still, they've much to gain if you reclaim the throne. So long as they believe that, they'll fight for you."

"*When* I regain my throne," Boudain said. "I appreciate your candour, though. While you may not trust men who seem too eager to please, I don't trust those who tell me what they think I want to hear. It's men like you I want around me now."

"There are men better able than I—"

"I won't hear any more of that, Villerauvais," Boudain said. "You were long considered the best, and in recent weeks you've proved that you still are. That you're no friend to the Prince Bishop is just about your best-known quality, which puts us in the same boat, so to speak. If he wins, we're both dead."

Gill nodded. There was no arguing that point.

"I know my father did wrong by you," Boudain said, "but I assure you, I'm not my father. You've already done this kingdom great service in slaying the dragons, and I'd like to be able to grant you lands and titles, and tell you to go and enjoy your rewards, but I can't. I have need of you yet. The Prince Bishop must be stopped, and Mirabaya will need the best of her sons and daughters to steer her back to safety. Can I count on you?"

"You already know you can," Gill said. He was determined to see Amaury dead and couldn't ask for a more powerful ally than the king. Underneath it all, he knew none of that mattered. The king had asked. He didn't have it in him to say no.

A group of riders led by Savin approached them with two spare horses. Dal Coudray threw Gill a belt and scabbard containing a sword. Gill gave a nod of thanks and drew it enough to take a look at the blade. It wouldn't win any prizes for craftsmanship, but the hilt was tight and the steel looked good. It would do until he could find something better. He strapped it on and felt fully clothed for the first time in days.

Boudain and Gill mounted. Escorted by Savin's honour guard, they rode through a small gap in the picket. A group carrying a number of banners broke away from the front of the waiting army and started toward them. Gill couldn't make out any of the banners, and was unlikely to recognise any of the sigils even if he could. There was a time when he might have, but that had long since passed—being able to identify his peers didn't seem like a necessary skill anymore.

Gill couldn't guess what was coming next, and he reckoned none of the others could either. He was impressed by the king, though. This was a high-pressure moment and came soon after his body and mind had been subjected to tremendous abuse. None of this showed on his face—he looked as carefree as a man riding out for a picnic.

Curious to see if the young king would be able to maintain his sangfroid as the confrontation developed, Gill kept his horse close beside Boudain's. He held his reins in a casual fashion, with his right hand conveniently close to the pommel of his sword. There was just enough tension in the air to make him think he'd soon be getting another look at its munitions-grade blade.

The king didn't wave or greet the approaching riders; he simply drew his horse to a halt when they were within earshot. An awkward silence descended, until eventually, one of the opposing noblemen, all of whom were bedecked in three-quarter armour, spoke. For Gill, the fact that they were already in their armour said more than anything that would come out of this man's mouth.

"I'm glad to see you well, your Highness."

"I'm glad to be well, Cousin Aubin."

There was no warmth in either voice.

"No greeting for me, Cousin Chabris?" the king said, a slight, ironic smile on his lips.

The man next to Aubin, the younger of the two, and about the same age as the king, blushed and doffed his hat, but said nothing.

The king shrugged. "What brings you both here?"

Aubin glanced at Chabris. "We sought to parlay with Lord Savin."

"What good fortune that you find your king here, then. You may camp your men in that pasture," Boudain said, gesturing to an open area south of the village. "I'll need a complete manifest of your troop numbers and supplies, by sundown."

Neither Aubin nor Chabris said anything and the awkward silence returned.

"So," Boudain said, after he had allowed the discomfort to draw out. "You didn't come here to rally to my banner. Why, then?"

Aubin opened his mouth to speak, but the king cut him off.

"You must have heard I was here, and most likely also that I was very ill. You put your differences aside and rode here to make sure Savin couldn't use me as a figurehead to build a more powerful army. Or to make sure I didn't get the chance to heal. Perhaps both?"

Chabris flushed from shame, but Aubin's face twisted spitefully. "You're bewitched," he said. "Possessed by a sorceress. You have no legitimate claim to the throne. Not any longer."

"That's quite an interesting appreciation you have of the law, there, Cousin Aubin," the king said. "Completely wrong, of course, but it goes to show your spying seems to have improved since that day you got caught peeping at the ladies swimming in the lake at the summer palace."

"You can try all you like to embarrass me, Boudain, but it won't change a damned thing."

Gill raised an eyebrow at the use of the king's given name, and moved his hand a little closer to his sword. Any semblance of respectful discourse was now far behind them.

"There was no magic cast on me but to undo that which had been done by my enemies. Transfer your troops to my authority and return to your estates, and I promise to forget this conversation happened," the king said calmly.

"You've had magic done to you," Aubin said. "You're not my king, or anyone else's, Boudain. Not anymore." He looked to the Count of Savin, who sat on his horse next to the king. "My Lord Savin, I make now the offer we came to deliver. Join your forces to ours and ride with us against this tyrannical warlock."

"Who'd be king?" Gill said.

Everyone looked at him and he felt suddenly self-conscious.

"If you win," Gill repeated, "who'd be king?"

"Well," Aubin said. "I'm of the senior branch."

"But through the female line," Boudain said. "Savin is the senior by age, and dear Chabris is senior through the male line. How many civil wars do you plan on fighting to untangle that mess?"

"We all have the best interests of the realm at heart," Aubin said.

Boudain barked out a laugh. "Then assign your troops to my command and return home. You have until sunset to make your decision. After that, your names go on my list next to the Prince Bishop's." He turned his horse and started back toward the village.

Gill moved immediately to follow his king, but Count Savin hesitated and the honour guard remained with him. Faced with a larger army, the rewards of supporting the king through this trial instantly became less likely, but switching sides didn't necessarily offer any better position. Gill knew as well as anyone how nobles—particularly those with a claim to the throne—operated. He could see the gears turning over in Savin's head. He knew as well as Gill did that even in the best-case scenario, only one of the cousins would live to see the end of this civil war. He was just trying to work out the likelihood of that being him.

With a nod as he passed, Gill said, "You ride over there to join them and I'll make sure you're dead before sundown." He smiled at Savin's outraged expression. "Hope that helps make your decision easier."

He urged his horse forward, catching up to the king, who had never looked back. A moment later, Gill heard the jingling of harness and glanced over his shoulder. Savin and the honour guard were following them back to Castandres.

They have twice our number, at least," the king said, when they got back to the illusory safety of the pickets. "If they choose to attack, what do we do?"

"Numbers aren't everything," Gill said, not sure what else he could do to allay the king's concerns. "Troop quality counts for a lot, and attacking a defended position is always a big ask for peasant levies."

"I doubt Savin's troops are crack guardsmen," the king said, looking around at the troops, who bore all the hallmarks of being levies themselves—improvised weapons, mismatched clothes.

Some men had the look of soldiers—probably mercenaries or members of the count's personal retinue—but there weren't enough of them to make a difference. They might hold back an initial assault, but without a solid force to back them up, Gill didn't reckon they'd last a whole lot longer than the levies.

All in all, it didn't look good. Gill knew they were going to have to get creative. Of course, Aubin and Chabris might conclude it better to side with the king once they'd had the chance to properly consider the idea. . . .

"Savin!" the king said. "Council of war in the tavern."

Gill watched Savin carefully. He wasn't convinced of the man's loyalty. A quick escape might be his best option at this moment. While nobles didn't tend to place much worth on their levies, the count would take his best troops with him. Guillot wondered if it would be worth arresting Savin now, before he had the chance to cause any trouble, but that wasn't his call to make.

The king waited for the senior nobles to assemble in the tavern.

He was starting to show some signs of agitation, but that was only to be expected. He had never fought in a battle before, much less commanded the opening clashes of a war. As with all heirs, he'd attended the Academy, but Gill doubted if he had done much more than pay lip service to his studies. This was as big a challenge as an experienced king and commander could expect to face. To have to deal with it at such an early stage of his reign would test him severely.

"Is everyone here?" Boudain finally said, when the taproom was full.

"Everyone of consequence," Savin said.

"Can we expect any more troops to arrive in our support?"

"Possibly, Highness," Savin said. "But in truth, I wouldn't count on it. Not in time to make any difference."

The king scratched his chin and stared into the distance. To Gill, it was clear that Boudain was doing everything he could so as not to appear out of his depth; he wondered if anyone else could see it. Other than the Count of Savin, who was older, most of the men in the room looked to be a decade younger than Gill. Few, if any, were old enough to have served in the last war. For them, this probably all seemed like a great adventure. Those that came out the other side wouldn't think that way any longer.

"I, uh," Boudain said, strain showing on his face. He looked across the gathering and his eyes stopped on Gill. The strain was replaced with an expression of relief. "Villerauvais! Villerauvais is one of our most experienced soldiers. He's already made some interesting suggestions. How would you proceed in these circumstances?"

Every eye turned to Gill. He wanted to swear, but couldn't with everyone looking at him.

"Aubin and Chabris are inexperienced commanders at the head of a levy army," Gill said, doing his best to sound more confident than he was. He didn't know much about either man, but reckoned he would have known more if they had distinguished themselves in any way. "We're defending a position, rather than attacking. These three factors are strongly in our favour. As is the fact that Aubin and Chabris are likely arguing at this very moment over what to do next. Division within their ranks is an even bigger asset."

He took a breath and looked around. Everyone seemed to be pay-ing attention and no one had spoken up in criticism. Yet. He took that to be a good sign.

"With a fixed position to defend, our task is simpler, our tactics fewer. There's only one, in fact, when you boil it down. Keep the enemy out. We repel their attacks until they break. With arguing command-ers and inexperienced, untrained troops, that will be far sooner than it might otherwise."

The room was completely silent. He wondered how many of the people gathered here knew who he was, and which version of his rep-utation they had heard. Would they have confidence in him? More importantly, did they have confidence in the king? The accusation levelled against him by the Count of Aubin was surely playing on everyone's mind. Would the king's entanglement with magic lose him the support of the few followers he did have?

"We'll divide the picket into four sectors for defence and hold a reserve ready to reinforce any sector that's coming under attack." He kept talking, outlining basic tactics, as his mind ran through the dan-ger that lurked closer to home. Although Gill had become more com-fortable with the idea of magic and fantastic creatures being abroad once more, it was unlikely anyone else was. Solène needed to be ready to flee at a moment's notice. If things turned against them, even the king wouldn't be able to protect her.

"My Lord Savin, if you could have your five most senior com-manders make themselves known to me, we can divide up our forces and allot assignments. In the meantime, have the men put to work reinforcing the pickets. We'll need a platform around the inside to allow our men to stand above the attackers and strike down at them. Get them working on it now."

Savin muttered something to Coudray, who left in a hurry, then pulled five men from the crowd, before ordering the rest to give them the room. Gill chewed his lip in consternation. His speech to the full room had been the easy part. Speaking in generalisations always was. Now he had to come up with specifics.

He walked over to the dead fire in the hearth and rooted around with the poker until he found a likely-looking piece of charred wood. Grabbing it, he walked to the largest section of exposed whitewashed wall. He hesitated for a moment before starting, but reckoned one day the tavern keeper might appreciate having the graffiti on his wall, and regale his customers with the day the king planned the defence of the village, and the first battle of what was sure to be a significant war, in that very room.

Working quickly, Guillot scratched some blocky shapes on the wall—the village—then drew a circle around that to indicate the pickets, although he had no idea what shape it actually was, or even if it completely enclosed the village. With a little luck, it would be by the time Aubin's and Chabris's men came knocking. That done, Gill drew one vertical and one horizontal line, breaking the diagram into four quadrants. Finally, he marked an "X" a short distance from his main drawing: the enemy.

He stepped back and regarded his work for a moment, refining his plan as he did, then wrote the numbers one to five down the side.

"We'll divide our force in two," Gill said. "One half will be split up between the four sections of the picket, while the other half will be held back in reserve to assist anywhere along the picket that's getting hit hard. The key to this battle is holding the enemy off until they break or decide that the cost of getting through is too high. There are more battles to be fought in this war, and we're not even facing the real enemy yet."

"Hold on, and hope they go away?" Savin said. "That's your plan?"

Gill knew this criticism was coming sooner or later, so it was no surprise. "What would your suggestion be, my Lord?"

"To fight like men," the count said. "We lead our troops out onto the field and give battle properly. With honour. Not like caged rats."

"Where their numerical advantage will allow them to envelop our flanks and slaughter us to a man?" Gill said. "The only way we limit their strength of numbers is here, behind our pickets. A man behind a wall is worth at least two trying to get through it. They won't want to commit to a full siege. They could easily wake up one morning and find the Prince Bishop's army at their back. With us at their front, they'd be wiped out before lunch."

"When do you expect them to come at us?" Savin said, sounding suitably cowed.

Gill shrugged. "Who knows? They might even decide that we're not worth the effort and march away. I think that's unlikely, though. So long as the king lives, he's a threat to anyone who wants the throne for themselves. I'm sorry to say it, Highness, but there are three men whose survival depends on your death. Likewise, yours depends on them dying."

"Lord Savin is right," the king said, finally breaking his silence. "We can't kill them in here, hiding behind our walls."

"Today isn't about killing them," Gill said. "Probably not tomorrow either. It's about surviving long enough to hit back at them. For that we need to be steadfast and patient. If you rush in now, Highness, you'll lose everything. We might rout your cousins on the open field if we go after them now—stranger things have happened—but we'll break ourselves in the process, and when it comes to facing Amaury, he'll smash us."

The king didn't like that idea, if the expression on his face was anything to go by. Gill didn't reckon he was going to like much of what happened in the coming days, but if nothing else, it would give Boudain the chance to prove he was up to the job of being king. If he lacked the resolve, perhaps it would be better if one of his cousins got the job. Beating Amaury would take grit and a willingness to get his hands dirty. If he didn't have that in him, this was the place to find out.

Gill allotted the assignments to Savin's chosen officers and sent them off to get organised.

"Now we need to find a vantage point to keep an eye on everything," Gill said. They wandered out into the village for a look around, but Gill was pretty sure there was only one place that fit the bill. There was a tall hayloft, and a clock tower on the village hall, but the church steeple was the highest point in sight. Gill wondered how the deacon would react to his coming calling again. And to him knocking some holes in the steeple.

The deacon seemed a little more relaxed about receiving visitors this time. So far, the army had behaved itself, and the presence of the king was another comforting factor. At least until word spread that a sorceress had cast magic on him. That wasn't a problem Gill had seen coming. With a little luck, they'd have dealt with Amaury before it became too much of an issue.

The deacon cried out in protest when Gill smashed out a few slates on each side of the steeple's roof, giving them a panoramic view of the countryside. The king's small army was hard at work strengthening and raising the pickets, and building the platform around the inside. Beyond, the enemy army was setting up camp. That could mean they planned to attack right away and were hoping to lull the king into a false sense of security by appearing to be settling in for the night; or, it might indicate that they would wait at least until the next day before attacking. Uncertainty had always been the part that Gill found hardest. That, and the waiting. Most things about war were hard, now that he thought about it. However, he suspected Aubin and Chabris would argue over the king's offer until the time limit expired, by which point it would be dark, and madness to attack with inexperienced troops.

"There's a lot of them," the king said, bringing his borrowed telescope to bear once again. "Can we really hold them off?"

"I'd like to say yes, Highness," Gill said, "but it'd be a lie. There's no reason why we can't, but so many things can go wrong when you've an untested army. Believe it or not, it'll be better if your cousins surround us. Our troops will fight a lot harder if they think there's nowhere to run."

The king laughed. "I'm not sure I like the sound of that."

"There's not much to like at a time like this, Highness."

"What do we do?"

"What men in our situation always do," Gill said. "They make the best of it."

"How many wars have you fought in?"

Gill tried to count, but realised that with few exceptions, all battles blurred into one. What constituted a war, anyway? He'd fought in battles that had cost hundreds and thousands of men their lives, but most would probably not have been considered wars. "Enough that I have trouble counting, Highness."

"I feel ashamed every time I think of you," the king said.

Frowning, Gill stared at his king.

"A man who has served his kingdom so faithfully should never have been treated the way you were," Boudain said. "I'm sure you realise the Prince Bishop had a hand in it, but my father should have been stronger. Should have been able to recognise who his true friends were."

"I . . ." Gill said. What was there to say to that? "Thank you, Highness."

"I appreciate you standing with me on this. After all you've done, and been put through." He returned his gaze to the enemy, and raised the telescope. "If we get out of this, I'll do everything I can to undo the damage the Prince Bishop and my father caused you."

CHAPTER
23

There were few spare moments when an army was preparing for battle, but when the commanders paused their discussions, Gill took the opportunity for a much-needed break. Putting into place the command structures for the village's defence was tedious but necessary work. Everyone had to know who was responsible for what. They couldn't risk the chance of something going unaddressed because everyone thought it was someone else's job.

An idea had been forming in Gill's mind for a while, and he allowed himself to follow it, which led him back to the seamstress's house, to ask her to sew a banner for the king. He wasn't sure why, but it seemed like the type of thing that might come in handy; if raised at the right moment, it might put mettle back into wavering troops. He knew only too well what a man would do for his king, and knowing that the king was with you in the thick of it might be the difference between fighting on or turning and running.

Task completed, he turned his mind to other necessities, like his swords. He'd left them sitting in the Wounded Lion in Mirabay. Like as not, they'd been stolen by now, along with everything else he'd left there. The swords, and Valdamar's armour, which was with them, were all made from Telastrian steel. Worth a fortune. The innkeeper had appeared to be one of dal Ruisseau Noir's confederates, so perhaps he had placed them in storage. It would be worth checking at the end of all this, assuming he survived.

Regardless, his predicament remained. He was without any of the accoutrements he needed to go into battle. He had returned the sword he had borrowed for the king's confrontation with his cousins and he had no armour. There was a smith in the village, but there was no time to have anything new made. The best he'd be able to hope for was some hammering of heated plates to make any armour he scrounged up fit better.

The army had a quartermaster of sorts. Gill knew the type, having encountered many of them with levy forces over the years. When the call to raise levies came, they were the men sent into their lord's armoury to dig out all the weapons and armour that had been dumped there the last time the levy came home. The more diligent lords—who were few, in Gill's experience—would have everything repaired, sharpened, and oiled, in anticipation of their next use, whenever that might be. Most would leave the gear to rot, knowing they wouldn't be the poor sods relying on it in the next fight.

What was serviceable in this quartermaster's care had probably been handed out long ago. The only saving grace was that no farmer-turned-soldier was going to be given a rapier—he'd be as likely to hurt himself with it as an enemy—so Gill was hopeful there'd be one he could have the blacksmith tweak to his tastes.

The quartermaster and his assistant were busy working on what was left in their meagre inventory when Gill got there. A quick look confirmed that he might be in luck with a sword, but as for armour, he could forget about it. Metal plate in a battle was always a comfort against the threat of the arrow or blade that you didn't see coming. He'd feel naked in only borrowed tunic and britches.

As the quartermaster approached, Gill gave him a hopeful smile. "What have you got left?"

"What do you need?"

Gill shrugged. "Everything." He realised the borrowed clothes he was wearing made him look much like any of the other levy men. "I'm a banneret."

"You're in luck, then. We have some side swords you can look over. Only leather cuirasses left, though."

"I'll take what I can get," Gill said. "The swords?"

The quartermaster rummaged in a hay-filled wooden crate, withdrawing three scabbardless side swords. He laid them down on the trestle-and-plank table for Gill's scrutiny. None of them were rusty, but that was about all he could say in their favour on first glance. The plain, three-ringed hilt design was of a fashion that displayed their age. They were old—probably out of style even in his father's time.

Failing the demands of fashion was one thing; far more important was the question of whether they'd survive their first meeting with another blade. He picked each one up, hefted it, and studied each blade, making mental notes as he went, adding up the pros and cons. In the end, one emerged as a clear leader. There were fewer flaws in the steelwork, and the weight was closer to what Gill was comfortable with. He wouldn't win any style awards in the officers' mess with it, given its guard of roughly welded bars, but he reckoned it would hold up when it counted.

"What about the cuirass?" Gill said.

The quartermaster's assistant appeared from the red-clothed stores tent with two mouldering cuirasses of leather that looked like they had been stored in a damp pool. His skin crawled at the thought of wearing either of them, and he couldn't see them being much protection. He gave a curt shake of his head.

"I'll take the sword," he said. "Thanks for your help."

Sword in hand, Gill headed for the blacksmith. The blade needed some work, and the balance wasn't quite right. The closer he could get it to what he liked, the better, but he didn't expect a man who spent most of his time making iron fittings and horseshoes to be able to work wonders on it.

The smithy was built of stone and slate, and open to the elements at the front. Heat radiated out from the forge, the glowing coals concealed underneath a black and grey crust of ash and charcoal. The blacksmith sat next to a sharpening wheel with a spearhead in his hands. There was a pile of similar points on either side of him—one sharp, one blunt, Gill guessed.

"I need some help with a blade," he said.

The smith looked up from the metal head he was holding against the rotating whetstone. He stopped pressing the pedals, and the wheel slowly came to a halt.

"It'll have to wait," the smith said.

"This isn't on the army's bill," Gill said. "I'll pay for it myself."

The smith looked at him with tired eyes. He'd probably been sharpening blades and shoeing horses nonstop since the army had arrived. Likely he hadn't seen a penny for his troubles, and was being motivated by the fear of saying no and the hope of being paid before the army left.

"What needs doing?"

"I'd like to take some length off the blade, rework the balance."

"I'm not a bladesmith," the smith said.

"It's not difficult work. I can guide you." Gill picked up a wax pencil from the smith's workbench and took his guard with the sword. He tried a cut and a thrust, pulling into a parry and back to guard after each one. That done, he made a mark on the blade, half a handspan from the tip.

"Cut it clean there, and rework the tip into a spearpoint, just like you're doing with those."

The smith nodded, staring at the sword. Gill stuck out his index finger and rested the blade on it, moving the sword backward and forward until he found its balance point. It was a little too far toward the tip for his liking, but the trimming and reshaping might solve that. He made another mark.

"This is where I want the balance to be," Gill said. "If the tip work doesn't bring it back far enough, add a little lead to the pommel. It's no great beauty anyway. Will a crown cover the work?"

The smith nodded. Gill knew it would cover the work three times over, but he wanted this prioritised, and a grateful smith did better work than a resentful one.

Gill smiled. "I'll be right back."

Gill wandered through the village in search of the Count of Savin. It was conspicuously devoid of villagers. Other than a few of the braver businesspeople who had ventured out in the hope of making some money out of the situation they found themselves in, it seemed everyone was shut up in their homes, unwilling to come out. Gill really couldn't blame them, and hoped that would be enough to keep them safe if the worst happened.

It didn't take him long to find Savin, leaning against a fence and chatting with three of his lords. They stopped as soon as they spot-

ted Gill, making him doubly curious about what they'd been saying. Savin had the look of a man stuck with a horse he hadn't wanted
to buy. Now he was caught in that uncertain place, trying to decide
whether to keep it and make the best of a bad situation, or sell it at a
loss for whatever he could get.

"My Lord Savin," Gill said, with as much geniality as he could
muster. "I find myself in need of some financial assistance."

Savin frowned at him.

"Our flight from the city being such, I was dispossessed of all
things and don't fancy going into a battle without a few comforts."

The count's frown turned to irritation. "Give him some money,"
he said.

None of his lords made to reach for their purses. After a moment,
Savin pulled a purse from the belt of the closest man and tossed it to
Gill, ignoring the look of indignation on the lord's face. Gill caught the
bag one-handed and smiled.

"Consider it a gift from the Crown," Savin said.

Gill nodded his thanks, but knew damn well that every expense
the count incurred—and more, plus interest—would be presented to the
royal treasurer for repayment the moment the king was back on his
throne. Thus enriched, Gill returned to the smith, who had resumed
his work on the spearpoints.

Rummaging through the purse, Guillot could see why Savin's lord
had been annoyed. It looked like he'd been gifted the man's full campaign float—at least twenty crowns in various denominations. An un-
skilled worker might make one crown a day if they were well paid.
Gill reckoned two were more than enough for the smith, adding a
margin of generosity for the rush.

He tossed two crowns to the smith, who dropped the spear tip he
was working on to catch them.

"I'm obliged, Lord," the man said, then got up and went to the
workbench, where Gill had left the sword. "The wax mark for the cut?"

Gill nodded, and the smith took a saw and made short work of the
blade. It looked odd with a square tip. He immediately took a file to it
and started working the cut end back into a point. It wasn't the ideal
way to make a blade, and meant that softer metal at the blade's core

would be exposed, but Gill reckoned he'd fare better with a weapon that felt good in his hand, even if the edge on its tip didn't last quite as long as usual. On a cheaper, munitions-grade blade such as this one, the difference would be less pronounced than on a sword made by a master bladesmith anyway.

The roughing-out done, the smith presented the sword for inspection. Guillot looked it over; judging by the colour of the metal, not too much of the softer core material had been exposed—one of the benefits of cheaper construction. As he had expected, the balance point had moved back, and already the weapon felt better in his hand. However, there was still room for improvement.

"Round off the transition into the tip a little more," Gill said. "Then I think we'll need to add a touch of weight to the pommel."

The smith got to work with the file again, pausing every few strokes for Gill's input, until it had the shape he was looking for. He tested the balance again, and reckoned it wouldn't take much more to get it right.

The smith drilled a small hole into the pommel, then melted some lead, which he poured into the hole. Once it had cooled, Gill tested the sword. It took a second filling of lead before it felt right. He made a few more cuts with the sword. Satisfied that it was as good as he could hope for, he gave the smith another crown for his efforts. It was time to return to the council of war to discuss what further preparations could be made.

CHAPTER

24

Tresonne had rustled up enough tarpaulin to completely cover the cage for the journey back to Mirabay. Exhausted though she was, Ysabeau's concern that the dragon might wake in transit was enough to motivate her to continue using magic—both hers and Hangdog's—to speed their return journey. As soon as they got back to Mirabay, the dragon would be someone else's problem, but the credit would remain with her.

When they reached the city gates, they discovered that the cage was too large to get through the city gate. More, the sight of two great ox wagons trundling along in tandem, pulled by teams of straining beasts and blocking the entire road, was too much to ignore. The guards stepped across the road, blocking the path.

"Who seeks to enter the city?" one of them asked.

"Agents of the Prince Bishop, Regent of Mirabaya."

"What's on the carts?"

Ysabeau smirked. "Best take a look for yourselves. You wouldn't believe me if I told you."

The guards looked at one another, then one walked forward. He cast Ysabeau a nervous look before approaching the covered cage, halberd in hand. Grasping the tarpaulin, he cast furtive looks at his fellow guards.

Everyone now gathered around the city gate was watching the goings-on, wondering what was under that cover. Ysabeau wondered if any of them could guess. She couldn't wait to see how they reacted.

Lifting the tarp and peering into the cage, the guard let out a loud gasp and fell back on his arse. He dropped his halberd and scrambled back, away from the cage. Ysabeau let out a cackle, as amused by his reaction as by the fact that he was the only one who had seen what was in there. Everyone else had to speculate based on his terrified reaction; she found their consternation delicious.

"Anyone else want to take a peek?"

There were no volunteers.

She turned to Hangdog. "Go to the palace and tell my fa—the Prince Bishop that I've returned to the city with everything he requested."

Hangdog seemed only too happy to get back into the city, and most likely to get as far away from her as he could.

"Take these three with you," she said as an afterthought, and pointed to the three academics, who looked equally delighted to have returned to Mirabay. After they disappeared through the gate, Ysabeau smiled at the guards.

The fallen man was back on his feet and whispering furiously at his comrades. The colour drained from their faces.

"Is it really?" one of them said to Ysabeau.

"Why don't you find out for yourself?" She gestured to the tarpaulin.

From his expression, she could tell he was trying to balance his desire to see a real live dragon against the danger of losing a hand, or perhaps a whole arm. Of course, the dragon was still asleep. It hadn't so much as budged the whole way back to the city. Were it not for the sporadic twitching of its nostrils, or the regular rise and fall of its chest, she would have thought it was dead. She'd given up wondering what was wrong with it, or why it slept. Soon enough, it wouldn't be her problem anymore.

The problem that remained, however, was getting the cage through the gate. It wasn't like they could lead it through on a leash, like a puppy. What about using the same method they had to get the cage out of the temple? Ysabeau looked up at the battlements, towering overhead. The wall was high—at least twice as high as they had to deal with at the temple, perhaps more. There would be far stronger and more sophisticated equipment available at the docks, but even still, it was a big obstacle. Perhaps floating it upriver and into the city would be the best approach. Still, that would be someone else's decision to make.

She wondered if they might be able to widen the gate, or if that would bring down this whole section of the wall. Her father's engineers would probably be able to come up with a solution. Best to leave them to it.

Ysabeau was surprised by how quickly her father arrived. She also thought it odd that he was dressed as an ordinary man rather than in his vestments and that his hair appeared to be dyed—she almost didn't recognise him. Had the city become so dangerous that he was required to wear a disguise when out in the open? He had four other "ordinary men" with him, but they all had the look of mercenaries. She raised an eyebrow when she saw him, but a quick shake of his head dispossessed her of the idea of asking any questions.

"Is he telling the truth?" the Prince Bishop said.

There was only one person he could be talking about. She smiled.

"If he's talking about that," she said, nodding toward the cage, "then yes, he is."

"Gods alive."

The Prince Bishop dismounted, handed his reins to one of his men, and walked toward the cage. When he lifted the tarpaulin, his reaction was far more measured than the guard's.

"I can't say I ever thought to see this," the Prince Bishop said. "Is it alive?"

His voice was firm, but it sounded forced to Ysabeau. "As best I can tell," she said.

"What's wrong with it? Why doesn't it move?"

"Your guess is as good as mine," Ysabeau said. "Perhaps it's hibernating?"

The Prince Bishop nodded. "Yes. Perhaps." He looked from the cage to the gate, then back again. "Getting it through the gate's going to be a problem," he said.

"I thought that myself," Ysabeau replied. "But it's not my problem." She flashed her father a winning smile, then urged her horse forward and into the city.

▲▲▲▲▲▲

Amaury didn't like how relieved he felt once he was back inside the palace walls. That meant he had to admit to himself how concerned he was about the situation outside. As unsettling as these realisations were, they didn't detract from his excitement at what Ysabeau had brought him. A real, live dragon. Caged and slumbering. It was beyond the realm of his imagination, and he had always prided himself on his ability to think big. The prestige it would bring was immense—enough, perhaps, to soften the blow of having let the king slip from his grasp. The satisfaction he had felt at preventing Gill from taking the Cup soured completely once he had realised the attempt was merely a distraction from the actual mission. Dal Villerauvais, it seemed, had more artifice than Amaury had ever given him credit for.

Word was yet to get out that the king was no longer in the city, but it would. Soon. The news could be dismissed as misinformation for a time, but eventually it would be undeniable. Considering how angry the citizens already were, he might be better off admitting it from the get-go, and trying to twist the information to his advantage, painting those who had taken the king as traitors.

The dragon had come just at the right time—Divine Fortune showing that perhaps she still did favour him. Showing the people this great trophy was the perfect thing with which to grab their attention, and distract them from everything else that was going on. At that moment the beast was being brought downriver to a site where it was to be loaded onto a barge for transport into the city. With three armies roaming the countryside, he wasn't going to risk disassembling part of the city wall, no matter how much value the prize might bring.

It hadn't taken him long to work out what to do with the creature—there was an old duelling arena on Southgate Road that would be a perfect home for it. He could have a sturdy enclosure built to cover the arena floor, leaving plenty of space for his citizens to come and view their great prize. His citizens. He wondered if they'd ever think of him as their liege. Their saviour—for that was what he undoubtedly was. When the Ventish marched south or the Ostians landed on their shores, led by powerful battle mages, the people would ask where the king was and why he was not protecting his people.

Thanks to Amaury, that day would never come—Mirabaya would have its own battle mages, far more powerful than anything the Ventish or Ostians could come up with. He feared the people would never appreciate the great service he had done them, at so much personal risk and sacrifice.

He knew that he had come too far to hand power to someone else. If whoever it was had an ounce of sense in their heads, they'd have him thrown in the dungeons as soon as they sat on the throne. There was no longer any question of ruling from the shadows, through a puppet king. Not anymore. In any event, he deserved this. All that he had done, all that he had sacrificed, was to make sure that Mirabaya was strong, and safe. No one else could do that. Only him.

Amaury returned to his office to draft the orders for his new dragon menagerie. As he took up his pen, his gaze fell on the wooden box containing the two Cups. They were of no more use to him personally, so he was sending them to the Priory. Their temporary boon would be of great use to his mages-in-training, and more importantly, they could give the Order's mages worthwhile power while they were carrying out the tasks that would build public support.

The mood in the city was ugly, and his health clinics had not yet achieved the effect he was hoping for. People were using them, but only in small numbers, only with reluctance, and always with fear. Even the healed seemed to resent magic. He was certain that would change with time, but time was something he was running short on. Eventually he was going to have to face his challengers on the field, and when that happened, the last thing he needed was a city that would turn on him as soon as his attention was directed elsewhere.

If kindness wasn't working, he would soon have to alter his tactics. A display of power might cow the people into obedience long enough for him to deal with other issues, but he knew that would cause problems of its own if not managed carefully. The residents of Mirabay needed to know what he could do if they didn't get in line, but he had to be careful not to punish them so severely they would resent him all the more. He would have to show them what the stick looked like, but make it clear the carrot remained available. Perhaps he could use the dragon in that regard? Might his new magical power allow him to yoke the beast to his will?

He desperately wanted to use his power, but now that he had access to it, he felt ill at the thought of what the effort might do to him.

His state after the encounter with Gill and Solène—unconsciousness, followed by pain and fatigue—remained a great concern to him. That there was still a price to be paid for his use of magic was obvious. Amaury had hoped the Cup would free him of such constraints, but it seemed that was not to be. Far more power, but still at a cost. He supposed that was right, in the grand scheme of things, but it was frustrating. It would take time to learn how to control it without killing himself before he could unleash its full potential.

If the gods favoured him, the inscriptions his academics had brought back from the temple would accelerate the process. Otherwise, he would continue to rue his decision to have Kayte dal Drezony killed as he stumbled along his journey of self-discovery.

CHAPTER

25

In Gill's experience, there was always a moment of calm before a battle—that last, momentary hesitation where everyone involved reconsidered whether they wanted to be there or not. For the men behind the pickets, the army staring at them from just beyond cross-bow range looked far larger than it had when it was at camp. For the men in the army, the pickets looked unassailably high, defended by men who would fight to the death. Everyone would be wondering why they had chosen to be there, and if the coins they were paid, or the potential for plunder, was worth it.

The ones carrying the seed of doubt in their minds would be the first to break if things started going wrong. As he scanned his de-fences, Gill wished there were a way to tell when a man was wavering. If one on the picket were to turn and run, the rest would follow. Panic was the greatest killer of armies he'd ever seen, and when dealing with levies, it was an ever-present threat.

These troops weren't men who'd grown up with their heads filled with notions of honour; they were farmers and tradesmen who wanted nothing more than to make a bit of extra money before re-turning to their families. If they had a bit of an adventure along the way, and went back with a few stories to tell, all the better. Dying for their king, far from those they loved—who would likely never hear how they died—didn't seem so noble when it was staring at you from a few furlongs away.

Silence prevailed, joined by an uncomfortable partner—tension. Beside Gill, the young king exuded tension like a reeking body odour. It was understandable—it was his first battle, and the fact that he hadn't soiled his britches meant he was already ahead of a great many men who had faced a similar situation.

"What do you think of," the king asked, "at a time like this?"

Gill snapped out of his musing. "Now? I wonder how the battle will play out. Once upon a time, I thought of my family. It's different for every man."

The king nodded thoughtfully. "Why do they wait?" He nodded toward the opposing force.

"There's no way to know. They might be having second thoughts. Your cousins might not be as confident in their men's resolve as they made out. They might be trying to come up with an alternative, or merely taking a little time to let their breakfasts settle."

"You think they might be considering surrender?"

Gill wanted to laugh, but recognised that the king was serious. "I doubt that. What with all that's . . . happened to you, I reckon they see too good an opportunity here. They'll come at us as soon as they've built up the nerve."

"This waiting is . . ." the king said.

"Always the hardest part," Gill said. "When things get started, it's almost easier. There's nothing to do then but fight for all you're worth."

As though they had heard him, the enemy started to move toward the village. It was difficult to tell from that distance how well they moved as a unit—they were still little more than a dark row of figures on a green field. The sound of marching and rattling weapons gradually grew to fill the air. It was an ominous sound all by itself. When you realised it was the sound of men coming to try and kill you, it was terrifying. Considering how many times he had heard it, and the effect it was having on him, he pitied the men who were confronting it for the first time. They had nothing to guide them but their imaginations, which were undoubtedly multiplying their fear of the unknown.

"I suppose we should be grateful they don't have any siege equipment," the king said.

Gill nodded. "It certainly wouldn't have made life any easier for us. We'll have troubles aplenty as it is." He didn't know much about the king's cousins. As with all senior aristocrats, they were Academy graduates, but being an Academy graduate didn't say a whole lot. They would have had the same military education and training as all others who graduated as bannerets, but a man who knows land and titles await him tends to be less diligent than one who knows that the lessons he's learning might save his life one day. One way or the other, he'd find out soon enough.

A crossbow bolt shot out from the pickets, followed by a shout to hold fire. Gill couldn't see where the shot had landed, but knew the enemy were still too far away for it to have hit one of them. Nerves were building; he hoped Savin's officers were up to the task of keeping their men under control until the action started.

"Sire, it might be best for us to return to the belfry to observe. You'll be able to command far more effectively if you can see everything that's going on."

"I want the men to be able to see me," the king said.

It was a noble intention, but not one that served them best. "There'll be a time for that," Gill said. "Until the enemy are fully engaged, or as much as makes no difference, it's best if you can see what they're up to."

Boudain nodded slowly, as though he was unconvinced, and thought it was cowardly to retreat to the comparative safety of the belfry. After a moment, Gill cleared his throat, and finally the king moved off. Gill followed.

Savin and a collection of runners also crowded into the small room at the top of the belfry, spilling onto the steps that led to the ground. When Guillot looked out, he saw that the enemy army had halted again. Skirmishers advanced from their line; an archer stepped forward and fired a ranging shot. As soon as it landed—mere paces from the pickets—a hundred or so of his colleagues rushed forward and fired the first salvo.

Gill wanted to shout at the men below to take cover, but they could all see what was happening, and it was their officers' responsibility anyway. He heard the orders and saw the men react. Thankfully, most of the arrows thudded into the picket or overshot and hit nothing but dirt. There were only one or two cries of pain, but Guillot knew there would be far more before the day was out.

The attack had come on the part of the picket wall that Gill had designated as "Sector B." It faced the approaching enemy, so it seemed the most likely point of attack. If the king's cousins focussed their attack here, then Gill could pull men away from other sections, keeping his reserve intact, ready to react to any change in circumstances.

"Do we just wait for them to dictate how it all unfolds?" the king said.

"Pretty much. That's the curse of defending a position. We'll start making life difficult for them soon enough. The captains on the picket will have their bowmen start to fire as soon as it'll be effective. They'll shoot down any of the skirmishers that get too close, but for now, we don't want your cousins to know how many bows we have."

"I'm not going to lie, Villerauvais," the king said. "I'm going out of my mind. How can you stand still and watch this?"

Gill shrugged. "Best to enjoy it as long as you can, Sire."

The king returned his gaze to the skirmishers, who were withdrawing once again, having completed their probing of the pickets while leaving only a handful of bodies lying on the grass. The captains had done as instructed, and their true number of bowmen would remain a surprise until the main force approached.

As soon as the skirmishers got back to their lines, the enemy archers began a consistent barrage. A moment later, the army moved forward. Gill had wondered if they would split their forces and attack two parts of the picket, but it didn't look like that was their plan. Gill wondered if the cousins were unwilling to share command.

He cast a glance at Savin, wondering if the loyal cousin was regretting having remained on this side of the picket. It was a big gamble for him. If they successfully fended off the attackers, Savin's fidelity would bring him riches and titles that would make him one of the most powerful magnates in the land. If not? He had passed up the opportunity to be king. When he spotted Gill staring at him, he raised an eyebrow, quizzically. Gill gave him a wry smile before returning his attention to the advancing army. No matter how the day went, Savin would probably feel like a loser. It made Gill glad he wasn't still trying to climb the slippery pole of court politics and position.

Volley after volley of arrows fell, peppering the ground, the picket, and any unfortunate whose effort to take shelter wasn't good enough. Under this cover, the enemy force advanced. Gill knew it was a sound tactic, so long as their commander remembered to cease fire before his troops marched into the kill zone. As soon as the rain of enemy arrows stopped falling, their own bowmen would be free to unleash a barrage of their own.

The air was filled with the sound of marching, the whistling of arrows, the thud of impacts, and occasional screams. Then the arrows stopped. It took the defenders a moment to react to the change, first with hesitant looks over the top by the officers, then with commands to return fire. Gill felt oddly disconnected from it all, up in the belfry. He couldn't claim that he would rather have been down with the troops manning the pickets, but all the same, he didn't like being stuck in the bell tower, observing. It was the best place to command from, and it seemed that was the role the king most needed him to fulfill.

The approaching line opened up in several spots along its length, to allow small groups of men carrying wooden ladders to approach the fortifications. The invading army let out a roar and surged after them. Gill felt his heart quicken. The foreplay was over and the main event had begun. He held his breath as the cousins' army reached the picket—a bodged-together mix of quickly constructed palisades, overturned carts, and furniture; suddenly it looked far less imposing than it had only moments before. The first charge was a critical moment. It could all end in that one blink of the eye—this was when the attackers were at their most motivated, and the defenders most likely to decide running for the back wall was their best chance of surviving.

The men on the pickets fired volley after volley at the approaching force, but the enemy showed no sign of faltering. Whenever a ladder-carrier fell, another man took his place. When they reached the palisade, there was a collection of clatters and bangs as the ladders hit the barrier, followed by war cries. The first wave raced up, but most were shot down by the crossbowmen on the makeshift ramparts. The few that reached the top were cut down and toppled back to the side from which they'd come.

The attackers didn't look like soldiers. They had proper weapons and wore patchworks of leather armour, but everything about them said they were a peasant levy. Gill wondered if they were a probing attack. It was what Gill would have expected from an experienced commander—some halfhearted attacks with expendable troops, to work out where the defences were strongest. However, the main body of the army was closer to the pickets than Gill would have expected if that tactic was in use. Instead, it looked like they were throwing their full force against this spot, in the expectation of a quick win thanks to their greater numbers.

He chewed his lip in agitation as he watched. Was it ever thus for commanders? Gill had never spent a battle behind the lines before. He'd always commanded infantrymen, starting with a small squad when he was a young ensign and working his way up to a regiment when he was a well-known captain. That had always put him in the thick of the action, focussed on his small slice of the battle, rather than the entirety. As much experience as he had, just like the king, this was all new to him.

The men kept coming, their weight on the ladders preventing the defenders from throwing them off. They were all shot or cut down, falling to the ground within reach of their goal. Gill could see the growing sense of confidence in the men behind the pickets. They were holding off the initial wave with light losses, and were starting to believe that they would be able to do so until the enemy had enough. Then the first man made it over the wall.

CHAPTER
26

The first man was cut down quickly in an act of overkill common among frightened and inexperienced troops—his body was hacked to fragments. His comrades only saw him going over the palisade and making it into the enemy compound—the goal for which they were all fighting. It was inspiring, emboldening. If they could have seen what happened to him on the other side, they might have thought twice. As it was, they had seen him go over, which meant they now believed it could be done. They came at the picket with renewed enthusiasm. When a second man cleared the barrier, Gill's stomach twisted.

"We need to move the reserves to contain this," Gill said. "We can take troops from the northern sections and build a second reserve unit if we need it."

The king nodded. "Do it," he said. One of his newly appointed adjutants scribbled the order on a notepad, tore off the page, and passed it to one of the runners, who set off as fast as he could.

There were a half dozen of the attackers on the picket now, with more men coming up behind them. The fighting spilled out into the compound as the defenders did their best to contain the breaches, but once the enemy started coming over the pickets and gaining a foothold, the king's forces were in trouble. It wouldn't take long for the reserves to reach the fighting, but this was the turning point. With the pickets breached, the defenders would either consider their last line of safety lost—and therefore, the fight lost—or they would double down to push their foes back. That they had not yet broken was a good sign.

Gill hoped the fact that they knew the king was with them might embolden them some.

He felt as though his hands were tied, his role in this battle as unfamiliar as if it were his first. There had been times in the past when it had seemed as though he had become detached from his body and was watching things unfold from a distance, even though he was right in the middle of it all. This time, that was no mere feeling, it was exactly how things were. He was no general, and felt like a fraud pretending to be one.

"Permission to lead the reserves, Highness," Gill said.

"I . . ." Boudain hesitated.

It was an unfair thing for Gill to do. If the king admitted to needing Guillot at his side, it would show weakness in front of the others. Yet because of his past experience, Gill would be at his most effective leading the counterattack, and far more useful in that role than he was in the belfry.

"Very well," the king said. "Return to me as soon as you've pushed them back beyond the pickets."

Gill nodded, then shoved past the messengers and the Count of Savin's retinue to get down the stairs. The fresh air outside was as welcome as the prospect of moving onto familiar territory, even if it meant placing himself in danger. He found the reserves on the village square, preparing to move off to support the south wall. A young captain was trying to order them into a cohesive unit, but was struggling to impose his idea of military formation on a bunch of farmers who clearly had no idea what he was talking about half the time.

"I'll take over here," Gill said.

The captain shot him a look of relief. Guillot assumed that it was his first battle too, and that he was glad to be unburdened of the responsibility of saving the defence.

"What's your name?" Gill asked.

"Jean-Paul," the younger man said.

"Stay to the rear and urge the men on."

He nodded and Gill turned his attention to the levy. He held out his sword to create a boundary. "Line up here and ready your weapons."

The men jumped into action at the sound of a confident command.

As soon as they were in some semblance of order, Gill ordered them to advance. He set the pace and, as he moved off, checked over his shoulder to make sure they were keeping up with him. He could hear Jean-Paul barking at them to move faster, which was having the desired effect.

The battle was hidden until they were clear of the village. The situation had worsened since Gill had come down from the belfry, with far more enemy troops within the pickets. They'd formed a pocket on the inside of the palisade, allowing more men to safely crest the top and get into the fight. Gill surveyed the field quickly. This situation required no tactical finesse. The task was simple—push the enemy back over the palisade.

"When I tell you," Gill shouted, "I want you to roar for all you're worth. Make them think you're the angriest bunch of bastards this side of the Loiron."

He led the men on at a brisk trot, keeping them moving too fast to consider the reality of what they were doing. Better that they were stuck in it before they had time to think too much.

"Shout!" Gill ordered. "Loud as you can!"

His men gave it their best as he ran them straight to where the defenders looked the thinnest. Battles like this were not so much about skill at arms as weight of bodies. There was enough space to stab with daggers and short swords, but anything larger was all but useless in such close quarters. If they wanted to get their enemy back on the other side of the pickets, they needed to kill enough people to make the survivors flee, or to physically push them back until they had no option but to retreat over the wall.

"Push forward, lads!" he shouted. The men groaned and strained and roared, and pushed as hard as they could, but the enemy kept coming, adding bodies to their mass, and Gill found himself taking small steps in the wrong direction.

"Push, you bastards!" he shouted. He grabbed a spear from the ground; holding it horizontally, he pressed forward on the men before him, trying to drive them on. The front row were already too closely entwined to use their weapons, and the fight had degenerated into a grappling contest, with the men thrown to the ground killed by those in the rearward ranks who still had space to use their weapons.

The melee was a confusing scrum of bodies. There were too many men coming over the wall, and the pocket they were occupying was growing, allowing them to be bring more men to the fight. There was no denying what was happening, and the longer they fought on such a wide front, the more the advantage would swing against them. Gill looked back at the village: the cluster of buildings around the square provided a number of choke points, where they'd be better able to defend against greater numbers.

He'd considered this in preparing their defence, but part of him had hoped that they might be able to hold the enemy at the walls. He'd wanted to instill the idea in his fighters that the pickets would be enough to help them hold off the enemy, and keep them safe. Confidence in that thought would help them achieve it, but even a fool could see that was no longer believable.

"Fall back!" Gill shouted.

The men didn't need to be asked twice. They peeled away, turned, and ran back for the village with such haste that he was worried they wouldn't stop. He charged back himself, hoping to get there before them so he could rally them at a choke point.

A few of the fleeter-of-foot got back to the village before Gill, and as he'd suspected, they didn't stop to take up new positions. All he could do was hope that those coming behind him did—or at least, didn't try to kill him if he stood in their way. He spotted a small reserve waiting in the square; they appeared unnerved by the withdrawing troops, who looked far more like they were routing than merely retreating.

"Let no one else by," Gill shouted. "Add any men that reach you to your force. We'll plug all the streets. We'll hold them here until they break." He threw in the last part in the hope of undoing some of the damage of the fleeing troops. He had some reputation, both as a dragonslayer and as a soldier who had been considered a national hero once upon a time, although many of the men were too young to have much memory of that. Nonetheless, they weren't going to believe they could win if he didn't pretend he did, so pretend he would.

He turned and held his arms out to stop the retreating troops and soon gathered enough to block the street, then started issuing commands to put them into a semblance of order. Some had dropped their weapons, but most still clung to a spear, axe, or sword. Gill did his best to ignore the approaching enemy as he tried to put the men with spears and shields in the front, while those with cutting weapons stayed in the rear rows, poised to chop at anything that came within reach.

One thing caught his eye, however—a banner he recognised. The one the Count of Aubin had been flying when they had met for their parley. The sight of it set Gill's mind racing. There were any number of reasons that Aubin might choose to come in for a closer look, but one stuck out in Gill's mind. As long as the king lived, he remained a threat, possessed by witchcraft or not.

Aubin was going to want to make sure Boudain was captured or killed. It was something he needed to see with his own eyes.

Gill had planned on saving the king's banner for a special moment, that point where a little morale boost could make the difference between victory and defeat, but now, he realised, he could use it like a flame to draw a moth. He grabbed a spear from the soldier next to him, pulled the banner out of his tunic, tied it on, and raised it as high as he could. The two blue dragons rampant on a white field fluttered proudly on the gentle breeze, announcing to everyone who recognised the king's sigil that he was in the thick of battle. The deception was hardly honourable, but neither was sedition, and when it came to war, winning was all that mattered.

There was a chance he was inviting an arrow in his direction, but everyone would know that the standard-bearer was not the king and that shooting him down was an empty act, for such a man was easily replaced. Better to leave the banner flying, so they would know where the true prize was.

He didn't have much of a vantage point where he was standing, but he was taller than most, so could see over their heads. A group of well-armoured men was clustered around Aubin's banner, exactly as Gill had suspected. He would have liked a little more time to consider a plan to draw Aubin in. Killing a commander could swing the balance of a battle faster than anything else.

The surest way to lure him was to make it look like the king's party was in trouble. The only problem there was that unlike the group around Aubin's banner, those around Boudain's looked distinctly less convincing. He spotted the young officer from earlier, and gave up trying to remember his name after only a moment's effort.

"You!" Gill had to shout three times before the young man realised he was the one being called. "Get up to the belfry and send the Count of Savin's retinue down here to join me. Then get all the troops from the northern section and form them into a reserve on the square before the church. Understand?"

The captain nodded, but didn't look like he appreciated the seriousness of Gill's order. With so much going on, and the fact that he'd just experienced his first combat, that was forgivable. "Get them down here fast," Gill added, nearly snarling. "Or I'll have their guts out myself."

Now the fellow set off at a run, disappearing into the church a moment later. Gill turned back to the enemy. Aubin had slowed his attack, and was taking time to get his troops back under control. He was shrewd enough. Many inexperienced commanders would let their troops run amok once they'd had their first hint of victory.

It didn't take long for a group of noblemen to emerge from the belfry, their quality armour a marked contrast to what everyone else, Gill included, was wearing. They were moving quickly, but there was no mistaking their reluctance. They'd had a prime view of the battle as it had unfolded, and had no doubt watched plenty of men die. Now it was their turn to roll the dice.

"To me!" Gill shouted.

They responded, and as soon as they'd gathered, Gill raised the royal standard as high as he could.

"Look important," Gill said to one of the new arrivals who had a neat black beard that would pass for the king's at a distance. Gill could see that the noble was a long way from understanding what Gill was up to, but time was too tight to get everyone caught up.

"Gather around the banner, lads," he said. "You're the king's retinue. Act like it."

They looked at him with puzzled expressions, but did as they were told. *Now, how to get to Aubin,* he thought. An idea occurred to him, accompanied by the pang of regret that he hadn't come up with this plan earlier. Still, there was something to be said for an ability to react to circumstances as they unfolded. Plus, he could always claim it had been part of his plan all along, assuming it worked out. He turned to a group of levy men gathered in the square.

"Any of you lot done any hunting? Any poaching?" he said.

There was no response.

"Come on. I'm not the bloody sheriff. I need some men who're handy with a bow. Show me some hands!"

One or two rose hesitantly, followed by a half dozen more.

"Good," Gill said. "Find yourself some bows and ammunition if you don't have any already, then get up on these roofs." He pointed to the ones that would give the best vantage point over the approaching enemy. "When you get up there, I want you to look for the Count of Aubin's banner. It's the green one with the red prancing horses. When I give the signal, I want every man within ten paces of it filled with arrows. Understand?"

There was a general murmur of assent.

"Right, off you go, and be quick about it now. Stay out of sight until I call on you!"

Some went straight for the buildings, while others headed toward the stores.

With a roar, the attackers came forward, having re-formed into some semblance of order. Gill felt his heart leap into his throat, a sensation he was far more familiar with than seemed to make sense. It was so normal to him, he barely gave it a second thought. The forces met once more, and the chaos of battle resumed at the entrance to the village square.

"Rally to the king! Rally to the king!" Gill shouted. The men roared as though the king were actually with them. Considering how few of them would have seen the king close up, Gill realised that some of them probably thought he was. He couldn't tell if Aubin's party had reacted to his call, but it occurred to him that Aubin might be doing exactly the same thing as Gill was, in the hope of drawing the king out. The count himself might be safely tucked away behind his own lines. Still, there weren't many options left, and this one seemed like their best hope.

The enemy advanced behind an anonymous row of shields. The men behind the front row held their shields above their heads, creating an effective barrier against the arrows that occasionally skittered across the surface. There weren't many; Guillot's recent postings seemed to be holding to his orders and restraining themselves—often a difficult thing in the heat of battle when a good shot presents itself.

He could make out the Count of Aubin's banner following the troops—perhaps his plan was working? He had no idea how good his archers were, though, so he had to wait until the last possible moment to spring his trap.

"Give ground!" Gill shouted. It was risky. A pace or two backwards could quickly turn into a rout with inexperienced troops. "Slowly now," he yelled as they started to pull back toward him, hoping his voice could be heard by those who counted. "Hold there!"

The retreat stopped and the din from the front increased as the defenders started to fight for every inch. Gill looked at the rooftops, where his archers were concealed. It occurred to him that they might have taken the chance to run, but he was in the middle of it now, and had to act as though they were doing what they were told.

The count's banner was close enough, so with one final look at the belfry—where, hopefully, Boudain was watching—Gill gave the command. If this didn't work, he was out of options.

True to their word, a half dozen dark shapes appeared at the tops of the buildings and began firing for all they were worth. There were some shouts, and arrows thudded against shields, but the count's banner remained flying. The element of surprise didn't last long, and Aubin's men reacted quickly—Gill didn't hear a single scream of pain.

Enemy archers started to return fire, and a man on a roof to the right let out a gurgling cry, then tumbled down on top of the shield platform. He lay there, grotesquely twisted, for a moment, before the shields opened up and swallowed him. When Gill glanced up, the rest had disappeared from sight. He couldn't blame them. Their surprise attack had had no effect and they'd just seen one of their own killed.

His defensive line gave some ground, then held again. He knew that wasn't likely to remain the case for long. The reserve was still in the square behind him, but once they were out of the choke point of the streets, numbers would be against them again, and it would only be a matter of time before they were all cut to pieces. The futility of waiting tore at Gill. He shoved the king's banner into the hands of the man next to him.

Almost before he registered the thought, he was scrambling up and over his men, then across the platform of shields intended to stop arrows from above, not provide a walkway for a lunatic embarking on an ill-formed, last-ditch plan to snatch something from the jaws of certain defeat.

Before he knew it, he was back on the ground and face-to-face with the Count of Aubin's party. Three men-at-arms surrounded a core group—a couple of nobles and a man Gill recognised as Aubin.

Gill launched himself forward, trading on what little surprise he carried with him. The men-at-arms were slow to react. He lashed out with two savage cuts, one flowing into the other. There was little art to them, but it did not matter—the first two men-at-arms were dead by the time the third had brought his shield up. Even Gill was impressed by the speed with which he was moving. It seemed that some of his former ability was returning.

Kicking hard at the shield, Guillot sent the man-at-arms sprawling back, then cut at one of the noblemen, who appeared not to have realised he might have to actually fight that day. Gill took no satisfaction in killing a man like that, but it was war, and if one of them was going to die, Gill always did his best to make sure it was the other fellow. The man was dead before he had his sword out of its sheath.

Three men dead in the blink of an eye.

The remaining nobleman didn't seem to be in any hurry to step between Gill and his lord. He had his sword en garde and seemed to be hesitating, resolve teetering on the balance point of duty and self-preservation. His inexperience was telling: Any man who had tasted war knew that hesitation was a surer killer than making the wrong decision. So it was for this man.

Gill ran him through the chest and watched the count's banner flutter to the ground. Then he turned his attention to the blanched Count of Aubin. Moments before, the count had been witnessing his victory unfold, observing his moment of triumph over the king. Now he was faced with death.

It was Gill's turn to hesitate now. With Aubin's troops firmly committed to the attack, he and the count existed in their own little bubble, in which Gill was the arbiter of life or death. Here was a man who was Gill's social superior—a lord of the realm, the king's cousin, a man in whom royal blood flowed. Gill had never spilled royal blood before. Not that he knew of, at any rate. Should he present the opportunity to surrender? The king had already made that entreaty.

Aubin was a traitor, and they both knew there was only one way for that to end. *Better to finish it now,* Gill thought. The death of their commander would have the same effect as surrender once news of it spread. What point was there in fighting and possibly dying for a man not able to enjoy the spoils—or to share them?

The count drew his sword, which settled the matter. Gill preferred it this way. Like most noblemen, Aubin had been trained in the sword, but like many of them, he appeared to have little experience of using it. He made two uncommitted thrusts and backed away a little. Gill could tell right away that Aubin was trying to buy himself time, hoping for rescue. Gill had no intention of allowing this opportunity to pass by.

He lunged forward with a feint to Aubin's midsection, which the count brought his blade down to parry. Gill slipped his blade to the side and flicked it back, piercing Aubin's throat. The older man fixed Gill with wide eyes as he spluttered and fought to draw breath. Gill pulled his blade free and finished him with a neat thrust to the chest.

Aubin collapsed to the ground next to his banner. Gill took a moment to catch his breath, surveying his grim handiwork. It seemed that there was never any end to killing. He drew in a gulp of air and let out a bellow.

"The count is dead! Retreat! The count is dead."

He didn't expect the army to believe his claim and break immediately, but one or two would glance at where they expected to see the count's banner. Enough would see it soaking up the count's blood to spread the word, and the rout would begin. Gill wondered how the remaining cousin, Chabris, would react. Would he fight, or seek terms to save his skin—put the blame for their treason on Aubin, and try to wriggle his way out of it?

Gill looked back at the steeple and saluted with his sword. The enemy soldiers started to break and run. It wasn't the most conventional way to command a battle, but it had worked.

CHAPTER
27

Pharadon could smell that all was not right at the temple long before he could see it. There were too many unfamiliar scents, and more alarmingly, one that was familiar: that of the woman they had chased back to the city. Why had she come back? They had already stripped the place of its last treasure. Or had they?

He hadn't been looking for it up until that moment, but now that he did, he noticed the absence. Of the goldscale he could detect no trace. He leaned into the wind and swooped down to the opening that led to the temple, allowing his momentum to carry him down the ramp into the main chamber. His first glimpse confirmed his fear. The goldscale was gone.

The red dragon stared at the empty spot for a time. Both dragon and coin were gone. He feared that whoever had taken the coin was not using it for the intended purpose. Without the coin, the magic he had shaped around her would fade and break. She would grow weaker and weaker, until she came out of her slumber; shortly after that, she would die. He opened his mind to the Fount. Strong though it was in the temple, he was enlightened, and his mastery of it was absolute, so its power held no threat. He could see the faint trace of the path the goldscale had taken up the ramp and out of the chamber.

From there she had ascended vertically, and Pharadon could only guess that the woman whose scent filled his nostrils was responsible for having the goldscale hauled out, and away. He clambered out of the antechamber, his claws tearing away more soil and rotted boards from the edges of the opening as he pulled his bulk back to the surface. The trail led straight back toward the city.

Pharadon frowned. He'd hoped never to have to return to that place. Aside from anything, it stank. That didn't even take into account the danger he was risking, going there in human form, with most of his powers unavailable. Although the thought occurred to him, he couldn't bear to consider the possibility that the goldscale might have been killed. He could tell by the scent that she had still lived when they took her from this place. That was hope enough.

Alive or not, though, it wouldn't make any difference. The coin anchored her to the Fount, and ensured she drew the sustenance she needed in her slumber. Without that magical bond, she would die. He wondered what the humans had in mind for her. As he stared in the direction of the distant city, he was reminded of the fear of being the last of his kind.

It was something he found difficult to comprehend. Dragonkind were so long-lived. They had never been as numerous as humans, but with lives measured in centuries rather than decades, their population had been a healthy one. To think he might now be the last—a thought he had been able to avoid since waking due to the presence of the three young dragons. He couldn't sense the goldscale now, only the fading trace of the scent she had left as she passed.

There was no choice but to go to the city. What could he hope to achieve, though? In human form, he was feeble. While he was in his natural dragon form, every weapon in the city would be turned against him, and powerful as he was, that was too much for him to hope to defeat. Another way was needed. It occurred to him that if war was on its way, that might make it easier to free the goldscale— confusion and battle would obscure his actions.

That the people bringing the war to the city owed him a favour made the plan all the more appealing. Efforts could be coordinated to maximise his chances for success. However, that did not change the main reason he had left the humans as quickly as he could. Pharadon had no desire to be used as a weapon of war.

The image of a fire-breathing dragon flying over a city, incinerating all below, was the last thing he wanted humans to have burned into their memories. If there were a thousand dragons in the world, it would have been less of a concern, but given his assumption that there were only two, he did not wish to increase the human desire to hunt and eradicate anything they saw as a threat.

If he was to rescue the goldscale, it had to be as a human. That meant he would need as much help as he could get. Getting it without having to fight in their war might prove a far more difficult proposition. First, he had to make sure the goldscale didn't die before the rescue could be effected; where, he wondered, might he most easily find another gold coin?

▲▲▲▲▲▲

No one really knew how to contain a dragon, least of all Ysabeau. Yet that was the task her father had set her. She'd managed a couple of hours' sleep before there was a bang on her door and a new set of orders in her hand. No rest for the wicked, she supposed.

They had placed the dragon in the centre of the floor of one of the city's many open-air fencing arenas, then drafted every smith and craftsman in the city to build a cage around it. The one saving grace was that the beast remained in a deep slumber, no different from an oversize babe in a crib. Other than the fact that at any moment this babe might wake and slaughter her and all the workmen. It had been difficult to convince them to go anywhere near it at first, but with promises of money, and threats of flogging, she got them to work.

There was a great deal of prefabricated material in the city already, so it didn't take long for the preliminary skeleton of a domed cage to be welded together. Workmen were toiling hard to add bands of metal to the bare framework, to ultimately create something that would prevent the dragon from getting out and any overly inquisitive fool from getting in.

Ysabeau surveyed the ironworks with satisfaction. Her father intended this creature to be the great showpiece of his achievements. Her involvement in capturing the beast would go unannounced, but she had no difficulty with that, so long as the rewards still came. The old wooden benches built into the arena's stone tiers were being removed, to later be replaced with a gallery that would afford a clear view of the dragon. For now, though, the priority was getting the cage completed.

Judging by the crowds who had gathered outside, asking for a glimpse or wanting to know when the spectacle would be open to the public, it seemed her father was using the creature the right way. Whether it would prove enough of a distraction for them from all the other things that were going on was another question.

She could not dispel a lurking fear that led to images of a rampaging dragon slaughtering, burning, and eating Mirabay's citizens. Ysabeau looked over the strips of riveted and welded iron that in theory provided solid containment while allowing the citizens an unobstructed view. In purely physical terms, she was happy to take the word of the engineers who had designed it in record time, and the smiths who were busily welding and riveting the structure together, but there was more to it than that.

A dragon was not simply a strong beast. They were creatures of magic, and when that was added to the mix, there could be no certainties. She'd seen more than enough to know that magic could turn the most solid understanding of the world on its head. This was a creature of the old magic, not the diluted form she and the Spurriers played with. Her father might be capable of near-limitless feats now that he had drunk from the Cup she had brought back from the temple, but for the first time in that which she'd known him, he was displaying remarkable restraint in testing his gifts. Was old age teaching him patience, she wondered, or fear?

She supposed she would be the same. Such power could be daunting for anyone, particularly when you knew the power was as dangerous to you as it was to others. One way or the other, Ysabeau was glad he was demonstrating prudence. If the etchings were true, he had power equivalent to that of Amatus, the First Mage, who had helped found the Empire. Given time, her father could achieve truly great things. Too much haste, and he could prove correct every fear people had about the use of magic.

Would fate grant him the time and patience for the former? Her gut twisted with nausea when she thought of it, but then again, she had ever been a pessimist. She forced her attention back to the cage. The responsibility her father had placed on her carried with it the safety of every soul in the city. If the dragon woke and got out, it was unlikely to be happy with its captors.

The smiths had sworn blind that they'd forged the strongest steel that could be had, that a herd of stampeding Jaharan elephants couldn't break through. She'd seen a Jaharan elephant in the city's menagerie when she was a child. It was a fantastic beast, but it paled into insignificance next to a dragon. And it couldn't work magic.

Ysabeau reached out and touched a bar of the cage with her index finger. She pressed against it, and true to their claims, it didn't yield any flex. She opened her mind to the Fount and channelled energy into her desire to bend the metal. The rivets and welds surrounding her chosen spot groaned and the metal flexed. Releasing her hold on the Fount, she took her hand away.

The surrounding section of the cage had warped in, as though it had been struck a great blow. If she could bend it, with her limited magical ability, the dragon would shatter it as though it were made of glass. They needed to do more to safeguard the populace. There was no question that Ysabeau had killed many times, but everyone who met their end at her hand had deserved it in some fashion. The deaths of countless innocent men, women, and children was not something she wanted on her conscience.

Fear tickled her flesh with its icy-cold fingers as she considered the problem. How could they hold it within these confines when it woke? She paced along the stone steps, squeezing her chin between thumb and forefinger in agitation. She couldn't cast a spell to add a magical barrier to the physical one. She neither knew how nor had the power. Her father had the power, but he didn't know how either.

Shielding spells were within her ambit, but they were subtly different, and when it came to magic, a subtle difference was more than enough to make something utterly useless. Here they wanted to keep something in rather than out. It would also need to be permanent, and not connected to the caster. The rational part of her mind said that might not even be possible, but she knew that when it came to magic, the only limiting factors were the power they could draw on, mental discipline, and the caster's imagination.

The more complicated the magic, the more defined the thought processes required to achieve it. It would take them months, if not years, to work out how to create magic the like of which was needed here. That couldn't be the solution—they didn't have the time.

If only they had a limitless supply of Telastrian steel . . . For reasons that remained a complete mystery to Ysabeau, the famed metal had a strange relationship with magic, and in her experience could not be affected by it. It was an idle thought, however. They could melt down every Telastrian blade in the kingdom, and still not have enough to make a cage even a quarter the size of the one they had now.

She added chewing her lip to her list of agitated ticks as she began her second circuit of the cage. A thought occurred to her. Perhaps they didn't need the cage to be *entirely* made of Telastrian steel. . . .

She smiled and stopped squeezing her chin. It would mean confiscating a few swords, which wouldn't be popular, but being popular was certainly not a claim her father could make.

Food supply to the city has been interrupted, your Grace."

Amaury regarded his new chancellor with tired eyes. Grand Burgess Girard Voclain was a competent businessman who had crawled his way out of the slums around the docks on ambition and ability, so Amaury knew the problem was not his fault. It was the king's whoreson cousins, carousing around the countryside at the head of their little armies, stealing whatever caught their eyes.

"How much is getting to the city?" Amaury said.

"Less than ten percent of normal."

Troubles were mounting faster than the Prince Bishop could deal with them. It was as if everyone were trying to sabotage him. Probably they were. He needed time to show them all the good he could do, that he was the right man to lead them, but he was beginning to fear he would never get that opportunity.

"How much supply do we have in the granaries?"

"Two weeks. Perhaps twice that with rationing, but that won't make the citizens happy."

"The citizens are only happy when they've got something to be unhappy about," Amaury said bitterly.

Voclain gave him a crooked look, to which Amaury replied with an apologetic nod. They both knew where ignoring the citizenry's mood could lead, and acting recklessly would lose Amaury the support of the men he relied on the most. No one wanted to meet their end swinging from a gibbet or resting on the headsman's block.

"Keep the rations at the usual level," Amaury said. "We can review again in a few days if supplies haven't returned to normal. What's next?"

The new commander of the Royal Army stood up. There were so many new faces around that it took Amaury a moment to remember his name. Duchain. General Didier Duchain. The commander of his old Guard. Amaury tried to recall why he hadn't migrated over to the Spurriers, but could not.

"The uptake on the mercenary contracts we put out has been less than expected," Duchain said.

Amaury let out a strained breath. "How much less than expected?" He'd hoped they'd all be taken up.

Duchain swallowed hard. "Three-quarters, give or take, but I'm hopeful that more will sign up in the coming days. I'm in correspondence with one captain who seems to think he can put together a force of nearly ten thousand men. If that's the case, our needs will be met easily. It seems all the talk of dragons and magic has put off the bigger companies. Lots of less risky work to be had; for instance, the Auracians are at each other again, according to the latest."

"Auracians," Amaury said. He stood from behind his desk, his instinct being to walk to his window, as he so often did when considering new troubles. However, he had relocated to the king's offices and no longer had that luxury. He hesitated a moment, and then, feeling slightly foolish, sat back down. *This is not how it was supposed to be,* he thought.

"What's the status of the Royal Army?"

Duchain grimaced. Would he ever be the bearer of good news? Amaury wondered.

"The Royal Army was not in a good state of readiness, what with it being several years since the last war. Desertions stand at a little over fifty percent."

"So what you're telling me is, that if I had to fight a battle in the morning, which right now looks like it could very well happen, I'd lose."

Duchain nodded with a solemn expression, then took a deep breath before speaking. "I don't think you would be able to field a battle-effective force, your Grace."

Amaury smiled thinly. It was all he could do to stop himself swearing to the heavens. The way sentiment in the city was heading, he needed what troops he had to maintain order. To take them out of the city to fight a battle might mean facing a city in revolt when he returned.

There remained the bigger problem of the king. Even if Solène couldn't undo whatever it was he had done to the king's mind, so long as Boudain lived, he remained a rallying point for the opposition. Not to mention, it emphasised the tenuous legality of Amaury's regency.

That was something he needed to address, and soon. By taking up arms, the king's cousins had made themselves useless to the Prince Bishop. The more distant relatives didn't have a strong enough claim to the throne for Amaury to place any of them upon that seat. As much as he had given up on the idea of wielding power from behind someone else, the fact that the option was no longer available was oddly comforting—it was one less difficult decision to make. Or to get wrong.

With the king—incapable or not—in someone else's hands, Amaury needed to firm up his rule. Regent wasn't enough anymore. Whoever had Boudain could easily cook up a forged document and claim that it superseded the one putting Amaury in control.

"Before we close business for the morning, gentlemen," Amaury said, "there's one more matter I wish to raise. With the king kidnapped, the regency, not to mention the kingdom itself, has been placed in a position of great jeopardy."

He scanned the faces of the men before him for any reaction. He didn't know if he was fooling anyone or whether he was fooling only himself. They showed no signs of disbelief, so he continued.

"In order to ensure the good management of Mirabaya and the safety of her subjects, stronger measures will be needed until the king has been recovered. With this in mind, I intend to propose the following interim measure."

He slid a piece of paper toward the seated officials. They looked at one another until Duchain took the initiative and picked up the document.

"Appointment as Lord Protector of the Realm?" Duchain said.

"Precisely," Amaury said. "A temporary measure to ensure consistent governance and keep the throne secure for the king and his ultimate successor."

Amaury leaned back in his chair and gave them a moment to digest the idea. These were his men. If they didn't go for it, no one would. He knew it was too soon to declare himself permanent ruler. He needed to weather the current storm, and then, in a year or two, with fewer threats on his doorstep, he could push through whatever was needed to make him prince of the realm, as well as prince of the church.

"It seems to make sense, your Grace," Duchain said. "Any old bandit could forge the king's signature now."

"Precisely," Amaury said. "The document also outlines the mechanism by which the protectorate reverts to a regency, and from there to a kingdom, but that's all simple enough." He paused to gather his thoughts. "There may be some pushback on this, from any number of quarters, but it's important that we make clear how vital this measure is for the kingdom's prosperity."

▲▲▲▲▲▲

Pharadon wasn't sure what to make of the scene before him. He stood, uncomfortable and weakened in human form, staring at a sign proudly announcing that in a matter of days, the Regent of Mirabaya would proudly unveil the greatest trophy of war the nation had ever known. A captive dragon, alive, but cowed by the greatness of Mirabaya's power and by the prowess of the Order of the Golden Spur. People wandered past, some stopping to read the sign. One or two passed comment, but Pharadon ignored them. He was in no mood for conversation.

Although he could go no farther than the external wall of the incipient menagerie, he didn't need to see the goldscale with his own eyes to know she was there, to know that she was suffering. As he allowed his senses to drift beyond his body, he felt her heartbeat as if it were his own, but slow and strained, as though each great thump threatened to demand too much from her frail body. She didn't even seem to be aware of his presence. Her state pained him—emotion raged within, not something to which he was accustomed.

He was filled with the overwhelming desire to return to dragon form and tear the goldscale from her cage. He knew that was folly. There were many humans in the city, many soldiers. He needed time

to recover from this transformation before he could attempt another.
Freeing her and lifting her away would take far longer, and attract
much more attention, than rescuing an enfeebled king on a misty day.
He would be shot from the sky and cut to pieces. As tempting as it
was to try, Pharadon knew it was a reckless act doomed to fail. Not
only would the goldscale descend into barbarity, she would die before
she'd ever had the chance to live.

Right now, he couldn't even get close enough to place a gold coin
beneath her body and thereby prolong her life. Still, there was no way
he would sit back and do nothing. He turned and headed toward the
city gate, eagerly awaiting the moment when his powers had been restored enough to allow him to return to his natural form.

As he walked, he considered his options. A daring rescue attempt
was clearly out. If he had a Cup, he could enlighten her, which might
be as much cruelty as a kindness—the greater awareness enlightenment brought would enhance her suffering, but it would allow her to
sustain herself more from the Fount, and buy him more time to work
out a way to free her.

In the time it took for Pharadon to walk several miles away from
the city and wander off the road in preparation for his transformation, he did not manage to come up with any good options. What
were the chances of there being more Cups? He remembered there
being others, and was still confused by finding only one at the temple
when he had expected far more. During the wars, he could remember
a faction of dragonkind wanting to use the Cups as weapons, while
the majority refused to allow such barbarity. Perhaps they had been
used; perhaps they had been hidden to prevent that from happening.
It was impossible to know—Pharadon had gone into self-imposed ex-
ile before the war had ended.

Might Cyaxares, the high priest at the temple, have hidden some
of the Cups, to keep them away from mankind? He realised he might
as well spend his time searching as sit around wondering if any remained. There were some obvious places to search, but the plan felt
tenuous at best. As his body morphed back into that of a dragon, he
comforted himself with the thought that perhaps as he flew, he might
come up with something better.

A flight through the cool night air usually settled him and allowed his mind to focus. This night, that relief did not come. As countryside became hills became mountains, his heart felt heavy. He might be chasing a hope that was impossible; there might be nothing he could do for the goldscale. The thought made him want to cry out in despair—the idea that he was the last of his kind was too terrible to bear. More so when there was another still alive. No matter what happened, he had to spend what little time was left doing whatever he could to save her.

Pharadon had not known Cyaxares particularly well, but he knew where the ancient dragon's territory had been, which was as good a place to start as anywhere. The intention behind the concealment worried Pharadon. If Cyaxares had intended to hide them from dragonkind, the task might be impossible. If he had only intended to keep them out of the hands of humans, it would be far easier.

Some sort of magical concealment would have been employed, and Pharadon hoped that the magic would have degraded over the years— it was unlikely Cyaxares would have thought the Cups would need to be hidden for more than a short time. A century or two at the most; little more than the blink of an eye for a dragon. Pharadon tried to think where he would hide something precious to narrow down the search area. The obvious answer was somewhere in his mountain's caves, with his other valuables, as was the practice of all dragonkind. That didn't seem likely in this instance, however. It was too obvious.

Pharadon had no idea where Cyaxares's mountain was, only that it would lie deep within the mountainous terrain that had once been his territory. There should have been four Cups at the temple, but there had only been one. Four was an important number to dragons. There were many legendary reasons; some said Araxion, first of the enlightened, had tasked four of his comrades to go out to enlighten others, but Pharadon had always suspected the true reason was because they had four talons on each of their forelimbs.

Whatever the reason, four Cups had always been kept at the temple. When one was used, it was immediately replaced by the priests. That meant three remained unaccounted for. Had they been used as weapons, Pharadon suspected the skies would be filled with his kind and the lands below would have been devoid of humans. Hidden in a safe place seemed their most likely fate. The only challenge was finding them. A needle in a haystack, as humans might say, but Pharadon had a lodestone of sorts.

As he flew, he let his mind drift onto the Fount. His consciousness floated along its ethereal waves, carried along like a vessel navigating a great ocean. Even after having been awake for some time, he was amazed at how strong the Fount had become during his slumber. It was difficult to fathom, but was a joyous thing—it spoke of life and wonder and fecundity. In any other circumstances, it would have been a great time to be alive. As it was, the threat of loneliness spoiled it.

His senses picked up every ripple, every shallow, every depth of the Fount as his great wings carried him high above the mountains, and the miles dropped away behind him. He spotted what appeared to be a new Fount spring that had formed during his hibernation. That was a rare thing indeed, and something he would have to investigate if time ever permitted. A goldscale, a Fount spring—so many wonders, but none of his kind to revel in them. It filled his heart with a sadness.

On and on he flew, letting the song of his kind, which perpetually drifted along with the Fount, distract him from the harsh reality he found himself in. He didn't think he could ever grow accustomed to the mountains without so much as a trace of other dragonkind present. It felt as though something fundamental was missing, like the tops of the mountain peaks, or the snow.

He lost track of how long he had been flying, part of his mind searching, part convinced he would never find what he was looking for, and part wondering what life he could make for himself as the last of his kind. Then he felt it. Like a dense knot in a sheet of cloth, Pharadon sensed what he was looking for.

CHAPTER
29

Picking over the scene of a battle was an ugly thing, all the more so with an inexperienced victor. A disciplined force might have held ranks until they were given the order to pursue, but as soon as Boudain's motley force caught the scent of victory, they charged. Cutting down the retreating force as they ran, men stopped only when their attention was caught by an attractive piece of plunder.

In other circumstances, Gill would have done his best to stop them and reorganise, but he thought it unlikely Chabris—whom he had not seen on the field of battle—would be able to rally his fleeing army, so there was no chance of a counterattack.

The king and his small retinue arrived, and Boudain surveyed the grisly sight of his dead cousin. The young king appeared unmoved.

"I've sent some horsemen to chase down Cousin Chabris," the king said. "I'll put down good money that the snivelling little turd will do whatever I tell him, if he thinks it'll save his skin."

"Not everyone reacts to the threat of death with courage," Gill said.

"Indeed, unlike you," the king said. "I couldn't believe what I was seeing when you ran across the tops of those shields. That's a story that'll be told for some time, mark me. You won the day for Mirabaya. Again."

Looking down, Gill shuffled his feet. He couldn't deny how good it had felt. For a moment he had been possessed of much he had thought was gone forever—valour, speed, prowess. It was an intoxicating feeling that he wanted more of, but he wasn't sure what to make of it. Would he become a bigheaded fool once more? Lose sight of the things that were truly important? Was there anything left in his life that *was* truly important?

Before he could say anything in response, the king continued. "Unlike my father, I don't forget good service, and yours has been beyond what could be reasonably asked. Despite that, I'm afraid there will be more calls on your great talents in the days to come." He looked out past Gill. "Ah, here comes my darling cousin."

Raising his head, Gill saw the finely armoured nobleman being escorted on horseback toward them, hands bound before him. This encounter would be an interesting test of the young king's mettle, and Gill was curious to see what would happen. What kind of man was Boudain, really, and what kind of king did he intend to be? The next few moments would give strong indications of that, and the campaign to retake Mirabay would set them in stone. These were interesting times. Gill had very much hoped he had seen the last of those.

"My Lord Chabris," the king said, when his cousin was within earshot. "Your circumstances are sadly reversed. What do you have to say for yourself?"

"I, your Highness, I . . . Lord Aubin convinced me that you were bewitched. I can only apologise for my error in judgement and beg for your forgiveness."

The king let out a short laugh. "If you were convinced I was bewitched, what's changed your opinion? Surely there is little different about me than when last we spoke?"

"I . . . The gods wouldn't have given victory to a man possessed by darkness."

Gill cringed. If that was the best Chabris could come up with, the king would need to be of a merciful nature indeed.

"Guillot dal Villerauvais gave me victory," the king said.

Gill cringed again.

"A good, *loyal* man," the king said. "The type of man I need in my service, one that Mirabaya might be proud to call one of her own. You, though? Rebellion at the first hint of cause. Does that sound like the type of man I need in my service? A man of whom the people of Mirabaya might be proud?"

"No, your Highness. It doesn't."

"I'm glad we agree." The king turned to his retinue. "String him up. Brand him with the word 'traitor.' I want everyone who sees his swinging carcass to know why he's there and what happens to those who betray their king."

Two men-at-arms stepped forward and pulled the Count of Chabris from his horse. His jaw had dropped open and all the colour had drained from his face, but he remained silent until they started to drag him toward the village. He cried out for mercy, between mewling sobs that made Gill feel embarrassed for him. He was a traitor, and this was a traitor's punishment. It was harsh, but everyone knew that. Chabris would have known the risks when he chose to side with his cousin against his king.

Boudain showed no reaction to the cries, instead fixing his gaze on his remaining cousin, the Count of Savin. The message was clear, and Gill could see from the expression on Savin's face that it had been received.

"We'll need to clear the field before rot and disease sets in," Boudain said. "I want all recovered weapons and armour stockpiled, inventoried, and repaired where necessary. I'm granting an amnesty to any man who took up arms against me, ranked banneret or lower, so long as they agree to serve in the Royal Army until I have no more need of them. Any man of noble birth, I will review personally before deciding. Get to it."

There was a chorus of assent and the king's officers set off to go about their orders. That left Boudain alone with Gill and the Count of Savin.

"Well, gentlemen," the king said. "We have an army to build and a usurper to topple. Shall we?" He gestured back to the village where their temporary headquarters was, and Gill knew there was no question of refusing.

⏵⏵⏵⏵⏵⏵

Pharadon hovered over the peak containing the knot in the Fount. In many respects, there was nothing unusual about it—snowcapped, with jagged grey faces, it looked much the same as the others around it. However, there was a void within it, and in that void, Pharadon was certain, the Cups were waiting for him.

His certainty was built upon the decaying magic he could sense in the peak, with the Cups at its centre, like a gem in a rotting jewellery box. Someone had cast a spell of concealment here, and time had done its work, leaving only the shadow of what it had been.

There was something else, though. Something that stirred a memory in Pharadon, which came only slowly out of the recesses of his mind. His heart sank when he connected the reality to the reminiscence. Venori.

At first he was sure he must have been mistaken, but as he hovered there, the trace of them grew more distinct, and he came to accept that dragonkind were not the only ancient creatures to have returned to the world. Of all things, why did it have to be the Venori? The last of them was thought to have been killed when Pharadon had still been a young dragon. The last of a ferocious, and some would say evil, race that had warred against dragonkind since the beginning of remembered time.

The extermination of the Venori had created a stain on the collective conscience of dragonkind and had inspired much of their approach to dealing with humans—engage with them, show them the way to enlightenment, never again wipe a race of creatures from existence. And here they were again, while dragonkind teetered on the balance, most likely to slide into oblivion.

Pharadon wondered how the Venori had found their way to this place, then realised all that mattered was they were here. If he could sense them through all that rock, and from so great a height, they were likely to be many. He had been too young to fight them himself, but had listened long to tales of the battles between his kind and theirs.

They were said to live in groups. Some of the tales he had heard involved dragons being drained of their store of Fount and killed. He would need to be careful, but he was powerful, and he didn't intend to allow a few Venori to stand in his way. He might even be able to get in and retrieve the Cups without alerting them.

He spiralled down to get a closer look, gliding silently as he scanned the rocky peak for a way in. With dragons as large as they were, the cave would need a big entrance, or at least somewhere a dragon could set down and transform into a smaller creature. It didn't take him long to find it, or at least where it had been. Once there had been a large cave in the side of the mountain, but the mouth had collapsed at some point in the distant past.

It took but a moment to determine that magic had caused the cave-in—and done a thorough job of it. The effort of getting through the rubble would be substantial, and would certainly earn the attention of the Venori. It bothered him that the Cups and the Venori found themselves in such proximity. Had the magic drawn them? The Venori fed on the Fount—preferably that freshly drawn from a living creature.

Dragons provided the flavour they liked best, the main reason the two species had found themselves at odds with one another. Ironically, human beings had proved the Venori's second choice—it seemed to have something to do with the taste intelligence imparted. Their appetite and lack of compassion had made them the antithesis of the world enlightened dragonkind had envisaged. Who were the dragons, to have decided how the world should be shaped? Pharadon liked to think that were it not for the fact that the Venori sought to feed on his people any chance they got, they would have been left as nature intended.

He spotted a ledge and a small gap in the rubble. Pharadon landed and inspected the opening. There was no way he could get in while enjoying his natural form. It was big enough for him to enter as a man. However, his magical power would be so severely curtailed that facing down the Venori would be a foolish thing to do. He could feel them down there, lurking in the darkness. Worse, he could sense that they had already reacted to his presence.

The Fount might have grown strong enough to wake them, strong enough to sustain them indefinitely, but he could tell they hungered for that which was within him. They were working their way toward him through the passages hidden within the mountain, but if the stories were true, they wouldn't dare venture out in daylight. It was hard to put much faith in the stories when they also spoke of Venori draining all the life energies out of dragons, leaving them withered husks. As with all beings of magic, the creatures were vulnerable to Telastrian steel, but Pharadon didn't have any. In human form, there was no way he could go down there. Not on his own, at least.

▲▲▲▲▲▲

The smith's eyes nearly popped out of his head when a cart carrying a dozen Telastrian steel swords had turned up at the makeshift foundry beside the new dragon enclosure. Ysabeau thought he was going to throw up when she told him what she wanted done with them.

The swords themselves had been donated by noblemen now residing in the dungeons beneath the citadel on the Isle. There were a number of places an unfortunate could be incarcerated in Mirabay, but the citadel's dungeons were by far the worst. Unlikely though it was for a prisoner to emerge alive from any of the others, the citadel was a confirmed death sentence, a place of forgetting.

Stripped of noble rank, neither they nor their children would have need for the heirloom blades. The weapons would now serve a greater purpose—to contain the greatest spectacle in the land.

The smith and his team set to smelting the blades and reforging the steel into long wires that could be welded to the metal bands of the cage. The process was well under way when one of the workmen sent for Ysabeau.

The workers were all terrified of the Prince Bishop—perhaps rightly so—and every request that came to her was flavoured with hesitation. On this occasion, there was none of that, something that instantly caused Ysabeau alarm. She knew only too well what the stakes were. If something happened to the beast, or it escaped . . . She didn't want to consider the consequences, even if she wouldn't be around to see them—everyone here would lose their lives. There was no question of that.

"What is it?" Ysabeau said. She could see that the men had downed tools, and were vacillating between their fear of the Prince Bishop, and their fear of what lay in the still-incomplete cage.

One of the men turned to face her, and scratched at his scraggy black beard. "It moved, my Lady."

Ysabeau felt a chill run across her skin.

The dragon was curled up in much the same position in which it had been placed when they first lowered it into the old arena by crane. Its head rested on its foreclaws in an eerily similar fashion to a dog. Its nostrils flared gently and rhythmically as it breathed—there was nothing unusual about that. Ysabeau's gaze was fixed elsewhere, and her jaw had dropped.

The dragon's golden eyelids had retracted to reveal two crystal blue eyes that looked like great sparkling sapphires that reflected a flame. They held a captivating depth that made it hard to look away.

"I . . ." Ysabeau said. "I . . . We need to send word to my fa—the Prince Bishop. He'll want to know about this right away."

"Aye, my Lady," the workman said. He turned to his mates and whispered orders. One of the men headed off with haste, no doubt delighted to be putting distance between himself and the creature of nightmares, contained only by an unfinished cage.

"How much work is still to be done?" Ysabeau asked. Her heart was racing; her gaze remained locked on those two magnificent eyes. If it got out now, what kind of destruction and mayhem might it cause before they could kill it?

"One section left, my Lady," the workman said. "This one here."

"Get it finished. Fast."

CHAPTER
30

"What happens now?" Solène said.

Guillot shrugged. "The king doesn't have enough men to march on the city, but with his cousins out of the way"—he did his best not to glance at the body hanging from the tackle beam extending from the gable of the village's storehouse—"rallying troops to his banner should be easier. Amaury will be trying to do the same, I expect. Not sure how much success he'll have. Probably some in the environs of the city, but beyond a day's ride, the king will hold sway. A little time to build his army, then we march."

"So it's war then?"

Gill looked about and nodded. The village was a hive of activity. The smithy was being extended and any man who had ever swung a smith's hammer was being drafted to help repair weapons and armour. Heralds had been sent across the country to rally men to the king's banner, and spies had been dispatched to scout the countryside. Gill still felt drained by the previous day's battle. The energy that had coursed through his veins took time to wane, and although he had been exhausted when he had finally crawled into bed, the jitters and anxiety left behind—the thousand "what if"s—ensured it was hours before he eventually found sleep.

"I don't see any other way," he said. "All things considered, Amaury isn't going to apologise and step aside. He knows he'll swing for what he's done. If he's lucky, which judging by Cousin Chabris over there, he's not likely to be, I expect Amaury will be looking at an extended stay in Mirabay's dungeons before he's put out of his misery."

Solène grimaced.

"It's nothing he doesn't deserve," Gill said. "Nothing he hasn't brought on himself. He's not a man to feel sympathy for, no matter what you might think he's done for you."

She took a deep breath. "Everything he did for me had a price attached. That much was very obvious." She glanced at the king, who was standing outside the inn, deep in discussion with Savin and a couple of distinguished-looking men she didn't know. "I fear there's another price I'll have to pay now."

"A good king will always see things of value in people," Gill said, following her gaze. "And exploit them for his own gain. The best you can hope for is that he'll be generous in return."

"Will he want to use me or burn me at the stake?"

Gill raised an eyebrow. There was nothing flippant about her question.

"I saw the way the people of Mirabay reacted to the announcement of magic," Solène said. "The king will have a much easier return if he turns on it."

"You saved his life," Gill said. "That will count for something."

"Will it? Or will his memory only last until his next problem needs to be fixed—a problem that I'm part of?"

"Only if people know that about you," Gill said. "The first thing I'd be doing, if I were you, is burning any item of cream clothing in my possession."

She gestured to her clothes, which, like his, she had borrowed when they reached the village. "This is all I've got."

He nodded. The reminder of their lack of personal possessions made him wonder again about his swords. The fighting was far from over and he would far rather be walking into it with one of his Telastrian blades, though his altered munitions blade had served him well enough so far. Fetching them from Mirabay didn't seem like an option.

"The king owes you his life," Gill said. "I won't let him forget that. He'll ask much of the people around him over the coming days, but he'll have to remember what they do for him."

"I hope so," Solène said. "I'm going to spend some time with the wounded, see what I can do. The count's physician will talk me through what he knows of anatomy. I seem to have gotten the hang of doing more good than harm."

Gill gave her a reassuring smile, but wasn't sure who he was trying to reassure. He knew only too well how quickly kings could forget the good service done them.

"What's he doing here?" Solène said, looking startled.

When Gill turned to look, he saw Pharadon, in human form, striding purposefully toward them.

"I wish I knew," Gill said, "but something tells me in a few minutes, I'll wish I didn't."

Pharadon raised a hand in greeting. "I have need of you both, and of your Telastrian sword, Gill."

Gill forced a smile. Whatever it was, he was sure it wouldn't be easy. "I'm afraid I don't have any Telastrian swords at the moment."

Pharadon frowned, the expression far more fluid than it had been the last time Gill had seen it on the dragon's human face.

"The blade you carried when we first met?" Pharadon said.

"At the Wounded Lion, in Mirabay."

"Oh," Pharadon said. "It would be better if you had Telastrian steel."

"What is it you need our help with?" Gill said.

"Of course," Pharadon said. "I apologise for not making that clear. Venori. No more than a dozen, I think."

It was Gill's turn to frown. He looked at Solène, but she didn't seem to have any more of a clue than he did.

"Venori?" he asked.

Pharadon nodded, then seemed to pick up on Gill's look of confusion. "You have . . . *demons* in human mythology?"

Gill nodded. He hadn't thought Pharadon would bear welcome news, but even with all he had witnessed in recent days, Gill's imagination hadn't stretched nearly so far as to think demons might be their next problem. Dark creatures of the shadows that fed on newborns and tempted the wicked to ever greater depravity, they featured on the stained-glass windows of nearly every church in the land—hairless, pointed ears, flesh that looked as though it had been charred by the fires of all three hells.

He described this to Pharadon, who smiled broadly and nodded. "Venori. Demons. Time is of the essence," he continued. "You're certain your swords are at the Wounded Lion?"

"Certain," Gill said. "Unless they've been stolen."

"I'll return with them as quickly as I can," Pharadon said. "Be ready to leave when I do."

"My armour is there too," Gill said. "It would be great to have it back."

Without another word, Pharadon turned on his heel and strode away as purposefully as he had approached.

Gill gave Solène a bemused look and shrugged. She shrugged back.

"We'd be delighted to help, of course," Gill shouted after Pharadon.

⁂

"How much is there?" Amaury said, as he surveyed the front of the warehouse, peering out the window of his unmarked carriage.

"Enough to feed the city for three months, your Grace," Voclain said.

"A very good find," Amaury said. "This will take a great deal of pressure off until we normalise grain shipments. The Vosges has been secured nearly the whole way to the coast. Once that is finished, we will start bringing barges up from the port, but until then, I'll just be handing the grain to rebels and bandits. These stores will tide us over very nicely. How *did* you find it?"

Voclain blushed. "I, well, the warehouse is owned by a former business partner of mine."

Amaury laughed. "Let me guess, your partnership ended on less than ideal terms?"

Voclain shrugged.

"I don't care about the hows or the whys. All that matters is that we have it. Inform your former business partner that the Crown is requisitioning his stock. I won't brook any opposition. The city needs this grain, and if the owner refuses to do his patriotic duty and tries to stand in the way, make an example of him. Understand?"

Voclain nodded. "Perfectly."

"Good. Start distributing it to the mills immediately. The flour will have to be kept under guard until it reaches taverns, bakeries, and shops. People won't believe there's no food shortage unless they can see plenty of food on the market stalls. We need to make sure they're kept full. Get to it."

Amaury rapped on the roof of the carriage and the carriage rolled off, surrounded by some of Luther's mercenary hires, dressed in the livery of the Royal Guard. It had been Amaury's initial intention to put the Order out on the streets, visible as both a carrot and a stick, enforcing the rule of law, but carrying out good works around the city. As he'd mulled over the tactic, he decided that, for the time being, appearing to be the carrot was more important for the Order. There was unrest, which meant there would be violent crackdowns. Far better those actions be taken by men wearing the king's uniform, rather than that of the Order.

The captain of Amaury's bodyguard rode up alongside the carriage's window. "Back to the palace, my Lord?"

"No. I want to call in at the clinic on Northgate Road."

"Are you sure that's wise? The farther we get from the palace, the more exposed you are if there's trouble."

"There are plenty of soldiers and watchmen patrolling the streets and there's a big difference between random acts of destruction and attacking the Lord Protector of Mirabaya and his heavily armed retinue."

"I . . . my Lord, I must counsel against spending any more time out in the city."

Amaury wanted nothing more than to go back to the palace and lock every door, but knew he couldn't win the country that way. He had to be seen making good on the promises that filled every morning's news sheets. "You have my command," Amaury said.

"Aye, my Lord."

As the carriage rattled toward its destination, Amaury allowed himself a moment of calm. One by one, the problems he faced were falling before him, as had every other obstacle he had encountered in life. He was reshaping the kingdom to comply with his model of modern efficiency, to be aided by every benefit magic could bring. The more he improved their lives, the more problems he solved, the more likely the people of Mirabaya were to accept the Order—and Amaury as their ruler. In time, perhaps, they might proclaim him king by popular accord.

The master of the clinic at Northgate Road was a newly promoted novice whom Amaury vaguely recognised from his visits to the Priory—

one of the prospective mages dal Drezony had brought in, after the Prince Bishop had adopted a less hands-on approach to running the Order. There were three members of the Order in the clinic, and only five patients.

"How are they?" Amaury said, redirecting his concern from the venture's political success to the condition of the patients.

"They'll be fine," the master said. Amaury couldn't remember his name, and didn't bother asking. "And far sooner than any of them would have believed. I think one of them would have died if it were not for our help. This is a good thing we're doing, my Lord. The best thing, I think."

Forcing a smile and pointing at one patient, Amaury asked, "What happened to him?"

"Run over by a cart in the street," the master said. "Stove his chest in. If the internal injuries hadn't killed him, the fever it caused would have. Now? He'll go home tomorrow like it never happened."

Amaury nodded. This was the type of success the Order needed. The type of success he needed.

"You're doing excellent work," Amaury said, fixated on how few patients there were. He had ordered that three other clinics be set up around the city, and wondered if they were faring any better.

"Has it been this . . . quiet all the time?"

The master shrugged and nodded. "It will take time before people come to trust us. I'll be sending two of these patients home in the next couple of hours. They'll tell their family and friends what we did for them. Then I expect we'll get far, far busier."

Amaury wasn't as confident as his underling, but hoped he was right. "Keep up the good work." He returned to his carriage, and gave his next destination to the captain of his guard, who still wore a disapproving expression. The reality was—Amaury knew from personal experience—that if someone wanted to kill you badly enough, they would find a way. Here on the streets, locked away in his office in the palace, it didn't matter.

Drinking water in Mirabay was supplied by fountains dotted throughout the city. Amaury's personal supply was ferried in from natural springs several miles north of the city, as was the practice for most of the nobility and better-off. What came into the city was rarely clear, rarely smelled palatable. As for the taste? He couldn't say. He'd never dared drink it. Cholera was a regular visitor to the city. Hundreds of people died that horrific death each year, and the traditional methods of keeping the water clean enough to drink were haphazard at best, even when diligently carried out.

The problem had existed for such a long time that people had accepted it. No king had felt that providing consistently clean water to the citizens was a worthy expenditure. Amaury vaguely recalled the old king making some comment about "letting them drink wine," or something along those lines, no doubt hoping to maintain the tax revenues he made on the sale of wine. Generations of kings had sat on their thrones in Mirabay, but Amaury would be the man to bring the city clean drinking water.

His carriage arrived at the water tower in the city's northwest, into which water was pumped by the endless circling of beasts of burden. They turned a screw that carried the water to the top; the height gave it the force needed to push it out to the dozen or so fountains across the city. It was a miracle of Imperial engineering, a feat that modern engineers struggled to maintain. Hence the often brown, stinking effluent that emerged from the glorious marble fountains.

A group of men and women were gathered at the aqueduct, all wearing Spurrier cream and gold. This too had been a finely balanced decision. The last thing Amaury needed was the people deciding the sorcerers had poisoned their water. Equally, when spring-fresh, crystal-clear water started flowing from the fountains, he needed the Order to get the credit.

The mages were purifying the insides of the tower, piping, and aqueduct, stripping away the accumulated filth of centuries without interrupting supply. Conventional methods would have resulted in shortages and months of work. He watched a moment longer—although there really wasn't anything of interest to see—before ordering the carriage to return to the palace.

Amaury had only just reached his office's antechamber when he was approached by a messenger.

"Your Grace, there's been word about the king."

Amaury frowned and looked about for somewhere they could speak without being overheard. He beckoned for the messenger to follow him into his office, and closed the door behind him.

The messenger handed Amaury a note. He unfolded it and read. The king had recovered from his injuries and was in full control of his faculties. When this report had been written, Boudain was preparing for a battle against his cousins. That fight was probably over by now; hopefully he would soon receive word of it.

Amaury nodded slowly. If magic could cause the damage, there was no reason that magic couldn't undo it. Now that Solène was set against him, Amaury had suspected something like this might come to pass.

"You know what this message contains?" he said.

The messenger nodded. "I was told of the events it refers to."

Amaury nodded. "The king is in league with a very powerful sorceress. Exactly the type of person the Order and I have sought to stop from becoming too powerful. In a word, she has bewitched the king, but I fear the people aren't ready to hear such disconcerting news. Do you understand?" Amaury placed a hand on the aide's shoulder in an effort to add sincerity to his words. "You're privy to some very sensitive information. News will reach the city soon enough, but until then, I'd appreciate it if you'd keep this, and news of the sorceress, quiet. I hope to have the problem addressed before it becomes serious."

"Of course, your Grace," the messenger said, delight at being taken into the Prince Bishop's confidence evident on his face.

"Good lad," Amaury said. "Now, I'm sure you've plenty of important work to be doing."

The messenger nodded, smiled, and went on his way. Amaury watched him go, and wondered how long it would take him to reveal the secret that had just been shared with him. An hour? Two? By sundown it would be out, and would spread like wildfire, as the salacious rumours always did. Exactly as Amaury wanted it to.

CHAPTER
31

How did you get these?" Gill said, looking over his Telastrian swords—the Competition winner's blade; the Sword of Honour, for graduating top of his class at the Academy; and, finally, the Blade of the Morning Mist, the old family sword that he had recently learned had once belonged to Valdamar, the famed dragon hunter and member of the Chevaliers of the Silver Circle.

"It wasn't so difficult to convince the innkeeper to give me the items he was holding for you."

Gill didn't like the idea that magic could be used to persuade people to do what you wanted, and wondered if you'd be able to tell it was being done to you. He cast Solène a sideways glance. You really did need to trust the good faith of people who could do magic. It was an unsettling thought.

He checked over his armour, which Pharadon had also returned to him. Like the Blade of the Morning Mist, it too was made of Telastrian steel and had once belonged to Valdamar. Though Gill and the legendary hero had apparently been similar in size and shape, the armour had pinched somewhat at first. Now it felt as though it had been made for him, perhaps because of the magical metal's special properties.

"Time is something of an issue," Pharadon said, pulling Gill back into the now.

"You're going to have to tell me more about what you need us to do. You can't expect Solène and me to rush into something without any idea of what we're going to have to deal with."

"I found more Cups," Pharadon said.

Solène looked about nervously. "Best to keep that quiet," she said. "Perhaps they're best left where they are. Lost and forgotten."

Pharadon shook his head. "They are the only way I have to enlighten the goldscale. She's been brought to the city and placed in some sort of . . . menagerie. Time is running out."

"How are you going to free her?" Solène said.

"I haven't worked that out yet," Pharadon said. "Enlightening her is the most pressing matter. If I manage that, I can worry about other matters."

"Don't you need to bring her to the temple to do that?" Solène said.

Pharadon shook his head. "I brought her to the Cup to get her away from the slayers, rather than bringing the Cup to her. With the Cup I can carry out the ceremony anywhere. Even a cage in the centre of Mirabay."

"And these demons," Gill said. "The Venori. What are they? Really?"

"They are as I said. Demons. They feed on the life energy of other creatures. My understanding was that they were destroyed in my youth, but it seems that the magic of the world has brought them back, just as it did me and the other dragons."

"They've appeared in the same place the Cups were hidden?"

Pharadon shrugged again. "It's possible the concentration of magical energy attracted them. It's possible that it woke them. I really don't know. The Venori are little more than stories to me, and to sense them was shocking."

"Why do you need us? Can't you incinerate them?"

"It's not quite that easy," Pharadon said.

He described what he had found, and Gill could see where the difficulty lay. He wasn't at all enthusiastic about venturing into the shadowy bowels of a mountain, let alone a mountain filled with creatures that had given rise to human myths about demons. His life lately seemed to be about dealing with the worst creatures from childhood fairy tales. How had it come to this? At moments he wondered if he was dreaming it all—one of the wild and wicked dreams to be found at the bottom of a bottle of bad wine. He looked over at the mass grave that was still being filled, and he knew he was awake. No man dreamed of so much killing.

As unappealing as this task was, Gill owed Pharadon. Everyone, the king included, owed Pharadon, even if they didn't realise it. The dragon had behaved honourably, had helped them rescue the king, then heal the king. Now it was time to repay that debt.

If the goldscale was caged in Mirabay, that was undoubtedly Amaury's doing, and that was reason enough to interfere. Aside from Gill's sense of obligation to Pharadon, he had an overriding sense of unanswered injustice in the way Amaury was treating the dragon, keeping it from its enlightened state.

"I'll help," Gill said. "I don't speak for Solène, though."

"Of course I'll help," Solène said. "I'm not sure what I can do, but I'll help."

"Thank you," Pharadon said. "There isn't much time, so we should get moving."

"How far away is it? Will we get there and back in time?" Gill said.

Pharadon smiled. "It is quite far, but we will make it in plenty of time."

"Let me tell the king I'm going to repay the debt he owes you, and I'll be ready to leave," Gill said.

Pharadon smiled. "Excellent. I hope you're not afraid of heights."

⣦⣦⣦⣦⣦

"Is that it?" the Prince Bishop said.

"Well, yes," Ysabeau said. "So far, it is. But it's quite a big development. We weren't sure if it would ever wake. Now it's opened its eyes. Who knows what will be next?"

"Has the enclosure been completed?"

"It has," Ysabeau said. She didn't add that the last of the welding had been completed only seconds before her father had arrived. All that mattered was that it was done, that every precaution anyone could come up with had been taken.

"You think it will hold?"

"Who knows," Ysabeau said. "We've done everything we can. If we learn anything new, we can adapt as we go."

"Good," the Prince Bishop said. "I want to open to the public as soon as we can, so have your people clear up as quickly as possible."

"Yes, *Father.*"

"Lord Protector," he said, then blushed. "I'd prefer if you call me Lord Protector in public. It's important that people get used to it."

"Of course, Lord Protector," she said.

"Keep me updated." He frowned. "It looks thinner. Fatten it up."

He didn't wait for her to respond, instead turning on his heel and heading for his unmarked carriage, whisking his entourage of aides and guards along with him, leaving Ysabeau alone with the dragon. She looked again into the deep pools of the dragon's eyes. Her father was right, the creature was thinner. Far thinner. She had been so busy with everything else that she hadn't noticed.

Looking about, Ysabeau spotted her foreman coming back in; everyone had made themselves scarce while her father—*the Lord Protector*—was present. She couldn't say she blamed them. There were rumours going about the city that the return of magic was all down to him, that he dabbled in the dark arts and could kill a man with a single withering stare. It was laughable, or at least it would have been, were it not for the fact that the rumour gave even Ysabeau pause for thought. What might he be capable of when he finally chose to test his powers?

One way or the other, he needed the distraction of the dragon. The clinics weren't winning people over; the residents of Mirabay were refusing to eat food or drink water that they suspected had been touched by magic. In that, she was disappointed. The benefits were clear for all to see, they simply refused to accept them. You could lead a horse to water . . .

Those were her father's problems. Managing this dragon and its enclosure were hers. She caught the foreman's eye. He had proved competent in the preparatory works and she planned to keep him on to help her run things now that the construction was finished.

"Get me a side of beef," she said, then frowned. Might the dragon dislike beef? "One of bacon too."

"My Lady, there's a shortage of meat in the ci—"

"Get them," she said, "or it will be you and some of your men fulfilling that role in the cage. I don't care what it takes or costs. This beast needs feeding, and feed it we will."

She turned her back on him to show the conversation was over, and found her eyes locked on the dragon's once more. Each time she did, it made her feel uncomfortable, but she hadn't been able to work out why. She could see intelligence in the creature's eyes, dancing like a nascent flame. It wasn't just intelligence, though. There was something soulful about the beast. When Ysabeau looked into its eyes, she knew what they were doing was wrong, and felt ashamed.

She considered for a moment whether the creature was using magic to tug on her heartstrings, perhaps in an effort to convince her to set it free, but she knew her own mind, and heart, too well for that. She had done many questionable things in her life, but had always been able to rationalise it—she had never killed someone that didn't have it coming. On this occasion, she was struggling. Not because she wasn't creative enough, but because she knew what they were doing was unjustifiable. She reminded herself that these creatures had to be hunted down because of the death and devastation they had caused, but she knew also that her father's expeditions had provoked them.

As she looked into those eyes, she struggled to see the savage creature of nightmares. She saw more intelligence than she saw when looking most people in the eye. And more pain.

CHAPTER
32

Gill hadn't thought he was afraid of heights, but had really never had the opportunity to properly test it. When he was fighting the first dragon, he had been lifted up far higher than he had ever been before, but he had assumed the terror he'd felt rose from being locked in mortal struggle with a creature of nightmares. Now, dangling from one of Pharadon's claws proved he did indeed have reservations when it came to great heights.

Solène, in Pharadon's other foreclaw, seemed to be having the time of her life. Though she squinted to shield her eyes from the buffeting wind, her face was split by a toothy smile, and Gill couldn't think of ever having seen her look so happy. Watching her, he did his best not to allow his gaze to drift down. He wasn't sure how high they were, and wasn't willing to study the ground long enough to make an estimate. All he could think about was what it would look like if he impacted—little left but a red splatter, he reckoned. Certainly not how he would choose to go out.

They surged through the air as Pharadon's great wings beat with a powerful, steady rhythm. It was cold up that high; Gill's eyes watered as the wind whistled past his face. He wondered which of the mountain peaks below contained the Cups, and more importantly, the Venori. He had borrowed some warmer clothes from the stores at Castandres, but they weren't heavy enough to keep him entirely warm, and he worried his limbs would be frozen stiff by the time he encountered one of the demons.

Eventually Pharadon started down in a loose spiral that was centred over a peak capped with snow. He slowed and hovered above a ledge on the rock face, giving Gill and Solène time to realise he was about to release his grip. The drop to the ground was slight, and he had to do nothing more than bend his knees to absorb the impact.

With the humans safely on solid ground, Pharadon landed, his bulk filling most of the space. He immediately started to transform into a human, a process that always turned Gill's stomach. Unwilling to watch, he turned his attention to the opening in the side of the mountain. Even Gill's inexpert eye could see that it had once been much larger, that it had been almost completely sealed by a rockfall.

He approached and peered in. The light of day reached in for a few paces, but after that, the darkness was absolute, creating the kind of void that nightmares were made of. Even if Gill hadn't known for a fact that there were demons somewhere in there, the darkness alone would have been enough to set his imagination racing. Every instinct he had screamed at him not to enter.

"I'm ready when you are," Pharadon said.

Gill turned back, finding him in his now-familiar human form and appearing fully clothed. Gill drew his sword, Valdamar's old blade, and felt a momentary concern that he might lose the magnificent weapon somewhere in the dark depths of the mountain. Still, there had been no real choice—he needed his best blade if he hoped to survive.

"There's nothing to be gained by waiting any longer," Gill said. He looked at Solène, whose face was impassive. He wondered if she was as terrified by the thought of going in there as he was. "You know where the Cups are?"

Pharadon nodded. "I can find my way to them. I need you to protect me until I can get them back out."

"These creatures, do they use weapons?"

"I don't believe so," Pharadon said. "Your Telastrian blade should cause them fatal wounds, even if the blow itself would not normally have been mortal."

That's something, at least, Gill thought. "How do they behave?"

"They were said to swarm the creatures they seek to slay. The narrow passages in the mountain should be to our advantage, since they'll only be able to come at us one or two at a time. But there is something else they do, a form of mind control that subdues a living victim so they can feed. Be wary of it."

"Have they been here all this time? Waiting?"

Pharadon shrugged. "There's more magic in the world now than I've ever known. There are many possibilities when magical energy is so strong. It's possible that some of them went dormant all those years ago, and woke as I did, when the Fount grew so strong. Or, they may simply have come to be once more. All we can do is hope that there are not many, and that they will remain in this remote place."

"If they don't?" Gill said.

Pharadon shrugged. "Eliminating them will be left to your kind now."

"How dangerous are they?"

"They slew nearly as many of my people as humans did. It took centuries for dragonkind to bring them under control and then eradicate them. That they are present at all is . . . chilling. When your people are done with your wars, turning your attention to the Venori would be a very good idea. Before they become too numerous and powerful to stop."

Gill nodded slowly. It seemed there was always a fight for another day. "Is there anything else I need to know?"

"They are intelligent creatures, but their hunger will be stirred so deeply by my presence that they will be driven by that, rather than calculated thought."

Wonderful, Gill thought. *Intelligent creatures driven by insatiable hunger.* He knew Pharadon was trying his best to paint a bright picture of the task ahead, but his words did little to ease Gill's concerns.

Gesturing at darkness, he said, "Can you do anything about that, Solène?"

She nodded, then frowned for the briefest of moments. A great globe of light appeared several paces away, filling the passageway with light and making it appear marginally less foreboding. Gill could still see nothing but bare rock ahead. Pharadon seemed to be expecting Gill to take the lead, so, with a curt nod, he drew his sword, held it at the ready, and stepped into the tunnel.

The whistle of the chill breeze cut off instantly. Sheltered from its cold touch, he instantly started to feel warmer. Wondering if the light had anything to do with that, he held his hand out toward it but couldn't feel any heat being given off.

He edged forward, his footfalls echoing, heartbeat thumping in his ears. A moment later Pharadon's and Solène's footfalls joined his. Another globe of light appeared farther down the tunnel. Gill was glad that he didn't have to rely on Leverre's short-lasting trick that allowed him to see in the dark. Creatures that dwelled under the ground were going to be far more comfortable in darkness than Gill ever would be, and he hoped that the globes of light would put them off. As it was, the light would certainly alert the creatures to their presence, although Pharadon seemed to think the demons were already aware of them.

The passage led down at a shallow angle. At first one side of it looked similar to the rock face above the ledge—rubble and dust—but it soon took on the look of a natural cavity in the mountain, with jagged edges. The roof was high above and the tunnel was wide enough for two people to walk side by side. Gill wasn't sure if that was really a good thing—after all, the narrower the passage, the harder it would be for the Venori to swarm him.

It was difficult to gauge how far into the mountain they were getting, or how far they had descended. Gill was beginning to wonder how far they would have to go before they encountered signs of the Venori, when his query was answered.

▲▲▲▲▲▲

The noise was indistinct at first, something Gill thought he might be imagining, but it grew steadily, coming from farther down the passageway where darkness still ruled.

"They're getting close," Pharadon said.

Gill was tempted to ask what he should do, but he supposed the answer was obvious—kill anything that came toward them. He paused for a moment to steel his nerves, and adjust his posture to as relaxed a fencer's stance as he could muster. A moment later, he saw the first of them come out of the darkness.

At first Gill thought it was a man, albeit a pale, naked man—but the differences quickly made themselves clear. The creature was completely hairless and looked emaciated. It had pointed ears, sharp, elongated teeth, and eyes that emitted a faint red glow. *So this is what a demon really looks like?* Gill thought. He wondered how many more creatures from childhood tales he was destined to encounter before the year was out. He would have to get out of the tunnel alive first, of course, before he could enjoy that particular pleasure.

He was so caught up in the sight of his first demon that he allowed the creature to get perilously close. Solène urgently calling his name startled him out of his bemusement; he shifted his weight to balance more readily on his feet and started to study the way the Venori moved, rather than what it looked like. It seemed slow, weak; not at all what Gill had expected. When he judged it within range, he lunged, taking a great leaping step forward and extending his sword with as much speed as he could muster.

The blade met thin air. Instinct pulled him back into a more balanced, defensive pose, as his senses searched for the creature he had been certain he was about to skewer. His eyes and the tip of his sword tracked the same spot as he looked from side to side. The creature had either vanished, or moved so quickly that Gill hadn't been able to see—one moment it was there; the next, it was gone. So much for it being weak and starving. Was it too much to hope that he had connected with it, and the Telastrian steel had done its job, banishing the demon back to whatever hell it had come from?

The sick feeling in the pit of Gill's stomach said otherwise, and paying attention to that sensation born of instinct had saved his life on more than one occasion.

"Does anyone see it?" Gill said.

"No," Solène said. "It was a blur. Then gone."

"The Venori were known for their ability to move faster than the eye can follow," Pharadon said.

That tidbit would have been a bit more help a few minutes ago, Gill thought. Still, he couldn't have executed his lunge any faster, and even in his prime it would have been a decent strike. As pleasing as it was to realise his form was coming back with ever greater consistency, it didn't answer the question of where the demon had gone. The only comforting thought, as he stared into the darkness beyond Solène's magical light, was that the Venori would likely go for Pharadon first. Not a particularly noble thought, but an attempt to feed might keep the creature still long enough for Gill to cut it down. Somehow, he doubted Pharadon would be open to the idea of being used as bait.

"Keep your eyes peeled," Gill said. If the demons could all move like that, he knew they might be in trouble.

Gill's skin tingled and his body felt as though it were held in a vise. He had thought he had known true terror walking into the first dragon's cave, but this was worse. He wondered if his association with Pharadon had tempered those memories, and made dragons less a matter of nightmare. Perhaps it was simply that there were different levels of fear, and that once a danger had passed, the emotional experience inevitably faded. His first battle had been the most frightening thing imaginable—he had thrown up on his way to muster—but the first dragon had made that seem like a mild concern.

Now, he struggled to remember what all that fuss was about. What was an army of men, or a single dragon, compared to a horde of hungering demons? *How do I get myself into these situations?* Gill wondered. *Are the gods punishing me for past hubris?* It was difficult to get past the notion of divine intervention, though Gill had long since lost his faith. How could any man be as unfortunate as he, or have the world attempt to kill him so many times, if some great force was not behind it all? Might the powers of magic be conspiring against him?

There was still no sight or sound of the creature. Gill wasn't fool enough to think that he had frightened it off. Most likely it had gone to get its friends, or worse, was watching him at that very moment from an unseen vantage point. The thought sent a shiver across Gill's skin.

"We should push on," he said. They were either going on or turning around, and he knew the latter wasn't an option. He started to inch forward again, his body tense at the thought of the Venori flying out of the darkness at him.

CHAPTER
33

As he edged farther and farther into the mountain, the madness of what they were trying to achieve struck him. Even if they made it to the Cups, could they really expect to get back out again? It was true that he wasn't constrained by the usual limits of what he could achieve with his sword, that Solène's magic would be equally important, if not more so. But still. . . .

He heard Pharadon and Solène talking quietly behind him, and realised what his role there really was. Just as in the days of the Empire, the union of mage and banneret had happened once more. Gill—technically the most skilled swordsman of his generation—was there, Telastrian sword in hand, all to make sure Solène had the time she needed to shape the magic that would get them through this experience alive. No doubt that was the topic of the conversation behind him.

Gill had to admit he felt a little emasculated. He'd always been the one looked to when the impossible needed to be achieved. His renaissance over the past weeks had let him imagine that he could be that man once again, but now he realised that was unlikely. Magic was the future, one way or the other, and his kind would only ever serve as an adjunct to that, as had been the case in the distant past. He had struggled enough to find a place in the world he knew—how would he fare now? *Still,* he thought, *I might not make it out of here alive. Always a silver lining. . . .*

Solène's light reached only so far down the craggy passageway; beyond that lurked the Venori. He wished they'd come out, so he could at least kill some of them. He always felt better after getting the first splash of blood on his blade. Confirming that he could kill one of these demons would go a long way to settling his nerves. Until he did, they would continue to seem invincible.

While his footsteps echoed sharply off the rough rock sides of the passageway, the whispering between Solène and Pharadon seemed very distant. Even though Solène continued to create magical lights every time he moved from the embrace of the previous one, it felt as though the darkness was closing in around him. He heard what sounded like a laugh ahead, a warm sound, full of kindness and joy. It was a laugh he had heard before. He squinted into the blackness beyond the magic light.

"Auroré?" he muttered. The joy of hearing something he valued above all else flooded through him, overwhelming the part of his mind that screamed this was impossible. Gill quickened his pace.

No sooner had he stepped beyond the range of Solène's last light than he saw movement, a flash of a shape moving away from him. But something remained—its scent. He knew the smell. It was a perfume, made by a single parfumier in Mirabay. Gill had bought Auroré a bottle on her birthday each year. He breathed deeply, drawing the scent into his lungs. How long had it been since he had smelled it? There was no way she could be here. She was dead. But the sound? The smell?

"Gill? What are you doing here?"

The rational part of Gill's brain told him that Solène had spoken, but everything else said it was Auroré. It was *her* voice. There was no mistaking it.

"Auroré?"

"I'm here, Gill. I've been waiting for you for so long. We've been waiting for you. Our son is here."

My son? Gill's heart raced. This couldn't be happening, but there was so much he had seen with his own eyes over the past few weeks that couldn't be happening. Yet it had happened. Magic. Dragons. Demons. Now Auroré? His son?

A light bloomed farther down the tunnel and he hurried toward it, only barely aware of Pharadon and Solène behind him. The light grew as he progressed, a warm, welcoming glow that spoke of an open fire with a pot of inviting broth hanging over it. And there she was. There was indeed a fire, with a cauldron hanging over it. Auroré sat beside the blaze on a small stool, cradling a newborn boy on her lap.

"Gill," she said, looking up and smiling in that way that made Gill's heart melt. "We've been waiting for you."

"How? What?" Gill said. The boy should be older, he thought, but with magic, there could be many reasons for his appearance. Auroré, too, did not appear to have aged. Gill felt shamed. Time had not been kind to him, and although he had trimmed some of the bulk at his waist, his hair showed traces of grey, and the years he'd spent at the bottom of a bottle had lined his face. What would she think of him now? What would she think of the man he had become, so far removed from the one she had fallen in love with?

"I'm so glad you're finally here," she said. She placed the child in a crib beside her stool—a crib that Gill would have sworn was not there a moment earlier. More magic. She smiled a smile that would make a starving man forget about food, and opened her arms. "My love, I'd lost hope that you'd find us."

Gill returned her smile, as his heart filled with a warmth it had not known in so long. Perhaps the gods were not punishing him for hubris after all? He lowered his sword, walked forward, and surrendered himself to her embrace.

⁂

"Gill! Get back," Solène shouted. She couldn't believe what she was seeing.

He had rushed ahead, forcing her and Pharadon to run to catch up. When they came upon him, he was standing in the middle of a small chamber. Solène cast a light just in time to see Gill, as though in a trance, lower his sword and walk forward as one of the Venori emerged from the shadows. Guillot walked straight into its arms. The creature lowered him to the ground and knelt over him.

"What's he doing?" Solène said.

"The demon must have bewitched him," Pharadon said. "The magic I spoke of. Now is the time to use it. Quickly."

Solène felt a flash of panic, and wished that Pharadon retained his great abilities while in human form. Everyone was relying on her now. As they had when she'd helped first rescue, then cure, the king. She had never considered the responsibility that magic might bring with it. She had always thought of it as a terrible burden, and it still was—it was only the nature of that burden that had changed.

She furrowed her brow as she concentrated. She had sworn she would never again use magic to kill, but this seemed different. She silently mouthed the words that would focus her thoughts and saw a lance of blue energy shoot across the small chamber. It struck the Venori in the chest, blasting it against the far wall, and leaving a large hole in the creature where its approximation of a heart usually resided.

Gill lay senseless on the chamber's floor. After checking to make sure the Venori was dead, Solène knelt beside Gill. His eyes were open, staring into the distance, and he seemed completely unaware she was there. There was an expression of deep contentment on his face.

"What did it do to him?" she said.

Pharadon knelt beside her. "This is what I spoke of. It enraptured him."

"Will he recover?"

"Most likely, but this type of magic is anathema to me. I do not know how it works."

Solène gently slapped Gill's cheek. "Gill? Can you hear me?"

He mumbled and stirred, but his eyes and mind were still far away.

"What can we do for him?" she said.

"All magic fades. I don't expect this will last long. Its intent is only to stun the victim long enough for the Venori to feed."

"Well, we can't wait. What if more of those things come? We have to do something to get him on his feet again."

"A mild shock, perhaps?"

"A what?"

"Flush him with a small amount of the Fount. That should revive him."

"How much?" Solène said, not sure she liked the idea but unable to come up with any alternatives.

Pharadon shrugged. "I do not know how much will be needed for a human."

"What happens if I use too much?"

"The same as always happens when too much of the Fount passes through a living thing."

"Burnout," Solène said under her breath. "Wonderful."

She did her best to imagine how much would send a tingle across her skin, and focussed that thought on Gill. Indecision was as likely to get them killed as making the wrong decision. He jerked awake.

"Auroré?"

As he searched about him, the look of happiness on his face faded. "What happened?"

"The demon did that enrapturing thing to you," Solène said.

What was left of the smile on Gill's face disappeared completely. "That sounds about right," he said. "Where is it?"

"I killed it," Solène said, gesturing to the creature's corpse by the rock wall.

"At least we know they can die," Gill said.

"We should continue on as soon as you're ready," Pharadon said.

Gill hauled himself to his feet, cast a glance at the Venori corpse lying at the side of the chamber, and shuddered. A moment before, he had thought it was his long-dead wife. Auroré's smell was still in his nose, the sound of her voice in his ears; the sensation of her touch lingered on his skin. How could he have been so utterly fooled? How could he have allowed it? And how had the Venori known so much about him? Above all, the most frightening thing was how much he wanted to be back in that state.

The pain of her death was fresh in his heart, making it difficult to think of anything else. She had been so real. Every detail. At what point had reality blended into illusion? That was concerning—there was no clear transition. No point he could identify as the moment he had walked from the real world into one the demon had created. If he couldn't tell when that was, how could he prevent it from happening again?

The only consolation was the visible evidence that they could be killed. He would have preferred to be the one who had done the killing, but a dead demon was better than a live one. Gill gave the body one final look before moving toward the passage leading deeper into the mountain.

"I'm ready," he said. He didn't believe what he said and wondered if his companions did. Surely they were as concerned as he was by what had happened. "Wait," he said, second-guessing himself. "The enrapture thing. Is there anything you can do to stop it happening again?"

Solène blanched. He'd seen the same reaction from her before— it was the one she had every time she was asked to try a new piece of magic that might have a negative impact on someone. Gill wondered if she'd ever get over it, but knew she was still haunted by the first time she had killed. She'd done it to save him from the Prince Bishop's men, but the justification didn't seem enough for her. Some people never got over that kind of thing. Those with good souls. Gill wondered what that said about him.

She and Pharadon entered into a heated discussion, which continued for some time. At last they both started to nod and Solène turned to Gill.

"I think I have a way to allow you to see what's born of magic, and what's not," Solène said. "Hopefully it will work."

"Hopefully," Gill said, doing his best to muster some enthusiasm.

Solène muttered some words and Gill waited to feel different, but when he realised she was done, and he didn't, made his best effort to appear emboldened. She cast a globe of light in the passageway and Gill started down it, determined to claim the next kill.

He had not gone far before another creature peeked out of the darkness. For a moment it appeared stunned by Solène's light, but it adapted quickly and continued to approach, albeit more cautiously. Gill took his guard and advanced slowly. The demon regarded him with hungry curiosity for a moment. Suddenly it became covered with a coruscating blue light. Magical energy. It was a beautiful thing to see, and Gill realised what it meant—the Venori was trying to use its tricks on him again. Whatever Solène had done to him, it had worked.

Gill began to lower his sword, aping an expression of stupefaction. The Venori moved forward, lips pulling back to reveal pointed, elongated canine teeth. It thought it had Gill in its spell. Gill burst into motion. If the creature was surprised, it didn't have the time to show it. Gill had run it through the chest, pulled his blade clear, and taken its head from its shoulders in the blink of an eye. The body teetered on its feet, then collapsed to the ground.

There were two more Venori right behind it. Perhaps realising that their friend's trick hadn't worked, they split to opposite sides of the passageway, moving so quickly that they were in new positions before Gill could blink. His only advantage was that in such narrow confines, even their unnatural speed couldn't take them far from his blade.

He slashed left and right, attacks intended to do nothing more than harry, but the Telastrian steel blade made contact on both sides, yielding glancing cuts. The howls of pain the creatures let out suggested far more serious injury. They recoiled from him, smoke billowing from the wounds.

They were focussed on their agony, and Gill had never been one to pass up a good opportunity. He skewered each one through the heart, then took their heads. As he watched the second one tumble down the passageway, he started to think they might make it out of the mountain alive. Perhaps even with what they'd come for.

"Are there many more of these things?" Gill said, as he stepped over the bodies.

"Some," Pharadon said. "I'm not sure how many. All this rock makes it more difficult to tell. Particularly when my powers are weakened."

Gill cast Solène a glance; she shrugged. One way or the other, there were four fewer than when they arrived. Would their intelligence overcome their hunger? Might the deaths of four of their kind persuade the rest to scurry deeper into the mountain and leave them in peace?

They continued moving farther into the mountain for what seemed like an age. Gill couldn't work out how many times they had spiralled around, only that there was a gentle left-hand turn to the passageway as it dropped.

Down and down they went, into places that had probably never before been touched by light. Were it not for Gill's presence, he reckoned they still wouldn't be—Solène and Pharadon would be able to use their magical tricks to see in the dark.

▲▲▲▲▲▲

"Eat it, you dumb beast," Ysabeau said. She stood, arms akimbo, staring into the cage. The golden dragon stared back at her with mournful eyes, completely ignoring the cow carcass that Ysabeau's men had lowered into the cage. There was nothing wrong with it—the cow had been slaughtered only that morning—but the dragon didn't show even the slightest interest.

"That cow would feed a family for a week," Ysabeau said. She felt foolish barking at the creature, but some instinct within her said that it might understand at least the sentiment of what she was saying, if the great chunk of raw meat wasn't enough.

She was starting to become concerned. If they couldn't get the dragon to eat, it was going to die. Already she could see the outline of its ribs on its flank, its scaled hide stretched across its skeleton. Her father was gambling heavily on the effect that the dragon would have—the boost to his reputation and the distraction of seeing what could only be called a wonder of the world. If it died, he would blame someone, and that would be her. There were no other targets.

How could she get it to eat? There was no way she was going to climb into the cage and force-feed it and she doubted if any of her men would follow an order to. They were due to open the exhibit the following morning, and no one was going to be amazed by a lethargic, half-starved creature curled up in its cage.

Feeding it and livening it up were her pressing problems, but they weren't the ones that concerned her the most. Looking into the dragon's deep blue eyes told Ysabeau all she needed to know of its torment. She kept reminding herself that given the chance, this creature would slaughter livestock, raze villages to the ground, and kill scores of men, women, and children. Looking at it, though, that was hard to believe, and the memory of the other dragon at the temple—the one who spoke and changed into human form—made her wonder how much they really knew about dragons.

Might there be different types of dragon, some a danger and others not? Were they capable of higher thought? Certainly this dragon's eyes contained far more intelligence than many men she had encountered over the years.

"Eat, damn you," she muttered under her breath. The dragon just lay there, staring at her. Ysabeau swore in frustration. She'd not left the old arena since the dragon had been installed there; she'd been sleeping in a tent in the workers' camp. Now she decided she'd had enough of the place, that she needed a break from those mournful, accusatory eyes.

She left without a word to her work crew—she was sick of them too, and she had no doubt they would be delighted by a few hours out from under her harsh glare.

Ysabeau had never been one for wine or ale—waiting for others to get drunk had always been a favourite tactic—but she felt as though she could use something to take the edge off the tension that gripped her like a vise. As she walked toward a tavern she knew, she realised the city was in a similar state.

The violence she'd heard of soon after her return to Mirabay seemed to have abated; perhaps her father was starting to get a grasp on things. Yet there was still an uncomfortable air of tension on the streets, though she didn't feel unsafe, exactly. The ordinary business of the city seemed to be continuing. Maybe now that the agonised initial adjustment period was over, people were coming around to the new reality. That almost seemed too much to hope for, but Mirabay had always been a city of passion, where emotions ran high and the mood swung from one side of the balance to the other in moments.

The Little Palace had always been a favourite of Ysabeau's, even when she was too young to be allowed in. It was a place of agitators, anarchists, and intellectuals. Over the years, she had killed at least a dozen men and women who had gained notice within those walls, removing those whose voices were loud enough to make the wealthy and powerful uncomfortable. At times she had wondered at the morality of it—cutting down voices championing the rights of the poor, the downtrodden. People like her. Her mother. Her friends. The half brother who had died in the night one bad winter, starved and frozen.

Such moralising rarely lasted long. She knew reality too well. No one really wanted equality, or rights for the downtrodden, they simply wanted to lift themselves up. Become the ones doing the shitting, rather than remain the ones getting shit on. Those foolish and naive enough to listen to their mellifluous words wouldn't reap any benefit, just get killed during the process. People like her. People like her mother. Her brother too, had he lived.

Better cut those hollow words out of their throats before they convinced other people to get themselves killed. It wasn't so hard to justify how she had made her life when she thought of it like that.

The Little Palace was quiet that afternoon. There were plenty of people about, but there was no noise, no lively discussion or passionate speech, merely groups huddled around tables, drinking and talking quietly. Intensely. Ysabeau sat and ordered a drink. One of the dandies, who appeared to fancy himself as an intellectual, or at least liked to give ladies the impression he was, made his way over, wire spectacles perched rakishly on his nose in a way ironically similar to a dandy banneret who wore his sword low on his hip and walked with a swagger.

She forced a smile as he sidled up next to her at the bar as her glass of warm spiced wine arrived. She had ordered it from habit—it was the drink of Kate dal Drenham, her Humberland alter ego, a woman who wore silk skirts and had perfect hair and makeup. As for Ysabeau dal Fleurat, in her leather riding britches, boots, and a swordsman's tunic—Ruripathian whisky was more suited to her, but it was expensive and difficult to come by, not something to be found in the Little Palace, where claims of penury were worn like badges of honour.

She looked at her unwanted drinking companion and wondered what about her appearance had said "come and have a drink with me." It certainly wasn't her expression. She'd have thought that said something far, far different.

"Gerard Planchet, at your service," the bespectacled dandy said.

Gerard Plonker, more like, she thought.

"What brings a beauty like you to so dreary a place as the Little Palace?"

If he thinks he's poetic and charming, he ought to get a refund on his rhetoric classes. She flashed him her most radiant smile, the one she reserved for men whose decision-making she needed to relocate below their belt, and did her best not to laugh when she saw his overeager reaction.

"I've not had reason," she said, drawing out her words with a level of delectation that she realised ought to shame her, "to geld a man for irritating me in over a week. I started getting twitchy, so here I am."

Planchet's grin widened, and he made as though he was about to laugh, until her facial expression convinced him she wasn't joking. She brushed back her cloak to reveal the three daggers neatly strapped to her hip.

"I . . . If you'll excuse me, madame, I think I see someone . . ."

She watched him walk away and almost smiled when he cast a furtive look back to make sure she wasn't going after him. She turned her attention back to the spiced wine, and the question of how she was going to get the bloody dragon to eat.

W e're close," Pharadon said.

Gill kept his eyes peeled and looked dead ahead. They hadn't encountered any more Venori and he felt like they were long overdue. Pharadon was certain there were more of them down there, and Gill would prefer to be done with them rather than live with the thought of them lurking in the darkness, ready to attack at any moment. They couldn't be that hungry if they were showing such restraint. . . .

The tunnel opened out into a large cavern. The light from Solène's globe didn't reach as far as any of the walls, imparting an air of uncertainty. How big was this chamber? What lurked in the darkness? Gill reckoned they'd reached their destination.

"The Cups are here," Pharadon said. "They're here."

Gill could sense the relief in his voice, and realised that up until that moment, the old dragon hadn't been sure they'd get this far. Given what they'd seen of the Venori, Gill didn't understand Pharadon's worry. He wasn't ready to start underestimating them yet—he had too many fights under his belt to think he'd seen enough of them to form a worthwhile opinion. Nonetheless, he wasn't quite as terrified of the demonic-looking creatures as he had been on entering the mountain tunnels.

"The Venori?" he asked.

"They're around. I'm not sure where."

"Let's get what we need and get out of here fast, then," Solène said. "I could live quite happily not seeing one of those creatures ever again."

She cast another light, illuminating more of the cavern. Other than their footfalls and breathing, the only sound was of dripping water, falling from the countless glistening stalactites lining the roof. Gill felt a shiver run over his skin as he looked up at them. If one fell, it would spear right through whatever it hit.

The new light fell on an object sitting amongst a cluster of stalagmites. It looked like a chest, but it had slowly been swallowed up by the mountain. Only the top remained visible, its metal bands and latches and wooden frame looking unnaturally fresh considering how long it must have been here. Magic, once again. Was there anything it could not do?

"What happened to the chest?" Gill said, unable to work out how rock might have grasped it as it had.

"The water falling from the roof," Pharadon said. "It's gathered around the chest and is starting to turn it into a stalagmite. We may have to break it free."

Loud hammering was something Gill would have preferred to avoid, though he realised the Venori were attracted by other things. He scanned the cavern as he advanced on the rock-encased chest, but there was no sign of the Venori, nor any trace of them having been there—not that Gill had any idea of what he should be looking for.

"I think it's safe," Gill said, fully aware that Pharadon probably had a better sense for where the Venori were than he did. Still, he was there as the muscle, and he reckoned he should at least maintain the illusion that he was protecting them.

Pharadon moved forward and inspected the chest. His face broke into a smile when he placed his hands on it. Opening the latch, the dragon in human form gave the lid an experimental tug; it opened as though the hinges had been oiled that morning. He let out a sigh of relief.

"They're here," he said. "Intact and unused."

"Gather them up and let's get out of here," Gill said.

"How many are there?" Solène asked, craning to see.

"Three," Pharadon said as he picked them up, one at a time, and deposited them in pouches in his cloak that appeared to form out of nowhere as Pharadon required them.

"Three Cups," Solène said.

Gill didn't like the consternated tone of her voice.

"You'll use one of them on the goldscale," she said. "What will you do with the others?"

Pharadon shrugged. "It doesn't really matter. Once the goldscale is enlightened, the two of us will be able to enlighten any other juveniles we come across. We'll have no need of the Cups. I have no interest in shaping the types of magic the old temple priests created. They're of no use to me. Would you like them?"

"No!" Solène said, her harsh voice echoing around the cavern.

The question had been innocently asked, but the strength of Solène's reaction allowed Gill to piece together her concern. They had fought so hard to stop Amaury from getting his hands on an unused Cup. Now there were more, and who knew what might happen if they fell into the wrong hands.

"No," Solène said again. "No human should have that type of power."

"What they offer is not so great a step beyond where you already are," Pharadon said.

"Might they help us against Amaury?" Gill said.

"Giving anyone else that type of power would be an act of madness," Solène said. "Who would you trust with it?"

The king was Gill's first thought, but he quickly dismissed it. Solène was right. The Cups were too dangerous to let out into the world.

"Can you destroy them?" Solène said.

"I . . . I'm not actually sure," Pharadon said. "I don't know if anyone's ever tried. In any event, I'm not willing to risk any of them until I've brought the goldscale to enlightenment."

"We can't let anyone use those Cups," Solène said.

The tension in the cavern rose instantly. Gill watched Solène carefully. Whatever she did, he would follow, but he wondered if this was where their common cause with Pharadon came to an abrupt end. A lot of unpalatable courses of action flashed through Gill's mind. Pharadon would be tough to take down, unless Gill could get to him before he left his human form.

The silence that followed Solène's declaration seemed to stretch for an eternity. Gill was glad he was already holding his sword—this was the moment he would have drawn it otherwise, and that rarely defused a situation.

"Once the goldscale is enlightened," Pharadon said, "we can try to destroy the other Cups. If we can't, I'll take them far into the mountains, where your kind will never find them."

Solène nodded slowly, and Gill let out the breath he'd been holding, as quietly as he could. The sound of footsteps flooded the cavern. The Venori had decided it was time to make their appearance.

In the open space, Gill was concerned that they might be swamped by the demons, that their incredible speed would make them impossible to hit. At least Solène's issues with killing didn't seem to extend to the Venori. He didn't fancy his chances of fighting them off alone.

The three of them gathered at the chest. It sounded as though the creatures were coming from the passage they'd used to enter the cavern.

"Are there any other ways out of here?" Gill said.

"Plenty," Solène said. "I've no idea where any of them lead, though."

"Looks like we're fighting our way out, then," Gill said. They were surrounded by the pool of light created by Solène's magic, which showed neither the edges of the chamber nor the Venori, though Gill could hear them shuffling around just beyond its periphery. His skin crawled as he thought of them, out there, concealed by the darkness, balancing the danger against their hunger. That they wouldn't *actually* eat him, merely drain him of the vital Fount energy within his body, was no less disconcerting than the idea of having them gnaw on his bones.

"Why aren't they coming at us," Gill said.

"I don't know," Pharadon said. "The Venori are almost as much of a mystery to me as they are to you."

Guttural sounds echoed about the cavern—the demons were talking to one another.

The tension was reaching a breaking point. If something didn't happen soon, Gill would rush into the darkness and let the dice fall where they may.

"Cover your eyes," Solène said.

CHAPTER
36

Gill had fought by Solène's side enough times to not ask, "Why?" He trusted her, and covered his eyes with one hand just as the cavern exploded with light. It would have been silent, were it not for the pained hisses coming from all around him. If there was ever a better invitation to act, Gill hadn't seen it. As soon as the searing light fighting its way between his fingers faded, he charged.

The Venori were stumbling around, startled by the sudden illumination. Though Gill cut two down before they even started to come out of their daze, he didn't get long to congratulate himself on his swift reaction. He could see at least a dozen more, all beginning to regain their senses.

The massive discharge of magical energy had taken its toll on Solène—she was wavering on her feet as she recovered from the strain of the magic she had just shaped. Pharadon rushed to her side. With the dragon in human form, Gill knew that for the next few moments, he was on his own. There was a good chance the fight wouldn't last much longer than that.

He roared at the next group of Venori and rushed at the nearest. It jinked out of the way of his thrust, but Gill kept going, cutting deep into the one that had been behind it. The creature reacted to the touch of Telastrian steel the same way the others had, hissing in agony as its vitality quickly drained away.

One jumped on Gill's back, sending him staggering. He could feel the creature's breath on his neck as he twisted, trying to shake it off. No matter what he did, he couldn't throw it clear. He started to feel tired, as though his heart was struggling to find the energy to beat, and panic flashed through him as he realised what was happening.

He ran backwards with everything he had and slammed into the cavern wall. The Venori hissed, but still it clung tight. It didn't seem to be feeding off him anymore, but the sight of him weighed down with one of their kind was an invitation to others, who rushed toward him.

Again he bashed the one on his back against the cavern wall, while attempting to swing his sword at the two approaching from in front. His movements were restricted by the grasping demon on his back, and the ones in front were being a little more cautious. By now the Venori knew what his blade was made of and that he didn't need to make a killing strike to finish them with it.

Gill slammed the demon on his back against the wall one last time, then pulled the dagger from his belt with his free hand. It wasn't Telastrian steel, so he didn't know if it was a futile gesture. He stabbed at the Venori clinging to him as best he could, while waving his sword menacingly before him. The dagger connected with something fleshy and Gill dug it in as hard as he could.

His hand grew wet with whatever the Venori had for blood; the creature loosened its grip as it sought to get away from his blade. One more bash against the wall and it was off. He spun fast, whipping his sword around, then across the demon's flesh. Its scream of agony was enough to tell Gill that he could return his attention to the other two.

Whether enraged by the death of their comrade or overcome by their hunger, they launched themselves at Gill. The first was easy to deal with—it was moving forward with such speed that Gil cut clean through its midsection. The second was on him then, bowling him over backwards. Morning left Gill's grip with a clatter. He got to his hands and knees and scrabbled about for it in the gloom, finding it just as the creature leaped onto his back. The impact knocked the sword farther from Gill's grasp. He managed to hold on to his dagger, though, so rolled over, pinning the demon beneath him.

The Venori didn't seem to pay the blade any attention—all it was interested in was pulling Gill close enough to feed. It might not have feared regular steel the way it did the Telastrian variety, but Gill could cause plenty of mischief with it. He plunged the blade into the demon's throat up to the hilt, then pulled it sideways, severing all but a chunk of its neck, then hacked through the rest. Relieving the demon of its head seemed to do the job, as the body went slack.

Gill grabbed his sword and jumped to his feet. Solène had a pile of bodies around her now—more than Gill could claim, but he was happy to concede the tally to her, so long as she was recovered from her initial effort, and they got out alive. There were not many left—only two that Gill could make out. It looked like they'd managed to get the upper hand, but it wasn't time to relax just yet.

Gill joined the others, cutting down the last two Venori while their attention was fixed on Pharadon.

"Might be time to make a run for it," Gill said. No sooner had he spoken than the sound of charging feet echoed into the chamber from any number of directions. "Gods alive, how many of these things are there?"

"More than I could ever have imagined," Pharadon said. He drew one of the Cups from his cloak, crouched, and filled it with water from a cave pool. "One day soon, your kind will have to confront them, but for now, you must run."

▲▲▲▲▲▲

Solène felt a chill of fear run through her. She was torn between wanting to ask why, and not wanting to have the answer she already knew confirmed.

"The passage we entered through is clear," Pharadon said, "but there are many coming from deeper in the mountain. Too many. They will catch you, and kill us all." He lifted the Cup to his lips, drained it. He let out the sigh of a thirsty man refreshed, then dropped it to the floor. Reaching into his cloak again, he pulled out the last two Cups and offered them to Solène. "You must promise me two last favours. Enlighten the goldscale."

"I've no idea how," she said. "Why can't you do it?"

"I've done most of it," Pharadon said. "All that remains is for her to drink from the Cup. That is the spark that will light the fire. The goldscale is far enough along the path that she will accept the Cup willingly, but there is one condition."

"What?"

"That it is offered by one of the enlightened."

The colour drained from Solène's face.

"I can't. I don't want it."

"You are so close to enlightenment that this will make almost no difference. It will only free you from the fear of destroying yourself with your own power."

Solène shook her head. "That fear is what lets me know magic will never be the ruin of me."

Pharadon smiled grimly. "Using the Cup will also stop anyone else from obtaining its power."

Solène opened her mouth, but said nothing.

"The Fount has already called to you, Solène," Pharadon said. "It told you at the temple. 'In this place we are one.' You can be one with it, in this life and the after. Have faith in yourself. Enlightenment is meant for you. I beg you. Do this one thing for me. Save the last of my kind from ferity."

Solène swallowed hard. It made sense, and as noble a thought as her fear of magic being a good thing for her was, she knew it was naive. They day would come when she would regret turning down the benefits enlightenment would bring her. If it was as Pharadon said, and she already enjoyed most of the power it offered, why not have the safety benefits it brought also? She reached out and took the Cup, her decision made. "Now?"

"Is there ever a better time? The water is brackish, but it will not do you any harm."

Solène knelt and filled the Cup. She hesitated for barely a moment, then threw the contents down her throat and grimaced. It was salty and bitter, but no more than unpleasant—certainly nothing that would make her ill. She took a breath, wiped her mouth, then stood.

"Is that it? I don't feel any diff—"

The world flashed blue—the world, for she could see it all. More than see it, she could feel it, hear its beating heart as though it were a living thing, as though each living creature was part of one single entity. Everything seemed so simple in that moment. Solène remembered the voice in the temple—or perhaps she was hearing that same voice again now, it was difficult to tell. *In this place we are one.* Everything truly was one at that moment. All the differences and squabbles and rivalries of the world seemed utterly foolish and trivial.

The Fount surged and swirled within her, not like an untamed external force that she needed to tap into, as it had been, but as though it was part of her. Not just subject to her will, it *was* her will. It was like music and the touch of the sun on a warm day combined. It imparted a feeling of joy unlike any she had ever known.

For the first time in her life, Solène no longer felt alone, as the song of all enlightened creatures that had ever existed welcomed her. She couldn't understand them, but the sentiment was clear, like the welcome home by her parents that she dreamed of, but knew she would never have. It was a feeling of belonging. It was a perfect moment, one she wanted to remain in for as long as she could.

But there was darkness there also—darkness that balanced the light—and there was struggle, where the two met. That reminded her of who she was. Where she was. The peril they were all in. The realities of the world beyond that moment of perfection. She closed her eyes. When she opened them again, she was back in the cave, in a space lit only by the magical orbs of cold white light she herself had cast.

When she looked at Pharadon, he gave her a sad smile.

"You've made the right choice. Welcome. Now, take the last Cup and go. Don't look back."

She took the Cup from a hand that was already starting to elongate and become covered with red scales.

"Pharadon, I —" Gill said.

"Help her with the goldscale, Gill. You are one who does the right thing, and this is the right thing."

Gill's mouth opened, but closed again before any words came out. The footfalls were no longer echoes, but distinct sounds. The Venori were close.

"Go!" Pharadon roared, now twice the size of a horse and more dragon than man.

Solène and Gill made for the entrance. She could see the pain on his face, which mirrored that in her heart. Each step away from their comrade tore at her heart.

▲▲▲▲▲▲

The power the Cup had filled Pharadon with allowed his transformation back to dragon form to happen quickly, albeit painfully, with energy left over to shape magic. He didn't plan on using magic, though—his flame glands had gone woefully underused in recent days.

Once he was fully returned to his natural state, he glanced at the passageway leading out of the chamber—far too small for him to fit through now. Gill was standing at the mouth of the corridor, silhouetted by one of Solène's lights. He raised a hand in salute, then was gone.

Pharadon's heart felt heavy for a moment. He had slumbered for so much of his existence, missed so much of the joy of life. It was easy to regret such things when near the end. Oh, but this, *this* would be something that would have been sung about by his kind—a noble battle, a good fight, facing a great malevolence as the best of his kind had. There would be none to sing songs of what he did here, but he knew he would fly the Fount's breezes with his ancestors forever more, proud of the way he had lived his life. Prouder still of the way it had ended. His life, his deeds, would join the song.

He greeted the first of the Venori with a jet of searing flame that he knew would leave nothing but ash. Solène's light was fading rapidly; Pharadon's flame lit the chamber once more, this time bright red. The Venori charged, driven by the madness of their hunger and the succulence of the Fount that coursed through Pharadon's body. They hissed and screamed, but the sounds were drowned out by the thunder of his flame. The temperature in the cavern rose like a welcoming embrace. It was no longer an empty, dead place. It was his.

The next group to rush forward received the same treatment, but they were followed by more, crawling out of the darkness like rats. Soon the cavern was full with them, and Pharadon knew there was only so much fire he could create. But it was ever going to be this way.

The newly arrived Venori did not attack. Their numbers swelled until Pharadon realised that they were waiting until their forces were large enough to swarm and overcome him in a single attack. If he was being given a respite, Pharadon did not intend to waste it. He concentrated the Fount into refilling his flame glands to the bursting point.

At last they surged toward him, howling with savage hunger. Pharadon tried to smile, but couldn't in dragon form. How quickly he had become accustomed to being human. He lifted his right claw and plunged a talon into his throat, piercing both flame glands and allowing the entirety of their contents to mix in an instant. The cavern flashed bright as the energy exploded with tremendous ferocity, destroying all before it.

Now we are one.

Gill and Solène didn't stop running until they reached the mountain ledge. An incredible jet of hot air swept up the passage as they neared the exit. Gill felt the sickening realisation that it marked the moment of Pharadon's passing. It was difficult to comprehend the idea that a dragon—the creature of childhood nightmares—had saved his life.

Outside the cavern, they fought to catch their breath. At last Gill drew in enough air to speak.

"Are you all right?" he asked.

"Fine," Solène said, between laboured gasps.

It took him a moment to recall that she had drunk from the Cup, that she was now enlightened. He still wasn't entirely clear on what that meant, though he found himself hoping it might provide a solution to their most pressing problem. Pharadon had flown them to that distant mountain ledge. Not only was there no obvious way down, they were a very long way from civilisation. He didn't fancy their chances if they had to climb down and walk back to Mirabay.

"Do you think he managed to kill them all?" Gill said.

Solène smiled grimly and shook her head. "Most, but not all. Now that I know what to look for, I can sense them. There are more elsewhere, reawakening."

"Wonderful," Gill said. "We probably shouldn't stay here any longer. Is there anything you can . . . *do* about getting us out of here?"

"No," Solène said. "Wait. I. Oh . . . I think I can." She straightened and took a long, deep breath. "Take my hand."

Gill did as she asked. A gust of cold mountain air blasted him in the face and he closed his eyes against it. There were no mountains to be seen when he opened his eyes again. He and Solène stood on open grassland; the breeze was light and the day far warmer than it had been moments ago.

"Oh," Gill said, wobbling on his feet. "Wow, that feels very odd. Ooooh." The closest he could come to describing the feeling was that it was akin to the one he had after his third bottle of wine. The end result was the same. He threw up on the grass at his feet.

He felt a comforting hand on his back as he retched out the last of the nausea.

"Are you all right?" Solène asked.

"Ugh, yes. I think so."

"I'm sorry," she said. "I should have given you more warning."

"I doubt it would have made much of a difference," Gill said, standing up and drawing in a laboured breath.

"Probably not."

"When did you learn how to do that?" Gill said.

"I didn't. Not exactly. It's all part of being enlightened. When I want to do something, I know how to do it. It's strange. Overwhelming."

"Does that mean Amaury can do the same?"

"Maybe. Maybe not. Pharadon said something to me back in the temple, that many creatures can be enlightened, but not everyone is capable of *being* enlightened."

"What does that mean?"

"I'm not sure," she said. "But when I drank from the Cup, it felt as though I was being *welcomed* to something. Maybe that's it?"

"So there's hope?" Gill said.

Solène laughed. "There's always hope."

He did his best to smile, but he wasn't as confident as she was. If Amaury could do half what Solène could do, Gill didn't fancy their chances of beating him. With sword in hand and nothing else, Gill knew he would always best his old friend, but with magic added to the mix, what hope had he? An honourable death seemed like an empty promise.

Solène stared at the remaining Cup, which she held before her in the palm of her hand. "We can't tell anyone about this," she said. "They'll just want to take it for themselves."

"You're going to enlighten the goldscale?"

She nodded. "I promised. I'm going to see it through. One way or the other. Leaving so great a creature locked in a cage, never able to realise the potential of what it might have been. It's too horrible a thought."

Gill smiled as comfortingly as he could. "It's about as dangerous a task as you could take on."

She shrugged. "The right things are never the easy ones. What about you? What will you do now?"

"Report to the king, I suppose. After that, I'll help you however I can."

"I suppose I'd better come with you to the king, to back up your story!"

"I'd appreciate that," Gill said, not quite ready to see her march off alone to what could well be her death. He took a breath. "Do we have to do the *thing* again?"

Solène pointed behind him. He turned to see Castandres a short distance away.

"Ah," he said. "Impressive. Shall we?"

▲▲▲▲▲▲

Gill and Solène were challenged by sentries at the pickets, but were quickly identified and allowed through. The atmosphere about the town had changed dramatically in the time they'd been away. Gill wasn't sure exactly how long that was, considering that he'd spent a chunk of his absence in the bowels of a mountain with no sense of time on the outside, and had travelled a distance that would have taken days if not weeks, in the blink of an eye. Had that been instantaneous, or did even magic have to pay heed to the running sands of the hourglass? He suspected they'd been gone for only a day, but there was no way to be sure.

As word of their arrival spread, a runner appeared, demanding their attendance on the king at once. They hurried toward the inn, where his headquarters were still housed. On the way, Gill took note of the sense of purpose that prevailed throughout the village, as men prepared for their next move, which would undoubtedly be advancing on the city. Gone was the sense of uncertainty and disunity that had filled the camp when he had first arrived. It was encouraging. An army won and lost on morale, which existed now, and was infectious. Perhaps Solène was right—perhaps there was hope.

"General Villerauvais," the king said when they entered the tap-room. His voice sounded stronger than it had the last time Gill had heard it. The tone was also far more authoritative. Boudain was blooded now, and clearly liked the taste. He stood, surrounded by his officers and nobles, at the head of a large table that was covered with maps and lists.

"I, uh, yes, your Highness?" Gill wasn't sure when his promotion had come through, but he could think of worse things to happen. Or could he? he wondered.

"I'm glad to see you back safe and sound. You were successful in your endeavours?"

"We were, but I'm afraid I bring news that might not be best received."

"Go on."

"It seems that dragons aren't the only ancient creatures of magic that have awoken recently. We encountered humanlike beings called 'Venori.'"

"What are they? Will they cause us trouble?"

"Not immediately, your Highness," Solène said, "but they will come out of hiding in the near future and will need to be dealt with. As to what they are . . . I believe them to be the creatures that gave rise to our myths of demons."

Boudain barked out a laugh and looked at Gill, but cut his mirth short when he saw the expression on Gill's face.

"Demons?"

Gill nodded.

Boudain took a deep breath and paced toward a window, where he stopped, arms akimbo. "I wonder if any of my forebears have been so vexed." He chewed on his lip for a moment. "They are not an immediate threat, you say?"

"I don't believe so," Solène said. "But they will come, perhaps in only a matter of months, and when they do, we must be ready."

"Well, then," Boudain said, "right now, they're a problem for another day. When we take my throne back, you can tell me all about these Venori. Until then, I've a dragon of my own I wish to see slain, and we've been busy during your absence."

Gill frowned before getting the reference, and wondering again how long they'd been away.

"Over the past day, troops have arrived to bolster our forces, and reports have been received from spies and scouts," Boudain said. "Amaury has recruited a force of mercenaries who are marching up from Estranza. I'm given to understand that it is comprised of several companies and is a significant body of men. I'd hoped we might be able to move and take the city before they arrive, but I'm informed this is overly ambitious. As such, we need to stop this force from being added to Amaury's army.

"We have two options, as I see it. We can meet them on the field and destroy them before they link with Amaury's force, or we can pay them to turn around and go home."

"I must counsel against that, your Highness," the Count of Savin said. "It sets a terrible precedent. Every rogue band of mercenaries short of work will march into Mirabaya, expecting to be paid off. We must send them packing by force of arms."

Boudain tugged at his beard. "What do you think, Villerauvais?"

"I think that every soldier we lose fighting off the mercenaries is one less we'll have to fight Amaury. There's no reason to think mercenaries will see Mirabaya as an easy touch after this crisis is dealt with."

Savin let out a dismissive breath, and his smugness was mirrored by several of the other nobles surrounding the table. It was interesting how hungry they all were for another fight, having witnessed their first from the safety of the village church's belfry.

"You both have a point," Boudain said. "And I'm loath to put Mirabaya's sons at risk any more than is absolutely necessary. The funds so kindly bequeathed by my recently departed cousins are necessary to pay and feed my troops until I can gain access to the royal treasury again. Either way, I risk losing men, either to the sword or to desertion."

Only one involves them dying, Gill thought, but realised that the king would see it as much the same—a deserter forfeited his life in shame. A dead soldier gave his for glory. The latter really didn't seem to offer much more than the first to one so jaded by war as Gill. Still, that wasn't the way kings thought, and it wasn't the way they wanted their men to think.

"We ride to intercept the mercenaries," Boudain said. "Prepare the men to march."

There were the usual utterances of bravado as the officers filed out to pass the order on to their men. Gill made to leave, but the king caught his eye and gave a curt shake of his head. They waited until everyone else had left.

"I want you and Solène to ride ahead of the army and carry an offer to the mercenary commanders."

"Highness?" Gill said, frowning.

"I'm not a man to close the door on options. I can buy this enemy, I can't buy my next one, so I'll preserve the resources I have to deal with that for as long as I can."

Gill nodded, not sure whether to be impressed by the tactic or offended at the king viewing his soldiers—Gill included—as resources.

"I'll prepare the necessary paperwork for you to pay the mercenaries, and have it ready for you before the army marches. Solène can do whatever it is she does to speed you on your way under concealment."

"You're not sending coin?"

Boudain laughed. "Of course not. Once they have my coin, what's to stop them continuing their march north to take Amaury's? No. They'll be offered bonds under the royal seal that can be redeemed once Amaury has been put in the ground."

Gill could see the logic behind what the young king suggested, but likewise the glaring flaw, at least for the man negotiating the deal.

"That's all well in principle, Highness, but, with respect, why would they take the offer of a king who's not on his throne?"

"Greed, Villerauvais. Greed. I'm going to offer them a ridiculous amount of money. An amount that makes my bladder weak to think about, but I'm getting my throne back, and I'll do whatever it takes. My family have sat on the white throne for nearly a thousand years. I'll be damned before I lose it to that bastard. The offer will be too rich. Any mercenary captain who turns it down will be killed by his men before he can bark another order at them. I'll have the papers ready for you shortly."

Gill took a moment to reflect. He had forgotten what it meant to be a servant of the Crown, after so many years hiding in Villerauvais. Once you were sucked back in, there was no more refusing, no choosing what you did or didn't do. You were never asked if it was a convenient time, if your wife and child had just died. You were simply expected to do what was demanded of you. Here he was, jumping to attention every time, once again.

He took a deep breath to quell his anger, and saw Solène standing at the bar eating some broth. She too had made a promise, but not to Boudain the Tenth. She owed loyalty to no one, only to her word.

"Solène has other business to attend to," Gill said. "Our debt to Pharadon is not yet repaid, and only she can settle it."

The king looked at Gill for a moment, then nodded slowly. "I won't ever have it be said I don't repay debts, or leave a friend wanting when they are in need of my help. She has my permission, and blessing, to go."

Gill smiled thinly. He knew Solène was going to fulfill her promise to Pharadon whether the king permitted it or not, and there wasn't a damn thing Boudain could do to stop her.

"I'll let her know she has your leave, Highness," Gill said.

Gill joined Solène and gave her a sad smile. He wasn't going to be able to fulfill his obligation to her and Pharadon, and the only consoling thought was the fact that in reality, he could give her little assistance beyond moral support.

"I'm sorry, Solène," he said. "I'm not going to be able to go with you to enlighten the goldscale."

"The king has need of you?"

Gill nodded. "I should have said no."

"Could you have?" she asked, as if she already knew the answer.

He shook his head. "No, I don't think so. That's not how it works." He chewed his lip for a moment. "He wants you to help me, but I told him you couldn't. Your word to Pharadon is more important."

"I'm glad you feel that way, but I don't like leaving you if I can help."

Gill laughed. "I'm able to look after myself, and for what it's worth, I feel bad that I'm not going along to help *you*."

She smiled. "I can look after myself too."

"Do you think you can enlighten her?" he said.

"I don't see why not. I've plenty of tricks up my sleeve. Literally. But there's only one way to find out." The mirth left her eyes. "What about you? Can you do all of this, I mean. Defeat Amaury? Restore the king?"

"Like you say, only one way to find out."

"I suppose I'll see you at the other end of it all," she said.

Gill did his best to smile. "I suppose so."

While keeping ahead of a marching army was not terribly challenging, Gill had a long ride ahead of him and no support on the way. All things considered, he wasn't sure what type of greeting he would get at the royal way stations on the road. He wasn't even sure if staying on the road was a particularly good idea. You never knew where you'd bump into enemy forces, and that was a complication Gill was eager to avoid.

What he was going to say to the mercenaries when he reached them was another matter. The promise of payment from a king who might be dead in a matter of days didn't seem like a particularly attractive offer, and it was the type of message that could get the bearer killed. He didn't think his chances of success were particularly high, but with the king and his army already on the march, Gill didn't have much time to find a way to make it work before battle was joined. A lot of men would die if he didn't pull this off, and he couldn't help but resent the responsibility the king had placed on him.

He galloped for as long as his horse would allow it, making good time across the open farmland. Castandres and the army were long out of sight by the time Gill's horse slowed. The air was crisp and clear that evening. As he rode, Guillot noticed for the first time that the country had taken on the air of a land at war. The fields were empty and bore a look of neglect. Farmers tended not to bother when they were afraid of being robbed or killed, either right away or when the postbellum hardships came and people wanted to steal their crops. If you had nothing to steal, then there was a better chance you'd be left alone.

Gill couldn't deny the sense of importance being abroad on the king's business brought, even after so long, and so much disappointment in life. He had gone a long way, only to end up back in exactly the same place. He consoled himself with the thought that there was a higher purpose to his service this time. Amaury was a bastard, and people would suffer if he wasn't stopped. And perhaps, just perhaps, the young Boudain might have the makings of a good king. One way or the other, he had a job to do. He continued on, and turned his thoughts instead to what he would say to the mercenary captain to convince him to agree to the king's terms.

▲▲▲▲▲▲

Preparing to travel to Mirabay, Solène realised she was afraid. At first she thought it was because she was heading toward a city of enemies, any number of whom would try to kill her given the chance, whether that be the Prince Bishop—or Regent, as he now was—the Intelligenciers, or the thousands of people who were terrified at the prospect of sorcerers returning.

Then she thought it might be that she had no idea what she was to do once she reached the city. She did not know where the goldscale was, how she would get to it, or what she would do when she did.

Deep down, she knew neither of those thoughts were truly the source of her fear. No, the reason she was so scared, why she thought she might be sick, was that she was heading into a city filled with enemies who would want to kill her, that she had a task she had no idea how to complete, and that none of that bothered her in the least.

She was not being overconfident, she simply knew that there was no challenge she could not best. Solène was a born worrier—it was a consequence of living with a secret that others feared, that could get you killed. She knew this was the trait that had kept her alive for so long.

That feeling was gone. She couldn't think of a single thing that worried her. The irony was, that was the fact that was causing her concern.

Had she become so powerful that she truly could do whatever she chose? No one should have that much unfettered power. Least of all her. What would she do with it? Build an empire, as Amatus had after enlightenment? She supposed there was something in the fact that he had never claimed the title of emperor, but she did wonder if that was due to his self-control or if he had merely lost interest in temporal matters.

She thought of the moment where Gill had presented her with the problem of how they were going to get off the mountain without Pharadon. As soon as she had applied her mind to the question, she had the answer. It wasn't something she had known how to do before. It wasn't even something she had thought was possible before, but she immediately had known how to transport them from that lonely, windswept ledge back to Castandres.

Was that what enlightenment would mean for her? Always having a solution to every problem? It felt that way, and as comforting as that seemed, she could take no ease from it. She wished there had been more time to talk with Pharadon about enlightenment; without him, there was no one who could explain it to her. Even Amatus had not had to deal with that.

She wondered if she should borrow a horse and ride to Mirabay, rather than use the magical option she had immediately considered. Surely it was right to question the power she now had. If it became too familiar a thing, if using it became too commonplace for her, where might that lead her? Pharadon had told her to trust herself. She wanted to take comfort in that, to believe that she would never arrive at a place where she used magic so thoughtlessly it could cause harm to others, but she struggled.

Her mind flicked to a day not long ago, on a road not dissimilar to the one she was now looking at. Could she really still consider herself a good person after that? There had to have been a better way than to kill those people. Surely she could have disabled them, if only she'd taken a moment to think it through.

She'd killed that day. What was to stop her from doing it again? What was to stop her when killing was as easy as lighting a room, healing a child, transporting herself across half the country, or raining fire and hell down upon an entire city? She shuddered. She knew she was overreacting, but the thought of turning into someone like the Prince Bishop horrified her. She'd seen the look in his eyes when he spoke of the Cup or the temple; she'd seen how he used the power he'd already had. She had seen others like him, albeit on a smaller scale. A person had that avarice in them by the time they were full grown. Some were born with it, some learned it on the way up, but, she worried, might something like becoming enlightened give it to someone who hadn't had it before?

Solène was enlightened now and had full control over the chaotic power that had always resided within her. Fear of what that power—that curse—could do, both to others and to herself, had always made her be so careful with it. Now that fear was lifted. She no longer had to worry about what she *might* do. Instead, she had to think about what she *could* do. It was even more frightening a prospect.

She swore aloud—this would only change her if she allowed it to. She was no more likely to rain fire and hell down on a city now than she would have been when she was a teenage girl. Indeed, she was less likely now; if she chose for it not to happen, it would not. Before, she could never be sure what would happen—an errant thought could cause her magic to do things she had never intended. Now that she was enlightened, that could not happen. Her magic would obey her exactly.

She chewed on her lip a moment, stared toward the horizon, and decided it was time to believe in herself. Long past time. She enjoyed the tranquillity of her surroundings a moment longer: she was standing in a field near a stand of trees, just far enough from the village not to be bothered by the ruckus of an army preparing to march. She closed her eyes, and when she opened them, she stood in Mirabay, on a cobbled street, surrounded by the heaving vibrancy of the home of tens of thousands of people.

Your Grace, a protest started this morning," Amaury's secretary said. "It's grown larger throughout the day. It's not safe to take the carriage out. The captain of the Royal Guard has suggested you take a wherry from the palace dock if you insist on going out into the city."

"This is getting beyond a joke," Amaury said. The city had never been run so well, yet the people protested. Every day, street cleaners, teachers, traders, and the countless other people who were the cogs of the great machine that was Mirabay gathered in places around the city, in protest. Yet the streets were clear of rubbish, there was food in the marketplaces and clean water to be had from the fountains. Could they not see what a wonder that was? His temper flared. All these distractions were keeping him from learning more about his power, and how to properly use it. He had achieved the goal of so many years, but had not the time to explore it.

"I'll address them directly," he said. "It is long beyond time that I did."

"Now?" the secretary said.

"Seeing as I already have an audience gathered," Amaury said.

"I . . . Are . . ." His secretary saw the expression on the Prince Bishop's face. "I'll inform the captain of the Guard and have everything prepared."

Amaury nodded, then waited for his secretary to leave before allowing himself a sigh. Why could people not realise when they had a good thing? He stood and went to the mirror concealed behind a cabinet door. If he was going to appear before the people, he needed to make sure he looked the part of Regent. The comfortable britches, shirt, and tunic he was wearing might be fine for sitting in his office dealing with underlings, but for presenting himself to the people, more of a statement was needed.

The usual place for the monarch to address their citizens was a palace balcony that looked out over a natural amphitheatre formed by the sheer side of the hill the building sat on. The square beneath had become a traditional location to congregate and protest, somewhere Amaury had often thought would be wisely built on to prevent this. He supposed the people would always find somewhere to gather and protest. At least here, he could easily address them, and do so in complete safety.

He allowed himself a smile, knowing that he had no need of a natural amphitheatre to make himself heard. His voice would carry across the sea now, should he choose it. Still, the balcony was where people were accustomed to seeing their king, so that was where they would see Amaury.

Sitting down again, he waited for his secretary to return to escort him to the balcony, while mulling over what he was going to say. Of course, announcing the opening of the dragon menagerie to the public would be part of it, but that was only an appetiser.

Telling the people they were a bunch of ingrates who couldn't tell a gift from a kick to their delicate parts didn't strike him as the best approach, no matter how true that was. Also unwise, he thought, would be revealing how precarious the city's food supply was, or that magic was instrumental in keeping people from starving by preventing their stores from spoiling.

How, then, would he win over the hearts and minds of so many enraged people? The answer was obvious, of course. It was time to stop pussyfooting around the great power he had won for himself and start actually using it. He had no intention of continually wasting it to keep the populace in line, but a nudge toward his way of thinking, simply to get the ball rolling, seemed reasonable.

He wasn't altogether comfortable with the idea. He had no desire to do to the city's residents what he had done to the king. People incapable of working were useless to him and to the kingdom. How to avoid that when he was so much more powerful now? Or was he? He *felt* like he was, but until he actually did anything with his power, he couldn't be sure. The academics were still translating the rubbings they'd taken at the temple, and despite their daily updates, they'd yet to turn up anything of use. Amaury was beginning to give up hope. If the enlightened had taught their initiates how to use their new gifts, it seemed they hadn't carved those lessons into the walls of their temple.

He needed a test subject, someone whose opinion was contrary to his own and who was unimportant enough to not be missed if Amaury destroyed their mind. The problem was, he'd been very effective in making people who disagreed with him disappear in recent weeks. *Still,* he thought, *I might be in luck.* He scribbled a note and rang the bell on his desk. Then, remembering his secretary was preparing for his speech, Amaury left his office and grabbed the first servant he could find.

"Renaud and Canet," Amaury said. "I believe they are still in the palace dungeons. Have one of them fetched up to my office as quick as you can."

"Of course, Lord Protector." The servant blanched. "I'm sorry, Lord Protector. Who?"

"Renaud, the former chancellor. Canet, the former captain of the City Watch. They should still be in the cells below the palace. Take this release order. I only need one of them. I don't care which." He paused. "The one who stinks the least. Perhaps give them a quick rinse and some clean clothing. I don't want them leaving a stench in my office. Be quick."

"Yes, Lord Protector."

The servant headed off, clutching the release order, and Amaury found himself in the odd position of hoping at least one of his two former adversaries was still alive. Back in his office, he started to prepare. Desire was the spark and focus was the fuel—dal Drezony had explained it to him a hundred times. Easily done when the worst consequence was a pop and a flash of light, but maintaining that singularity of thought when you knew an errant idea could bring the building down around you made it significantly more challenging.

Still, the only way to learn how to ride was to get up on the horse in the first place, and Amaury had been creating uninspiring lights for several years. The unintended—although ultimately welcome—consequence of his magical assault on the king was an anomaly. A mistake made did not necessarily mean it would be repeated.

Before long there was a knock on the door, and a damp, but still filthy and bedraggled, Renaud was pushed in by two palace guards.

"Renaud, you're looking remarkably well, all things considered," Amaury said.

"I hope you burn in each of the three hells," Renaud said.

"Good to see you too. Please, sit."

The guards shoved Renaud into a chair.

"You may leave us, thank you," Amaury said. Knowing better than to question him, they did as they were told.

"Why did you bring me here, Amaury?"

"I want you to sign a document stating that you wholeheartedly support my appointment as Protector of the Realm."

"I'd rather walk back to the dungeon and heat up the torturer's irons myself," Renaud said. "Even if I sign it, I'll be back in a cage before nightfall."

"Brave talk," Amaury said. He wanted Renaud to be as opposed to him as he possibly could. He didn't want the man to entertain even the slightest hope that he might be able to strike a bargain. "And you are right. You will die in that cage, Renaud, and you will most certainly be back there long before nightfall, no matter what happens next, but let me put it another way.

"You wholeheartedly support my appointment as Protector of the Realm. You *want* to sign a document saying as much." Renaud's face twitched, once, then again. Amaury concentrated on his desire to the exclusion of all else. He changed the thought slightly, refined it, focussed it.

"I . . . I was delighted to hear of your appointment as Protector of the Realm," Renaud said. "I'd be honoured to make my sentiments public."

"Ha!" Amaury said, sitting back in his chair and throwing his hands up in delight. He had it now. "Perfect, and I appreciate the gesture, Renaud, but it really isn't necessary." He rang the bell on his desk. The guards entered. "Take Renaud back to the cells. I won't be needing him again."

They took the prisoner by the arms and led him out again; there was a bewildered expression on his face. Amaury watched them go, considering what he had just done. It appeared he achieved the desired effect—but not by framing it as a conscious want. Instead, he'd had to develop the thought into a more visceral desire. That seemed to run contrary to what dal Drezony had believed. Still, what had she known? She was a little more skilled at creating magical lights than anyone else, but that was about it. There was so much more to magic than she had been able to comprehend, and it was now all at his fingertips.

He took a deep breath and drummed his fingers on his desk. He didn't want to get ahead of himself. He had convinced one man who hated him. That was a long way from convincing thousands of people at one go. Or was it? His words and thoughts had addressed Renaud. From the balcony, his words and thoughts would address a mass of people. One target in both cases, after a fashion. The power he needed was all there. He could feel it. But to allow so much to course through him? The thought sent a shiver across his skin.

CHAPTER
40

It didn't take Solène long to find out where the dragon was being kept. A few topics dominated Mirabay's conversations, and the great golden dragon, being readied for public display, was one of them. Despite the anger and tension that filled the city, people talked about it excitedly—who wouldn't want to see a living, breathing creature that up until a few months previously had been a thing of legend?

From a vantage point across the street, Solène surveyed the building—an old, open-air duelling amphitheatre that despite extensive and obvious recent work still showed signs of having been neglected for many years. Looking at the lattice, ironwork dome, she wondered how they hoped to keep the creature contained by such means. Reaching to the Fount was now as natural an act as drawing a breath; the Telastrian steel welded into the bands appeared benignly, strips of darkness outlined by the glowing blue energy of the Fount. *Clever,* she thought. She suspected some of her former brothers and sisters from the Order must have been responsible for that. She couldn't imagine the labourers had come up with it by themselves.

They presented a problem—the labourers. Solène could see a number of them moving about and was confident there were even more she couldn't. That she would have to wait until darkness was a given. Even with magical help, she wouldn't be able to do what was needed with watchers nearby. Once the alarm was raised, all hell would break loose, and that might mean the dragon not getting away. Solène had no idea how long it would take the goldscale to adapt to enlightenment—would it happen instantly, as it had with her, or would it take longer because the dragon was coming from a baser state? She needed to make sure time was available if necessary.

Solène had decided to try to find somewhere to wait until dark when people around her began to chatter excitedly, as if sharing important news. She couldn't quite make out what was being said, so she went in search of one of the city's many criers. When she found one, he was repeating the same message over and over—the Lord Protector of Mirabay would be making an announcement to the people that afternoon.

The sun was already high overhead and people were starting to head toward the palace. Returning to the old amphitheatre, Solène saw that the labourers had stopped work and were talking to each other. A moment later, they set down their tools and disappeared from sight. She smiled when she saw them filing out of the entrance. It looked like she was getting the opportunity she needed.

She waited until the men had disappeared, and then, ever cautious, Solène draped herself in a magical shroud that made her almost impossible to see. She crossed the street and entered where the workmen had departed. A dark tunnel ended in steps that led up to light beyond. Two armed men stood at the opening, silhouetted by the light, but as soon as she spotted them, they crumpled to the ground in a slumber from which they would not wake for hours. Solène's eyes widened—she had put them to sleep almost without thinking—her desire had become reality as soon as it had entered her head. As satisfying as that was, it was proof that she had to be more careful with her thoughts than ever before.

She hurried into the amphitheatre proper, with its circular stone tiers of seating rising up and out like ripples on a pond. Nearly completed timber scaffolds supported a viewing platform around the top of the amphitheatre. The arena's floor was covered with the domed cage that Solène had seen from outside. Contained within was the goldscale. Solène's heart sank when she saw her. The vibrant, healthy-looking creature she had seen at the temple was now a shadow of its former self. It was curled up and mournful. Its flesh was stretched tight over its bones, and Solène could make out the shape of its ribs beneath its gleaming scales. It was a tragic thing to see, and she was terrified that she had come too late.

Solène checked the amphitheatre over again to make sure she was alone—it looked as though the two sleeping guards were the only ones who had remained behind. She wondered what the Prince Bishop planned to say, but her curiosity could wait. With luck, he would be gone soon and whatever he said would be rendered irrelevant.

Her first obstacle was getting to the goldscale. She walked around the cage's perimeter until she found a small, human-sized gate. Though the gate was locked, Solène didn't even have to touch a finger to it to open it. The recently greased hinges turned without a sound, and Solène was inside. She wasn't sure how the goldscale would react to her being so close—it was still a base creature, and Solène very much doubted it had received good treatment from other humans.

She approached slowly, not sure if it was asleep or awake. An untouched, fresh-looking carcass sat on the sandy ground beside it. If the dragon woke hungry, hopefully it would choose that, rather than Solène. The dragon's eyes opened lazily, first a thick gold outer eyelid, followed by a wet, gossamer-like inner lid that hinted at the brilliance of what was beneath. When it too opened, Solène's breath was taken by the magnificence of the two gleaming azure orbs.

"I'm a friend," Solène said, not knowing if the creature understood her, or even heard her. "I'm here to help you."

It continued to stare at her with its intoxicating blue eyes, but didn't move.

"Your friend sent me to help you," Solène said. "Pharadon, the red dragon. He said you are ready to be enlightened, so I brought you this to drink from." She took the Cup and a small leather flask from a pocket in her cloak, and held them out to show the goldscale. It did not react.

Solène filled the Cup with water from the flask and proffered it to the goldscale. No response.

"You have to drink from it," she said.

It gave no sign that it heard her.

Even with its mouth closed, Solène could see some of the dragon's fangs, and had no desire to get too close. It seemed she had no alternative, however. She gritted her teeth and got down on her hunkers, then shuffled forward in as unthreatening a way as she could. The last thing she wanted was to get eaten by the dragon she was trying to help.

"You must drink this," Solène said. "It will help you." She extended the Cup, doing her best to keep her hand from shaking and spilling every drop before it reached its intended destination. Where the dragon's mouth opened slightly—where those fierce-looking teeth could be seen—she did her best to pour the water in. Some splashed against her face and dripped to the ground, but Solène reckoned enough got to where it needed to go.

The Cup empty, Solène dropped onto her backside, drew her knees up to her chin, and looked at the dragon. It appeared no different. *What do I do now?*

After what seemed an age, the dragon's inner eyelids slid down, then up again. Solène thought she might be imagining it, but something about them seemed different—the vibrant blue seemed sharper, more defined.

"So weak," the dragon said, its voice rasping and sibilant.

"It worked," Solène said, allowing herself a laugh. "I'm Solène. What can I do to help you?"

"Gold."

Solène frowned. "I don't understand."

"Gold," the dragon said again, its tone strained and airy.

Wracking her brain, Solène remembered Pharadon asking for gold at the temple before placing a coin under the dragon's head. She hadn't asked why, but it was obviously important. She pulled her purse from her belt and whisked through it with her index finger, praying that she would spot the glimmer of gold. She let out a breath of relief when she did, and fished the coin out.

As gently as she could, she pushed the coin in under the dragon's jaw, then sat back to wonder what it did.

"Has that helped?" she said. She allowed herself to see the Fount, and instantly understood. Just as Telastrian steel seemed to soak up, store, and discharge the Fount's energy, gold similarly seemed to serve as a conduit for the magical energy. Ambient energy—a beautiful swirling blue glow—drifted toward the coin, then was sucked into it and channelled into the goldscale. For a moment she watched the process in fascination, until she realised the dragon had spoken again.

"I'm sorry?" Solène said.

"Ashanya," the dragon said. "I am Ashanya."

Solène let out a laugh of joy. "I'm Solène," she said, once again.

"Thank you for helping me." The dragon's voice was still weak and thin, but she seemed a little less lethargic now. "Where is the redscale?"

Solène smiled sadly. "I'm sorry, Ashanya. He's gone. He asked me to come and help you. We need to get out of this place as soon as you're ready. As soon as we can."

Ashanya lifted her head, then tried to stand but lurched to one side. Solène could see the strain on the dragon's face as she forced her weakened limbs to obey her, but eventually the goldscale stood on all fours, wavering gently as she struggled to maintain her balance.

"You should eat before we go," Solène said. "We have a long journey ahead. You'll need your strength."

Ashanya nodded, and lowered her head to sniff at the carcass. "Step away," she said.

Solène did as she was asked, and Ashanya let out a narrow jet of intense flame. The air filled with the smell of cooking meat, reminding Solène that it had been some time since she'd had a decent meal herself. While Ashanya ate, Solène turned her attention to the cage. With the reinforcement of Telastrian steel, there wasn't much she could do to it magically. Any Fount energy she directed at it by way of magical craft would be absorbed and dispersed. Short of taking conventional cutting tools to it, she couldn't think of a way through, and there certainly was not the time for that.

She looked around for any sign of weakness, but the work all looked solid, each crossing of the cage's bands being both riveted and welded. She turned back to Ashanya, who was finishing her meal.

"Can you break through this?"

Ashanya looked up at the cage, still chewing, then back at Solène, and shook her head. Solène scratched her chin for a moment, then smiled. Ashanya was enlightened now. Just like Pharadon, she could take on human form. An alarming thought popped into her head. If enlightened dragons could take on human form, did that mean *she* could . . . ? Solène shook the idea from her head—there wasn't time to think on it now.

"You have to change form into a human, Ashanya," Solène said. "Then we can walk out of here."

Ashanya frowned, her face remarkably expressive. "I don't know how."

"You're enlightened. A few moments ago, you didn't know how to speak, but now you can, because you've been listening to humans, and learning, even if you didn't know it. You've seen many of us, you know what we look like." She grimaced, remembering how Ashanya was forced to defend herself in the temple. "You know what we are, inside and out. You can shape the magic to make it happen now that you're enlightened. You just have to desire it."

Ashanya nodded, and her eyes narrowed in concentration. For a moment, nothing happened. Then her body started to change. It wasn't an enjoyable thing to watch—indeed, in that moment, Solène was glad that her stomach was empty—but the process didn't take long. In only a matter of seconds, a raven-haired woman with dark eyes and full lips stood before Solène. There was something familiar about her, but Solène couldn't put her finger on why. She was thankful that Ashanya had also managed to create clothes.

"This way," she said. "Quickly." She led Ashanya through the gate, past the unconscious guards, and into the tunnel that led back out to the street. Just as they reached the exit, two armoured men stepped across the threshold. One of them fixed his stare on Solène.

"Who are you? What are you doing here?"

Solène swore silently—it must have been time for the next shift of guards to take over. The men were still standing out on the street— visible to passers-by. If she knocked them out, people would see and the alarm would be raised. If she and the dragon had been only seconds quicker, they'd have been free and clear.

Then Ashanya stepped forward and the guards did a double take.

"I'm sorry, my Lady," one of them said. "I didn't see you there."

"Get back to work!" she barked.

Ashanya's voice sounded completely different, but Solène did her best not to show her surprise.

"Of course, my Lady. Sorry, my Lady." They both shuffled past and continued down the corridor.

"We need to get out of here," Solène said. "Fast. They're about to find the other guards."

Ashanya nodded and both women started to run.

CHAPTER
41

*A*t least I'm a big draw, Amaury thought, as he stepped out onto the balcony. There were people as far as he could see, filling the square beneath the balcony and funnelling into the streets beyond. He couldn't begin to speculate how many were present. *Better make this good,* he thought. From the balcony, he had a magnificent view over the top of the city, one he rarely bothered to appreciate. Now that it was his, he viewed it with considerably more affection and a sense of almost paternal pride.

Mirabay was a beautiful city, with the river flowing lazily through its centre; before him, the cathedral stood imperiously on the Isle, and beyond it, on the left bank, the spires of the university rose above the rooftops. The parapets and imposing towers of the city walls stood, foreboding, defiant, a statement that the city would stand for ages and never be taken by force. Mirabay was the finest city in the world, and it was Amaury's job to make sure everyone knew that.

Ysabeau had arrived at the palace a short time earlier to report that the menagerie was ready to be opened to the public. He intended to play up this good news in his announcement. He had captured the dragon. He had kept the people safe and he had brought this great trophy back to Mirabay so that all could share in his magnificent achievement. He had wondered if he should charge them for the privilege. The kingdom's coffers were always strained, all the more so now with the mercenaries he was having to hire to bolster his manpower. The dragon could prove to be a major source of revenue—there was not a person in the city who would not want to see it, and he was certain it would draw visitors from miles around.

Thinking further, Amaury realised charging to see the dragon was not the right move if he wanted it to help him calm the populace. It would fan the flames he wished to extinguish.

He took a deep breath, forced a broad smile, and walked forward to the edge of the balcony. The greeting he received was unwelcome, but not entirely unexpected. The gathered people started booing. There were insults mixed in—occasionally a voice rose loud enough for Amaury to make out individual words. Some he found particularly cutting— "limper" was one he'd always particularly disliked, and added to his irritation that he still hadn't had the chance to apply any of the Cup's power to his old injury. The pain was as pronounced as it had been in some time, and attending to it was long overdue. Perhaps today, when he was finished here—there was little more he could do to prepare.

"People of Mirabay," he said, in his most stentorian tone. The crowd didn't quieten. If anything, the jeering and booing grew louder. "People of Mirabay!" Still no reaction.

Amaury took a moment to stifle his rapidly growing anger, then shouted "Silence!" His voice boomed out, startling even him. Had he used magic? He wasn't sure. One way or the other, it had worked. The crowd had fallen silent. It was eerie to see so many people and for things to be so quiet.

"People of Mirabay," Amaury said. "I've chosen to speak with you today to ask for your patience and support during this time when changes are taking place in our city. As a true son of Mirabaya, I promise you all is happening for the best. It will make our kingdom stronger, our homes safer, and ensure a better quality of life for one and all."

"Bollocks!"

It was only one voice, but it wasn't the reaction Amaury had hoped for. What to do? Respond? Carry on as though nothing had happened? He chose the latter.

"Many of you will have already seen the benefits these changes can bring. Treatment for illnesses and injuries that would have been incurable before—"

"Doesn't seem to have worked for you, you limping bastard." A different voice, from elsewhere in the crowd.

Amaury smiled wryly. *Should have healed myself before I came out here, and danced the bastards a jig,* he thought.

"Water is clean and safe to drink," he continued. "Food is fresh and plentiful. These are just the first of many benefits of this new age we now live in."

"Sorcery is wrong!" a man called.

"It's an abomination!" a woman shouted.

"You're an abomination!" Several voices.

Laughter.

The hecklers were in different parts of the crowd. They were growing bolder and Amaury knew he didn't have long to bring the people around to his way of thinking. He reached deep, focussed his thought.

"Why don't you limp off that balcony, you bastard!"

"Silence!" Amaury roared, his anger finally getting the better of him. He watched in awe as the sound of his voice moved through the air like a wave and crashed down onto the crowd, smashing through them like a cavalry charge. There was blood, there were screams of terror and agony. Amaury watched in amazement as his word left a trail of absolute devastation in its wake before it faded to nothing, like a ripple diminishing as it spread through a pond.

It didn't take long for the stench of carnage to waft up to the balcony, but Amaury was still too enthralled by what had just happened to pay it any notice. What he had just done. Ysabeau came out from the palace and joined him on the balcony.

"Gods alive," she said, her eyes wide as saucers. "What happened."

"I . . . I'm not su—" Amaury said before stopping himself. "I did it. Magic. My magic." He held up his hands and looked at them. He had unleashed tremendous power, yet had felt no adverse effect. He hadn't burned himself out, the expected consequence of using too much energy. In fact, he'd barely even noticed he had done it. He felt no different. No fatigue, no dizziness. Nothing. What a fool *he'd* been. This power had been his for days, and he'd been too afraid to use it.

"Why?" Ysabeau said.

She went to the balustrade and looked down. Amaury paid her little attention. He was still trying to absorb the fact that the power that had worried him for so long was his to use as he saw fit. If he

could unleash such devastation with no noticeable personal consequences, then the things he needed to do on a day-to-day basis would
be no problem at all. There would be no more disagreements, no more
need for bodyguards, no fear of moving about the city. He had everything he needed. Everything he wanted.

"Father," Ysabeau said, "why? How could you? All those people.
There must be hundreds lying there. Thousands, maybe."

"They brought it on themselves," Amaury said. "If they'd just accepted that the world around them is changing, there'd have been no
problem. Some good might even come of it—the rest of them might
have learned their lesson.

"But none of that matters. Don't you see? The power I have now, it's
incredible. I'm untouchable."

"Don't you care?" Ysabeau said. "All those people. You're Lord Protector of the Realm. That means you're supposed to *protect them.*"

"Don't be so naive," Amaury said, disappointed. He expected more
from his own child.

"I can't believe this is what you had planned," she said. "It's barba-
rous."

Though Amaury kept his face impassive, to himself he had to admit that she had finally hit a sensitive spot. He hadn't planned what
had happened. Far from it. This was a glaring demonstration that he
had absolutely no control over this power. A shiver ran over his skin.

"I can't believe I'm the one who brought you the means to do this,"
she said.

"Statecraft can be a messy business," he said. "Ruling can require
hard choices and harder acts."

"Oh, I've heard that before," she said. "I didn't believe it then and
I don't believe it now." She shook her head. "I've seen terrible things.
I've done terrible things. But I can't be party to this."

She walked away, leaving Amaury alone on the balcony. As he
watched her go, he realised that the magic *had* done his bidding. The
people had, indeed, been silenced. He merely needed to develop better
control over his desires, just as dal Drezony had always maintained.
Perhaps she had been right about some things, after all.

He looked down at the square below. Most of the crowd was gone, having fled the horror. A great red stain streaked across the square, which was littered with bodies. The magic had not killed everyone it had touched, he saw. At the fringes of the bloodied path his magic had taken, there were wounded. Even from this distance, he could see that many were horribly injured. Some people were helping those who were hurt, while others wandered around checking the bodies. He wondered if anyone had started looting the corpses yet. It was only a matter of time before that started, and part of the reason he found it so hard to muster any sympathy for the fate of ordinary citizens. They cared about one another even less than he did. Once the shock had passed, all they would see was the chance to find a coin or two.

A child wandered amongst the dead, slipping every so often on the blood and viscera. She stopped beside one body, then reached down and shook it. She tried several times to rouse the person, but there was no response. At last, she stood up and stared straight at Amaury on the balcony. He had never seen so much hate in such a young face. For the first time it occurred to him that this act might not have a pacifying effect.

He turned and went back inside. If there was going to be trouble, he needed to be prepared for it. The new mercenaries should be no more than a day or two from the city; their arrival would be a weight off his mind. Desertions from the palace guard, the royal regiments, and the City Watch had been heavy—not that he felt he could trust them anyway. The Order's new recruits would have to serve as a stop-gap; his hopes of keeping them away from the dirtier side of maintaining the peace were well and truly gone.

"Your Grace," a clerk said, as soon as Amaury went back inside. "We've had word from the king's camp. He has defeated his cousins and is preparing to march."

Amaury had expected as much. The king's cousins were even bigger idiots than Boudain was. "Where to?"

"The message didn't say."

"Keep me updated."

For the first time, he regretted siting the Priory so far away, in that old monastery on the left bank of the Vosges. Originally he had placed the Order there to keep them away from the palace's meddling, but now it was an inconvenience. He needed them close now, but for the time being, there was little he could do about that.

Reaching his office, Amaury sent for the officers of the Order. He had to start preparing his cream-robed magisters for the war that was on its way.

PART THREE

CHAPTER
42

Gill spotted the mercenaries the next morning. It was as big a company as he'd ever seen. At a very rough estimate, there must have been ten thousand men, including the baggage train. He doubted it was a single company—more like an amalgam of several smaller ones. That meant there was going to be more than one leader, a command council of some sort, with absolute command awarded to an elected member only in times of action. It would make dealing with them more arduous, but delaying this force was almost as useful as getting them to turn around. Perhaps that should be the true focus of his offer?

A mercenary company on the march was always dangerous to approach. The reputations all such companies bore for looting, pillaging, and murder were well earned, even though some companies behaved far better than others.

He'd dealt with mercenaries a number of times during his career, fighting both with and against them. He had no strong opinions on them one way or the other. They were very much like any other segment of the world—there were some good ones, some bad ones, and plenty in between. He was pretty sure that in a force of this size, he'd find some of all. It didn't matter if the commanders were good men or not. They only needed to prize the value of a coin, or the thousands of them the king was offering if they turned around.

Gill stopped by a stand of trees and cut down a slender branch, which he used, in conjunction with a piece of cloth torn from his sleeve, to fashion a flag of truce. He was less likely to be targeted by overeager scouts if he looked like he was on official business.

With his new banner flying haphazardly above him, Gill continued toward the mercenary column. They had some outriders, but Gill hadn't encountered any advance scouts. Either they were very stealthy or the company's commanders were confident that no one would challenge so large a force. This behaviour wasn't unheard of, but it was arrogant and foolish—Gill knew of more than one force that had been attacked on the march. He wondered what was making them so confident, but answering that question could wait.

Once he was spotted, a group of riders broke away from the main column and galloped toward him.

"Who are you?" one of the men said, as soon as they were within earshot.

"Banneret of the White Guillot dal Villerauvais. An emissary of the king. I need to speak with your captain."

The rider gave Gill a curt nod, indicating that he was also a banneret. "Banneret of the Starry Field Carlos dal Dorado. The king, you say?"

"Yes," Gill said, returning the nod, acknowledging the Estranzan equivalent of his title. "The King of Mirabaya. This is a kingdom."

"We were given to understand that he is dead and that there is a regent in place. A regent we've been hired by."

"I'm afraid your information is incorrect," Gill said. "If you'd be so good as to bring me to your captain, I'll be happy to explain all."

The rider cast a glance at one of his comrades, then looked back at Gill.

"Follow us," he said. "And you can dump that ridiculous-looking flag."

Gill discarded the branch and shirt cuff, then dropped in beside the riders.

"Quite a big force you've got here," Gill said. "What company are you?"

"Black Spur, Red Lance, and a few smaller ones to make up numbers," dal Dorado said.

"Who commands?"

Dal Dorado and one of his comrades laughed but made no reply. When they got closer to the column, dal Dorado held up his hand.

"Captains!" he said. "Messenger from the King of Mirabaya."

"Thought he was dead," one of the men at the front said.

Gill shrugged. It was becoming clear to him that the mercenaries had either been supplied with very out-of-date information or been completely lied to. It occurred to him that he needed to be careful not to give away too much. Should they choose to reject the king's proposition, it was better that they remain as ignorant as possible.

"I bring an offer from Boudain the Tenth, King of Mirabaya," Gill said. "To whom do I have the honour of speaking?"

"Captain Carenjo of the Black Spur," said one.

"Teloza of the Red Lance," said the other.

Gill took the sealed papers from his tunic and held them out, still not sure which of the two men he should give them to.

Eventually Teloza, a man with a thick salt-and-pepper moustache, dressed in fine crimson clothing, leaned forward in his saddle and snatched the papers from Gill. He gave the seal a cursory inspection, then broke it open with no ceremony. He took what felt like an age to read the contents, during which Gill did his best to appear the disinterested messenger. Eventually, the mercenary captain looked up from the pages.

"Promise of payment to go home?"

"I believe that is what the king is offering," Gill said.

"If this is some sort of prank," the captain said, "I'll have you strung up from that tree over yonder." He pointed at the stand of trees where Gill had made his flagpole.

"I assure you, on my word as a Banneret of the White, this is not a prank," Gill said. "The king's offer is in good faith."

Teloza handed the papers to Carenjo, who clearly didn't like having been made to wait. The body language between the men did not speak of a solid working relationship. In the ordinary course of their contract—marching their troops to Mirabay, where they would be dispersed about to bolster Amaury's regular forces—it wouldn't be a problem. If they were to march into battle, Gill didn't fancy their chances of providing cohesive command. It was as sure a route to disaster as any he could think of, and any self-respecting captain would have avoided winding up in this position. Clearly whatever Amaury

had offered was enough to make them throw caution to the wind. Gill
had to wonder if the king's offer could make them turn their backs
on it.

"This is derisory," Carenjo said. He crumpled the paper and
dropped it to the ground.

Gill grimaced. "I take it that's a no, then."

"We've made a contract with the Lord Protector of—" Gill burst
out laughing and Carenjo cast him a filthy look.

"I'm sorry," Gill said. "I didn't realise that's what he's calling himself these days."

"The Lord Protector of Mirabaya," Carenjo continued, "and we
will hold true to it. What else does a company have, if not its reputation for keeping its word?"

Gill shrugged. He could think of a couple that had made a perfectly good living by changing sides whenever it suited them. Clearly
the king's offer hadn't been tempting enough to make them change
their colours. Gill wondered if there was anything he could do to convince them, but given that he wasn't in a position to change the offer
or to add to it, it seemed that his hands were tied. He really was nothing more than a messenger. Still, he couldn't let it lie without doing
something.

"Perhaps you might sleep on it, gentlemen," Gill said. "An offer
from a king is, after all, an offer from a king. I dare say the *Lord Protector* won't be in that role for much longer."

"Perhaps," Teloza said. "Perhaps not. We're losing the light, so
should set camp for the night. We can discuss the matter further with
the junior captains over supper, but I doubt our answer will be any
different. You're welcome to remain and sup with our officers," Teloza
continued. "Banneret dal Dorado will show you where."

One thing armies the world over were good at doing with little encouragement was setting up camp. The faster it was done, the sooner
they could get fed and into their bedrolls. Gill made idle chitchat with
dal Dorado as the companies settled in. He noticed they paid only lip
service to setting up pickets or posting sentries. Clearly they weren't
expecting trouble, and Gill supposed they were right. It was unlikely
they would face an enemy until they met the king's army, most likely

below the walls of Mirabay. There were no other forces in the field that a company of this size would have to worry about.

Supper was good. That was always the case with mercenary companies, in Gill's fleeting experience. When men were hired, rather than levied or conscripted, they had to be treated a little better if you wanted them to stick around and fight for you. The menu was fresh beef, potatoes, and a vegetable stew of some Estranzan recipe that was a little too spicy for Gill's taste, but it was the best meal he'd been offered in quite some time, so he ate it all gladly.

It was late, with the sun having long fled the sky, when Teloza and Carenjo appeared from the command tent and strolled to where the officers had messed. The other officers had been eyeing up their tents for some time by then, but were obligated to entertain their guest until their commanders had agreed upon a response.

"Our answer remains the same," Teloza said. "In consideration of the royal dignity, we've written a letter. Please inform His Majesty that we are sorry, but our word is our bond, and we have signed a contract with the Lord Protector."

Gill took the letter. "I understand. I'm sure His Majesty will appreciate the respect you've shown."

"You're welcome to remain here for the night, if you'd prefer not to set off in darkness," Carenjo said.

"Thank you for that kindness," Gill said, "but I should return immediately."

"I understand," Carenjo said. "Your mount was fed and watered while you ate. I hope the gods see fit that we shall not meet on the battlefield."

"I do also," Gill said, with a grim smile, knowing now that it was likely. "With your leave?" Gill gave dal Dorado a traditional banneret's salute—a click of the heels and nod of the head—then left to find his horse.

CHAPTER

43

Gill had always enjoyed riding on a clear night, beneath a star-filled sky. Setting aside the obvious dangers of his horse stumbling on an unseen obstacle and throwing him, he reckoned it was one of his favourite things. The fact that he didn't have two fire-spewing dragons chasing him, as he had on his previous nighttime ride, was an added bonus.

There was a hunter's moon—the usual spectral white and grey taking on a red hue. There was something foreboding about it, as though the moon were mirroring the wounds of the land beneath it. Gill tried to ignore the thought and focus on the fresh, bracing air . . . and the bad news he was bringing to his king. Boudain was a clever young man. He must have realised that this was the likely answer.

It took a little while for Gill to realise that the night was unusually quiet. Deathly so. The racket he was making as his horse ambled along would have been enough to frighten off anything but the most determined of predators, but even still, it felt unnatural to hear nothing. When he rode over the next rise, he realised what had kept all the nocturnal life quiet.

Glimmering red under the hunter's moon was a host of heavy cavalry. He brought his horse to a stop and tried to make sense of it. Should he flee before he was spotted? A gentle whistle told him it was too late for that.

"Banneret dal Villerauvais." The voice came from behind him.

Gill grimaced when he realised he'd been followed. Probably ever since leaving the mercenary camp.

"I'm to bring you straight to the king," the man said. "This way, if you please." A horseman loomed out of the darkness in a way that gave Gill pause. Was Amaury the only person training up people skilled in the magical arts?

As Gill rode along beside the whisperer, he thought about asking how long the man had been following, but realised he didn't actually want to know. The bigger question was how the king had managed to put together such a large body of horsemen in such a short time. True, men had been coming into the village steadily, and the king had retained most of the cavalry his cousins had brought, who had not played a role in that first battle. Even so, it was impressive. In the darkness it was impossible to make anything approaching an accurate estimate, but it was formidable. That they were in full battle array was telling.

The king was dismounted but fully armoured, and in discussion with several of the men Gill recognised as having become his general staff.

"Gill, they said no?" Boudain said.

"They did, your Highness."

"To be expected. Still, it was worth a try."

"Where did all these men come from?"

Boudain smiled, his teeth flashing in the moonlight. "Impressive, isn't it? Every horseman we could cobble together. Less than half the royal heavy host, but all things considered, I'm delighted. Some were donated by my cousins, but a remarkable number have been deserting their regiments. The rest are the feudal hosts who answered my call to raise their banners. I'm sure we left many behind by setting off ahead of the infantry when we did, but I'm hopeful this will be enough to do what needs to be done. Tell me, how many are they?"

"Nigh on ten thousand. I'd say at least seven of that fighting men, perhaps as many as eight. Looked to be about two thousand horse. Two large companies and several smaller ones. The two main captains don't seem to get along, particularly when it comes to who's giving the orders." Gill smiled. He'd been wondering why the king had sent him on what was nothing more than a message run, but now he knew. Boudain had wanted an experienced, trusted eye to appraise the enemy force. Why he hadn't just said that to begin with was beyond

Gill. Still, he knew only too well that it was never worth the effort, trying to understand why kings behaved as they did.

"If we catch them by surprise, Highness," one of the officers said, "I think we'll have the measure of them. There's not a mercenary company in the world that will stand before a charge of Mirabayan heavy horse."

Gill did his best not to let out an incredulous laugh. Not only was that statement a load of nonsense, Gill had seen the proof that it was with his own eyes. More than once. Still, if the mercenaries were caught unawares and before they broke camp, it wouldn't go well for them.

"We will proceed with the attack as planned," the king said. "Villerauvais, we brought your armour. A destrier and a lance too, if you wish to join us."

With all the reputation he had for swordsmanship, Gill had never been a cavalryman, although he had trained in fighting from horseback extensively while at the Academy—everyone did. Charging with the lance wasn't his preferred method of fighting, but a well-executed charge could be devastating and was their best chance to get rid of the mercenaries with minimal losses to their own forces.

Gill had to admit that Boudain was impressing him. He had known of the king's reputation when he was still a prince, and there had been general concern about him in court circles. The swordplay Boudain had enjoyed most was not the type taught at the Academy, but he seemed to have been able to navigate the web of potential scandals he had created without being caught.

A squire appeared, leading a horse, with what looked like Gill's armour bundled up on the saddle.

"When you're ready," the king said, "we'll advance."

The squire went about fitting Gill into Valdamar's armour. The lad was clearly expert in what he was doing, and made far faster work of it than Gill would have on his own. After a moment of trying to help, he realised things would go quicker if he simply stood there and let the squire do his job. This was the job poor Val would have done with his eternal enthusiasm, and Gill felt a pang of regret that the lad hadn't achieved his dream of becoming a banneret. So many dead who didn't deserve it, yet Gill remained. He wondered if his continued life was some bizarre divine punishment, if he was damned to watch those he cared about die before their time, or if that was simply the way of the world, as the wheel of fate turned and thinned out the herd.

"You're set to go, my Lord," the squire said. "Does everything feel as it should?"

"Yes. You've done an excellent job. Thank you."

Gill eschewed the lad's offer of help to mount. He was in the best shape he'd been in years and intended to take full advantage of it.

"I'm at your convenience, your Highness," Gill said, once firmly established in the saddle.

Boudain nodded, looking every part the warrior king in his finely polished armour. Gill wondered where he'd gotten it and what unfortunate nobleman was now wearing whatever he had cobbled together from the scraps in the village. It would be a shame to own so lovely a suit, yet be killed while wearing rusty, mismatched plate. Gill was thankful Pharadon had retrieved Valdamar's suit. Not only would it have been a terrible shame to lose it, Gill had come to place quite a bit of stock in the protection it offered. It had proved itself where a suit of Jauré's—as fine a suit of armour as money could buy—had failed. Compared to all the smooth, shining plate around him, his suit was dated-looking, but he had long since realised that substance was much more important than style.

"The regiment will advance at the trot!" the king said.

Boudain's force lacked the cohesive unity of motion Gill was accustomed to, but considering this regiment had been cobbled together over the past couple of days, their advance wasn't too bad. If they had been planning on charging a prepared line of infantry, Gill wouldn't have been happy, but an unexpecting mercenary camp was an entirely different proposition.

The noise they made was jarring in the otherwise peaceful night, but by the time the enemy heard them, it would be too late. Gill reckoned it would take them an hour to reach the mercenaries. By then, men would be in deep sleep, and sentries would be getting bored.

There was little talk as they rode. Some of the horsemen, Gill knew, were riding to their first battle. A number of them would have witnessed the slaughter during the battle at Castandres, where the king's cousins had held their cavalry in reserve. Gill wondered if having seen battle but not participated was worse than being completely new to it. Those men knew the horrors of war but didn't realise that it was possible to survive, if you fought as hard as you could. And were lucky.

The moon had dropped and lost its red hue by the time the mercenary camp drew into sight. There would be plenty of red on display by the time the sun rose. It saddened Gill that Carenjo and Teloza hadn't taken the opportunity to turn around. They had made their choice and would have to live with it. That was the lot of soldiers, and Gill wasn't going to lose any sleep over what had to be done. He had learned the hard way that honour counted for little when you were in a fight for your life.

When the king raised his hand and swiped it forward quickly, Gill didn't think twice. He urged his horse forward, as did the men to his left and right and those in the three ranks behind him. They increased speed to a canter that took them across the open farmland.

The first cry of alarm sounded, and in response, there was a call from the king's side.

"Chaarrrrge!"

Blood pounded through Gill's ears, syncopating to the beat of his horse's hooves. He pulled the visor down on his helmet, allowed his horse to surge forward, and lowered his lance.

The line had grown ragged—to be expected in an undrilled body of horsemen—but it wouldn't matter. The charging wall of man and horse mowed down the few sentries, and the first screams rose. Gill could see some movement amongst the fires in the camp. This was not a sight any man wanted to wake to.

The weight and momentum of the horses was as much a weapon as any sword or lance. They smashed through tents and men like living battering rams. Gill's lance caught a man stepping out of his tent square in the chest and punched straight through him, pulling the shaft from Gill's hand. Gill drew his sword as he rode on, trampling and cutting through row after row of tents.

It felt like it took forever before he was through the camp and galloping into the darkness on the other side. He had lost count of the
number of men he had ridden over or cut down by the time he got
clear. If the others had performed half so lethally, then the mercenaries would not be able to recover from that first shock assault. Nonetheless, the fight was not simply about winning—they needed to do it
with as little loss on their side as possible.

The attackers' line was well and truly broken now. Some had, like
Gill, charged through and out the other side, while others, in the heat
of the moment, had forgotten the purpose of a cavalry charge and had
stopped to cut down whatever came within reach. Gill looked about,
trying to spot the king, but there was no sign of him.

Gill hoped the man was well-protected. If Boudain were to be
killed that night, everything they had done would be for naught. Still,
there were times when a king had to stand with his men and show
he could get his hands dirty, if he hoped to earn their loyalty and respect. This was definitely one of those times—the only tricky part was
surviving it.

Seeing that the other horsemen who had come through the camp
with him were idling around, he shouted, "Form up!"

There was a risk in charging through the camp for a second time,
since so many of their comrades had stopped midway and were now
obstacles. But leaving their force disorganised increased the possibility that they might be picked off piecemeal and routed.

Seeming eager to have some direction, the men gathered around
him. The inexperience of both the king and his advisors was showing.
It didn't look like Boudain had appointed any lower-level officers, so
as soon as men were out of contact with the king's party, they were
beyond his command.

That might be fine for now—the devastation they had caused on
their first pass through the camp virtually guaranteed their victory—
but facing the well-drilled army that Amaury would bring to the field,
they'd be annihilated.

The men looked expectantly at Gill. He surveyed the mercenary
camp, and realised there was no need for another charge. The mercenaries had been caught utterly wrong-footed; Gill wondered how

many men lay dead beneath the shrouds of their collapsed tents. Small groups of horsemen wheeled back and forth, armour and swords flashing red in the light of the campfires. The air was filled with screams and cries of anger. For a moment, it occurred to Gill that the three hells must look similar to what was going on before him. There was no fighting anymore, only slaughter. That was something Gill would have nothing to do with.

CHAPTER
44

By the time dawn greeted them, the king's retinue had restored one of the larger tents for his use. While the rest of the force breakfasted and picked over the spoils, Boudain entertained his senior officers at a liberated mercenary campaign table. A preliminary count indicated they had lost no more than a couple of dozen men—an extraordinary result considering how many people must have died during the hours of darkness.

There was not a trace of a living mercenary. Gill wondered how many had gotten away under cover of darkness, and he was glad that the king hadn't ordered a pursuit. There was nothing to be gained by cutting them down, and it showed that Boudain hadn't let bloodlust overwhelm him.

Once they'd broken their fast, and completed the task of disposing of the corpses either by mass burial or burning—the better choice was an unappetising topic of breakfast conversation—the plan was to move to a campsite that didn't reek of death. There, they would get some well-earned rest before continuing on to join the main army, which was marching toward the city.

Gill sat quietly and ate ravenously. Even though his involvement in the fight had been limited to a single charge, he was starving, and thankful for his second meal from the mercenaries' larder. There were going to be more hard days ahead. The king was still untested against an experienced and seasoned foe, and after the chaos of the previous night, it was clear none of his retinue had much more command experience than Boudain himself.

"As soon as we've finished breakfast," the king said, "I want a fast inventory to be made of what is salvageable from this camp. My army is perilously under-resourced, so we will take as much as we can. Food, tents, weapons, armour. I believe the baggage train is largely intact from last night, so we shall make full use of it."

Gill nodded. It was a sensible idea and showed forethought, another hopeful sign. If some of Boudain's new officers showed similar aptitude, Gill might be able to go home all the sooner. Wherever that might be, now.

▲▲▲▲▲▲

The pile of reports on Amaury's desk all said the same thing—there was no more trouble on the city streets. The problem was, there was nobody *out on* the city streets. Indoors, they could be up to anything— plotting, hiding, obeying. He had no idea. The voice of worry in the back of his mind said it wasn't the latter.

Curious to see for himself, he climbed to the top of one of the palace's turrets and looked out across the city. It was deserted. Not a single person could be seen moving about the place. He was sure there were some, somewhere, but it was remarkably disconcerting to see the streets so empty. When he came down from the tower, he noticed that the palace was also far quieter than usual. While there seemed to be fewer servants about, more pronounced was the virtual absence of any of the court parasites and hangers-on who cluttered the place up most of the time. Those who were present gave him a wide berth—Amaury had even seen one servant stop in their tracks, turn, and head in the opposite direction upon seeing him.

He knew the reason, of course, and it was a bitter pill to swallow. If only the people had listened to him, listened to reason, nothing bad would have happened. As it was, he fully expected he would have to give another, similar lesson in the days to come. It was unpleasant, but nobody had ever said ruling was supposed to be enjoyable. It was a duty, placing the best interests of the state ahead of what one might desire personally, but that was his burden, and he was stuck with it now.

His secretary popped his head around the door after a cursory knock, with an expression on his face that said Amaury wasn't going to like what he was about to hear.

"Lord Protector, I'm afraid it appears that the dragon has disappeared."

"Pardon me?" Amaury said, genuinely nonplussed.

"The cage. It's empty. There's no sign of the creature."

It took Amaury a moment to process the news. There was only one conclusion he could come to. *That little bitch,* he thought. Betrayed by his own daughter, simply because she hadn't the stomach to see through the things that needed to be done. He should have left her to rot, all those years ago. He had been too sentimental by far, taking her in and trusting her as he had.

"Mobilise the City Watch. Every last man of them. I want the city gates closed and locked until we have the dragon back where it belongs. Tell the Watch to keep an eye out for my dau—Ysabeau dal Fleurat. She has some explaining to do." He was about to add that the Intelligenciers should start investigating, but of course they were no more.

"That's the other thing, Lord Protector," his secretary said, the fear in his voice palpable.

Amaury noted that the young man was still standing behind the door with only his head visible.

"The Watch appear to have deserted their posts," the secretary said.

"All of them?"

The secretary nodded.

Amaury closed his eyes and stifled a swear. "The Royal Guard then. Assign the Watch duties to them."

"Very good, Lord Protector."

As soon as the door closed behind his secretary, Amaury let out the curse he'd been holding back. The sooner he could get his mercenaries onto the streets, the better. He got up and paced around his office. *What in hells has Ysabeau done with the dragon? It's not as though it's easy to sneak about and hide. . . .*

⁂

Solène didn't like to admit—even to herself—how relieved she was when they got out of Mirabay. The feeling increased with every step away they took, and they kept going until the moon was high in the night sky. Only then, under cover of darkness, could Solène finally accept that they were free and clear, could she honestly tell herself that she had carried out her promise to Pharadon.

She hadn't thought beyond this point, however, and had no idea where to go or what to do next. She looked at the dragon, still moving somewhat awkwardly in its human guise. The beautiful, dark-haired woman regarded her surroundings with wide-eyed wonder. Only an hour earlier, this woman had been a golden dragon, not yet over the threshold of true self-awareness. It must have been an incredibly jarring experience for the young dragon, and Solène felt remiss for not making more of an effort to comfort her through it.

"Are you . . . all right?" Solène said.

"Perfectly, thank you," Ashanya said. "I'm listening to the song of my kind, and learning from it."

"The song of your kind? Other dragons are talking to you?" Solène could barely remember hearing something she'd have described as a song when she became enlightened, although she couldn't understand any of it. The memory felt so distant now that she had to search it out.

Ashanya shook her head, an odd, jerky movement with none of the natural rhythm of a real person. "No, not directly to me; their song is carried on the Fount. I can hear it now."

"What does it say?" Solène said, genuinely intrigued.

"All sorts of things. Stories of my kind, lessons they learned. It is a comfort."

She looked at Solène, who noticed that despite her human form, Ashanya's eyes had returned to a piercing crystal blue.

"It worries me that I might always be alone," Ashanya said.

Solène gave her a sad smile. What could she say? There were no assurances she could make; there was no comfort she could give. She had no idea if there were any more slumbering dragons or hidden clutches of eggs, waiting for the right moment to hatch. Part of her hoped there were.

"The song says there might be others, but not when they will come into the world. If they emerge, will you help me? The song says it takes a Cup, or two of the enlightened, to bring another dragon into the light. There are no more Cups, just you and I. Will you help?"

"Of course," Solène said. "I promise that I will always answer your call, if I can." It felt odd that she had made more promises to dragons than she ever had to other humans. "What will you do now? Where will you go?"

Ashanya looked toward the mountains. "Back there. Home. I will call you if I find others."

"I've heard the song too," Solène said. "Will I ever come to understand it?"

Ashanya shook her head. "Not that of dragonkind. Are many of yours enlightened?" She shook her head again, and forced an expression that looked like sympathy. "No," she said, answering her own question. "The song says only one other. Not enough to be able to hear their voice on the Fount."

Solène realised Ashanya must be talking about Amatus. It was incredible to imagine that one day she might be able to hear his thoughts and experiences, to learn from them.

They walked in silence away from the road until there was no chance of being seen, even at that late hour. Ashanya had started to revert back to her normal form before Solène noticed. She had to step back a few paces to get away from the dragon's rapidly increasing size. Solène wondered how Ashanya was able to change twice in such a short period of time, but reckoned that the Cup must have imbued the young dragon with a massive amount of energy, which was clearly not yet depleted.

Ashanya gave Solène a nod and stretched her wings. With a rush of air and dust, she was in the air. Solène shielded her eyes for a moment, then watched as Ashanya flew higher and higher, until she was no more than a speck, glinting in the moonlight like a dream.

When she could see no more trace of the young dragon, Solène began to wonder where she should go, what she should do next. If she went back to the king, he would expect her to fight for him, and even now, she couldn't bring herself to do that. She couldn't use her magic to kill. Once that dam was broken, there was no going back, and she knew the only thing easier than doing it the second time would be the third, then the fourth. There would always be a good reason to kill someone. The only way to resist was to say never and refuse to budge.

Her new power would enable her to be a healer the like of which the world had not seen since Imperial times—an idea she felt strongly drawn to. Surely the king would be satisfied with that? Still, if she was patching men up so they could rush straight back into the carnage, how different was that from doing the killing herself?

Was she powerful enough to prevent the coming war altogether? Could she force the king and the Prince Bishop to come to terms, or use magic to prevent them from fighting at all? That, though, was the first step to tyranny; it was no different from what the Prince Bishop was doing. She swore. Enlightenment was supposed to be a gift, but it felt more like a curse. She was rapidly coming to understand why Amatus had supposedly removed himself entirely from Imperial politics. She felt like removing herself from society completely. Where would she draw the lines? How would she recognise when she was about to cross one?

Perhaps a little time would help her find a role. Maybe a small bakery somewhere quiet and out of the way was an idea she could make herself excited about again. It was a good, honest life, and she smiled at the thought that her bread and cakes would be unrivalled. Still, there was something about it that rang of defeat, of giving up, of wasting the potential enlightenment brought. Was she being unreasonable? Too hard on herself? She started to walk again, still with no idea of where she was going to go.

There was little time for reflection once the task of stripping the mercenary camp was complete. Gill oversaw the acquisition of the baggage train, which was, happily, a far easier task than he had expected. As they were still on the march, the mercenaries had left all but what they had needed for the night on the wagons that followed the company. Luckier still, most of the draft oxen had survived the attack—certainly enough for them to get what they needed moving.

Gill had never been a logistician or a member of a quartermaster's corps, so other than gathering up everything that looked good and getting it moving in the right direction, he really didn't know what was expected of him. The goods probably needed to be catalogued, but he had no intention of doing that himself, nor did he intend to be responsible for issuing it all to the troops. His talents lay elsewhere, and if the king didn't know how to use them properly, what point was there in sticking around?

He was concerned about the attitude he saw amongst the cavalry. Morale was high, which was good, but to hear the men talk, one would have thought they had won a great victory, not slaughtered men by the hundreds before they were able to get out of their tents. As a strategic victory, it was a great one, but for any man to consider himself a blooded warrior after that was dangerous. They still had not been truly tested in battle.

As they rode, Gill realised he had turned into that wary old warrior who saw doom around every corner, the man who had escaped death many times whilst seeing friends and comrades drop like flies.

To him, the inevitability of death seemed certain. Someone had to be the voice of caution, but Gill didn't want the job.

▲▲▲▲▲▲

The infantry force that had marched directly to Mirabay from Castandres was already camped within view of the city's walls by the time Gill and the cavalry got there. Unlike the mercenary commanders, whoever the king had put in charge of his infantry had done a proper job of setting up and securing the camp. Of course, there was a good chance they'd be spending quite a bit of time here—not just one night.

A ditch and embankment had been created, and men were working on constructing a palisade along the top. Gill was impressed—whoever it was had clearly paid attention during the relevant classes at the Academy, unlike Gill during Logistics.

As they grew closer, Gill saw something that came as quite a surprise. Not only were there far more men around the camp than he had expected, many of them wore the various liveries of the permanent regiments, all of whom Gill had expected to be facing on the battlefield.

There was a serious problem in the city if that many troops had sneaked out. The thought brought a smile to his face. Anything that vexed Amaury was all right in Gill's book, and this could be the thing that tipped the balance in their favour.

Once his ox wagons passed within the camp's perimeter, Gill headed for the central axis, where he expected the command tent to be, given the organised, textbook placement of everything else. Sure enough, it was there, and the king was poring over maps on a campaign table, surrounded by his staff.

Several personal banners fluttered from spears driven into the ground by the tent, but Gill didn't recognise any of the sigils. That meant that none of these men were from the major noble families, so they all had a great deal to win by fighting on the king's side.

He thought of having his flown with the others, but realised he didn't care. For so many years, seeing his banner flown, bearing his family's sigil, had been a great source of pride. Now it seemed like another one of the pointless diversions people clung to so as to separate themselves from those farther down the ladder. A banner didn't do you any good when you were facedown in the mud, bleeding to death. All it was good for then was a souvenir for your mother, wife, or children. Or perhaps a trophy for the man who'd killed you.

Gill's arrival attracted one or two glances, but went largely unnoticed. Walking closer, he saw that the maps being reviewed were plans of the city. The king and his staff were discussing potential weak points in the walls and considering ways past them, such as using the river, or the sewers, to enter the city. All these things had been considered before, however, not least by those who had designed the defences. In the best of times, Mirabay was a near-impossible nut to crack. It would take months of siege, or an assault by many times more men than they had.

Now that Amaury had used the Cup, the situation had changed. Gill had no idea how the Prince Bishop's magic might be used to draw out the siege. If he could conjure up food and clean water, the city might be able to hold out forever. He wondered how long it would take for the collection of boys-playing-soldiers gathered around the table to realise that.

The thought of magic made him wonder how Solène had fared. He reckoned the disappearance of the dragon would have been pretty big news in the city—from which so many of the soldiers in camp had come. He decided to walk around the camp and see if he could learn anything. It would be some time before the younglings at the table looked for advice from more experienced heads, and Gill suspected that was why the king's cousin, Savin, was not present.

As Gill walked along the lanes, between tents and livestock pens, it struck him that he was preparing to lay siege to Mirabay. He'd never imagined doing anything like that—the closest he'd ever gotten was a dream of tearing the city down, brick by brick, after his arrest.

A standard military camp was laid out in a pattern of small "town squares"; each square was formed by a specific unit's tents and centred around their cook fire. Several squares constituted each regiment's section of the camp. Gill stopped at one fire where the men wore the blue tunics of the Royal Guard.

"Have you lads just come from the city?" he asked.

Though all looked up, only one spoke. "We have. What of it?"

"Just wondering how things are there, is all," Gill said. "I hear the Prince Bishop caught a dragon."

"All the dragons in the world couldn't make me raise a sword for him," the man said, a sour expression on his face.

"Things are bad?"

"They are. Hopefully not for much longer, if we can get our hands on the great Lord Protector. After what he's done, I'd like some time with him myself."

"What did he do?"

"Magic." The man spat the word out. "Killed thousands in Balcony Square. One word, and thousands dead. Even more hurt. After that, me and the lads cleared out. We weren't the only ones, as you can see." He waved a hand, gesturing at the whole camp.

Gill grimaced. He didn't think much of Amaury, but it was hard to believe he'd killed thousands of people in cold blood. Was it a sign that the man wasn't able to control his magic? Considering how worried Solène had always been about that, it seemed a likely explanation. Still, thousands of people? There was no way back from that. No matter what happened in the coming battle, Amaury would never be accepted as ruler of Mirabay. It might take a year, it might take ten, but one day, he'd get a dagger in the back. Until then, neither the city nor the country would be at peace.

"And the dragon? Did you see it?"

"Nah, a few of the lads did, though. They were on duty guarding it. Said it just lay there asleep the whole time. Then it went missing. I mean, how in three hells does a dragon in a cage go missing?"

Gill smiled and nodded. "Yeah, strange, that. Good talking to you."

He walked away, smiling. The dragon's disappearance meant Solène had most likely succeeded—and gotten away without trouble. He wondered where she was now, and what she was doing. He'd have felt a lot happier going into what lay ahead with her power at their side, but he could understand why she might stay away. There was no way she could get through the battle without blood on her hands. The only way to avoid that was to stay away. That was the right choice for her.

His mood had been greatly improved by the news that things weren't going well for Amaury, even though the thought that he was letting his magic off the leash and killing people was worrisome. Guillot wondered if that news had reached the king.

Boudain could not afford a lengthy siege if Amaury was slaughtering his citizens. Then again, a long siege was never really a good prospect—it was always worst on the innocent inhabitants on the inside, and Boudain would not be welcomed back into the city if he had spent months starving it.

As Gill headed back toward the command tent, it occurred to him that someone should tally the soldiers who had come to the camp from the standing regiments. Every one of them was one man fewer for Amaury. If enough had defected, that might make those still with him think twice when it came time to fight. Even so, Amaury had been buying mercenaries for months, and destroying the big company didn't mean he would be short of troops.

Once again, Gill was glad he wasn't the one making the decisions.

CHAPTER
46

Amaury glanced over the anatomical diagram one last time. He was so familiar with it by this point that he reckoned he could draw it himself. There was no one in the Order with the power to do what he sought to do, and no one he trusted enough to anyway.

He had already run his final few queries past both a surgeon and a professor of anatomy at the university. There was nothing to be gained by delaying any longer. Amaury focussed his thought and directed the Fount to his hip and the injury that Gill had left him with, all those years before. The injury that set him on course to his current predicament.

Power flowed through him. His skin tingled as though touched by a cooling breeze; he felt a sense of incredible wellness, such as he'd never felt before. Amaury held his focus for a moment, then was overcome by a sense of panic. He was flooded by memories of what had happened on the balcony, how he had created magic that he had not intended. Shutting his mind to the Fount, he scrabbled at his clothes as he jumped to his feet.

He pulled his britches down far enough to expose the scar. There was nothing there. Not even a blemish. His mind caught up and he realised that he should have already known it had worked—there had been no pain or tightness when he'd leaped out of his seat. The discomfort was such an old companion that most of the time he barely noticed it, but now it was entirely absent. Unable to contain himself, Amaury pulled his britches back up and jogged across the room. His hip felt loose and strong—as good as it had when he was a young man. Laughing, he jogged the short distance back to his desk.

There was a knock, and the office door creaked open. His secretary peered in and gave Amaury a quizzical look.

"Lord Protector?"

"I, uh, I was just testing something," Amaury said. "What is it?"

His secretary took a deep breath. *That expression of doom, again,* Amaury thought. He sat down and braced himself.

"An army has been sighted a short distance from the city," his secretary said.

Amaury shrugged. "That was to be expected. Now that they're here, we can get on with things." *Not so bad, after all,* Amaury thought.

"That's not all, Lord Protector. The mercenary company on the way to the city was attacked and dispersed. They won't be coming."

At that, Amaury's heart sank. All the joy of finally healing his hip was sucked from his body. "Get out," he said.

When the door closed behind his secretary, Amaury cradled his head in his hands. He wanted to scream. After he managed to get his anger under control, he began to think of next steps. He needed to scout the enemy force, find out how many he had to deal with and the composition of the king's army.

Where is Solène? he wondered. Was she another weapon that would be brought to bear against him? It was a concern, but he reckoned he had the measure of her—after all, he had drunk from the Cup and she had not. He could deal with her.

He reached forward and rang the bell on his desk. It was time to get to work.

Solène had walked through the night and into the next day. She'd noticed that since she'd become enlightened, her need for food had diminished, as though the Fount itself was providing her with sustenance.

She was still in open countryside, having avoided one or two villages along the way. She had no desire for human company. Her sense of being a pariah was as strong as it had ever been. She had magical power that almost no other person had ever had. Even before she'd become enlightened, she'd been running away from her magic, hoping that one day she would wake up and it would be gone. Instead, her choices had somehow led her to a point where it was stronger than she had ever imagined.

How could she hope for a normal life now? How could she be satisfied by being the best baker she could be when all she had to do was close her eyes and think to create hundreds of perfect loaves? Cakes, pastries, whatever fancies and delicacies she chose, no matter how complicated. There would never again be the reward that came from honest toil and effort—she could have whatever she wanted with only a thought.

Yet she couldn't think of a single thing she wanted, other than to be rid of this curse once and for all.

Could she do that? Solène shut her eyes and focussed. *Rid me of this power. Of this curse.* She repeated the thought over and over. She felt the Fount swirl around her, in her, through her. After a moment, she opened her eyes and looked around. She felt no different. She focussed her mind again—a random thought, the first to enter her mind—and a bolt of lightning shot from her fingertips into the sky. It hadn't worked.

She let out a sigh and wondered what to do next. She knew there was much good she could do, but that didn't change what an enormous burden she now carried. All she could do was follow Pharadon's advice—to believe in herself. To use her power in the best ways she could.

Her friend—the only person in the world she could call that—was riding off to attempt to rid the world of a tyrant, a man who had become far too powerful for Gill to have much hope of defeating. Gill understood that, yet Solène knew he would do his best to succeed, without hesitation or complaint. Helping Gill meant facing every fear she had, and Solène didn't know how she would remain true to herself. She turned back to face the direction she had come from. She would have to find a way. She knew where she needed to be. What she had to do.

▲▲▲▲▲

As the river barge drifted downstream, needing only the gentlest of guidance from the ferryman, Ysabeau watched the spires, walls, and towers of Mirabay shrink into the distance. She knew in her heart this was the last she would ever see of the city, but to her surprise, the thought didn't bother her in the least. During her year away, she had thought she missed the city, but she realised that she had missed the idea of it, not the reality.

It had been a relief when she had returned to the dragon cage and found it empty. She had intended to release the magnificent creature, regardless of her father's desires. Those great, blue, mournful eyes would be with her forever, would make her question much of what she thought she knew about the world. Her father had to know by now. She wondered how he'd reacted.

Putting her back to the city, she looked downstream. The barge would take her to the Port of Mirabay, and from there?

She had spent enough of her life living by the blade. Perhaps it was time for a change. She reckoned that, between her magic and the sharpness of her mind, she could turn her hand to whatever she chose. Not just what she thought might impress her father.

Ah, her father. Ysabeau knew the people had long since abandoned him. She only regretted that it had taken something as terrible as the massacre for her to do the same. He'd manipulated her, just as he had everyone else. Just as he had her mother, taking what he wanted before abandoning her, never caring what the consequences might be.

The Prince Bishop had always claimed he had not known of Ysabeau's existence until after the Intelligenciers had arrested her. Her mother had called on him as a last resort. The thought left a bitter taste in Ysabeau's mouth. He could have checked in on her mother at any time over the years, had he a shred of decency in him, but he hadn't. She wondered if he'd have shown any interest in her if the City Watch had arrested her, if she'd been taken into custody for theft rather than on charges of witchcraft. Probably not.

She'd been useful to him. A disposable tool. Nothing more.

There would be no more backwards glances, Ysabeau determined. No more regrets. No more need for acceptance. Only what lay before her, whatever that was.

An army on the morning of a battle was a magnificent thing to behold. Armour and weapons were polished, banners and flags freshly cleaned. By the end of the day, they'd be covered in mud and blood, and half the men now laughing and joking, doing their best to show how unafraid they were, would be food for crows. Gill couldn't help but think that if Amaury was one of those men, then it would all be worth it. Sometimes all that carnage, all that suffering, really was the only way to address a problem.

The king's new army was cobbled together from his traitorous cousins, nobles who had come out of the woodwork only when the king looked likely to win, young bannerets and aristocrats with nothing to lose but everything to gain, and now, it seemed, hundreds and hundreds of men who had deserted the city. It looked like well over half the Royal Guard had come over, and there were a couple of other regiments that were showing good strength. No one had a clue how many men Amaury would bring to the party, nor what type of magical malfeasance, but Gill reckoned things at that point could have looked quite a bit worse. By the end of the day, no doubt they would.

They were arranged regiment by regiment, in as much order as the newly appointed and inexperienced commanders who led most of them were capable of imposing. A quick glance could tell which were the standing regiments with seasoned sergeants, and which were not, even without the guide of banners and tunic colours.

The cavalry skulked in the background, ready, but useless unless

Amaury chose to bring his army out onto the open field. It remained the great uncertainty, how the tyrant would respond to the army at his door. Gill didn't know what he would do if their situations were reversed—remain behind the safety of his walls, or deal with his enemy head-on. As it was, the king had asked Gill to remain with his staff, on hand to offer whatever advice Boudain felt he needed.

Gill still wasn't comfortable with this—he found it hard to believe he was now one of the men influencing the big decisions. By comparison, standing on the front line with a sword in hand was almost an attractive proposition, facing all the danger that entailed. Of course, that was nonsense, but it was the role Gill knew and understood. With each day, he continued to struggle to make sense of the world. He'd always thought that was something that would get easier. It seemed that was another thing he was wrong about.

The army advanced a little closer to the walls, but halted out of range of bowshot. So much of what was happening was second nature to Gill, the sound of the march, of the movement of men and horses and armour, drums and pipes and shouted orders, that for brief moments he lost sight of the fact that they were advancing on Mirabay— their own city. He wondered if everyone felt the same way, or if each man viewed the day through his own lens.

As the moment they all waited for grew inexorably close, the tension in the air thickened. They had not been stopped for long when the gates opened, much as Gill had expected they would. No man who wants to hold on to a city will stand by while it is destroyed, and Amaury, for all his flaws, did seem to want the city to stand.

Troops started to rush out of Mirabay, many wearing colours that Gill didn't recognise—most likely some of the smaller mercenary companies that Amaury had collected over the previous weeks. After them came the cream and gold of the Order. No one was sure what they were capable of, but word of what had happened at Balcony Square had spread quickly, fuelling anger and bolstering the men's resolve to fight. There would be little quarter given to any who fought for Amaury that day, and less for his mages.

Gill could see some of the younger commanders glancing back

toward the king's banner, and all his gallopers, who remained stock-still with no orders to deliver. The eager young officers might wonder why Amaury was being allowed bring his army out and form them up, but to advance into the killing zone beneath the walls and into range of all of its artillery would spell disaster for the king's army—they would be devastated by ballista bolt, catapult shot, and arrow.

By the time the so-called Lord Protector's forces had finished mustering below the walls, there were more men gathered there than Gill had hoped for. Far more. In fact, to the casual observer it looked like the Royal Guard was present in full strength. Gill supposed Amaury could have dressed mercenaries or conscripts in spare uniforms, but from a distance, it was hard to tell.

A group of horsemen formed up at the front of the enemy army; squinting, Gill reckoned he could make out Amaury amongst them. A white flag was raised and the horsemen started forward.

The king looked about, assessing his staff. "Savin, Coudray, with me. You too, Villerauvais."

The small group started forward, and Gill felt a pang of regret that his banner was not flying. Suddenly it felt as though something had been left undone.

Gill didn't recognise any of the men with Amaury, when the two parties met. They were all hard-looking types who'd obviously seen a few fights in their time.

"I was pleased to get news of your recovery, your Highness," Amaury said.

"I'm sure you were," Boudain said. "I thank you for parading my army before the city walls. I presume you've done so to hand them back into my charge?"

Amaury laughed and shook his head. "No, your Highness, I'm afraid not. It's common knowledge that you've been bewitched by a powerful sorceress. It would be a disservice to all the right-thinking people of the kingdom to allow you back on the throne."

Boudain nodded slowly. "Bewitched? Is that the best you could come up with?"

"The truth is rarely as fancy as we might like it to be, but truth it is, and it would be a crime to allow a bewitched man to rule a kingdom," Amaury said.

Gill shook his head in disgust. He wondered if Amaury had told so many untruths over the years that he was starting to believe them himself.

"We both love this city," the Prince Bishop continued, "and this kingdom. If there is any shred of your true self left in there, I beseech you: order your men to put down their arms and return home. Those of the standing regiments will be welcomed back to their barracks with no questions asked. A man who loves Mirabaya will not tear her apart to possess her."

"You've always been full of shit, Amaury," Gill said, unable to hold his tongue any longer. "But you're really surpassing yourself today."

"General Villerauvais, please," Boudain said.

Amaury turned his attention to Gill and raised an eyebrow. "General? My congratulations on your advancement. I'm glad to see you here today, Guillot. Very glad."

"Want to even out that limp?" Gill said, placing his hand on the pommel of his sword.

"Gill!" Boudain said, then turned his attention back to Amaury. "I will allow you an hour to collect your belongings, Richeau, and depart the city, and the country. Never to return."

Gill noted the use of Amaury's surname, rather than any of his titles, but was surprised at the amount of restraint the king was showing, in marked contrast to Gill's own outburst. Despite his efforts to appear calm and in control, Gill knew Amaury too well to be deceived. The strain showed on his face.

"I don't think so, your Highness," Amaury said. "Now that we've dealt with the formalities, perhaps we can get down to it?"

"Gladly," Boudain said sharply, the contempt with which he was being treated finally seeming to have overcome his reserve. "You will not live out this day."

Amaury turned his horse to leave, then cast a quick glance back. "We shall see!" With that, he galloped back toward his troops, his retinue in tow.

Boudain watched him go a moment, then looked at Gill. "One way or the other, that bastard does not see the sunset."

"You have my word on that," Gill said.

As he rode toward his own lines, Amaury decided he was satisfied with his illusion. Even he couldn't tell who was real and who was not among his troops. The products of his imagination had passed muster so far, however, and it wasn't as though they were going to be doing any actual fighting. He turned to face the king's army once again. The king, and that smug bastard Gill, were at the centre, nicely contained and marked out with a number of fluttering banners.

It was a beautiful sight, really. So many men and horses in glittering armour. Beautiful, colourful flags flapping lazily on the gentle morning breeze. In a moment, all would be carnage. A scene from the three hells made real in the world. The feeling of power was intoxicating. A king had brought a full army against him, and there was nothing they could do to stop him. In a few moments, most of them would be dead. Those who weren't would be running away as fast as they could.

When word of what he had done spread, no one would dare challenge him ever again. No one. Mirabaya would reign supreme, with Amaury benevolently guiding it in the right direction.

He took a deep breath and reached out to the Fount. He held out his arms, ready to revel in the joyous sensation of its embrace. But it was not there. He opened his eyes and looked about in consternation. His men—the real ones—were giving him odd looks. He must have looked a fool, his arms outstretched, an expression of rapture on his face. The expression changed to one of confusion and dismay. Where was the Fount? Why was it not there for him to call on?

He stilled his panic and tried again. Nothing. What had happened? With all of the people in Mirabay, it was usually so powerful. He could hardly have drained it creating his fake army, could he? No, that was nonsense. It must be nerves, the distraction of a stressful day. He ignored the eyes that were burrowing into the back of his head, and tried to rid it of any distraction. Another deep breath. He opened his mind to the Fount.

"Where in hells is it!"

"Lord Protector?"

"Nothing, never mind," Amaury said. He looked around, but his illusion remained. There was no reason for it not to; he had cast it with an enormous amount of energy. But what was going on now?

This wasn't supposed to be how it worked—he had drunk from the Cup. The power was his. The power of Amatus. Perhaps the problem was temporary. But with an army facing him from across the field, there wasn't time to wait for circumstances to change. Time. He needed to buy more. But how? Then it hit him, and the idea was good enough to actually make him smile.

"They've raised the flag of truce again, your Highness."

"So they have," Boudain said, shielding his eyes with a hand as he squinted toward Amaury's position. "What in hells does he want now? Hasn't he antagonised us enough?"

"Amaury's capacity for that is . . . substantial," Gill said, focussing on the rider who was coming toward them. "It's only a messenger. Not Amaury himself this time."

"Well, I'll be damned if I'm riding out to meet him," Boudain said. "He can come to us. Anyone got any booze? My armour feels like it was stored in an icehouse and I could use my knackers to chill a whisky. I could do with something to warm me up."

There was a chuckle of laughter from the others. Even Gill broke into a smile. A man who could kill the tension at a moment like that was a man whom others followed. The young king continued to impress Gill. It was a strange thing, how a man—a king—could give you hope. Even a young one, like Boudain.

Someone passed the king a small silver flask. Boudain nodded his thanks and took a swig, then offered the flask to Gill. Guillot thought of refusing, but today was not the day to be seen doing that. He covered the opening with his finger as he tipped it up to his mouth. He caught a whiff of the contents, but no more—Ruripathian whisky by the smell of it. A good one, too, and happily not chilled by the king's knackers. He handed the flask back to Boudain, who passed it on to Savin.

The armoured messenger drew his horse up a short distance away.

"His Grace, the Lord Protector of Mirabay, wishes you to hear his offer," he said in a clear voice. "In consideration of the devastation a battle would wreak upon the people of Mirabay, he suggests an alternate solution: to settle this matter with a single combat, the result of which he will abide by, on his bond and word as Banneret of the White and as a loyal son of Mirabaya."

"Pah," Boudain said. "He's a treacherous maggot. But I'll listen. Who does he suggest do the fighting?"

"Banneret of the White, former champion to the king, Guillot dal Villerauvais."

Gill raised his eyebrows in surprise.

"And his champion?" Boudain said.

"His Grace, the Lord Protector, intends to represent himself."

Now the king raised his eyebrows. "Well, that is . . . unexpected. A moment, if you would."

The messenger nodded and rode off a short way.

"Villerauvais, what do you make of it?" Boudain said, turning and speaking quietly to Gill.

"I honestly do not know," Gill said. He couldn't work out what Amaury was playing at—it looked as though he had superior numbers. Why would he take a risk like this? Surely his desire to get at Gill couldn't be so great as to overwhelm his sense. And patience—if he won the battle, like as not, Gill would be dead by sundown.

"He'll use magic, won't he?" the king said.

"Of course he will," Gill said. "He's a cheating bastard. Always was."

"Still though, do you think you can beat him?"

"I . . . I don't know. Without magic, yes. With it? I don't know."

"I suppose we can still fight it out if you lose. No offense intended."

"None taken, your Highness," Gill said. If Amaury brought magic to bear in this fight, there was no way Gill could win, but how could he say no to a proposition like this? Every man standing around him would think he was a coward. "If he beats me, it will be because he's used magic," Gill said. "I'll agree to fight on your word that if I lose, you charge across the field and kill every last one of those bastards."

"You have it," Boudain said.

"Then you have your champion, your Highness."

Boudain gave Gill a grim smile, then looked at the messenger and called out, "Our answer is yes!"

CHAPTER
48

It simply wasn't the done thing to wear armour to a duel, and one of this importance needed to be conducted entirely within the expectations society placed on them, so Gill set about stripping off his suit. The air felt cool without it on, but he wasn't sure if he was just imagining that, a phantom of how exposed he felt being on a battlefield with no plate steel between him and his enemies.

Gill had never thought he'd fight another duel again, nor that he'd ever again have use for the blade he'd been awarded for winning the Competition. The blade would have been Amaury's, had Gill not beaten him that day. It seemed like the perfect choice for this fight. His two other swords had been brought along with the infantry's baggage train, which was safe back at the siege fort. Gill sent a galloper to fetch the duelling blade, and did his best to appear nonchalant as he waited, feeling like every eye in two armies fixed on him.

The duel was going to be a spectacle, the like of which had not been seen in some time. Considering the size of the two armies present, Gill reckoned the audience would rival the one for the Competition's final. It had been some time since he'd fought with so many eyes on him, and he wasn't sure how he felt about so much attention. He didn't want to be the big name anymore. He just wanted to go home— but home was a place that no longer existed. There was a time when all he'd wanted was to get away from Villerauvais, to be the swordsman everyone talked about. How times changed a man.

"How are you feeling?" the king said.

"As well as can be expected," Gill said. "I've beaten him before. I can do it again."

Boudain nodded intently.

"All I can ask is that you give your best," Boudain said. "I know you will, whether I ask or not—you've done that time and time and time again. Mirabaya owes you a debt I fear she will never be able to properly repay."

Not unless she can bring back my wife and child, Gill thought. *My village and its people.* "To serve is payment enough," he said, knowing he could say nothing else.

"Spoken like a true hero," Boudain said. "May the gods smile on you. They certainly won't on that bastard. Prince Bishop my arse."

Gill laughed and looked across the field to where Amaury was likewise preparing. Their seconds had already picked out a suitable patch of ground and were marking out the standard competitive dimensions. That wasn't usually done in a duel of honour, which this most closely resembled, but Gill supposed the stakes were rather higher. *No pressure,* he thought.

He wondered what was going through Amaury's mind. He always wondered that about his opponents before a duel—whether they feared him, respected him, held him in contempt. In this situation he was fairly confident it was the last, but Amaury was a fool if he thought a little magic would change things between them. He had never beaten Gill in a duel, fairly or otherwise, and Gill was determined that that would not change. With a limp, and swordplay skills that must be as rusty as Gill's had been when Nicholas dal Sason had called on him all those weeks earlier, Gill felt confident. Magic was the great unknown. There was nothing Gill could do about that, so he simply tried not to think about it.

Of course, it really didn't matter. He was going to fight Amaury, and that was all there was to it. Win or lose, he simply had to get on with it. *Nothing to be gained by waiting,* he thought. *Better put on a good show.*

He swished his sword left and right, then stretched his neck, trying to look as confident and purposeful as he could. Every man in the king's army who could see him was watching intently. His second had returned from inspecting the ground and now stood next to him, waiting.

"I'm ready," Gill said.

His second, a young officer who was standing too close when the need had arisen, nodded and headed across the field to convey the message. Gill started to walk toward the marked-off area, certain old habits and mannerisms finding their way back to him after a long absence. His heart pounded and his skin tingled, reminding him why he had lived for this once. The sensation was like nothing else.

He had reached the duelling area before Amaury started to move. The Prince Bishop had stripped down to shirt and britches, and walked easily, with no trace of a limp. That came as a bit of a surprise, but Gill realised he should have expected it. With so much magic, there was no way Amaury was going to carry that old injury any longer than he had to. It made no difference to Gill. If he needed to rely on his opponent's weaknesses, he had bigger problems in store.

Gill watched Amaury approach, taking his time, no doubt thinking that it would antagonise Gill, make him angry, careless. Ever the gamesmanship with Amaury. What he didn't know was that Gill enjoyed the pause. His second hovered silently a few paces away, but had the sense or experience of such matters to know there was a time to leave your principal in peace. Gill stood in a bubble of his own creation, feeling his heart slow and his senses waken. His mind was shutting down the parts used for day-to-day life, leaving only what mattered for this life-or-death struggle.

"I bet you never thought we'd find ourselves in this situation again," Amaury said, as he reached Gill.

Gill shrugged. He'd thought of Amaury far more over the years than he cared to admit, but indeed, this wasn't one of the situations he'd envisaged.

"When you're ready," Gill said.

"Both parties have been apprised of the code of conduct for this duel," Gill's second said. "All combat must remain within the marked area. This duel is to the death. Do both parties understand the rules as explained?"

"Perfectly," Amaury said.

Gill nodded.

"You may begin."

Amaury came at him straightaway, a thrust leading into a vertical cut that would have given Gill a cleft in his chin had he not been able to bounce backwards on the balls of his feet. Amaury was moving like a man half his age, and Gill regretted that Solène hadn't been around to give him a shot of rejuvenating energy before the fight. He backed away and circled to his left, watching Amaury's movement, trying to get the measure of him. He certainly wasn't rusty. *Is he better than before?*

The Prince Bishop came at him again. Gill parried, the chime of the two Telastrian blades ringing out like a musical note. Amaury had not had a Telastrian blade the last time they had fought, and Gill wondered briefly where he had gotten it—who he had stolen it from. Two more cuts that Gill parried, their clashing blades creating a song over the silent farmland.

Gill danced back and took his guard. *He's fast, and I'm slower than I was. He's not better than before, just hasn't slowed down much. I can live with that.* There wasn't enough difference in Amaury's speed and skill to put it down to magical enhancement, which was confusing. Amaury had never been one to play by the book before. Why would he start now, with so much at stake? It was time to find out. If Amaury intended to play by the rules, that would be the biggest surprise of all.

Guillot thrust, then followed seamlessly with flèche. Amaury dived out of the way; Gill passed by, then spun on his heels and took guard again. From the look on Amaury's face, Gill was faster than the Prince Bishop had expected.

"Still with the old tricks, Gill?"

"You didn't have an answer for them the last time," Gill said. He had never been one for verbal fencing, but if it made Amaury angry, he was happy to play along. He followed the barb with a testing thrust, but there was no real intent behind it. Amaury swatted it to the side—a cooler head would have ignored it.

Gill backed away a little more, keeping his guard up and his eyes firmly locked on Amaury. His old friend was tense. He had been rattled far too quickly. Was the pressure getting to him?

"How do you think history will remember you, Amaury? Tyrant? Murderer?"

"At least I'll be remembered," Amaury said, launching into a chain of thrusts, stamping his front foot with each attack.

Gill parried, revelling in the delicious sound the blades made when they connected. He moved back smoothly, allowing Amaury's attack to expend its energy, then riposted and drove the "Lord Protector" back across the duelling area with a series of cuts and thrusts that flowed into one another. A cheer erupted from the king's army and spread until the air was filled with roars of support.

Amaury slipped to the side, moving away from Gill. The intense look on his face gave Gill pause for thought. If he hadn't known better, he'd have thought Amaury was constipated. *That can't be it? Can it?*

The expression faded after a moment, replaced with one of frustration. Amaury came at Gill again, wilder this time. His blade work was loose, and Gill slapped the weapon off its attacking line each time, with the contempt with which a fencing master treated a weak pupil.

He backed off once more, more casual about it this time, letting his guard down a little, relaxing his stance. It was a signal of disrespect that Amaury could not miss.

"No magic to help you out?" Gill said. He knew he was playing with fire, but he couldn't help himself. If Amaury had power, and was going to use it, now was the time. But there was nothing.

Amaury roared and came at Gill again. He was fast, strong, and angry, but these were all things that could be countered by a cooler head and greater skill. Gill danced back, moving with a rhythm that syncopated with the chime of the clashing blade. There was a joy in this, the like of which could not be found anywhere else. This was the thing Gill had been made for; his body was responding out of instinct rather than conscious thought. It was a moment he had experienced only a handful of times before, but the promise of it made one seek it out relentlessly. It was harmony. It was perfection. Gill parried again, the sound of the blades meeting ringing out like a crescendo, then riposted and launched himself forward.

His blade moved faster than his eyes could follow. Amaury answered, his face a mask of furious concentration as he parried again and again. Soon he would falter—Gill knew it. They always did. He wondered again why Amaury had not brought magic to bear. If he would. When he would.

But he wouldn't, for it was over.

Gill drew breath deeply, his chest heaving. His form was perfect—knees bent, arms extended, back straight. His blade was buried in Amaury's chest to the hilt. There was a moment between them, where their eyes met, and both men realised what had happened. Amaury dropped his blade and opened his mouth to speak, but only blood bubbled out. Gill remained motionless, not sure of what to do next, unable to believe that it was finished, that he had done it. All those years of enmity, and for what? This moment? To watch his enemy—his onetime friend—bleed out under the shadow of Mirabay's walls.

Amaury's eyes showed fear and his face was a mask of pain. Gill wanted to say something, but didn't know what. He was angry, yet his heart was filled with sorrow. The life left Amaury's eyes and his weight collapsed on Gill's blade. He pulled the weapon free and allowed the body to fall to the ground. Gill studied the corpse for a moment, as though to convince himself that Amaury was truly dead.

Gill looked up. It seemed as though most of Amaury's army had already run, for they were nowhere to be seen. What little remained would not put up a fight. The day was won. He turned back to the king's army and raised his sword. The roar was deafening.

We found her by a tree not far from camp," the man said. He laid Solène's body down on the table in front of the king's command tent. The king and his staff looked on in silence. They'd yet to organise themselves for the march into the city, although a preliminary group had been sent to deliver the news of the king's victory to the citizens. The "Lord Protector's" army had proved much smaller than it had initially appeared, and now was dispersed or captured.

Gill had frozen the moment he had seen the soldier appearing with the limp form in his arms. He had recognised her right away, and all the joy and elation of victory had evaporated. He knew now why Amaury hadn't used magic. He didn't know how she had done it, but he knew that the day's victory was not his, but hers.

He fought down the wave of anguish and tears that threatened to overwhelm him. Unable to hold himself back, he went to the table and reached for her. Still warm. Still breathing. She was alive.

"Oh, thank the gods," Gill said, his voice laden with emotion. She was so pale, though. How much magic had she used? How could he help her? He looked around. There was a squad of Royal Guardsmen nearby.

"You," Gill shouted. "Go to the prisoners. Bring every man and woman in a cream-and-gold robe back here. Now!"

They shot furtive glances at the king.

"What are you doing, Villerauvais?" Boudain said.

"At least one of them must be a healer. They can help her. We have to help her."

Boudain nodded. "Get to it!" he said. "Find out if any of them are healers while you're at it."

"Get her somewhere comfortable to lie," Gill said. She deserved better than to be draped unceremoniously on the map table.

The king gave one of his aides a nod and the man headed off.

"She did this," Gill said. "She stopped Amaury from using magic to beat me. I'm certain of it."

"You have my word that we'll do everything we can for her," Boudain said. "I won't forget what she's done for the kingdom." He gave a grim smile. "What she's done for me."

It felt like an age before a man and a woman in the Order's robes were pushed before the king.

"You're healers?" the king said.

They both nodded, obviously terrified. They were no longer under Amaury's protection, and everyone knew what happened to sorcerers.

"You save this woman or you'll never see daylight again," Boudain said. "Understand?"

They both nodded again, and got to work. Solène had been transplanted to a cot bed in the king's tent. Gill hovered behind the Spurriers as they assessed her and got to work. He watched intently, trying to remember the occasions healing magic had been used on him, wondering if they were doing it right.

Gill did his best to hold his tongue while they worked. It seemed to be taking a long time. He wondered if they were any good—most of Amaury's best people seemed to have been killed during the past few months, but surely he had kept one or two decent ones back?

Solène stirred, then let out a short groan. Gill knelt by her side just as she opened her eyes. It took her a moment to focus, then she gave a weak smile.

"Did you win?" she said.

Gill burst out laughing. "I won. We won."

▲▲▲▲▲

Bauchard's seemed the obvious place to spend a few days recuperating. Short of the palace, there was nowhere else such luxury or comfort could be had, and Gill felt that he and Solène deserved no less.

It was no great surprise when a call to the palace came a few days later. As the carriage sent to fetch them rattled up the hill, Gill and Solène were able to look out over the city, which was slowly recovering from the turmoil of the past weeks. The Order of the Golden Spur had been disbanded, its remaining members arrested. They'd been placed under house arrest at the Priory until the king decided what to do with them, now that magic seemed to be out of its bottle, and likely impossible to put back in.

Gill could not help but ask something he'd been wondering about ever since his fight with Amaury, but hadn't found the right moment to bring up.

"What did you do, that day? To stop him using his magic?"

Solène smiled sheepishly. "I'm still not exactly sure. I think I funnelled the Fount away from the city, or at least from the area around him, so when he went to draw on it, there was nothing for him to use."

"Is that . . . hard to do?"

She laughed. "It nearly killed me. It seems being enlightened isn't quite the limitless power I thought it was. That's definitely not something I'll be trying again!"

"Hopefully there won't be any need to. I'm not aware of any other potential tyrants lurking around the place. I think now that Boudain is back in control, there's hope for the future."

"You like him?"

Gill nodded. "He's got all the makings of a good king. He wouldn't be the first who fell short of the mark, but I'm hopeful." There was more he wanted to ask her, such as why she'd come back, but it didn't seem appropriate. All that mattered was she had. She'd been there when it really counted, had put herself on the line for him.

A servant was waiting for them when they arrived at the gates. He led them to the throne room, where Boudain was once again installed, and very much in command. The room was full of petitioners and hangers-on—nobles and commoners both—part of the normal day-to-day business of court. When the king spotted them, he urged them both forward.

"Solène," Boudain said. "I'm delighted to see you looking well. You gave us all quite a scare."

"Bauchard's is an excellent place to recuperate," Solène said.

Boudain laughed. "Yes, I'm sure it is! But now, to business." He held out his hand and one of his officials gave him two folds of sealed papers. "For you, Villerauvais. I give you this charter for one hundred settlers to reestablish the village known as Villerauvais, to populate and improve its lands and create a vibrant and lasting community. In this, I add fifteen thousand acres to your demesne, and elevate you from Seigneur to Marquess of Villerauvais, Warden of the South."

Gill stepped forward and took the charters with a bow. He didn't know whether to be grateful or terrified. Marquess and Warden were not usually titles awarded in times of peace.

"Solène, I create you Baroness Bleaufontaine, with all rights, lands, and duties there attached." The king held out the second sheaf of sealed papers, which Solène bowed and took before stepping back beside Gill.

"Congratulations, Baroness Bleaufontaine," Gill said. "Solène dal Bleaufontaine has a nice ring to it."

"Thank you," Solène said, then whispered: "Where's Bleaufontaine?"

"Haven't a clue. You should probably find out before we leave, though."

"Probably," Solène muttered in agreement.

"And now to the next matter," Boudain said.

Gill's smile vanished. He knew it. There was always a catch.

"We have all seen the danger magic can pose if it is not properly controlled. I would prefer that we never hear word or see evidence of it again, but that is an unrealistic dream. Magic is out in the world, and we must take measures to ensure a despot the likes of Amaury dal Richeau can never become so powerful again. With that in mind, a diligent sovereign must make preparations to safeguard his people.

"In light of this, and concerning reports I have received, I have come to a decision. By deed under my seal, I hereby reconstitute the Order of the Chevaliers of the Silver Circle. As Master of the Silver Circle, I do so appoint Guillot, Marquess of Villerauvais, Marshall of the Silver Circle, and Solène, Baroness of Bleaufontaine, Seneschal of the Silver Circle. I command you to go forth, and with all resources and support the Crown can provide, reestablish this body of fighting men and women trained in both the martial and magical arts. They will protect the kingdom from those who seek to pervert the use of magic for their own gains, from our foes from other lands, and will defend us and our people against the creatures known as 'Venori,' which have recently been seen abroad in the kingdom."

The Venori. Perfect, Gill thought. He cast Solène a look, and she shrugged, with an expression on her face that said, "If not us, then whom?"

"What say you both?" Boudain asked.

Gill did his best to smile. "I am ever a servant of the Crown, your Highness."